closing in

closing in

a novel

Kerry Blair

Covenant Communications, Inc.

Covenant.

Published by Covenant Communications, Inc.
American Fork, Utah

Printed in Canada
First Printing: June 2002

09 08 07 06 05 04 03 02   10 9 8 7 6 5 4 3 2 1

ISBN 1-59156-012-8

Library of Congress Cataloging-in-Publication Data

Blair, Kerry, 1958-
    Closing in: a novel / Kerry Blair.
       p.   cm.
    ISBN 1-59156-012-8
    1. Government investigators--Fiction. 2. Rich people--Fiction. Deception--Fiction 4.
Arizona--Fiction. 5. Mormons--Fiction. I. Title.
    PS3552.L34628 C57 2002
    813'.54--dc21   2002023730
                                     CIP

ACKNOWLEDGMENTS

Quotes from the fairy tales by Hans Christian Andersen (1805-1875), translated into English by Mrs. H.P. Paull (1872), can be read courtesy of the Gilead Project (www.hca.gilead.org.il/) and the Eris Project at Virginia Tech (www.vt.edu/vt98/academics/books).

Excerpt from "Fly Not Yet" by Thomas Moore (1779–1852). (*Familiar Quotations,* compiled by John Bartlet, New York: Little Brown and company, 1910.) Some of Moore's poetry can be read courtesy of Classic Reader (www.classicreader.com).

Special thanks to Carol Hopper Holmes and others who added their insights, and especially to Shauna Nelson who always makes time to cross fingers and hold hands; Jessica Warner who encases my books so beautifully with her art; and Angela Colvin who translated many of *my* words and phrases into English and was a joy to work with every step of the way.

chapter 1

He formed many different words, but there was one word he never could manage to form, although he wished it very much. It was the word ETERNITY.

— The Snow Queen, Story the Seventh: The Palace of the Snow Queen & What Happened There At Last, 1845

"Pay careful heed to the beginning of this story," Libby James read aloud, "for when we get to the end of it we shall know more than we do now about love and greed and the ice that can freeze in our hearts."

She read *The Snow Queen*, but Libby's voice was like sunshine and held a promise of romance and mystery that most of the children in this shabby school library would discover only in the pages of the books she brought to life. The kids seated cross-legged on the worn, wooden floor were sixth-graders, and though most of them considered themselves too old for fairy tales, they leaned forward eagerly, basking in the warmth of Libby's smile and entranced by the luster in her wide pewter eyes.

But nobody in the room paid closer attention than their teacher, David Rogers, because nobody had more interest in how a story about greed would turn out. He was a newcomer to this small, predominantly Mormon town, and though he claimed to have come to teach, he had actually been sent to learn—learn, that is, what the beautiful bibliophile "Libby James" was actually up to.

David crossed his arms and leaned one broad shoulder against a bookcase as his gaze slid from the librarian's sleek, honey-colored ponytail down her tanned legs to her sandal-clad feet. Her dress showed taste and style and subtle curves. Her toenails were unpainted, he noted, as were her fingernails and lips. Not that she needed makeup. The glow that the Arizona sun had lent her delicate features was more complimentary than any cosmetic.

Though in person she scarcely resembled the stylish woman in the photographs, David knew that she *was* the suspect from his electronic case files. This Libby James was really Elisabeth Jamison, one of the richest, most powerful women in corporate America. Moreover, she was suspected of selling missile designs to terrorists.

"The story begins with a wicked hobgoblin," Libby told the children in a hushed, mysterious voice. "He was the worst. And he only came out from hiding when he wanted to cause mischief."

Which was, ironically, the opposite of what she'd done, David thought. The "mischief" at Jamison Enterprises—in the form of yet another sale of classified, technology-laden microchips to Iran—had coincided too perfectly with Libby's anonymous arrival in Amen, Arizona to be much of a coincidence. No matter how she told that story, the theme was treason.

"The antagonist in the story is the Snow Queen." Libby cast David a look cool enough to remove his eyes from her legs, at least for the moment. "Though she was made of ice, she was fair and beautiful and her eyes sparkled like bright stars."

She had that part right. Try as he might, it took more self-control than David possessed not to stare at Libby. She was an attractive traitor to her country; he'd have to grant her that.

But Captain Rogers didn't like traitors. It was that prejudice that initiated his covert move from NASA to the CIA and landed him here in yet another episode of "Mission: Improbable." He might be on board a space shuttle right now if not for what he'd seen—and overheard—on the last one. His well-developed sense of honor had taken him from the pilot's chair on the *Endeavor* to the Internal Affairs Center at NASA and from there to a Central Intelligence Agency office in Washington. Sworn in at the CIA, David had gone back to NASA undercover to help crack a major conspiracy.

David hadn't known what to expect after his former shuttle commander was arrested along with two foreign spies. Maybe a congressional medal or citation of valor? He'd wondered if either honor would cause his grandfather, the four-star admiral, to sit up and take notice—as his graduation at the top of his class at Annapolis and assignment to the space program had not. At any rate, David never found out because all he'd been given was another undercover assignment—this time to a godforsaken spot near the suburbs of obscurity.

He looked over his ragtag class and shook his head ruefully. Sure, he'd taken a sacred oath to protect and serve the United States of America—and he'd meant every word of it—but who'd have guessed he'd be asked to do it this way? Babysitting preadolescents while spying on a turncoat with the legs of a goddess and the face of a saint. It was downright funny when he thought about it.

"One day, when he was in a merry mood," Libby read, "the hobgoblin made a looking-glass which had the power to make everything beautiful that was reflected in it look hideous. The loveliest landscapes looked like boiled spinach, and people?—well, even one freckle on the nose appeared to spread over the whole of the face."

The children giggled at the face Libby made and even David grinned.

"This is what?" a man's voice asked quietly from behind him. "A hob—? Hob-gob-lin? You might tell me, please?"

Omar. David identified the man without looking.

Who else? David had been in town for only a day and a half and already he knew that Amen was not what it seemed. Sure, it *looked* like a little town dying in the desert foothills outside of Phoenix, but it was actually more like a thriving desert island inside the Bermuda Triangle. There must be *some* cosmic undercurrent of weirdness to account for all the misfits who'd washed up here—like this new Egyptian PE coach, for instance.

David turned. "A hobgoblin is a, a . . . " *What the heck is a hobgoblin, anyway?* Fairy tales hadn't been part of his curriculum in military school.

It didn't matter that David didn't know. Omar had turned away to listen intently to Libby's story. *And no wonder*, David thought. The century-old words rolled easily from her tongue and her expressive face told more than the words. She was a natural storyteller. No wonder she was so good at covering her tracks.

"As the clock in the church tower struck twelve," she read, "the boy Kay said, 'Oh! Something has struck my eye!' Sweet Gerda put her arm around his neck and looked into his eyes, but she could see nothing. 'I think it is gone,' she said. But she was wrong. It was not gone."

Libby's expressive face clouded as she continued, "It was one of those bits of the evil looking-glass. Poor little Kay had received a small grain in his eye, and another in his heart, which very quickly turned to a lump of ice. He felt no more pain, but the glass was there still." She closed the book slowly and smiled when the children groaned in disappointment. "It's almost three o'clock," she said, tapping the watch on her slender wrist. "Time to go home."

"But what happens next?" asked a redheaded girl.

"Kay is bewitched by the Snow Queen," Libby replied. "We'll read that chapter when you come back to the library on Wednesday."

The girl's pigtails swung out from her head as she turned toward David. "Can't you read the rest of the story to us in class tomorrow?"

Other kids joined in with "Yeah!" and "Please, Captain Rogers?"

David smiled. No way could he compete with Scheherazade up there, but he *could* read, and he'd had a heck of a time today filling all those hours he was supposed to be teaching. He'd killed most of the time telling stories about NASA, but he hadn't told them well. David was an ace pilot and a passable secret agent, but he was a lousy public speaker. Lecturing, even to eleven-year-olds, unnerved him. The girl's suggestion was a godsend. "Sure, we'll read the story," he told the class. To Libby he said, "Can I use your book?"

Her fingers tightened around the dog-eared pages. At last she said, "You may check it out, I suppose."

Right, David thought as she rose to place the book on her desk, *you worry about me stealing fairy tales, and I'll worry about you stealing government secrets.* Still, he couldn't help but admire the way Libby formed his class into an orderly line at the door. A line was a novel concept; he'd brought them to the library in a mob. When the dismissal bell sounded, the children scattered to the seven winds.

David watched them go from the open doorway and let out an involuntary sigh of relief. Anybody who thought that NASA's infamous altitude chamber was the worst place you could spend a day had never been in charge of a sixth-grade classroom. He glanced at his watch and when he looked up he realized that the seven winds hadn't carried the children off after all. Instead, they'd been blown back toward the library with all their little brothers and sisters.

"He *is* an astronaut!" Calvin, a freckle-faced boy at the front of the pack, declared. He peered around David into the library for an unimpeachable witness. "Tell them, Miss James! Captain Rogers is *too* an astronaut, ain't he?"

"Isn't he," Libby corrected automatically. "Well, he *says* he is."

David started in surprise. Then he relaxed. No way was Elisabeth Jamison on to him. Even if she'd had him checked out, and there was no intelligence from headquarters to indicate that she had, at least not yet, his cover was flawless. He *was* an astronaut for crying out loud; he had the scars to prove it.

"I've flown the *Atlantis* and the *Endeavor*," he told the children. "Orbited the earth. Walked in space. The whole nine yards."

"He showed us pictures!" the boy exclaimed. "Let's go show 'em your pictures, Captain Rogers!"

If Calvin had pictures to back him up, the children were willing to believe. One little girl tugged on David's pant leg. "Can I ask you a question about outer space?"

David looked down into the dirty, eager face and smiled. "Sure you can. What do you want to know?"

"Where do you go to the bathroom?"

The group giggled. Behind his back, he heard Libby repeat the question for Omar. Suddenly, he felt his face warm without benefit of the afternoon sun. "We, er, well, the . . . facilities . . . are like a vacuum cleaner kind of thing and you take the hose and—" The laughter increased in volume and David regretted the graphic nature of his explanation. He was grateful to see principal Max Wheeler, a shaggy gray bear of a man, ambling toward the library for the faculty meeting. As one, the children stepped back to let him pass.

"This the organizational meeting of your fan club, Captain?" Before David could respond, a smile lit the older man's craggy features and he added, "Sign me up. Not every school can claim to have a real Buck Rogers on their staff."

David returned the smile as though he hadn't been called "Buck Rogers of the 21st Century" at least once a week since he got his pilot's license at the age of twelve. He was twenty-eight now, so he'd heard it—what—eight hundred times? Nine hundred? *Probably more like a thousand,* he thought, *but hey, something that clever never gets old.* "I'll, uh, show you guys the pictures tomorrow," he told the children as he turned to follow Max back into the library.

"Your book," Libby said when he paused at her desk. The way she extended the volume of fairy tales seemed designed to push him away.

David didn't budge. Instead he flashed his killer grin—the one reserved for NASA Public Affairs photographers and female senators on the Space Committee. He knew he was somewhat attractive, and he wasn't above using his good looks to his advantage. He didn't mind that saving the Free World called for a little flirtation when the flirtee was as lovely as Libby James. He leaned confidently across her desk. "What I'd really like to check out is the librarian."

The look she gave him suggested there was more space between his ears than he'd see in a lifetime at NASA.

Okay, he thought, *so it wasn't a great come-on.* He turned the charm up another notch. "What I mean is, can I take you to dinner tonight?"

"No."

The suggestion, he realized at once, was worse than the come-on. There was only one diner in town—The Garden of Eaten—and it had taken David less than two minutes to determine that what its cook lacked in olfactory senses she made up for in poor hygiene. Of course Libby wouldn't want to eat there. Nobody would want to eat there. He tried again. "Can I take you to a movie this weekend?"

"No."

"You've probably seen it." There was only one theater in town too, and it was showing *Camelot.* With his charm already on "high," and his ego on the line, David wondered what *would* be appealing to a woman like Elisabeth Jamison. Then he remembered where they were: Amen, Arizona, where the brightest light of the big city was the 60-watt street light in front of town hall. *No ballet. No symphony. No museum. Heck, there isn't even a bowling alley. What do people here* do?

"Can I walk you to church?" he asked finally. There were two of those. A new chapel anchored Main Street, and an old adobe house of worship—built by the pioneers Brigham Young had first sent to settle Amen—fell to ruin at the edge of town. When she hesitated, David wondered if it would help to "accidentally" flash his temple recommend. He'd already let drop at their introduction that he belonged to the Church.

"No," Libby said.

So much for flirtation. Not only was he not above it, he wasn't good at it. "Okay then." He tucked the library book under his arm. "Maybe I'll see you around school." He retreated before she could say "no" to that too.

As the other six teachers filed in for the meeting, David pulled out a chair next to the PE coach, dropped the fairy tales on the table and frowned at its cover. "You want to know who the *real* Snow Queen is?" he asked Omar under his breath. "It's Libby James over there."

Words spoken in haste are often lamented in leisure. That was the lesson Captain David Rogers would best remember from his first day at Alma Elementary School.

chapter 2

The word ALONE she understood very well, and knew how much it expressed.

— *The Snow Queen, Story the Fourth: The Prince & The Princess,*
1845

Libby slid into the chair farthest away from David Rogers and wished it were farther. They'd spoken fewer than two dozen words to each other and already she knew all about him. He was self-absorbed, cocky . . . and deluded if he thought she was going to give him the time of day, let alone a date. It was men like him—or at least a man like him—that she'd fled Los Angeles to avoid.

Why was it that since she'd turned twenty-five, worthy single men were so much harder to find than fudge sauce, and so much less satisfying? All the "eligible" men Libby knew were either divorced and looking for another chance to make an "eternal marriage" last longer than their car payments, or egocentric flirts like David Rogers who probably couldn't spell "commitment" to look its definition up in a dictionary. Libby had been engaged to a cretin in the not-too-distant past and wouldn't make that painful mistake again, ever.

Ever, ever, she told herself as she caught a glimpse of David's handsome profile from the corner of her eye. Despite herself, her chin gravitated after her eyes. *And why is it that You give men like* him *the huge spaniel eyes and thick, curly brown hair?* She was still awaiting God's explanation when David turned toward her and smiled. Libby looked quickly away, then propped an elbow on the table so she could lean her chin on her palm and cup her fingers into a blinder for her traitorous eyes. *Ever!*

Hoping to overcome a painful past, Libby had come to Amen to cultivate a life of books, gardens, and solitude. In another life she was Elisabeth Jamison, CEO of Jamison Enterprises, but as soon as she completed the corporate sell out that was in the works she could retire to eternal obscurity as Libby James. She'd worked for a life of her own choosing and planned now to cherish it. Alone. Words mean different things to different people. To Libby "alone" meant "sans a man" and that in turn meant "safe."

Max cleared his throat in preparation for yet another year at the helm of his slowly sinking ship of knowledge. Libby pushed aside her thoughts of Captain Rogers and smiled up at the principal in encouragement.

Two new teachers had replaced the ones who had fled back to the city after the previous term, Max reported. Omar had married the local veterinarian and David had come courtesy of a Teach for America grant to impoverished areas. Omar stood and bowed after the formal introduction while David made a gesture that approximated a wave. Libby applauded like the others, but with less enthusiasm.

"Isn't he so scrumptious you could eat him right up?" LaVerne Payton asked in a stage whisper that couldn't possibly have carried farther than Sacramento.

Libby tried not to cringe. She knew that with so little happening in Amen about which to gossip, LaVerne considered it her civic duty to generate intrigue as best she could. She and Captain Rogers would be the hottest topic in town unless she responded correctly. "He's very handsome," she said. "Too bad Dr. Jenn married him first."

"Not the Egyptian, Libby!" LaVerne cried. "The astronaut!" She thrust her chin forward rather like a gila monster about to take hold of prey in its powerful jaws.

Libby knew that, like the lizard, once LaVerne latched onto something, she might worry it to death but she'd never let it escape. Never let *her* escape, in this case. This was *his* fault. Unreasonable or not, Libby held Captain Rogers's arrival, his marital status, and even his good looks against him.

And what was he doing here anyway? This was *her* town. Her ancestors had left Salt Lake to settle it. Their son had discovered the rich ore deposits and improvised a way to mine the copper. This man, her great-great-great-great-grandfather, had built the Amen Mine, and while building it amassed the tidy nest egg that his son invested in the railroad, which his son rolled over into early aeronautics on the West Coast, and that his son parlayed into a fortune in defense contracts in the World Wars. It was his son, Libby's grandfather, who had made it a super-fortune with the rise of the Star Wars defense program, and her father who had nearly tripled the wealth manufacturing microchips in California's Silicon Valley.

Libby and her older sister, Geneva, had been born in California almost a century after the first of their ancestors left Amen. A quarter century later they returned—like generations of Jamisons before—to bury their dead in the family cemetery outside of town. They had come veiled in black to avoid the prying media cameras that followed them everywhere after their parents' brutal murder. Geneva Jamison had taken one look at Amen from beneath the layers of netting and vowed never to go back. Elisabeth Jamison had taken a longer look and vowed never to leave.

No one had seen Libby's face at the funeral, so nobody recognized it a few weeks later when she returned. Nobody but her bishop—and her eccentric next-door neighbor—knew that Libby James was Elisabeth Jamison. Max Wheeler was too intelligent and too intuitive to believe the fables Libby spun in his office when she sought a position at the school. When he told her that he would be her bishop as well as her boss, Libby sobbed out the story of her parents' murder and her recently broken engagement. Max hired her on the spot, granting her sanctuary in an anonymous, idyllic world of books and children. Each time she returned to Amen from a business trip to LA, she felt as though she were being cast back into the garden from someplace east of Eden.

If only the garden had remained serpent-free. Glancing at David, she figured she had to say something else to placate LaVerne, but she was wrong. Shenla Naylor swept Libby out of the spotlight and claimed center stage before the younger woman could blink.

"Libby's not the only single gal in town," Shenla said with an exaggerated tug on her wig of platinum curls. (She'd once had a walk-on role in a 1952 B movie and had maintained the "Hollywood mystique" ever since.) "And I think he's *real* cute." The wrinkles on her Max-Factored face overlapped as she smiled and batted false lashes. "Would you care to join *me* for dinner tonight, Captain?"

"Yes, thanks," he said without hesitation. "I don't think I'd survive another visit to the Roadkill Café."

This time Libby did wince. Talk about potential roadkill. LaVerne would no doubt quote Captain Rogers to her sister LaDonna, The Garden of Eaten's owner and cook. LaDonna, in turn, would hold a grudge against him until the morning of the First Resurrection. Possibly longer.

"Then we have a date," Shenla said with a wink at Libby.

Max soon adjourned the meeting to Libby's desk where she removed the lid from a tin of homemade applesauce cookies.

"Her cookies got more applause than we did," she heard David observe to Omar.

"Perhaps her cookies are more deserving of praise."

David took a bite. "You nailed it, Omar. This is the best cookie I've ever had."

Libby ignored both his praise and his Tom Cruise–patented grin. She turned her back on him to walk over to a shelf of perfectly aligned books. Dewey be darned; she began to pull books off the shelf and put them back on again just to pass the time until he left her library.

"I may speak with you?" Omar asked a few minutes later.

Libby turned to see that the cookie tin was empty and the room almost so. But not empty enough. David was still there, talking to Max but following her with his eyes. She looked down at her feet, then forced her own eyes to make the interminable climb back to his face. This was ridiculous. She was the head of Jamison Enterprises for goodness' sake. A mere glance from her in a boardroom could make a grown man blush and look away.

David Rogers didn't look away. Most disconcerting was an odd something in his eyes that hinted that, while he might admire her, he didn't like her.

Why not? she wondered, then in the next moment amended it to *So what?* She couldn't describe the lurch in her senses when he looked at her—or the sudden craving for fudge sauce—but it couldn't be attraction she felt. If she made a list of things she didn't want in her life right now she'd write "egotistical male" on it six or eight times. In red ink.

"Of course." She turned back to Omar.

"I have lived only here in Arizona," Omar continued, "but I would like to know about other places in your country. You, Miss Libby, were born in the northlands?"

"Um, no," Libby said, trying to pull her mind into their conversation and ignore the fact that David was listening in. "I grew up in California."

"There it is very cold?"

"No." She pushed an errant strand of hair back behind her ear. "I'm from Southern California. It's warm there year-round."

"It was your college education then that took you from your land of birth?"

"No, I went to Stanford." Libby considered the poor man's puzzled expression helplessly. "Omar, I'm sorry, but I don't understand what you're asking me."

"Neither do I understand," Omar said. "Captain Rogers told me that you, Miss Libby, are a snow queen. I ask your background only in my wonderment at how you obtained this title."

Suddenly Libby had no trouble meeting David's eye and knew at once that she had been wrong. The right look under the right circumstances *could* make him color and look away. She turned back to their colleague. "Captain Rogers was using an English figure of speech called a metaphor. I'm sure *he'd* be happy to explain it to you."

Omar looked past her toward David, but Libby didn't want to wait for the explanation herself. She'd been right about him from the first moment they'd met. What was it about her that could attract a cretin all the way from outer space?

As she brushed past David on her way to the door he said, "I meant—"

"*I* know what you meant, Captain," she said. She'd show him "snow queen." She'd show him "snow queen, ice princess and arctic empress" besides. "You've made it perfectly clear to *me*. It's Omar you've confused."

Libby looked around for Max Wheeler and saw him by her desk. "Lock up for me, will you please, Max? I just remembered I left some Eskimo Pies in the oven."

chapter 3

It is difficult to keep the thoughts together in everything; one little mistake upsets all our arrangements.

— The Snow Queen, Story the Third: The Flower Garden of the Woman Who Could Conjure, 1845

Okay, so he shouldn't have given a zero-star review to the diner, David thought as he stared down at the plate of charcoal toast and runny eggs that had been tossed on his table with a look that could have curdled the goat milk. And he *really* shouldn't have called Libby James anything but blessed yesterday—at least not in this town.

He pushed the plate away and looked out the window to avoid meeting the glassy-eyed gaze of a buffalo head that frowned down from its mountings above his booth. Across the street was the town square. David was surprised to note that Libby's statue had not yet been erected there. Probably it was just being polished somewhere else.

In the meantime, there was a veritable chorus of townspeople to sing her praises. Max Wheeler, for one. The kindly principal hadn't sent him packing after yesterday's snow queen incident, but David knew that he'd considered it. And it might have been easier to pack up and tell his chief at the agency that he'd botched the assignment than it was to apologize to his unhappy new principal and define "cad" for his baffled new colleague.

Shenla Naylor, another card-waving member of the Libby James fan club, hadn't heard his remark, so he still got dinner at her house with extra helpings of Libby testimonials. Did he know, Shenla had asked, that Libby made the sauce in those applesauce cookies herself *and* grew the nuts *and* ground the spices? (He didn't.) And did he know that she was simply the sweetest person ever born on the face of the planet? (Then why was she turning her country over to terrorists?)

David set his palm computer where his plate used to be, then looked around to make sure none of the men seated at the counter drinking Postum had turned his way. Finally, assured that the only creatures looking on with any interest were the ones mounted on the walls with the buffalo, he pressed a couple of buttons to call up the latest communication from the Phoenix office.

There was nothing new to look at. Elisabeth Jamison was as slick as the Teflon panels that lined the space shuttle—nothing would stick to her. *Or else*, said a quiet voice in his head, *there is nothing to stick.*

Try as he might after meeting her yesterday afternoon, David had had a hard time fixing Libby James on an "America's Most Wanted" list of murderers, thieves and international spies. She kept landing instead on a more personal "wanted" list. Not that he needed to worry about her staying there for long. David's little black book was famous in Houston for its uniqueness. All the names in it were written in pencil. Those that hadn't been erased had mostly faded away over time. It wasn't that he didn't like women. It was rather that—like the grandfather who had raised him—he didn't like them very close or for very long. His bishop back home often teased him about Brigham Young's assertion that an unmarried man was a menace to society, but David intended to remain a menace for a very long time. His attraction to Libby—if he had one—was a passing fancy at best.

Frustrated to have nothing to go on in the Jamison case, David stuck his palm computer in one pocket of his knapsack and removed his scriptures from another. If he'd learned only one valuable thing in the last couple of years, it was that daily scripture reading kept him centered. That's what he needed now. He had to keep his thoughts together and his mind on the job ahead. He'd been sent to this desert island of a town on a mission, and the faster he accomplished it the faster he could hail a rescue ship for civilization. Amen gave him the willies. At night it was darker than deep space, but the din of crickets in the trees and frogs on the river bank kept him awake. He missed the soothing sounds of sirens, jet planes, and the loud music from the apartment downstairs.

David opened the quad to where he'd left off reading, the sixth section of the Doctrine and Covenants. As he read the fourteenth verse, David experienced the vague internal nudge that he'd come to recognize as the Spirit trying to get his attention. He read the verse again:

Verily, verily, I say unto thee, blessed art thou for what thou hast done; for thou hast inquired of me, and behold, as often as thou hast inquired thou hast received instruction of my Spirit. If it had not been so, thou wouldst not have come to the place where thou art at this time.

David glanced up instinctively, but it was clear that the little voice that whispered "Amen" was in his head. He looked back at the page. The first part was unquestionably true. At a time of crisis during his space walk, the very moment in his life when he had most needed a Father with both compassion and power, David had inquired with desperation and the Lord had responded with devotion. It was the first step on his return to the church of his childhood. He'd been baptized about a year ago, recently been ordained, and then endowed in the Houston Temple.

Despite his recognition of the truth in the first lines of scripture, the words that commanded David's attention now were the last: *If it had not been so, thou wouldst not have come to the place where thou art at this time.*

Amen? This time it was a question, not a benediction, but it was something to think about.

To think about later, that is. If he didn't hurry he'd be late for school. Meditation would have to wait until he'd survived another day of trying to educate Attila's latter-day Huns.

David returned his scriptures to his knapsack and dug a dollar tip from his wallet. Then he reconsidered and pulled out a five. He'd gone back to the Garden of Eaten this morning when he realized that if he wanted to get anywhere on this assignment he'd better start rebuilding his bridges mighty fast. He hastily spooned most of the raw egg into his mouth and slipped the burnt toast into his knapsack. Then he picked up the check and headed toward the counter, keeping his eyes on the snarling lynx that hung above the cash register since the woman who stood behind it looked less welcoming. If ever he'd needed his charm not to fail him it was now. "That was a great breakfast," he told LaDonna and patted his tight, empty stomach to prove his point.

The chief cook, bottle-washer, and keeper of the menagerie was obviously torn. On the one hand, he had publicly insulted her cooking. That deserved nothing less than chronic indigestion. On the other hand, she had a very unmarried daughter, and Captain Rogers was the most eligible bachelor this town would ever see. The sound with which she took his money, then, was something between a growl and a purr.

David had gained ground and he knew it. "I'll be back tonight," he said. "I hope you'll serve that Magic Meatloaf I've heard so much about." *Not.*

"LaRae will make it especially for you, Captain," LaDonna said. "LaRae's my lovely, *unmarried* daughter." She gave David a shiny new quarter in change and a free peppermint before adding coyly, "I'll wager that after one bite of that meatloaf you'll be forced to admit that she's an even better cook than her mother."

Couldn't be worse.

"And her talents!" LaDonna exclaimed as she lay a dimpled hand to her fluttering heart. "You can't imagine the talents that girl has." She raised the hand to encompass the dead animals or the cosmos, David wasn't sure which. "Can you believe she did all this herself?"

"Shot them? Stuffed them? Hung them?" David paused briefly between each question, an excited nod from LaDonna nudging him on.

Her final "Yes!" confirmed all three.

He'd met lots of women, David thought on his way to Alma School, but never an amateur big game hunter/taxidermist/decorator. But no matter how varied and unique LaRae Flake's talents, they scarcely compared with Elisabeth Jamison's. After all, Libby was a professional; a professional CEO/librarian/traitor, that is.

He crossed town square and thought again of the high opinion Libby's friends seemed to have of her. Could a whole town be mistaken? He shook his head. Either these naïve townspeople were in for a shock, or the Central Intelligence Agency was. It would be interesting to see which it would turn out to be.

chapter 4

"Ink-pitcher!" cried the pen
"Writing stick!" retorted the inkstand.
And each of them felt satisfied that he had given a
good answer.

— *The Pen and the Inkstand, 1838*

"I need a favor, Libby." Max Wheeler laid his age-spotted paw next to the uneaten apple on her desk. It was lunch hour on Thursday afternoon, and the sound of children playing carried through the open windows, making Libby wish she were outside with them. "It's a big favor."

Libby looked up and noted that the twinkle in his eye belied his words of caution. "For you Max, anything."

"Good. I want you to go into Captain Rogers' classroom this afternoon to—"

"No." She looked resolutely down at the catalogue that lay open before her. "I'm busy. We need knew encyclopedias." She circled a set—perhaps the only ones still being bound in this age of CDs and wide Internet access. Her company was on the cutting edge of cyber-technology, but Libby valued words on a page she could touch, hold, and turn with her fingers.

Max began again, "Captain Rogers has got to be one of the world's worst teachers."

"Glad to hear it," Libby said without inflection. "Fire him."

"There's nobody to replace him with and you know it."

She knew, too, that Max liked the man. It was the only real lapse of good judgment she'd ever seen in him.

"He's a nice enough guy," Max continued as if reading her thoughts. "The kids like him. He'll do okay once he knows what he's doing. He just needs help."

Libby turned the page to look at globes. "So I noticed."

"Could you—?"

"No. Send Shenla. I'll take her class."

Max shook his shaggy head. "It's the second day of school, Lib. Shenla needs to hit her stride with her own kids."

Libby turned another page and circled an atlas. "'Hit her stride'? Shenla taught those children's parents. She probably taught their grandparents!"

"Precisely," Max said, trying another tack. "She'd overwhelm poor Captain Rogers with her experience."

"Max," Libby said firmly, "no." The old man shrugged his shoulders in defeat and turned toward the door. "Fine. Hide behind your stacks of books to lick your wounded pride."

"Pride!" Libby exclaimed. "Surely you don't think— " Words were lost in her indignation. "I am *not* hiding from Captain Rogers!"

Am I? She looked down at the catalogue but didn't see it. Instead she saw herself hurrying across the playground in the mornings instead of playing her usual game of tetherball with the girls, and then saw herself eating lunch alone in the library instead of in the workroom with the rest of the faculty. *Why?*

Because I'm busy, of course. She certainly wasn't afraid to face David Rogers. She'd been called worse than a snow queen by a competitor—in the headlines of *The Wall Street Journal,* no less. She'd been called worse by the detectives she'd hounded to solve her parents' murder. Even her ex-fiancé had called her worse—often, and in public.

Why, then, had two little offhand words from a stranger cut so deeply? Only because she'd let them. And she'd let them because she feared they were true. What if she never *could* trust another man after Karlton?

Above all else, Libby hated her insecurities to show. And they must show now or Max wouldn't be here. He didn't ask her to trust Captain Rogers, after all. He didn't ask her to date him. He only asked her to help him with his class. "Okay," she agreed.

"That's my girl!" Max said. "Could you go right after lunch? I think he's been having a little trouble teaching math."

Libby saw from the open door to his classroom that Captain Rogers didn't have any trouble that a little simplification and a fully equipped riot squad couldn't solve. He stood at the blackboard with his back to the class, apparently outlining the theory of relativity. While he scribbled equations and talked to himself, the class hollered back and forth, wrote notes, and tossed spitwads.

Libby cleared her throat. Then she rapped on the door frame. Finally she raised two fingers to her lips and whistled like a riot cop. Thirteen surprised faces turned toward her. The noise and notes and spitwads disappeared.

"Good afternoon," she said as she walked into the now-quiet room. She gathered a stack of books from the shelf as if it were part of everyone's daily routine. "I hope I'm not interrupting."

David lowered the hand that held the chalk. "Uh, no," he said. "They were finished with math a long time ago."

She couldn't help but notice that the embarrassment on his face was mixed with relief. She carried her armload of books up to the front of the room and set them atop his bare desk. Almost bare desk. Somebody had brought him a half-dozen crab apples from the tree at the edge of the school yard. Or, more likely, somebody had brought them to throw at his classmates and David had intercepted them one by one.

She turned to the class. "Mr. Wheeler suggested that since you're sixth-graders, it's time you learn library science. We'll begin with spelling."

"Is that what 'library science' is, Miss James?" a boy called out.

"We raise our hands in class, Calvin," Libby said. "But yes, spelling is the root of library science. How can you look up a book if you can't spell the words in the title?" She rewarded the few bobbing heads with a warm smile and the rest of the children nodded too. "Take out your workbooks please."

A girl's hand shot up. "We haven't got any workbooks, Miss James."

David soon realized that not knowing he had a cupboard full of supplies was only the first of his failings. He watched Libby issue materials with a proficiency that would put a naval commissary to shame, then took mental notes as she taught spelling. His confidence began to grow. Teaching couldn't be as hard as he'd thought. In fact, Libby made it look easy. By the time the spelling lesson ended, he had mostly forgotten his failings, but when she mentioned history he gulped audibly. With luck, none of the kids had been listening to this morning's lesson.

He wasn't lucky. Libby wasn't the only traitor in residence. Alma School was full of them.

"Captain Rogers said that history is 'vastly overrated,'" a girl—David didn't know who, but *would* when he started using Libby's new seating chart—volunteered. "What did he mean, Miss James?"

"I meant—" David began.

"That it's all in the way you approach it?" Libby asked.

David hesitated, unable to look away from her pretty, faintly accusing face. "Okay," he said at last.

"You're studying American history this year," Libby told the class as she turned away from their teacher. "It can be fun." She considered for a few seconds, then opened the history book. "Perhaps you could study transportation—the way people have moved from place to place over the years." She showed a picture of the *Santa Maria*. "You could learn about sailing ships first and later Conestoga wagons and steam engines and—yes, Calvin?"

The boy's eyes were bright. "Can we learn about space shuttles?"

"Yes," Libby said. "Finally you can learn about space shuttles." She glanced at Captain Rogers. "And since you have your own expert here, you can study space in science too. There's a long section on astronomy in your book."

"There is?" David asked eagerly.

"Yes. And you can check science fiction out from the library to read in English."

David was as elated as the kids. Issac Asimov beat Emily Dickinson by a moon shot. After he'd told them yesterday that most of her sonnets could be sung to the tune of "The Yellow Rose of Texas," the lesson had gone quickly downhill. But now there was hope on the horizon. And if things ever got really out of hand, there was always "library science" to fall back on.

When the final bell rang more than an hour later, David looked up at the clock in surprise. The morning had seemed to last six and a half days, but the afternoon had evaporated. He expected Libby to leave with more alacrity than the kids, and was surprised and pleased when she lingered in front of the cupboards. He walked over to thank her for coming in.

"Max sent me."

It didn't take a rocket scientist to figure out that her earlier warmth had gone home with the children. He watched her pull out a stapler, scissors, and a long roll of black paper. "I appreciate your help," he ventured. "I'm not much of a teacher."

"Then why are you here?"

He stepped back. "I, uh . . . NASA sent me."

"Why you?"

After Monday's fiasco, she probably wouldn't believe he'd been sent to charm her, even if he could tell her the truth, which of course he couldn't. "I've been grounded since my space walk," he said, reciting the CIA script. "It was either Teach for America or man a desk for NASA."

He was ready with more of the almost-true explanation, but Libby didn't ask for it. Instead, she stuck the paper under her arm without further comment and carried it across the room to the bare bulletin board. He watched her unroll and cut the paper, and tried not to stare at her legs when she kicked off her sandals and climbed atop a desk to staple the paper into place. "Do you want me to do that?" he asked.

She climbed down silently, handed him the stapler, and returned to the cupboard. A moment or two later, feeling his eyes on her back, she turned. "You can cover a bulletin board, can't you?"

"Yeah," he said. "Sure." It wasn't too difficult. The bulges were hardly noticeable when he finished.

In the meantime, Libby produced a veritable milky way of yellow and white stars. "It's a progress chart," she said as she climbed back up on the desk to staple stars over the worst of the wrinkles in the paper.

"A what?"

She turned and leaned against the board. "Surely you went to elementary school. You must remember *something* about sixth grade."

"I remember a few things," he shot back. "I remember that we stood at attention at the blackboard to do math and that we did twenty push-ups for every problem we got wrong." He didn't like the sound of his voice, but seemed powerless to stop the stream of words. "And I remember every latrine I scrubbed for forgetting to end a phrase with 'yes, sir,' and every lap I ran for lousy penmanship. I went to military school," he concluded, as if it might explain both his incompetence and his outburst.

"I went to finishing school," she replied.

David couldn't define the look that came over Libby's face with their shared confessions. He could only catch his breath at the beauty of it.

She lifted her shapely shoulders. "I think my school was a lot like yours except our uniforms were chic and we did declensions of Latin verbs for violating rules."

"I'd rather clean latrines."

Libby's lips parted in what could only be a smile; then, as if remembering herself, she turned quickly back to staple up her astral cutouts. "*Ad astra per aspera*," she recited. "That's Latin for 'To the stars by hard means.' It was our headmistress's favorite expression."

It was also, David thought, a fitting motto for his life; he'd have to remember it. As he handed Libby the remaining stars he wished he knew what to say to return them to that flash of near-intimacy. But the moment had passed, if indeed it had ever existed.

The bulletin board at last complete, Libby began to climb down from her perch. David reached out automatically to help her and, when she drew back, felt as if he'd been slapped. "Excuse me," he said. The tightness in his throat felt like rejection, but it came out as sarcasm. "I've been reading your book of fairy tales. I should have known that we swineherds aren't supposed to soil the lily-white fingers of you snow queens." He crossed his arms and took a step back. "Do you mind if I breathe in your presence?"

Libby pushed the desk she'd been standing on in line with the others, squarely between them, and right into his leg. "I don't care what you do, Captain Rogers," she said. "But I wish you'd go back to outer space to do it."

Even while nursing the pain in his shin, David admired the way Libby's silky hair brushed her shoulders as she spun on her heels. "Why are you so anxious to get rid of me?" he asked as she reached the door. "Are you afraid you might melt if I do touch you?"

The gust of air she created by slamming the door behind her blew the carefully stacked spelling papers to the floor, but didn't dispel the scent of vanilla and wildflowers she'd left behind. It was as unmistakable to his senses as the clear, perfect penmanship she had left on the chalkboard.

As he bent to pick up the papers, David caught a glimpse through the window of Libby stalking back toward her library. He paused to watch the woman he'd been sent to spy on and berated himself for letting his mouth again take over for his brain. He was supposed to be gaining her trust, not her loathing. What was his problem? Could it be Libby herself? Who was this woman that could beguile children, create order from chaos, and disconcert him more than he liked to admit?

"A traitor," he told himself. "That's what she is, Rogers, and you'd better not forget it."

chapter 5

It was late summer and the Ice Maiden was melting amidst the green verdure when Vertigo first made an appearance.

— *The Ice Maiden, 1861*

"We're going through with the sale of the company, Frank," Libby said into the cell phone. "Get used to the idea."

She was in the yard behind her house early Saturday morning, kneeling in the moonflower garden that was her pride, joy, and often salvation. Each time she stuck the sharp point of the trowel into the earth to wrest a weed out from among the flowers, she'd imagine herself removing an unwelcome thought from her mind. Until this call, all of the wilting herbage this morning had represented something to do with David Rogers—his broad shoulders, ready smile and, especially, his annoying habit of being everywhere she turned.

The most recent image to hit the pile of mental compost with a stickery broad-leafed weed was the mental picture of David escorting LaRae Flake into the movie theater last night. Not that she cared if they dated. For all she cared they could go to the temple next weekend. She'd be first in line at their wedding reception with a lovely *My Condolences* card for LaRae. What bothered her was the way Captain Rogers winked at her as they passed on the sidewalk. Men like him, with looks like that, ought to be required to wear signs around their necks; something along the lines of "Lovely to look at, delightful to hold, but watch out sweetie, he'll drop you cold."

Why, then, didn't she stop looking at him? "It's a bad move," the voice said into her ear, startling her back to the present.

Frank. Libby lay down her trowel with a sigh. Without doubt, her irritation with her latest brother-in-law, Frank Gordon, went too deep to be removed from mind with the weeds—even if she'd had a backhoe instead of a hand trowel. He was, nevertheless, the president of Jamison Enterprises, so ignoring him completely was impossible.

"The deal with SynQuest will be final by mid-October," she repeated calmly. "You have until then to find another job." *Or another con,* she thought. Frank had no job skills beyond "charm," and nothing to put on a resume besides "Figurehead, Jamison Enterprises." Libby didn't know what he had done with his life before he married her sister, but she hoped he'd go back to it after the sale and leave poor Geneva in peace.

"You're making a bad move, Elisabeth," Frank repeated. "One I guarantee you'll regret."

Libby sat back on the gravel path in surprise. What was that tone in his voice? She was used to Frank flattering her, wheedling her, and especially whining to her, but she wasn't used to this. "Are you threatening me?" she asked.

Calliope, her fluffy calico cat, had come around the low rock wall and padded silently to her side before Frank responded.

"Certainly not," he said finally, the tone moving back toward wheedle. "I'm only saying that it's not like you to think only of yourself. Genie's beside herself worrying about what selling the business will mean to her and little Chelsea."

Libby scratched the base of Calliope's ear and wished that it were true. Geneva had shut down emotionally since her second marriage, more so since their parents' death. It seemed to Libby that the greatest remaining worry in her sister's life was that she might break a silk-wrapped fingernail between spa sessions. Libby loved her sister, but was hard-pressed to know how to help her. Genie refused to see a doctor or go to counseling, and their heart-to-heart chats were now few and far between.

Her niece, on the other hand, Libby both adored and understood. Through some remarkable blessing of genetic hopscotch, Chelsea Dumont was as sensitive as her mother was detached, and as faithful as her father was fickle. She was also only eleven years old. She'd been five when her father, Jerrold Dumont, had left Geneva with a child but without most of her inheritance. She'd been nine when her mother married Frank and thereby proved that marrying Jerrold wasn't the stupidest thing she would ever do.

"Frank," Libby said, "you know as well as I do that Geneva has nothing to worry about. She might never have all the money she wants, but she'll always have all she needs." She nudged Calliope further away from the flowers—the feline was a notorious nasturtium nibbler. "And Chelsea's portion of the sale's proceeds will go into her trust fund." The ironclad trust fund. The one that Leonard Kelley had helped her establish to make certain that nobody but Chelsea could ever touch it. Before Frank could respond, she concluded, "The sale is going through. SynQuest officers are taking over. End of discussion."

"Leonard doesn't like it."

The words went straight from her ear to her heart. "He hasn't told me that."

But he had hinted at it, and it was the only thing that gave her pause. Leonard Kelley was more than her attorney and financial advisor; he was her ally, her defender, and her unofficial fairy godfather. He'd helped gather up the pieces of her broken heart when Karlton betrayed her. And he'd been the first one there when her parents died. Libby did not believe that she could have lived through that first dark day when Martin and Lorraine Jamison were found by the Coast Guard—murdered and left adrift on a small yacht—if it had not been for Leonard. She knew too, that he had been more responsible for holding Jamison Enterprises together since that day than she had, despite the "CEO" after her name on the company letterhead.

"He thinks it's a mistake," Frank said, pressing his advantage. "He's waiting to tell you so in person."

"Then let him tell me." She tucked the phone under her chin, picked up the trowel, and went determinedly after another weed. "If that's all, Frank . . . "

Unfortunately it wasn't all. Still, she thought as she paused to focus for a moment on the flowers instead of the weeds, what a blessing it was to conduct business under a clear, blue sky rather than in the elegant oak-paneled office in downtown LA. She was grateful that Leonard encouraged her to do most of her work at home on her computer. With his help she'd telecommuted successfully all these months. But the strain on her nerves was still beginning to show. She could feel the tension every time she sat down to work on JE transactions.

As Libby half-listened to Frank, she made a mental note to go over the new defense contracts again, though she couldn't say why. She'd sat in front of her laptop for more than three hours last night, as she did most nights, but this time her attention was focused on trying to pin down a niggling uneasiness. Everything *seemed* in order at Jamison Enterprises. The documents dealing with sensitive government intelligence were a pain, with miles of red tape and checks and balances in triplicate, but nothing about them had changed.

Had they? Why was it that every time she looked at them or even thought about them she felt uncomfortable and vaguely worried?

"Are you listening to me, Elisabeth?" Frank asked impatiently.

Libby considered for less than a moment. "No," she said and turned off the phone. She could ignore both Frank and the contracts for now. Until the sale of the company the business wouldn't go away, but she didn't have to deal with it when the breeze was so warm and the sky so blue. She rose and brushed the soil from her jeans. It was a beautiful Saturday and she wasn't going to waste another minute of it talking to Frank—or mooning over an astronaut. She'd learned from her parents' death how short life can be, and she'd moved to this small town to remind herself every day that the things in mortality that matter most aren't *things*.

She walked back toward her house with Calliope padding along behind. They both knew that Libby had a real vocation to tend to here in Amen, one that had nothing to do with the Fortune 500.

Or, for that matter, with romance.

chapter 6

Once upon a time there was a prince who wanted to marry a princess. There were princesses enough around, to be sure, but it was difficult to find out whether they were the real ones.

— The Princess & The Pea, 1835

David pulled to a stop in front of the Sam The Secondhand Man store and swung open the door of his Hummer. With Wal-Mart so far away it might as well be an outpost in another galaxy, this establishment was the sole purveyor of everything but food in the Amen metropolitan area.

Not that David thought he needed anything for his "furnished" bungalow. His landlord, Homer, had generously provided a cast-off Army cot, a three-legged card table (David propped the legless side on the windowsill) and a single folding chair, all of which suited his tenant just fine. What he had come "shopping" for was information, though he might pick up a bed—if he could find one with a decent mattress—a desk for his computer, and a few other things to make his visit look innocent. He needed to check out everyone in town who knew Libby James, and that, of course, was almost everybody.

He'd been on a fact-finding mission last night when he took out LaRae Flake. The date might not turn out to be the greatest sacrifice he'd make for his country, but David bet it would be darn close. Throughout the movie she'd gripped his arm with buttery fingers, chewed popcorn with the same grace and good manners God had granted to nanny goats, and told him everything she knew about virtually everything. It hadn't been much. The night would have been a total bust except for the revelatory look on Libby's face when she saw them together. He wouldn't go so far as to believe he'd made her jealous, but at least he'd caught her off guard, and that was more than he'd been able to do the rest of the week.

This morning David had moved on to "Sam the Secondhand Man," and his expectations for success had grown. Not only was Libby apparently the shop's best customer, but he'd learned that the owner was often gone from Amen, supposedly buying and selling wares in every small town in southern Arizona. Might he also be acting as a courier for Jamison?

David crossed the junk-filled yard, pushed open the warped store-front door and blinked. As his eyes adjusted to the dim light, he blinked again. It looked like a Goodwill store gone bad. Only a plank-wide spot of floor marked the path between solid walls of curios balanced atop books that had been stacked on furniture that now sank into the heaps of worn rugs. It would take more than the Salvation Army to save this place.

"Morning," somebody announced from behind a desk, a plastic rubber plant, six stacks of dime novels and an empty birdcage. "Help you?"

David struggled to rearrange the astonishment on his face into an amiable smile. "Hello," he said, stepping forward to extend his hand over the books under the plant and around the birdcage. "I'm David Rogers. I'm new in town."

"Heard you were here," the man said as if David were a strain of Asian flu or a new species of locust.

When the man didn't offer to shake, David dropped his hand back to his side. But the smile remained, as did his determination to learn all he could. He'd get the pleasantries out of the way first. "You must be Sam."

"Nope."

"Sorry. I assumed you were the store owner."

"Am."

"Sam was your father?"

"Nope."

The sign out front said, "Sam the Secondhand Man." David knew it did. "Sam's the guy you bought the place from?"

"Nope."

"Okay," David said, willing to play along a little longer, "Sam's your brother? Uncle? Partner? Wife? Cousin? Dog?"

"Nope."

It finally occurred to David that he wasn't going to win Twenty Questions even if they doubled it. "So, who's Sam?"

The man leaned across the desk to spit toward a brass spittoon at David's feet. He missed both the spittoon and his customer's shoe, but he was closer to the latter. "Secondhand Man."

David took a cautious step back from the puddle on the floor. *I'm an officer in the United States Navy,* he reminded himself. *I work for the CIA. I can handle this guy.* "Then who are you?"

"Guy that owns the store."

Great. With the "pleasantries" out of the way, David thought he'd better try another tack. "Mind if I look around?"

"Nope."

He reached for the first thing he saw—something shiny and silver—and pulled an oversize pair of ice tongs from the heap of stuff, thinking they might be handy for dropping icebergs into oceans.

"You plannin' to birth cows?" the man asked.

Or maybe for that. David dropped the tongs. "No, I teach school. Over at Alma Elementary." The man didn't respond. "Do you know any of the people over there?"

"Yep."

Still trying to look like the average connoisseur of the bizarre, David picked up a lamp that had been made from a bowling pin. As he pretended to examine it he asked, "So, do you know Libby James?"

"Yep."

"She seems like a nice person."

"Is."

David set down the lamp. Either this guy was naturally quiet or he had a nasty case of lockjaw. "Have you known her long?"

The man's eyes were slits above his grizzled cheeks. "You come in to shop or talk?"

"To shop," David said. "Have you got any, uh, beds?"

"Down the hall on the right."

David retreated to the "bed room" to regroup and find something he could buy. Maybe the guy would open his mouth a little more if David opened his wallet. He located a semi-rusted frame and a passable box spring, but a mattress was another matter. After eliminating the ones already staked out by mice and vermin, he still had a few possibilities left. He'd just cleared enough space on the floor to lay a mattress down flat when he heard a familiar voice from the front of the store.

"Where *were* you this week?" Libby asked the old man. "South America?"

David leaned out of the room and saw her enter the store. Perhaps it was because of the open door, but the whole place had brightened. He'd heard the expression "light up a room with her presence" but he hadn't believed it until now.

He stepped into the hall and watched Libby, her back to him, replace the birdcage with a small wicker basket. "I don't know what you traded the drug lord for that rig out on the street," she laughed, "but you got the worst end of the deal. What a piece of junk."

"Hey!" David objected. "That's my truck you're talking about." Libby James could think or say anything she wanted to about him, but when she disparaged his HMV it got personal. What space shuttles are to hang gliders, that baby was to automobiles.

Libby spun in surprise at the sound of his voice, but recovered quickly. "Why am I not surprised it's *yours*? There are three parking places on the entire street and you take two of them."

"He's been askin' about you, Lib," the junkman volunteered. He uncovered the basket she'd brought him and the aroma of fresh-baked muffins filled the room.

David shot him a look, but he didn't blame him. If those muffins tasted half as good as they smelled the man would be loyal to Libby for life. David said, "We were just making conversation."

She stiffened. "Next time talk about the weather."

"I feel a cold front moving in now." *Good thing looks don't kill,* David thought, *or I'd be collecting a Purple Heart posthumously.*

"I brought ya somethin'," the man told Libby suddenly. He scurried around the desk and started down the hall.

Libby followed and David tagged along. When they got to the door of the "bed room," the junkman halted. "Wait here for me, Libby," he said. "This you've gotta see in the light."

With the hall so narrow and David so close, Libby moved into the room and sat on the edge of his stack of mattresses.

He leaned against the door frame. "So tell me, Your Highness, how's that mattress? In your professional opinion as a princess."

Libby's gray eyes narrowed as she ran her hands over the mattress's surface. David knew it had a lot of lumps, very little padding, and uncoiled springs that must be pushing uncomfortably into her tailbone. He didn't know whether to wince or grin when she smiled sweetly and said, "I think it's perfect for you, Captain Rogers."

Before he could respond, the man returned with something the size and shape of a cantaloupe, wrapped carefully in an old beach towel. As the cloth fell away, Libby gasped and rose quickly from the mattresses.

"What is it?" David asked.

"A witching ball?" Libby asked the junkman with awe. "A real one?"

David stepped back as Libby brushed past him. "A what?"

"Got it down in Bisbee," the man told her. He held the orb as tenderly as he might a newborn baby. "Figured it was blown in the 1800's. Whaddya think?"

David thought it looked like an overgrown Christmas tree ornament.

"It's beautiful," Libby breathed, running her fingers over the pearlescent glass. "Oh, Guy! It's perfect."

Guy? David thought. *So he really is the "Guy" that owns the store.* "Perfect for what?" he asked. It was too big to be a fishing float and too small to drop in Times Square on New Year's Eve.

"Thought you'd like it," the man told Libby as a road map of fine lines crinkled across his face. "It's yourn if you want it."

"If we can arrive at a fair price," she teased. "What are you asking?"

Guy's grin showed a crooked row of tobacco-stained teeth. "Whaddya think it's worth?"

"What *is* it?" David asked again. He wondered if he'd lost his voice. Nobody seemed to hear him.

"Forty-eight?" Libby suggested. "And four?"

Guy pulled the cloth back over his find. "I'd say it's worth seventy-two, missy, and six and three—and one of 'em's gotta be blueberry."

David ran a hand through his thick hair. Whatever the thing was, it had remarkable magical properties. It made Libby speak nonsense and caused him to be invisible. While Libby considered Guy's counteroffer, David tried once more to be noticed. "Dare I ask what you want for a mattress?"

The man's eyes flicked toward David for a nanosecond. "Ten bucks."

Glad to know he was still present after all, David said, "So is that in chocolate coins?"

"What's the man talkin' about?" Guy asked Libby.

"I have no idea." Then she offered: "Twelve and two and one blueberry today, with the rest on my account."

"Twenty-four today?" Guy asked hopefully.

"No." When he grumbled and turned away she laid a hand on his shoulder. "When I paid you all at once for the Blue Willow platter you made yourself sick."

David noted that the man didn't move away from Libby's touch, though he muttered, "No guarantee it'll be here when you git around to payin'."

"I'll take my chances." Libby patted the prominent shoulder blade before withdrawing her hand. "But it'll be late this afternoon before I can pay you. I'm on my way out to the McKrackens' house now. You heard that Aaron's home?"

"Didn't hear," Guy said. "Nobody in this town tells me nuthin'."

David could empathize with that.

"I thought you might like to come out with me," Libby suggested. "You can take him a few of your books. You know how much he likes science fiction."

"You take what you want," Guy said.

Libby's voice lowered, "It wasn't your fault he fell, Guy."

"It were my ladder."

"It was an accident." When the old man's eyes remained steadfastly on the floor, she said tenderly, "I'll take him a few of your books today with your best wishes and tell him you'll bring more out yourself later."

Guy grumbled as he started up the hall to retrieve the books, but he nodded.

David paused, pretending to examine a sturdy oak desk, as Libby followed Guy to an overflowing bookcase. He watched her fill a paper sack with fiction by Asimov, Bradbury and Pohl, and smiled when he finally inferred from eavesdropping on their continuing negotiations that Libby paid the junkman in cookies, bread and jam.

When she left a few minutes later with a hug for Guy and scarcely a backward glance in his direction, David sat down on the desktop. Was it his imagination that when she left the room his heart rate slowed and his senses dulled?

"You look like a whipped pup," Guy observed from his perch behind his own desk. He was devouring another of Libby's muffins; crumbs cascaded down the front of his dirty shirt.

"I . . . uh . . . uh . . . yeah." David tried to gather his thoughts. From the start the plan had been to pretend an infatuation with Libby to make all the questions he would ask about her around town seem innocent. His plan was working better than he thought. At this moment he almost believed it himself.

"You want a mattress?" Guy asked.

"Yeah," David said. "And a box spring and frame." He pushed himself up from the desk. "I'll take this too. You got a lamp?" When Guy raised an eyebrow, David looked around. Stupid question. *The Guy Who Owns The Store has everything.* "Does that bowling-pin lamp work?"

"Yep."

"I'll take it." He motioned toward the wall. "Is that ship's wheel for sale?"

"Yep."

"Sold. Got any scrap lumber?"

"You building a boat?"

"As a matter of fact I am." If Nephi could build a ship without any previous experience, David figured he could too. Especially with the added advantage that his boat didn't have to float. He'd begun to plan the project the afternoon Libby came into his class. He meant to transform one side of his classroom into the cabin of an ocean schooner that would convert to a prairie schooner later in the semester and eventually into a space shuttle cockpit. He'd set out to show Libby James history in the making, but it was the kids' enthusiasm that really sold him on it. With just one crash course in library science, and one week of getting to know Calvin and the rest of the gang, David had discovered that sixth grade could be fun the second time around.

He helped Guy excavate the lumber and furniture and load it into the truck, then followed him back inside to the ancient cash register. Libby's basket sat beside it. "How much for a muffin?" David asked impulsively.

"Five bucks."

David's eyes widened, but he pulled an extra bill from his wallet. At that rate of money-to-muffin exchange, what he was going to ask for next might cost him more than he'd paid for his Hummer. "What about the, uh, witching ball?"

"That 'air's Libby's."

"I know," David said quickly. "I want to buy it for her. She helped me out at school last week and I owe her something. I saw that she admired it and thought I could leave it for her as a surprise while she's gone today." That would maybe gain him a couple of brownie points *and* give him the chance to nose around her house a little.

"Druther have her bread than your money." But the way he said it was an invitation to barter. They both knew that if Guy worked this thing right he could have Libby's bread *and* David's money.

"Twenty bucks?"

The old man snorted, but he didn't push the tray back into the cash register. "Fer a gen-u-ine Victorian witching globe? Folks use to hang 'em in their gardens to ward off evil. Makes 'em all kinds of valuable in these here wicked days."

"Thirty bucks?"

Guy examined the dirt under his fingernails since the offer clearly wasn't worth his attention.

In the end, David spent more on Libby's witching ball than he did on his bed, desk, and lumber, but he didn't begrudge Guy a penny. It had paid for itself already by giving him an excuse to visit her house. If it scored him a few points with her it would double or triple in worth.

On the other hand, David thought as he carried it out to his truck, if Guy were right and it really could ward off evil maybe he ought to keep it for himself. Elisabeth Jamison might not fit the Mata Hari mold, but with that pseudo-saintly persona she'd built around herself, she could be more dangerous. Having his very own anti-bewitching ball might indeed be as the junkman had said: *all kinds of valuable.*

chapter 7

"If you are a poet, you can make soup on a sausage stick," said the mouse.

— Soup on a Sausage Stick or A Great Deal Out of Nothing At All,
1858

"Aaron's in back," Tansy reported to Libby as she helped to lug the large box of food up onto the ramshackle porch of her family's home. "Mom's with him. Dad's out in the fields." As they set the heavy load beside the door, she couldn't resist a peek inside the box. "That's more food than I've ever seen at one time!"

Though the excited words made her want to cry, Libby smiled at the twelve-year-old girl. "There are a couple of baskets of laundry and a bag of clothes in the backseat of my car. Get them for me, okay?"

"Okay!"

Libby watched the girl's red-orange braids bounce against the thin, faded fabric of her T-shirt as she flew down the stairs and across the dirt drive to the car. Then she turned and walked around the porch to the rear of the house.

Although it was early September, it was still in the mid-90s on the open desert, and probably warmer still within the small, uninsulated home. Aaron's bedroom was on the north porch where his mother hung dampened blankets to provide shade and to turn any passing breeze into a poor man's evaporative cooler.

Libby paused to watch Hannah bend over her son. The tenderness of her care and hopelessness of her position again brought tears to Libby's eyes. She wanted to do—and could afford to do—so much, but these proud people would accept so little. What Libby had done, in hiring a doctor for Aaron after his accident, she had done anonymously.

Libby held the paper sack of books in one arm and tapped gently on the side of the house. Hannah turned and straightened. Libby forced her brightest smile for the pale, drawn woman and her newly paraplegic teenager. "Hi!" she said. "Tansy told me you were back here. Are you up to entertaining a visitor?"

"Sister J-James!" Aaron struggled to raise himself on his elbows, but his mother gentled him back into the pillows.

"Libby!" she said. "We're always glad for your visits. You know that."

"It's not only a social call," Libby said as she approached the side of the bed to take Aaron's outstretched hand in her own. "I've brought you more laundry and mending, Hannah. I hope you have the time."

"I'll help," the boy offered at once. "B-before the accident, Mom was t-teaching me to wash and iron for my m-mission."

Libby saw Hannah look away. She knew her friend's concern for Aaron's success on a mission was much graver now than it had been over the slight stutter that had persisted since his childhood. "Good for your mom," she told Aaron.

"It's only f-four more years," he reminded her. "I'll b-be walking by then for sure."

"What did the doctor say?" Libby asked because she thought Hannah would expect it. She already knew from the doctor that Aaron would likely never walk again.

"That doctor's a good man," Hannah said quickly. "Didn't think there'd be men like him around that'd work for what we could pay." She took Libby's hand when Aaron released it. "Thank you for telling us about him."

Libby looked down at the splintered porch. "I'm glad you like him."

Hannah smiled at her son. "He says we can expect Aaron back out in the fields before the spring corn comes up."

Libby's lips parted, not so much at the falsehood as at the obvious faith with which it had been uttered. After a moment she managed a weak, "I hope he's right." Aaron was looking at the bag, so Libby put it on the bed, grateful to change the subject. "Guy sent you books," she told the boy, removing thick copies of *Foundation Trilogy* and *The Martian Chronicles* from the sack. She smiled at his obvious excitement. His sister could never get enough food, but Aaron would forget to eat if only he had something to read. He'd read almost everything on Libby's overflowing shelves by now, but science fiction and fantasy were his favorite reads, and she'd had little to offer besides fairy tales and Tolkien.

"Tell G-Guy I said thanks."

"You can tell him yourself," she said as she removed several more books from the bag and stacked them on the bedside table. "He'll be out to see you soon." She wondered if she was being as optimistic as his mother and if her assertion had any more chance of coming true than Hannah's. Aaron had fallen from a ladder while working at Guy's store and the old man seemed determined to blame himself even when nobody else did.

"I'll be b-back to work before he knows it!" Aaron tucked *The Martian Chronicles* under his pillow.

Just then Tansy skidded around the corner of the house. Several new shirts and jeans and a dress or two were clutched to her chest. "These are for me, aren't they?" she asked breathlessly. "Please say they're for me!"

"They are," Libby affirmed, sending the girl into squeals of delight, but causing her mother to frown. "My sister keeps sending me her and Chelsea's castoffs," she told Hannah hastily. "I've given their clothes to lots of the girls in the ward."

Hannah shook her head as Tansy showed off her clothes for Aaron and rattled on about how she'd look as good as Chelsea on the girl's next visit to Amen. She and Libby's niece had been inseparable last summer. Hannah finally smiled at her daughter's happiness and said in resignation, "Must be nice for some people to have more money than they know what to do with."

"Shopping is about the only thing my sister still seems to enjoy," Libby said, glad that she could be mostly honest about the source of the back-to-school wardrobe. She was glad too, that Genie enjoyed *something* that served others. If one had a compassionate service assignment that required only impeccable fashion sense and a Platinum VISA card, Geneva was the woman to call.

Tansy had finished showing Aaron her new clothes and was hugging them close while she looked politely at his books. "It's all outer-space stuff," she observed with her nose wrinkled in distaste.

"I'm g-going up to live on the new space station someday," he reminded her.

Tansy turned immediately to Libby. "Tell Aaron that my teacher's a real astronaut. He won't believe *me*."

Libby was surprised at the sudden, uncomfortable prick of feeling at the mention of David Rogers. She told herself that the emotion was annoyance, but while it might feel that way now, it hadn't at first.

"It's n-not t-true is it, Sister J-James?" Aaron asked, his stuttering more pronounced in his indignation. "T-Tansy's always m-making up things. He's n-not a real astronaut?"

"He's a space shuttle pilot," Libby acknowledged to Tansy's crow of triumph. She smiled at Aaron's sudden flush of color. "He flew the . . . I don't know . . . *Endeavor* and *Atlantis*, I think." Libby colored a little herself. She did know, as a matter of fact. She'd looked up his missions on the Internet—out of idle curiosity, of course, and nothing more.

"W-What's he like?" Aaron asked eagerly.

"I told you!" Tansy exclaimed. "He's wonderful. He's funny and smart and a real hunk! Isn't he, Sister James?"

It was warm out there on the porch, Libby realized. "He's . . ." Three pairs of eyes regarded her quizzically. What was Captain Rogers—besides good looking? Charming, possibly. Egocentric, probably. Irritating, certainly. He was also Tansy's teacher. "I don't know Captain Rogers," she said diplomatically. "We've only barely met."

"C-Captain Rogers," Aaron repeated to himself. "G-Gosh, I wish I could meet him."

"When you feel good enough to go back to church you'll meet him," Tansy said encouragingly.

"C-can I go tomorrow, Mom?" he asked anxiously. "I c-can get myself in and out of the t-truck."

That was fantasy and Libby was relieved to see that even Hannah knew it. Aaron's mother shook her head. "Not tomorrow. You just came home from the hospital. The doctor said another few weeks of bed rest."

"Maybe Captain Rogers would come out to the house," Tansy suggested. "Can we invite him, Mom? Sister James brought lots of food, so we could invite him to dinner and—" The words stopped abruptly when she saw the way her mother looked at Libby.

"I knew you wouldn't have time to bake or go to the store," Libby inserted, "so I brought a few things out. But I brought extra laundry too." She began to relax only when Hannah did. "Estelle's feeling a little under the weather, so I brought a week's worth of her things as well as mine. I hope you don't mind the extra work."

"I'm glad for it," Hanna said simply. "Keeps my hands busy."

If only, Libby thought, she could bring something to keep this mother's mind busy and off her broken heart.

"*Can* we invite Captain Rogers?" Tansy asked again, more meekly.

Hannah looked from her daughter to her silently pleading son. "I don't think so," she began helplessly, "you know your father doesn't like strangers in our home."

It might have been the understatement of the century. Mortally offended by nobody-remembered-what, Moses McKracken had fired a load of birdshot into his home teachers' backsides more than a decade before and had sworn to do it again to any others assigned in this dispensation. Hannah and the kids could go to church, but the Church had better not follow them home.

Except for Libby. On Tansy's twelfth birthday she'd told Moses down the barrel of his gun that as Young Women's president she visited *every* girl in the ward and that included Tansy. If he was the kind of man who shot a lady he could do it now and explain himself to the marshal and his Maker at his leisure. Moses had held his fire and liked and admired Libby ever since. Once in a while he even listened to her, as long as the conversation never turned religious.

"Dad would have to let Captain Rogers in to see Aaron if Sister James brought him," Tansy pointed out.

"Yes," Hannah agreed, "I suspect he would." As one, they turned to Libby.

"Oh," she said quickly. "No. I hardly know Captain Rogers." And what she knew, she didn't like. Was determined not to like. The McKrackens were still looking at her. She said, "I . . . he . . . we . . . I mean . . . " What did she mean? She looked from Tansy's hopeful face into Aaron's more hopeful one and regained her senses. "I could ask him, I suppose. Sometime."

"Tomorrow?" Tansy urged.

"Not tomorrow," Libby said, horrified at the thought. "He . . . I . . . "

"Not tomorrow," Hannah said. "Aaron needs his rest tomorrow." She spoke to Tansy, but she looked at Libby. A smile played upon the corners of her lips, but if something was amusing, Libby didn't know what it was.

"B-but sometime, Sister James?" the boy pressed.

Libby managed to nod. "Sometime," she agreed, thinking that she would need divine help to keep her word.

Fortunately, she would get it.

chapter 8

*There once was an aeronaut with whom things went
badly; his balloon burst, tumbled the man out and broke
into bits.*

— *The Flea & The Professor, 1873*

"Need a hand?" David's landlord asked as the younger man pushed
the box spring through the narrow front door and paused to wipe the
sweat from his face with the back of his arm. David knew that Homer
had watched each labored step he took between the Hummer and the
bungalow before finally coming out to offer his assistance.

"I've got everything but the wheel," David said.

"Happy to oblige." Homer strolled down his steps and over to the
Humvee to retrieve it. "This remind you of the Navy?"

David might have told him that despite his naval commission the
only time he'd spent on open seas was when he practiced landing
fighter jets on the decks of aircraft carriers, but a vibration from the
satellite phone in his pocket saved him the trouble of telling Homer
anything. He pulled it out, checked the digital display and saw that it
was the CIA chief in Phoenix. In other words, his boss. "I've got a call."

"I didn't even hear it ring." Homer peered at the device in David's
hand. "That's the dangest thing I ever saw. Phone, you say?"

"Yeah." Phone. Internet. Satellite tracking. Tape recorder. And some
other stuff that David didn't remember how to work. You couldn't pick
one up at Radio Shack quite yet, but the technology was amazing.
Probably too amazing for a guy who taught sixth grade to be showing
off. David hit the "delay call" button and stuck it back in his pocket.

"Can I see it?" Homer asked.

"No."

He looked wistfully at David's pocket. "Thought you had a call."

"They'll call back."

By the time they did, David had managed to get rid of Homer. Or so he hoped. To make sure he wasn't overheard, he walked to the center of the hall away from the doors and windows before pressing the "accept call" button. "Rogers."

"What have you got?" The local agency chief, Preston Wescott, was nothing if not direct. David didn't have time to frame a response before he added, "You didn't file your weekly report."

"I haven't been here a week."

"Fridays, Rogers. The reports are due on Fridays."

David sat down on the scuffed wooden floor and made a mental note to buy a broom when he went back to try pumping Guy for more information. The top layer of the Alma School playground had sifted through the torn screens on his windows and begun to collect in drifts on the floor. If he didn't devote at least some time to housekeeping he'd eventually need a camel to make it from the bedroom to the bath.

"So what have you got developing?"

A possible crush on the subject, David thought, but didn't figure that was what Wescott wanted to hear.

"Rogers?"

"I don't have anything yet," he said. "I can't find a person in town with an unkind word to say about Libby James."

"Saint Elisabeth," Wescott said derisively. "That's what the boys working the case from this end call her. She's squeaky clean, Rogers. That tells us something."

David wished he knew what.

The chief told him. "People who seem too good to be true usually are."

"Maybe," David began. "But—"

"It's a clever facade."

Not to mention a good one.

"You two an item yet?"

We're about as close as Little Red Riding Hood and the Big Bad Wolf.

David's silence apparently gave him away. Wescott chuckled. "Come on, man. Turn on that legendary charm we picked you for."

Yeah, that's worked.

"You've at least put the bugs in her house."

"No," David said, "but I'm on my way over now."

"Time," Wescott said, "is something we're running out of. When that sale with SynQuest goes through, her trail will be covered for good. We need to nail Elisabeth Jamison now."

* * *

Nailing Elisabeth Jamison to a charge of espionage was roughly as easy as nailing Jell-O to a tree, David thought as he walked the few blocks to her house. Wescott himself would admit it. Why, then, wouldn't the CIA consider the notion that it might be so difficult because she was innocent?

Even as David asked himself the question he knew the answer: *somebody* was selling Iran the microchips used to develop their surface-to-air and sea-to-land missiles. (The only plants in the world with the technology and contracts for those missiles belonged to Jamison Enterprises.) *Somebody* was exchanging their allegiance to the flag for a handful of diamonds offered by a madman bent on destruction of all the flag stood for. (The diamonds were going into a safe-deposit box in the Caymans that still bore Libby's father's name.) *Somebody* was compromising homeland security in this age of terrorism and risking hundreds of thousands of innocent lives. Somebody—no matter who it was—had to be stopped.

Frank Gordon was one of those somebodies.

David knew that Libby's brother-in-law had a list of priors and aliases that stretched from New York to LA and back again. What he didn't know was if *she* knew it. Gordon was so good at racketeering and re-creating himself that it had taken the massive data banks of the United States government to find a link between who he was and who he pretended to be. Libby might not know herself. Or she might.

Certainly her integrity was not above question. As he passed the church, David shifted the glass witching ball from one hand to the other. After all, she lied to the whole town about who she was. She even lied to her bishop.

And so had he, he realized uncomfortably, though he hadn't known Max Wheeler was his bishop at the time of their first interview. He thought he was lying to a principal. There was a difference, right? Besides, it wasn't as though he could have told the truth, even if he wanted to.

So, Brother Rogers, what brings you to Amen?

Well, Bishop, I'm here to deceive you and the rest of the town, pretend to teach school—badly—and spy on Sister James. You don't have a problem with any of that, do you?

David didn't like the way the CIA used his membership in the Church to their advantage, but had finally resolved it in his own mind as an uncomfortable means to a righteous end. After all, the espionage business wasn't defined in black and white. That was one of the things David disliked most about it. But he'd never set out to become a spy—it had happened rather accidentally—and as soon as this assignment was over he'd go back to a pilot's seat at NASA where he belonged. In the meantime, whenever he felt himself slipping into a gray area, he'd say a prayer, listen for the Spirit, and hope that the Lord did indeed judge a man on the intents of his heart.

He prayed for guidance now—and a little luck—as he approached Libby's house. Her home was just like her: beautiful, understated, and classic. A low rock wall surrounded the yard, and paving stones led from the gate to the steps of the veranda. A huge, century-old cottonwood tree stood sentry in front, towering above the flowers, herbs, and well-trimmed blackberry brambles.

David glanced in every direction to assure himself that the street was as empty as it appeared before vaulting the wall from the side and circling to the back of the small house. Here the profusion of plants was even greater, with gravel walkways winding between the lovingly tended gardens. One of the plots was smaller than the rest, but more unique, planted entirely in shades of gray-green, white, and muted gold. It was as good a place as any to leave his gift, so David looped the globe's chain carefully around a tree branch and let it dangle above the foliage. Nailed to this tree, as to several of the others, was a box roughly the size and shape of a bird house, but lacking any openings that David could see. He considered the oddities for a moment, then walked quickly over to the house to do what he had come for, before Libby returned home.

As he approached a back window a calico cat looked up at him suspiciously from beneath a wicker rocker. "It's okay," he told the cat. "I'm one of the good guys."

The cat didn't believe it. She mewed her protest as David pressed his nose against the screen, trying to read the papers Libby had left spread out around the laptop computer on her dining room table. They looked like contracts, and David knew that he needed to get a better look at them. He reached into his pocket for a lock-picking tool as he walked over to the door. He had just inserted the thin metal tool into the lock when he heard a car pull into the gravel driveway in front of the house.

So much for her being gone until late afternoon. At least he hadn't been caught *in* Libby's house, and he did have the witching ball to explain his presence in her backyard. When he heard her car door open, he walked around the house to where she could see him.

"Hello," he said. David thought for a moment she might drop her bag of groceries, but she recovered quickly and her eyes narrowed.

"I'm sorry I trespassed," he added with a grin, hoping to lessen the impact of his crime by mentioning it before she could. "I brought you something. When you didn't answer your door I thought you might be out back."

She clearly didn't trust his motives any more than her cat did.

"I hung it in back," he said. He took a couple of steps toward the backyard and was somewhat surprised when she followed. "There." Suspended above the silvery foliage, the antique globe was as luminous as the moon at midnight.

"The witching ball," Libby said in surprise.

"Is that an okay place for it?" he asked. "You can move it wherever you want."

"You hung it above the moon garden," Libby said softly. "It's perfect there." She blinked at David as if seeing him for the first time. "But I can't accept—"

"It's a thank-you-and-sorry-we-got-off-on-the-wrong-foot-peace-offering kind of thing," he said before she could finish refusing it.

"I've been acting like a jerk, and besides I owe you big-time for helping out in my class last week." He figured he must look suitably humble and sincere since, truthfully, that was how he felt. He took a step toward her. "You were great to come in and help me after . . . everything. Things will go a lot better from now on because of you."

"The kids like you," she said. If the note in her voice wasn't approval, at least it wasn't disdain. He watched her gaze linger on the glass ball before looking back up at him. "But you didn't have to—"

"I wanted to," he said quickly. "Here, let me carry your bag." She hesitated for a moment before passing him the sack. The paper was warm from her touch and smelled—like her—of vanilla and sunshine. He wouldn't have carried it any farther than Pakistan.

As they reached the porch, David didn't see that the cat had moved from beneath the rocker to take advantage of a patch of late summer sun. Nor did it occur to the pampered feline that she was not the center of the universe to be considered in each thought and movement of mankind. When David accidentally stepped on her long, fluffy tail, Calliope yowled her outrage and was across the yard and scaling the apple tree almost before he could recover his balance.

David looked after the cat in dismay. Here he was trying to up his approval rating with Libby James and it was probably dropping faster than the cat was climbing. The calico was about halfway up the tree now, perched on a branch that didn't look capable of supporting its rather hefty weight. David had never owned a cat—or known anybody who did. What did you do when you'd chased a cat up a tree? Did you get a ladder, or call the fire department and let professionals take over?

Calliope blinked accusingly and moved further out on the slender branch as if to prove how perilous her position was.

The darn cat was going to fall. David knew it. There was no time for even the ladder. He'd put Libby's pet in mortal danger and he'd have to save it himself.

Libby's mouth parted in surprise as he pressed the shopping bag back into her arms. Then he sprinted across the yard and grasped the branch over his head to chin himself so he could wrap his leg over the limb. No problem. He was in great shape and he knew it. He only hoped that Libby would recognize it.

She called after him from the porch. "It's all right, Captain Rogers. Calliope will—"

"I'll get her!" he promised. He stood on the lower branch of the gnarled apple tree and reached for the next. Chivalry existed outside Libby's fairy tales and he'd prove it. "Don't worry."

An apple hit him on the top of the head on its way to the ground. Calliope looked down with interest.

"No, really—" Libby began.

David didn't hear the rest of the assurance. Nor did he see Libby drop the bag on the veranda and take an anxious step forward. He'd come eye-level with the cat.

Libby said louder, "Captain Rogers, don't—"

It was too late for the warning. He'd already reached for Calliope. A second later he yelped in pain. The cat leapt across his shoulders, scurried effortlessly down the tree, and disappeared into the hedge.

"Are you all right?" Libby called. When there was no answer she moved closer and said, "Captain Rogers?"

David hadn't moved and he didn't intend to. So much for chivalry. He'd forgotten that quests were seldom undertaken by the village idiot. Apparently there was a reason he'd never seen a cat skeleton in a tree. He stared resolutely into the foliage. Rather than face Libby James, he would stay right where he was and quietly bleed to death from the perpendicular gashes that beast of hers had left across his forehead.

"Captain Rogers?" she asked from only a few yards away. "Shall I get you a ladder?"

She wouldn't let him stay where he was, he realized, because his mangy corpse would mar her beautiful landscape.

"I don't need a ladder," he said. "I can at least get *myself* out of a tree." He reached for the branch Calliope had vacated and discovered it was every bit as weak and untrustworthy as it had looked. When it broke off in his hand he lost his balance and slid gracelessly out of the tree to land on his rear in the pansies. Libby cried out in alarm, but whether for him or her flowers he couldn't say.

"Captain Rogers! Are you all right?"

Did she have to keep calling him *Captain Rogers?* Didn't she know by now that like almost everybody else in the world he had an actual first name? David tossed the broken branch onto the lawn in frustration. She unquestionably knew enough about cats to have told him that what went up could come down, even if he had been too stupid to know it himself. She'd deliberately stood back and let him make a fool of himself, he concluded.

"Are you hurt?" she asked.

"Yes," he shot back, "I'm hurt, okay? My face is shredded, my tailbone's bruised and my pride is fractured. Are you happy?"

"Come into the house," she said gently. "I'll put something on your wounds."

"Salt?"

"No." She extended her hand. "Hydrogen peroxide. It will sting more."

Slowly, he raised his head to see her eyes dancing. She might be a little amused by the situation, but she wasn't gloating. He accepted her outstretched hand and let her help him to his feet. Nothing was seriously damaged except his ego, and that didn't hurt as much when he returned her smile. He followed her into the large, airy kitchen but hesitated in front of the chintz-covered chair she pulled out from the table for him. "I think I have most of your garden on the seat of my pants."

"Sit," she said. She opened a cupboard. "I'll get you an aspirin." She brought him his pain reliever on a little Blue Willow plate with muffins and a tall glass of lemonade.

He held the lemonade in one hand while Libby held his other wrist and tended the scrape on his arm. Sunshine poured in the wide windows, a beautiful woman held his hand, and his mouth was blissfully full of gooseberry muffin. David wondered if he had died in the fall from the tree. This seemed an awful lot like heaven.

"It's not too bad," Libby said as she patted the wound dry with a clean, fluffy cloth before applying the bandage. Her attention moved next to his forehead and she raised her fingers to brush a curl back from his temple. "This is going to hurt a little more, I'm afraid."

Hurt? Not a chance. He was reluctant to admit to himself just how good her touch felt. Except for that one. "Ouch!"

"Sorry." But she didn't stop rinsing the scratches with the promised peroxide despite his protests. "I have something that will take the sting out," she said as she walked over to the windowsill. She returned with scissors and a potted cactus with long, spiked ends. David eyed it dubiously. Libby snipped off an inch-long tip of the plant with a smile. "It's an agave plant. Aloe vera. It's better than anything you can buy at the drug store."

As she squeezed the healing fluid onto the bandage and leaned close to apply it to his head, David scarcely felt the cooling effects. His mind was on the graceful curve of Libby's neck and how many millimeters it was from his lips. He had trouble remembering the topic of conversation when she added, "I'm sure you'll survive, but if you have any swelling you should call Jenn."

"Isn't Jenn the vet?"

"Yes. That makes her the only person within fifty miles with a medical degree."

"Welcome to Amen," he said. Watching Libby return items to her first-aid kit after finishing her task, it finally occurred to David that he had a job to do here himself. He reached discreetly into his pocket for one of the tiny listening devices. He could slip it under the table while her back was turned. If he asked to use the bathroom perhaps he could move through the house and place others as well. In the meantime, it was the first chance for real conversation he'd had with her. He would, of necessity, have to begin by asking questions he already knew the answers to. "Have you lived in Amen all your life?"

"No." She closed the lid on the medical kit and put it back in the cupboard.

"You moved here with your family?"

"No."

"What brought you here?"

She turned to face him. "I came to run the library at Alma School."

She was clearly as adept at half-truths as he was. "Where are you from?"

"California."

"Been here long?"

"Awhile."

He grinned ruefully. "I'll bet you and the junkman have some real meaningful conversations."

"Excuse me?"

David had picked up another muffin and bit into it just as Libby tilted her head. A slanted ray of sun from the window turned her hair to spun gold. David stopped chewing, and perhaps breathing. Finally he managed, "I mean that neither of you talk much."

Her lips curled up at the corners. "Might it be you, Captain? Do all your 'conversations' take the form of interrogations?"

"Maybe," he admitted. "That's what I was used to growing up." Though he was supposed to be gathering information, David found himself sharing it instead as he told Libby about Admiral Benton Rogers, the grandfather who had raised him. Pretty much all he'd ever heard when he was "home" between sessions at military school was a barrage of questions followed by a few brief instructions and then a brusque, "Take care of yourself," as though he hadn't been taking care of himself for as long as he could remember. "I guess I wasn't raised on much conversation," he concluded. "Sorry."

Her face had softened. "No, I'm sorry. I've been rather cool toward you since we first met and it isn't . . . well . . . it isn't because of anything you've done."

If it wasn't him, he wondered, what was it? There was something in Elisabeth Jamison's background that he hadn't seen in her extensive files, but he could see now in her expressive eyes. Something that had hurt her, perhaps even more than her parents' death. Or, he realized with a start, maybe it was *someone* who had hurt her. Someone like him?

Before he could say anything, the back door flew open and a broad-hipped woman in a flowered muumuu and fuzzy bedroom slippers blocked the sunlight.

"Grab the rolling pin, Libby!" she trumpeted. "The rascal won't get past me!" She brandished a badminton racket in one hand and a wicked-looking pair of knitting needles in the other.

"Estelle—" Libby took a step toward David as the woman did.

"Already got him good, did you?" Estelle asked, taking in David's bandaged arm and forehead. "Good for you! I'd have been here sooner but I was dressed in my unmentionables." She aimed the needles toward David's heart. "Guess we've caught us a skulker, haven't we, Lib?"

Libby cast David a sheepish glance. "No, Estelle," she said, covering the old woman's hand with hers to urge her to lower the weapons. "This is Captain Rogers. He's a new teacher at Alma School. He brought a gift over to put in my garden. He hurt himself . . . rescuing Calliope."

So Libby *had* noticed his attempt at chivalry, misguided as it had turned out to be. David felt a little like Sir Galahad.

"He was skulking," Estelle insisted. "I saw him."

Libby managed to free the badminton racket from her neighbor's plump fingers. "No, he was in the garden looking for a place to hang the witching ball." She turned to David for confirmation.

If he'd been trapped in a tunnel with the al-Quaida David would have felt more at ease. "I was—"

"He was peeking in your windows," Estelle reported. "I saw him through my spyglass." Her expression was earnest and David expected his goose was cooked. "You know how vigilant I am, Libby. I've got to be vigilant. Those ten tribes could return from the North Star before we know it!"

David wondered if he'd heard right. Did the woman just say she expected the ten tribes to return from *outer space*? Forget his goose being cooked, this witness for the prosecution was Mother Goose herself. When Libby turned to him he flashed her a conspiratorial grin. "Talk about lost. No wonder those tribes haven't found their way back."

Libby didn't return the smile.

"He was fiddlin' with the back door," Estelle insisted.

"You were trying to break into my home?"

As unlikely as the accusation must seem to her, David saw little disbelief in Libby's expression. There was only anger and, worse, a lot of pain. It was as though she *expected* to be betrayed by a man.

David's throat felt suddenly thick. "I . . . no. Your, uh, neighbor must have seen me . . . knocking on the door to see if you were home."

"Show her those little doodads in your pocket, Captain Skulker," Estelle challenged.

"Get out," Libby said. Her tone of voice invited no excuse or response.

Whatever guy had hurt her, David thought, had done a heck of a job of it.

Estelle's face fell. "We're not going to call the marshal?"

"Leave," Libby told him.

David rose and walked to the door. Perhaps Estelle got in a jab with one of her needles when his back was turned—he could have sworn he felt something pierce his conscience, and reminding himself that he worked for the good guys did nothing to dull the sensation. The cat hadn't believed it when he'd told her, David recalled as he stepped carefully over Calliope while crossing the veranda.

He wondered how much longer he would believe it himself.

chapter 9

The sea creatures looked at the telegraph wire.
"What is that thing?" they asked, "and what is it not?"
Aye, that was the question.

— *The Great Sea Serpent, A New Wonder Story, 1872*

"Caught in the act!" Estelle lamented after David left. "And you let him walk away scot-free!"

Libby closed the kitchen door. She had overreacted and she was already sorry for it. What must Captain Rogers think? It was just that Estelle's wild accusations had dredged up all the old fears Libby had of again being deceived, deluded, and duped by a man. Suddenly, nothing had seemed more important than getting David out of her home—and keeping him out of her life. Feeling somewhat weak-kneed, she leaned against the door.

"You okay, Lib?" Estelle asked, sticking her knitting needles into a front pocket of her dress. "You look pale. You're not afraid of that man, are you?"

"No," Libby said. "Of course not." She was afraid of herself and of the stirrings she had felt as she watched David climb her tree thinking he was saving her cat. Captain Rogers was all ridiculous macho ego, she'd thought at the time, though the muscular package it came in was pretty darn attractive. Later, as she'd tended his wounds and he'd told her about his childhood she'd realized that Tansy was right. Captain Rogers *was* funny and smart. He was also—like her—a survivor.

Estelle broke into Libby's thoughts. "Why do you suppose he'd be skulking around your house in the broad daylight?"

Why indeed? Libby knew that she must look skeptical because Estelle flushed.

"I don't miss *anything*, Lib!"

"I know you don't, Estelle." But Libby also knew that Estelle genuinely believed that the Ten Lost Tribes of Israel would "return" to Amen, Arizona. According to Estelle—who had been misquoting a vague passage from her patriarchal blessing for the last sixty-seven years—the tribes lived on a not-far-distant planet and awaited the divine mandate for their return. Estelle didn't know what the signal would be, but felt it was her duty as a stalwart daughter of Ephraim to be ready with a hearty homecoming back to the earthly fold. Certainly Libby knew that her friend was delusional, but thought it a harmless fantasy as delusions go. Estelle was devout in the Church and as good a neighbor as anyone could hope for. If she was also a little bit crazy, well, Libby found it endearing.

"You believe what you will, Libby James." Estelle folded her arms across her ample bosom. "I believe what I see and what I read in the holy scriptures."

This time Libby agreed readily. She believed what she saw too, and she thought she'd seen guilt cross David's face. But maybe, in retrospect, it was more surprise at being accused of being a Peeping Tom. Whatever it was, Libby regretted the way she had thrown him out of her house. Would she be hyper-suspicious of every man she met for the rest of her life because of Karlton Fisk?

She was still asking herself that question an hour later when Estelle went home. She feared that the answer was "yes." She was suspicious of everything lately.

Libby sat at the dining room table, pushed away the contracts, and rested her elbow on the table and her chin in her palm as she stared at the pile of papers. She hadn't seen anything unusual when she went over them yet again. The vague doubts she felt must be prompted more by her nerves than by the Spirit. Is that where her doubts about Captain Rogers came from too? Impulsively, she reached for the phone and dialed the number she knew best."Elisabeth!" Leonard Kelley boomed a moment later. "How's my girl?"

"Good, Uncle Leo."

"Uh, oh. What is it?"

Libby bit her lip in vexation. She mostly called him Uncle Leo when she felt confused and alone and a little sorry for herself. "I wonder if you could do me a favor?"

"For you, Princess, anything." His voice was so warm and familiar it felt to Libby like a security blanket. "You called to ask for the moon? It's yours. You want it gift wrapped or in a bag from Saks?"

Libby smiled. Then she looked out the window and saw the witching ball hanging like a lunar pearl above her garden and the smile disappeared. "I want you to call a private investigator and have him find out everything he can about a Captain David Rogers."

It was so quiet she could hear the scratch of his pen on paper—the silver-inlaid fountain pen she'd given him last Father's Day, no doubt. "Who is he?" Leonard asked when he'd finished writing.

"An astronaut," Libby said. "A space shuttle pilot—from the Navy, I think. He came to Amen last week to teach at the school."

"You don't like him," Leonard asked cautiously, "or you *do?*"

Libby gazed out at the globe and remembered all the times she'd peeked out the library window to watch David play football with the boys in his class. She remembered how open and honest he'd been with her this afternoon. But she remembered too, how odd he looked at her sometimes and that her first impression had been that *he* didn't like *her*. "I don't know," she said.

"I'd be glad to think you'd found someone after—"

"It's not like that," she interrupted. "It's not like that at all. I only want to know where he came from and what he's doing here." She turned away from the window. "Find out for me, Leonard, will you?"

"You've got it, Princess."

"And, Leonard, have you had a chance to look over the new defense contracts?" She pulled the papers back in front of her.

"They're on my desk now."

"Is anything . . . different . . . about them?"

"We're making a little more profit," he said. "That should make the good folks at SynQuest happy."

Did the tone of his voice change when he said "SynQuest," Libby wondered, or was that her imagination too? "I feel funny about it, Uncle Leo."

"You're going to have to define 'funny' for me, Elisabeth."

She sighed. "I can't. I only feel that something isn't right with the whole thing."

He hesitated some time before he said, "It looks hunky-dory to me." Then he teased, "Are you sure this Captain Rogers hasn't addled that analytical little brain of yours?"

"Yes!" Libby said, and hoped she was as sure as she sounded. She was almost relieved when he changed the subject back to SynQuest and the upcoming merger. *Almost* relieved. Frank had been truthful for once. Leonard wasn't one hundred percent behind the sale. Libby listened to his concerns and noted that his words were so carefully chosen that they sounded rehearsed. He was walking on eggshells trying not to upset her.

"I'm thinking of you, Princess," he concluded, "and Genie and Chelsea. Jamison Enterprises is your heritage."

No, Libby thought, that little adobe chapel her ancestors had built with their bare hands was their heritage. The multi-story Jamison Enterprises complex in downtown Los Angeles was something else. Increasingly it felt like an albatross that she couldn't get from around her neck fast enough. It surprised her that Leonard, who understood everything about her, didn't understand this.

"We'll discuss it another time," he said, sensing her unspoken resistance. "Plenty of time to reconsider."

In the meantime, he had a list of things that did require her immediate attention. Libby took careful notes. When their business was complete and Libby turned off the phone a few minutes later, she stared down at it absently. *Was* she doing the right thing, or was Leonard right? Had her long absence from the day-to-day operations at Jamison Enterprises clouded her thinking?

She at last stacked the contracts to the side and turned her attention to her E-mail. She wouldn't think about the sale now. If Leonard was wrong about her heritage, he was right in saying she had time to decide about selling her company. What she didn't have time for was daydreaming.

Libby knew she wasn't the kind of CEO her father would have liked her to be, but it still took many hours a week to be what she was. Though Frank (in his dreams) and Leonard (in reality) ran the company, they reported to her. She, in turn, was careful to keep up appearances. The corporate world thought she was jet-setting around the globe—sunning herself in Majorca or shopping in Paris—when actually she was working at a school library in Amen. She presided in person at the quarterly board meetings and was careful to make her presence known electronically every other day but the Sabbath.

Sunday. Libby's heart skipped a beat and thoughts of business left her head. It was just her luck that David Rogers belonged to the Church. She'd have to see him six days a week instead of five. What must he think of her after the scene in the kitchen? And what if he'd bought that horrible mattress she recommended at the second-hand store? Maybe if she kept a chapel's length between them at all times tomorrow she wouldn't have to explain herself.

It wasn't much hope, but it was all she had.

* * *

David had practiced half a dozen different ways to explain himself to Libby without calling Estelle a liar or crazy, though he suspected the latter was true.

I looked in your windows and tried your door because I thought I smelled smoke . . . ?

But that—and every other explanation he came up with—was so lame he couldn't say it while looking at himself in a mirror. No way could he get the words out while looking at Libby. He walked up the sidewalk toward the church with roughly the same enthusiasm as the cranky two-year-old next to him being dragged to worship by his mother.

He felt worse once he was inside. LaRae Flake was waiting in the lobby and attached herself to his arm tighter than the seal on an air lock. However, her dragging him along might have been the only thing that got him to the chapel door once he saw that today's greeter was Libby's neighbor, Estelle of the Ten Tribes.

"Welcome, Brother Skulker," she said with true Christian charity. Although her only weapon was a vinyl scripture case, David gave her as wide a berth as he was able.

LaRae tugged on an elbow still sore from his fall from the tree. "Did you get my messages?" Neither the words nor the tug registered since he was watching Libby adjust a music stand up by the organ. Her dress was the color of the autumn sky, and he thought her silky hair held the light of distant galaxies. It fell over her shoulders as she leaned forward, struggling with the stand. David took a step toward her.

Only the yank that nearly separated his arm from his shoulder caused him to pause. "We sit in back," LaRae said, the words curt and clearly enunciated.

David allowed LaRae to lead him to a seat back and center. He greeted LaDonna and LaVerne and tried not to gape at the former's lynx jacket. Clearly nothing went to waste in that family.

The music stand in place, Libby took her seat and looked steadfastly down at a hymnal in her lap.

LaRae stuck the point of her bony elbow into his ribs. "What happened to your face?"

He raised his fingers to the bandage on his forehead and remembered Libby's gentle touch. He couldn't seem to take his eyes off her. "Libby's cat scratched me."

"A cat scratch can kill you," LaRae said in a tone of voice that implied she hoped it would.

David wondered if Libby would care if her cat killed him.

The point of LaRae's elbow struck again, possibly puncturing his left lung. "Dinner's at two. I'm making dumplings to go with the gopher."

It might have been the only thing she could say to distract him from Libby, but it worked. His head swung toward her. When she smiled he thought that he'd never seen more teeth on a human being. Like her Aunt LaVerne, LaRae Flake was all mouth. "You didn't say 'gopher,' did you?"

Stiff, copper-colored ringlets bobbed as she nodded happily. "You've never had gopher, David? Well, aren't you in for a treat! Daddy traps 'em in the garden and skins 'em fresh." She reached up to puff out the sleeve on her frilly pink dress. "Well, fresh yesterday. We don't butcher on the Sabbath, naturally."

"Aren't gophers *rodents?*"

"Waste not, want not."

David might have eventually sputtered a response, but LaRae put a finger to her lips to shush him. "The bishop's standing up. It's wicked to talk in sacrament meeting." She folded her freckled hands primly in her lap. Then she saw Libby James glance down at David, so she wiggled a little closer.

Since he was already against the end of the pew, there was no place for David to go. He tried to ignore LaRae and smile politely when Bishop Wheeler read in his membership. He wondered if it was the Church or the CIA that had been responsible for getting the records here so quickly. Probably it was the CIA.

During the administration of the sacrament, David opened his scriptures and removed a picture of Christ from between the pages of 3 Nephi.

. . . And it shall be a testimony unto the Father that ye do always remember me. And if ye do always remember me ye shall have my Spirit to be with you.

David remembered that as a boy, while his mother prayed during the sacrament, he would look at this picture and try to think about Jesus. When his parents died in an accident, David was sent to his grandfather. That was when his contact with the Church disappeared. All that was left for many years when he thought about Jesus or tried to pray was the feeling that, like his parents, his Heavenly Father had left him. Still, when it was time to pack a few personal items for his first trip into space, David had looked for his scriptures for the first time in twenty years. They—and this picture of Christ—were the only personal effects he took along and were all he needed at a time of crisis to change the course of his life.

He fingered a well-worn corner of the picture as he bowed his head and thought about what the gospel meant in his life today. With the acceleration of his heart at the sight of Libby James to indicate that he might be falling for her, and the CIA still convinced she was a traitor and spy, his faith in the Lord might be the *only* thing David was still sure of.

chapter 10

"But suspicions are nothing when a person is really true, and everyone should persevere in acting honestly, for all will be made right in time."

—The Silver Shilling, 1862

"So, Brother Rogers," Bishop Wheeler said, folding his hands atop the walnut desk in his office, "what brings you to Amen?"

If forced to cite one completely normal person in the town, David would have named Max. Until now. He shifted in his chair as the bell rang to announce the beginning of Sunday School. "I, uh, came to teach at Alma School." *Remember?*

"We're glad to have you."

So you do remember.

"Why Amen?"

"NASA sent me." They'd had this conversation already. But on that day Max had been his boss. Today he was his bishop, and it felt entirely different. The only thing more unappealing than this interview was the thought of LaRae's gopher dumplings.

"Did they?"

"Well, yeah." David looked at Max's hands, at his polished desk—anywhere but into his eyes. He'd had very little training before embarking on his new career in counter-espionage and none of it had covered lying to Church authorities. "I just came to work . . . " His gaze happened upon a picture of Christ. *If ye do always remember me ye shall have my Spirit to be with you.* Even so, the next words out of

David's mouth simply amazed him " . . . for the CIA." He rested his elbow on the desk and dropped his forehead onto the palm. *Stupid. Stupid. Stupid.*

"Nothing leaves this room," Max said quietly.

And that would be a good thing. David knew he could be arrested for what he'd just revealed. On the other hand, as he recalled, the questions in the temple recommend interview dealing with honesty and sustaining priesthood leaders weren't multiple choice.

"Are you spying on Libby?"

David raised his face. Bishops were supposed to be inspired, but this guy was downright omniscient. "Yes," he admitted quietly. "She isn't . . . I mean she is . . . She's really . . . " He'd blown his own cover in less than half a second. Why couldn't he bring himself to blow hers?

"You're trying to say that she's Elisabeth Jamison?"

Even as David's eyes widened, his heart lightened. So she hadn't lied to her bishop. At least not about her identity. He nodded.

"It had to be her," Bishop Wheeler mused. "There's nobody else in Amen to spy on."

Except maybe Libby's neighbor, David thought. *Somebody ought to keep an eye on that nutcase.*

Max's bushy brows met above his nose. "But why? Does it have something to do with her parents' murder?"

"Not directly," David said. "It has to do with somebody at Jamison Enterprises helping Iran develop weapons of mass destruction."

The bishop was incredulous. "Surely you don't suspect Libby?"

David shrugged uncomfortably. "The diamonds are going into a safe-deposit box in the Caymans. The box has the Jamisons' name on it."

"I'm not asking what the CIA thinks," Max said. "I'm asking you. Do you believe that Libby James might be capable of murdering thousands of innocent people?"

When you put it that way . . . . But, really, what did he know about Libby James? David determined to put aside his growing personal feelings for her—whatever they might be—and remain objective. Above all, he would remember the agency's motto: Guilty until proven innocent. This time he looked Max squarely in the eye as he said "No."

The bishop nodded approvingly. Then he leaned forward. "What will the CIA do if you blow your cover?"

You mean if they find out I've blown it. He said, "Besides shoot me for treason, they'd probably have to arrest Libby now and try to prove their case in court later. They don't have enough evidence to convict her or they wouldn't have sent me, but they have enough circumstantial evidence to arrest her."

"And ruin her life," Max said. "There's your answer."

"Where?" David asked. "What was my question?"

"You wondered if you should stay undercover and do your job, and the answer is yes. I know for a fact that you'll never prove Libby guilty, but you might be able to prove her innocent." He reached across the desk and laid a hand over David's wrist. "She needs your help, Captain Rogers. Take care of her."

It wasn't the worst offer he'd ever had, but there was one small problem: Libby would run off with a swineherd before she'd accept his help.

"It won't be easy," the bishop continued as if reading his thoughts. "You'll have a hard time gaining Libby's trust."

You don't know the half of it.

"Estelle tells me you were 'skulking' around Libby's house yesterday." The chuckle was scarcely contained.

So you do know the half of it.

"May I suggest that you be a little more subtle from now on?"

"I'm a shuttle pilot," David muttered. "I'm not James Bond."

"The problem is that you're a man," Max said. "An attractive single man, and Libby doesn't trust attractive single men."

David looked up. He'd read every word of her case file more than a dozen times. He knew where she was born and where she'd gone to school and how she'd spent her summer vacation, but he still didn't know *anything* about her.

"She was engaged before she came here," the bishop said.

Lucky guy, David thought. *I hope he's dead.*

"She thought she'd found the perfect man," Max continued. "The guy, Karlton something-or-other, was a returned missionary. Problem was, he didn't mention that he'd returned in disgrace. He lied about his mission and his temple recommend, then tried to get Libby to elope with him to the Caribbean and be sealed later. Smart girl; she held out long enough for one of the other women he'd used to turn up—with a new baby and an old story. Karlton was in love all right, but it was with Libby's money. It's taking her a long time to get over it."

David reconsidered. *I hope he's alive. I'd like to kill him myself.*

"To say she's cautious," the older man concluded, "is to put it mildly." He leaned back in his chair. "But what about you? Your church records show you've never married."

"I haven't been on many third dates even."

Max smiled. "As half the women in Houston can attest?"

David picked a piece of lint from his tie. "Something like that."

"Libby's like a daughter to me."

The words carried enough weight to raise David's chin from his chest. "I understand."

"Now, about why I asked you in to the office today . . . "

There's more?

" . . . I want to call you as the Scoutmaster. Ezra's the Young Men's president, but he's not as young as he used to be." David knew that "Deaf Old Ezra," as he was known around town, hadn't been as young as he used to be since the middle of the previous century. "We've got a dozen deacons now with more energy than the Palo Verde nuclear power plant. A couple of the livest wires are in your class at Alma."

That David already knew. Calvin-of-the-crab-apples was one of them.

"What do you say?"

"Uh—" It wasn't eloquent, but it accurately expressed his feelings.

"Good!" The bishop swiveled his chair around to a low bookcase behind his desk. When he turned back he had a stack including some guides for priesthood leaders, the *Boy Scout Handbook, Activities for Youth,* and a trio of Aaronic Priesthood manuals. From his desk drawer he added *For the Strength of Youth* and *Duty to God* pamphlets. "Any questions?"

"Uh—"

"Excellent. We'll sustain you next week, but you can get started right away. Let's go into the priesthood meeting and I'll introduce you to the boys you don't already know." He pushed back his chair. "Except for Aaron, of course. You'll have to go with Libby to meet Aaron. Otherwise his father will fill you full of birdshot." By now the big man was on his feet and around the desk. "Come on, Brother Rogers. Bring your books."

He mentioned Libby in connection with the birdshot, David reminded himself through his shock. It wasn't much to hold on to, but it was something.

"Oh!" the bishop said on his way to the door, "I almost forgot."

David cringed.

"The wife wanted me to bring you home for lunch after church today. About two?"

"Oh. Thank you!" David told the bishop—and God.

Wheeler paused with his hand on the doorknob. "The Flakes invited you for gopher, I take it?" When David nodded, he shook his head. "Well, let me tell you, LaRae's gopher and dumplings sure beat her skunk chops."

He's kidding. David wanted to laugh but found he couldn't. "You're kidding, right?"

The bishop pulled open the door.

"You *are* kidding?" *He must be kidding,* David decided as he followed the bishop into the hall. He'd be sure of it if he didn't have his hands full of books, a quorum full of unruly deacons to oversee, and a new mandate from the bishop to spy on Libby James. Things in Amen only kept getting stranger, but *skunk chops*? He *had* to be kidding.

chapter 11

Now these thoughts were great and daring, as our thoughts usually are at home, before we have gone out into the world and encountered its storms and tempests.

— *The Philosopher's Stone, 1859*

Libby paused with her hand on the doorknob to the faculty workroom. It was Friday afternoon and in another moment she was going to turn the handle, open the door, walk in the room, and start over with David Rogers.

She could do it. She knew she could. What she couldn't do was continue to hide in libraries to avoid him asking her for yet another date. He'd started asking last Sunday, in spite of the fiasco the day before, and now people were beginning to talk. Libby wouldn't accept any of his offers, but it was because she didn't care to date, not because she was afraid that he was right—that she *might* melt the first time he touched her hand.

In a second she was going to open this door and prove how unaffected she was by his attention. She'd be casual and cool and put the last of the awkwardness behind them. Then she'd be professional at school and at church she'd call him "brother" and mean it.

"I'm telling you, Omar," David was saying as she opened the door, "those three pigs I saw must have their own gang. They have big muscles and hairy chins and—" the words ended abruptly as he saw Libby.

"Leather jackets?" she prompted. *That was good*, she told herself. *Keep it light.*

"He is telling me of animals that attacked his vehicle last night," Omar offered when David didn't respond. "He describes, I believe, fierce mutant werepigs."

"They're peccaries, Omar," Libby said with a smile. "In Arizona we call them javelina. They come into town sometimes looking for food." *Go on about your business,* she commanded the body that seemed pinned in the doorway by Captain Rogers' gaze. She walked calmly to the copy machine. *Good. Now keep talking.* "You must have left food in your truck, Captain."

"I guess," he said. "The Scouts ate their s'mores back there last night."

"The javelina probably smelled the leftover graham crackers." Libby thought that she could go for a leftover chocolate bar herself. Not that craving chocolate meant she was nervous. She wasn't. She turned quickly, lifted the lid of the copy machine, and laid the paper she'd brought in on the glass. If only David would stop looking at her with those Hershey-colored eyes of his. And if he'd stop being so nice all the time and go back to being his old obnoxious self, that would help too.

"How many blank copies do you plan to make?" he asked.

"Oh!" She'd been so busy trying to appear as though she was concentrating on her work that she hadn't noticed she'd put her original in upside down. She flipped it hastily, reloaded the paper into the drawer, and hit the "ready" button. The stupid machine jammed on the first copy. She ripped open the service door and stared blankly at the mechanical innards. She'd fixed this copier a dozen times or more—but now her brain was as hopelessly jammed as the machine.

She was so intent on trying not to scream in vexation that she didn't hear David move. Only the sudden prickling of every nerve in her body told her that he was leaning over her shoulder.

"Let me take a look."

Libby did *not* want to stand here next to him. The problem was that with all her senses filled with his closeness, there were no sensory paths left to control the basic motor skills necessary for movement.

"There's the problem," he continued, indicating a rumpled paper lodged between two metal rods.

His thumb brushed her bare arm as he reached around her for a release lever inside the machine, and Libby's reflexes returned in a rush. She jumped to the side and clasped the flesh that he'd touched as if it were burned.

"Sorry," he said. "Did I shock you?"

It was impossible to tell what he was thinking, but she was grateful a moment later when the handsome, bemused face receded back into the machine.

Get a grip, Libby commanded herself. She took a deep breath and moved close enough to see that he had removed only part of the paper. "You have to turn that wheel-thingy to get the rest."

"Where?"

Emboldened to be so close and yet so in control, Libby reached down and turned the knob herself. "Here. It feeds the paper through and—" Her fingers flew from the knob to her lips. She hadn't seen David's tie so near the mechanism and she'd just wound it into the machine. Though he tugged to free the fabric, he was firmly tethered to the copier.

He managed to turn his head enough to look up at her. "You planned this, didn't you?"

"I didn't know—"

"The same way you didn't know your cat could get itself out of a tree?"

"I . . . you . . . " Unable to look at the scabbed scratches on his forehead, and knowing that the knob turned only one way, Libby fled to retrieve scissors from the supply closet. "Here, let me."

He caught her wrist. "You've done enough. Omar, disarm her for me before she 'innocently' removes my tonsils."

Libby placed the scissors meekly in Omar's hand. She winced when he cut the tie and David rose with only a knot and three or four inches of silk left around his neck. "I'll replace the tie," she offered.

"With what? A noose?" He removed the ruined fabric from around his neck and then removed the rest of it—as well as the crumpled paper—from the Xerox machine and closed the side. He pressed the restart button and nodded approvingly when the first copy came through successfully. He glanced at it and saw his name on the short list. "My library book's overdue? Already?"

"The check-out period is one week."

"I haven't finished it yet," he protested. "I got sidetracked by Scout manuals."

"You're reading the fairy tales?" she asked in surprise. He hadn't impressed her as the "once upon a time" type.

David grinned. "Oh, it's a very instructive book." He turned to Omar. "Hans Christian Andersen had women nailed."

"Your meaning?" the coach asked. "It is what?"

Libby wondered the same thing.

"My meaning, my friend, is that the moral of every fairy tale is don't turn your back on a woman." David leaned against the copier and crossed his arms over his chest. "Take *Thumbelina* for instance. There's this mole—a heck of a nice guy; quiet, faithful, a good provider, and head-over-heels in love with a homeless girl. He offers to marry her and give her everything she'd ever need, and what does she do? Ditches him for a flower fairy."

"It wasn't exactly like that, Omar," Libby began.

"Yeah, it was," David said. "But at least the mole escaped alive. The Brave Tin Soldier only looked at a fancy dancer and he ended up as a heart-shaped lump of metal."

"Tell him about the Little Mermaid," Libby said. When Captain Rogers didn't immediately respond, she told Omar the gist of the story herself: "She gave up her life to breathe the same air as some narcissistic prince, then spent the rest of eternity trying to get her soul back."

The Egyptian looked from Libby to David. "And in *The Snow Queen*?" he asked. "That boy and girl, their story is sorrowful as well?"

"The Snow Queen had typical female expectations," David told him. "All she asked the guy to do was one little *impossible* job."

"She gave him a puzzle," Libby countered. "He was supposed to spell 'eternity' from pieces of broken ice. It only *seemed* impossible because Kay was male and thus the concept of eternity was beyond his comprehension."

"And even when he *did it*," David continued, "he didn't get the prize. The Queen promised him the world and a new pair of skates besides. But do you know what he got, Omar? He got—"

"Gerta," Libby inserted, determined to tell the story as Andersen had meant it—a tale of hope and faith and true love conquering all. "Gerta melted the ice in Kay's heart and that made it possible for him to solve the puzzle at last. By that time he'd grown up enough to—"

"To know that if he found the girl he loved he already *had* the whole world," David concluded.

Libby stared at him in surprise. "Well, yes."

"Then there is something on which you agree," Omar said. "Shall we leave it at that, please?"

"Yes," Libby said again, thinking that Omar hadn't deserved to be caught up in this strange allegorical crossfire in the first place. And her cool, professional persona was as frazzled as her nerves. Her opinion of Captain Rogers was not unlike the most volatile stock in her portfolio: plummeting one minute and rising the next. Unfortunately, unlike the stock market, she couldn't ever correctly predict what he might do next.

"Do you have plans this afternoon?" he asked.

"Yes," she lied without hesitation.

"Tomorrow?"

"Yes." She retreated to the door.

"Sunday afternoon?"

"Yes."

"Three years, five weeks and two days from next Tuesday—at say, 4:17 in the morning?"

"Yes."

"She has nothing against me personally," David assured Omar. "She's very busy." He turned back to Libby, "Any possibility your plans might change if I swear in front of this fine witness that I'm not asking you for a date this time?"

"You're not?" *Oh, please don't let that have sounded like disappointment*, she prayed, realizing that disappointment might be what she felt.

"No," he said. "I'm asking because Aaron McKracken is one of my Scouts. I'd like to go out to meet him, but I understand from Max that I'd better not try it without a Kevlar vest and/or you to protect me."

She'd been out to the farm twice this week and Aaron had asked dozens of questions about Captain Rogers. She should take him out this afternoon, and she knew she should. If only—

If only nothing, she told herself firmly. She'd promised Aaron. This way she wouldn't have to ask David herself. "As a matter of fact," she said, "I'd planned to drive out to the McKrackens' farm this afternoon. Could you leave in thirty minutes?" When he agreed, her grip on the doorknob tightened reflexively. Keeping her promise meant twenty minutes alone in a car with him, but she'd drive fast. Really fast. And she'd keep her eyes on the road and her mind on driving.

Sure she would. The same way she'd come in with a vow to remain calm, cool, and collected and now struggled to leave with palms so slick she could scarcely turn the doorknob.

Thank goodness Wall Street couldn't see her now.

chapter 12

She was so lovely anyone could see she was a real princess. The soldier could not stop himself from kissing her, for he was a real soldier.

— *The Tinder-box, 1835*

David knew that Geneva Jamison drove this year's Lamborghini—when she wasn't in the backseat of her chauffeured limo—and yet her sister drove a '98 Mazda. Libby had the window down, preferring it to the old, faulty air conditioner. And David wondered if Libby knew how attractive she looked with the wind lifting silken strands of hair back from her long, graceful neck and was simply trying to drive him crazy. If that was her plan, it was working perfectly.

But that probably wasn't her plan. Her eyes were focused on the road and her lips were drawn into a thin, determined line. David forced himself to look out the passenger window. Indian paintbrush bloomed from the roadside up to the base of the mountains to the east. The sky was a deep, perfect blue with a few puffy clouds dotting the horizon. A small herd of antelope looked curiously at the passing car and a hawk swooped in lazy concentric circles over a nearby bluff. It was a nice view, David thought, but better on his left. He turned back to Libby. "Tell me about Aaron."

"Who?"

He'd talked from an orbiting shuttle to people in Houston who'd seemed closer than she was now. She was pressed against her door to leave as much space as possible between them. David suppressed a smile at the recognition that, if nothing else, he made the fair maiden nervous. "Aaron," he repeated. "You remember, the kid we're going to visit."

"Oh!" Libby's attention shifted from the road for a fraction of a second. "Well, Aaron's remarkable. He's almost fourteen and very bright . . . "

David listened gratefully to the first essay answer he'd received from Libby. She talked about Aaron's goals in life and the recent accident that had made many of those goals unattainable. When they turned off onto a narrow dirt road and he commented on an odd-looking cornfield, she explained that Aaron's father was trying a method of farming practiced by the Anasazi Indians twenty-three centuries before. His fields had a triple crop of corn, beans and squash. The corn stalks served as bean poles and the broad leaves of the squash covered the ground to hold in moisture.

Libby turned down a lane that led toward a small farmhouse. "I hope this is Moses's best crop ever."

David understood her concern for the family as he looked at their roof. It was clearly missing a shingle or twelve.

Libby said, "The McKrackens deserve a blessing if anybody does."

"Maybe if the family patriarch stopped taking potshots at the stake president—"

"You don't know anything about Moses McKracken," Libby said quickly. She stopped the car and opened her door before David could reach for his handle. "We'll only stay a few minutes."

He looped his knapsack over his shoulder and followed Libby toward the house. A sad-faced hound and its beaming young owner met them halfway.

"Captain Rogers!" Tansy cried. "You came! Did you bring the pictures like I asked you to?" When he nodded she took his hand and pulled him forward. "Okay then! Aaron's in back. He's gonna be so surprised!" She tugged harder to move David around the house a little faster. "He's been talking about meeting a real astronaut for a whole week now. It's all he talks about! He makes me tell him every word you say in class. Every *word*. You have the pictures, right? I wish we'd known you were coming today, we'd have—"

"Tansy," Libby said with a smile, "breathe."

They rounded the final corner. "Aaron! It's *him*, Aaron! It's honestly him!"

A shock of dark hair fell over Aaron's forehead as he turned. He tried to struggle up but Tansy had David to his side so quickly he didn't have time to complete the effort.

"Here he is! Sister James brought him, just like she promised! He brought the pictures, Aaron, and—" her orange braids flew horizontal to her scalp as she spun toward David, "you *do* have the pictures, don't you?"

Libby placed a hand on the girl's shoulder. "Go tell your mother that we're here." When Tansy didn't immediately obey she said, "Scoot. I'll introduce Captain Rogers to Aaron. You won't miss anything."

"I'll be right back!" The screen door banged shut behind her.

"Captain Rogers," Libby said, moving to the boy's side, "may I introduce Aaron McKracken?" She smiled down at the youth with affection. "Aaron, this is Captain David Rogers, the man Tansy's been telling you about."

David extended his hand. "Pleased to meet you, Aaron. I'm your new Scoutmaster."

"Y-you-you are?" Aaron's eyes were on the hand that was clasped in David's. When the space shuttle pilot released it, he looked at it still. "Th-that's g-great."

"I hear you're interested in the space program."

"Oh, y-yes! S-Sister James b-brought me all this st-stuff." He indicated a sheaf of papers spread out on the nearby bed. "I've r-read all ab-bout you."

Most of it, David saw at a glance, had come off the NASA web site. But there was at least one page that hadn't. It must have come courtesy of that private investigator Leonard Kelley had hired to check him out. Libby saw the paper the same time he did. She moved over to the bed and rearranged Aaron's collection into a neat stack—with the PI's picture of him on the bottom.

David pretended not to notice. "Sister James tells me you'd like to be an Eagle Scout. Do you have the astronomy merit badge?" When the young man's head swung back and forth, David smiled. "What say we work on that one together?"

"C-could we?"

"It'll be my pleasure."

The back door opened with another bang to reveal Tansy and
Hannah. "Where're the pictures?" the girl asked anxiously. "I didn't
miss the pictures, did I?"

"Let your mother say hello to Captain Rogers," Libby said. "Then
you can all look at the pictures together."

Hannah untangled her lean hand from her apron to extend it to
David. When he released it, she twisted it back into the fabric. "Good
of you to come, Captain Rogers. Tansy speaks real high of you." She
cast Libby a long, grateful look. "Good of you to bring him, Lib."

David said, "I'm glad to be here. I've looked forward to meeting
Aaron." At a little yelp from Tansy he added hastily, "And to visiting
my favorite student."

He accepted the wooden chair that Hannah proffered and soon
was removing a folder of photos and articles from his knapsack.
Aaron was such an appreciative audience David didn't know how long
he spent answering the boy's questions before he realized that Aaron's
stutter had disappeared—as had Libby and Hannah. Even Tansy and
her dog had drifted away at some point. "Well, Aaron," he said, "It
looks like nobody else is as interested in Whipple bumpers and zeolite
systems as we are."

Aaron seemed genuinely amazed. "I could listen to you talk all
night! And you haven't said anything about your space walk yet."

That was because David never said anything about his space walk.

"I remember it," Aaron said. "We watched it in science and history.
Everybody talked about it for days. I bet you weren't even scared."

Because he liked Aaron so much, David was reluctant to climb
down from the pedestal. It wasn't easy, but he said, "You're wrong,
Aaron. I was plenty scared." He expected to see disappointment on
the youth's face, but he saw something else. Hope?

"I'm sc-scared too, Captain Rogers. I'm scared I'm not ever g-
gonna walk again. I'm sc- scared I'll never get *any* of my d-dreams."

David had never been good at platitudes at a moment's notice, so
he was at a loss. There were lots of things he supposed he could say to
console him, some of them even true. Instead, he looked mutely into
the boy's frightened face. Suddenly he felt at peace, and then David's
mouth opened apparently without instruction from his brain. "Your
dreams will come true, Aaron."

The next thing he knew Aaron's head was on his shoulder and his arms around his neck. He returned the embrace and felt prompted to add, "You'll walk again." Over the top of Aaron's head he saw Hannah and Libby pause behind the screen door. Hannah smiled broadly, but Libby's eyes widened in concern.

I didn't just promise this paralyzed kid that he'll walk, did I? Looking at Libby, he knew that he had, and his former confidence faltered. Who did he think he was, anyway?

"We need to go," Libby told him. "We've stayed too long already."

She means about three words too long.

"Stay," Hannah urged. "It's beans and corn and bread for supper, but there's plenty. We'd be honored to have you and Captain Rogers eat with us."

"Please stay!" Aaron echoed. "I want you to meet my dad."

The one with the shotgun. David suspected that at this point Libby wouldn't stand between them.

"Oh, Hannah," Libby said, "another time." She stared helplessly from the look of disappointment on her friend's face to the look of near devastation on Aaron's. "You see, I . . . I mean he . . . you . . . well, we . . . "

You, me, her, us what?

"Please, Libby?" Hannah urged. "It would mean a lot to Aaron."

Libby turned toward David for backup. He knew that a gentleman would invent a pressing engagement to get her off the hook. "I'd like to stay," he said, willing to risk a little petty caddishness—and even birdshot—if it meant spending another hour or so with Libby.

* * *

"Haven't you ever shucked corn?" Tansy asked David a few minutes later as she sat between him and Libby on the porch steps. When he shook his head, she deftly removed the outer husk from the ear she held, brushed away the corn silk, and snapped off the stalk before depositing it in a large enamel basin. Then she took another ear off the stack and handed it to him.

Libby didn't look up from the corn in her lap. How could David have promised Aaron he'd walk? And why couldn't she be angry about it? Try as she would to be reasonable, Libby felt stirrings of peace creep into her heart—peace and a somewhat begrudging admiration. David had spoken too quickly, and undoubtedly foolishly, but he'd spoken from his heart and she had a difficult time faulting him for that.

Tansy picked up another ear of corn, pulled down the top for a quick peek inside, then returned the ear to the pile and grabbed another.

"She's looking for one with red kernels," Aaron told David.

Despite herself, Libby smiled. Tansy wasn't the only girl around who had a crush on Captain Rogers. All the girls in the Young Women's program had been swooning since last Sunday. Libby's smile faded quickly, however, when the girl found what she was looking for and passed it to her with a triumphant grin.

"You shuck this one, Sister James!"

"What's so special about that one?" David asked

"At a c-cornhusking party," Aaron explained, "you find an ear with red kernels so all the unmarried g-guys or girls have to kiss you."

"You keep it, Tansy," Libby said. Her cheeks felt warm and she suspected more than the setting sun.

"You're the guest," Tansy insisted. "Husk it, Sister James!

"Tansy—"

David grinned broadly. "Tansy, if Sister James is afraid that one little peck on the cheek could make her—"

Libby tore the husk off the corn and tossed it in the pot before he could finish the sentence.

"Now you have to kiss her, Captain Rogers!" Tansy sang out. She scooted out from between them and looked on happily.

"Well, if I *have* to—"

Libby closed her eyes. When she felt David's lips linger at a spot along her cheekbone, it was all she could do not to raise her fingers to the place and try to calm the pulsing in the temple above. She turned toward him instinctively and when she opened her eyes, found that his face was still only inches away.

Libby knew now why she never allowed herself to look into David's eyes. The longer she gazed the more she saw reflected there. They were dark as night but the amber flecks within made her think of bright stars. Neither of them moved—or could move—to break the enchantment, and Libby wondered what might have happened next if Aaron hadn't said, "My turn!" The sudden words made her blink, draw back, and break the spell.

Or almost break it. She couldn't quite shake the remnants of magic powerful enough to draw her eyes to his again and again, over the course of the meal, in spite of Hannah's knowing looks and Tansy's constant chatter about the upcoming school carnival.

After dinner, David set his plate aside as he, Aaron, and Tansy looked toward the last rays of the setting sun. "Red sky at night, sailor's delight," he told the kids. "Red sky at morning, sailors take warning."

"Warning about what?" Tansy asked.

"Storms. Before meteorologists got involved, sailors used to forecast the weather by looking at the sky."

"Farmers have always looked around," Moses observed. He'd been remarkably accepting of Captain Rogers, Libby thought, for a man who distrusted practically everybody. But David wasn't everybody. He was Tansy's teacher and Aaron's hero. And he was an astronaut. Even Moses had to admire him for that. "Spiders are the best weathermen in the business," the farmer continued. "When you see spiders working like mad on their webs, then you know you're in for a real gully washer."

Libby followed David's gaze over to a large web in the corner where a wolf spider had been busy since late afternoon. Anchoring one corner of the web was a bundle of shingles that had been there since before Aaron's accident.

"Not that I need a spider," Moses concluded, rubbing his knee. "This gimp leg of mine'll tell me it's gonna rain quicker than anything."

Libby saw David consider the shingles and the spider. Finally he motioned toward them with his chin. "I couldn't help but notice that bunch of shingles over there."

Libby heard a low rumble begin in the base of the older man's throat. There was no possibility that Moses McKracken, with his badly palsied leg, could climb up a ladder to fix his roof, but there was even less chance of him letting a stranger do it for him. She appreciated David for wanting to help. She knew also that Moses wouldn't appreciate it.

"I noticed that you're one heck of a carpenter too," David said before Moses could erupt. "Aaron told me you built this house and made most of the furniture yourself." The admiration on his face looked genuine.

The rumble ended in a harumph of agreement or caution—Libby wasn't sure which.

"I can nail two boards together," David said, "but that's about it. You wouldn't believe the mess I'm making of the ship in my classroom. Ask Tansy."

"Ship?" Moses said. "Building a ship inside sounds like tomfoolery to me."

"It was kind of Libby's idea."

"Then it was a good one," Moses declared before Libby could protest.

David shook his head. "My problem is that I can't do it." He looked over at Moses. "Now on my teacher's salary, you know I can't afford to pay you what you're worth, so I was wondering if you'd consider a barter. I'll come out tomorrow morning and tack up those shingles, and then you come back into town and help me build a ship."

It was a great offer, Libby thought, but she knew Moses wouldn't consider it.

"You know how high that roof is?" the older man asked, pointing at the ceiling.

David pointed at the darkening sky. "I've been higher."

"What if you fall off and break your fool neck?"

"Then the deal's off."

No way was Moses going to go for this; he was only leading David on, Libby thought. She started when Moses said, "We could do it then."

"Good," David said. "I'll be here by nine."

"Thought you said morning."

"Eight?"

Moses leaned back in his chair. "My rooster's been getting up at five."

"Five?"

"Five's fine," Moses agreed with a twinkle in his eye. "But come ready to work. We ain't socializing like we did tonight."

"Star light!" Tansy called suddenly. "Star bright, first star I see tonight . . . I wish I may . . . I wish I might—have the wish I wish tonight!"

Libby watched her cross the fingers on both hands as she sent her girlish hopes and dreams out into the universe. *Grant her wish*, Libby urged the star as David told Aaron that it wasn't a star at all, but a planet.

Libby forgot about Tansy's wish as the sky deepened from azure to indigo and David pointed out constellations that winked into view one by one. His voice was low and rich and the stars he named reminded her of the amber flecks she'd seen in his eyes. She was so wrapped up in him that she jumped when Tansy materialized at her side.

"Do you know what I wished?"

The girl's whisper smelled of hope and youth and sweet corn. Libby pulled her close. "No, what?"

"I wished that you would fall in love with Captain Rogers."

All feeling left Libby's limbs and rushed to her heart.

"Wishing-star wishes always come true," Tansy said.

Libby drew in a breath but couldn't let it go. What if Tansy was right? She looked at David's broad shoulders and wavy hair, then back up at the sky. What if the girl's wish had already come true?

chapter 13

"Well, well, one is never to give an opinion, I suppose," grumbled the portrait.

— Ole-Luk-Oie, The Dream God, 1842

She must have been out of her mind to agree to this, Libby thought. Last May it had seemed that October was a lifetime away and that the annual school carnival would never come. But it had almost arrived, and if she wasn't crazy last spring to agree to head it, she would be by the time the task was complete.

She leaned across her desk in the library and tried to keep the impatience out of her voice. "LaVerne, I'm the carnival chair. We're going to sell hot dogs, sno-cones and cotton candy."

It was the fourth time in ten minutes that Libby had reminded LaVerne that 1) Max had put her in charge of this year's carnival and 2) nobody was sorrier than she was herself. What she didn't add was that 3) she'd been trying to run Jamison Enterprises for more than a year now, and even that multi-billion dollar behemoth was easier to deal with than this carnival committee.

"It won't *be* a carnival without LaDonna's bunny burgers," LaVerne pouted. "Everybody loves those bunny burgers."

"I know they do," Libby said over Shenla's derisive snort. "It's simply that last year so many people got sick from eating—"

"They shouldn't have eaten so much!"

"No," Libby agreed, "they shouldn't have. But this year we're going to remove the temptation—for their own good."

LaVerne looked down at the last item on her sister's long list of specialties. "Could we at least have porcupine meatballs?"

Libby hesitated. Most of the world made porcupine meatballs from ground beef and brown rice, but this was LaDonna's culinary menu. She couldn't discount the likelihood that the meatballs would be made from real porcupines and served on quills. "Hot dogs," she repeated tiredly, "and cotton candy and sno-cones."

LaVerne crossed the meatballs so thoroughly off the list that she left a hole in the paper. "Do you know what they put in hot dogs, Libby?"

"No," Libby said, checking "food" thoroughly off her own list as well. "And I don't want to. Let's move on to games." A Phoenix-based carnival company would deliver the booths, but Omar was to staff them.

"My job, it is done," he reported. "Almost done, that is to say."

"Um, good." Libby put a question mark by "games" and made a mental note to triple-check as Saturday approached. "Shenla?" This, thankfully, was the least of her worries. The annual raffle raised the most money for the school, probably because Shenla approached it with more gusto than Cecil B. DeMille ever brought to one of his productions. If there was *anything* of value to be found in Amen, Shenla found it, polished it, and presented it with a theatrical flourish—five tries for a dollar.

"I think we're good, Lib," she said. "I had a little idea this year that's going to be a real winner."

Libby smiled. "That's great, Shenla." She checked off "raffle" and leaned back in the chair. The meeting was over. "I hope you know how much I appreciate you all," she told the small committee, "you've been just—"

"Oh, *stow* it," LaVerne muttered. LaDonna's list fell to the floor when she pushed back her chair. "So long as you get what you want, Miss I'm-Perfect-Let's-Do-Everything-My-Way."

Libby's brow furrowed as LaVerne flounced across the room and slammed the door on her way out.

"Forgive her, Lib," Shenla counseled. "She has to live with LaDonna and LaRae. Job would snap under that kind of pressure."

Libby managed a weak smile. LaRae Flake was the new bane of her existence. Although Libby had never called David Rogers anything but Captain and had turned him down for dates how many times now—a dozen? a hundred? maybe more—LaRae *still* accused her of plotting to "steal her man." Libby wished that LaRae would *take* the man and go live happily ever after in never-never land.

In fact, she wished it fervently and fortified the wish every time she saw a falling star, happened upon a four-leaf clover, or spilled salt and tossed it over her left shoulder. But David stayed in Amen—building sailing ships for his class and monkey bridges for his Scouts and castles in the sky for Aaron.

Not to mention making it almost impossible for Libby to remember the careful plans she'd built for her own life. *I want to be alone*, she reminded herself every time she saw or heard of his kindness. *I need to be alone*, she whispered to herself as he kept her and the teachers laughing over lunch. *I like to be alone,* she'd say out loud every time he asked her for an ever-more endearing date—like to a frog-and-cricket concert, coyote opera, or tumbleweed ballet.

Though she chanted the magic word "alone" faithfully, Libby found to her dismay that each day its power over her mind grew less. Meanwhile, David's spell over her heart grew stronger still.

* * *

"I am speaking of the carnival," Omar explained from the door of David's classroom. "Might I assign yourself to the dunk-you machine?"

"I don't much like the sound of it." David didn't lay down his red pen. He had to finish grading these vocabulary papers because when he finished them he had history papers to score, English essays to decipher, and math quizzes to tally. Then he had a Scout meeting and, oh yes, there was that little matter of the CIA. The government still functioned under the delusion that he had time to work for them. Wescott expected him at an electronic meeting tonight at ten. In his spare time there was Aaron to tutor, Libby to pursue, and LaRae to flee.

"Miss Libby suggested that the dunk-you machine would be the best spot for you, Captain Rogers."

"She did, huh?" David couldn't suppress a grin. So, she'd been thinking about him. Another sign of progress. David had no doubt that as long as he hung in there, there was hope. On their way home from the McKrackens' a few weeks ago he'd invited her to stop for ice cream. (She'd said "No.") A few days later he'd suggested they go back out to the farm together to see the job he'd done on the roof. (She'd said "No thanks.") Since then he'd invited her almost daily to do any-and-everything he could think of. (She mostly said "No, I like to be alone.") But since her latest refusals seemed to lack the ironclad conviction of her earliest ones, David had every reason to believe that Libby would one day accept a date with him. (Most likely they'd play shuffleboard or canasta and then dine on strained lamb and peas at the Retirement Villa.)

And the funny thing was David knew he would wait. Although the CIA's pursuit of Libby was proving as fruitless as was his, they still pursued her as a suspect. His pursuit, on the other hand, had crossed the line from professional to personal weeks ago, and would never go back.

"Omar, you go tell Libby James that I'll sit on the seat over her dunk tank if she'll go out with me once for every dive I take. One date for every dunk. Got it?"

"Yes," Omar said. "I understand." He consulted the paper in his hand. "The Duck Pond would be more to your liking then? Or the, ah, Plinko Board?" David chuckled. It didn't take an astrophysicist to know that Libby would never go for his proposition. "I'll man the dunk tank, Omar," he said, "but I'm putting kids on that bench." Now that he thought about it, he rather liked the idea. After a few weeks of Scouts, there was more than one deacon he wouldn't mind watching drown.

"Very good," Omar agreed gratefully. "I will put you down."

David had graded only two more papers when Shenla appeared in the open doorway. "Knock, knock."

"Who's there?" he responded automatically. Then he looked up. "Oh, hello."

"Sorry I don't have a good knock-knock joke for you, Captain."

"Believe me," he replied with a grin, "I've heard them all since starting to teach sixth grade. There's no such thing as a good one. What can I do for you?"

"As you may know, I'm in charge of the raffle for the carnival."

Good, he thought, reaching for his wallet as she approached the desk. *This won't take long.* "Five dollars?"

Her face folded into a smile around her painted lips. "You don't know what we're raffling, Captain."

"I'm sure it's great. Give me five dollars worth of tickets." When she rested her huge straw tote bag atop his desk, David knew he wouldn't get rid of her that easy. "Ten?"

"I've been doing this raffle for years," she continued, "and I have to tell you, I've offered some rather unique and marvelous prizes. Last year, among other things, we raffled off a cow."

"Uh, great." David pushed the bill across the desk hopefully. "A good cow is precisely what I need." Maybe he could trade it for some magic beans.

Shenla clasped her hands as if applauding herself. "But this year I have the most fantastic prize of all. I have an astronaut!"

David set down the red pen.

Her crepe-papery skin quivered as she raised her arms theatrically to the cosmos. "I'm going to raffle off 'An Evening Under the Stars'— with you, naturally."

"Me?"

"Naturally," she repeated, in case he had missed it the first time. "Isn't that *inspired*?" She lowered her arms. "Do you have a space suit?"

"Not outside of Houston. They're kind of heavy to wear for everyday."

"But you have *something* official?"

"I have some NASA insignia," he said, "and a Naval uniform and—"

"You'll wear the uniform," she decided. "Do you have any medals?"

"I have—" What was he saying? "Uh, Shenla, what is it you want me to do?"

She sighed dramatically at his density. "Spend an evening with the winner, Captain, talking of the sun and the moon and the stars. Unless you don't like the idea." The look on her face told him there was something here he was missing. "I think it's *brilliant*."

"I'll do it for you," he said at last, wondering what was so brilliant about it. "But I'll be surprised if you sell any tickets."

"You will, will you?" Shenla wrapped a lock from today's titian-blonde wig around her index finger. "I think it'll be my best-seller.

Besides all the other girls in town who will buy tickets, LaRae Flake is probably good for fifty bucks herself."

"LaRae—?" The light finally dawned. David pushed the vocabulary papers aside and leaned across his desk. "Shenla, do you think you can get Libby to buy one of those tickets—*one* even?"

"Certainly I can, Captain Rogers. I'm an actress you know."

David pulled out his checkbook. "I'll take, uh, five hundred tickets right now."

Shenla held up a ring-bedecked hand in caution. "You know there's no guarantee she'll win even if you buy a thousand tickets. I can't fix the school raffle."

"I wouldn't ask you to," he said, but mostly because he knew it wouldn't get him anywhere. "But give me those thousand tickets."

Shenla smiled. "I need cash, dear boy. Libby's the carnival chair. She'll see the check. I don't want to explain why you bought so many of your own tickets. Do you?"

"No. I'll bring you cash tomorrow."

Shenla pulled a roll of blue tickets from her tote. "Your credit's good, Captain. Let's hope your luck is." She lay the roll on his desk. "That's a thousand tickets right there. Take as many as you like, but you'll have to write Libby's name on the back of every one you buy."

"No problem." He didn't have anything to do from midnight to six in the morning, and he could always sleep during math like the kids did. "Thanks, Shenla," he added when she reached the door.

She held up two fingers and crossed them. "Here's hoping!"

Here's hoping, David repeated to himself as he pulled his knapsack out from beneath his desk and stuck the roll of tickets into it. He allowed himself almost a full minute to imagine an evening under the stars with Libby before reaching for the vocabulary quizzes.

Optimist, Tansy had scrawled between the lines with a dull pencil, *a person who hopes he's got a chance even when he doesn't.*

David's pen paused and then passed on. Tansy's wasn't the textbook definition, but it hit too close to home to be marked wrong by a guy who was about to buy a thousand raffle tickets on the off chance that he would get the attention—if only for an evening—of a certain celestial school librarian.

chapter 14

"Examine your own heart," said the princess, "and if you do not feel sure of its strength, return with the East Wind who brought you here."

— *The Garden of Paradise, 1838*

Libby dropped the spiral notebook of carnival duties on her dining room table and pulled out a chair. She'd told herself this afternoon that running Jamison Enterprises was easier than coordinating a carnival, but it wasn't true, primarily because her sister wouldn't let it be.

A message on her laptop computer reported that she'd received more than a dozen E-mails since seven o'clock this morning. Half of them were from Geneva. After months of showing so little interest in the company that Libby had finally bought out her shares, Genie suddenly acted as though her life depended upon the future of Jamison Enterprises. It was too strange.

She ignored her sister to open the message from her niece, Chelsea, first. Chelsea was at the same boarding school her mother and aunt had attended, despite Libby's repeated pleas to keep the girl with her and let her go to school in Amen.

To: EAJamison@jamison.com (Aunt Libby)
From: chillygator@jamison.com (Chelsea Gaye)
Subject: I HATE IT HERE!

It was the same subject line every day, Libby thought with the inevitable tug on her heart. Unhappy in school, Chelsea lived mostly in a world of her own making. Even the books Libby sent lacked the appeal of the vivid stories her niece told to herself. Forget the protago- nists of literature; Chelsea created her own sweeping epics—and always cast herself as the heroine. (Why read about Scarlett O'Hara when you could *be* Scarlett O'Hara?) Yesterday she had been Joan of Arc and had sent Libby a message detailing the tortures of being wrongly accused of scholarship and cast into prison at the Kendicott Academy for Young Ladies. As usual, Libby had been torn between laughter and tears.

Today her niece was just Chelsea again, but a remarkably excited version of herself:

Mother says I can (may?) spend my fall break with you if you say I may (can?)!!!!! Can/may I? Pleeeeeeeeeeeeeeeeeeeeeeeeeeeaze?!???! Mother says we can go home together right after your board of direc- tors meeting—if it goes well. I can visit Tansy and Aaron and help you at school and work in the garden and play with Caliopee (sp?) and we can stay up late telling stories and . . .

Though Libby's eyes continued down the screen through the dozens of plans that came between telling stories and "I LUV U 4- EVER AUNT LIBBY J!" her mind stalled on the "after the board of directors meeting—if it goes well." Those must be Geneva's words to her daughter. The question was, what did they mean?

Libby reluctantly opened the first of her sister's messages. She read it through quickly and managed to swallow the lump in her throat by reminding herself how much Geneva had been hurting since their parents' death. Maybe the sale of the company added to the loss in her mind. Besides, wasn't Libby years past the time when having her sister call her things like "selfish" and "mean" should have the ability to sting?

By the end of the final E-mail, however, Libby was more angry than hurt and more determined than sympathetic. The arguments not to sell the company in the later E-mails didn't sound like Geneva at all. They had been coached—if not written—by her husband, Frank, and for him Libby had no tender feelings. She saw through the way he charmed Geneva and detested the way he bullied her.

Libby would never think of Frank Gordon as anything but a two- bit thug with good manners and expensive tastes, but his interest in Jamison Enterprises she could at least understand. As titular head of the company, he drew a princely salary and had the one thing he craved even more: prestige. As long as he was married to Geneva he wouldn't need money, but he'd probably never land another "job." There wasn't a secretary in LA who didn't know Frank's reputation. (And, as repugnant as the thought was, the secretaries probably knew it best.) At any rate, Libby expected Frank to grasp for the gold nameplate on his desk until the last second—but what she didn't consider was the lengths he might go to.

* * *

By the ten o'clock teleconference with the CIA, David had graded most of the papers turned in by his class and untied all of the knots left by his Scouts. It didn't pay to get those guys started. Teach them one little clove hitch and the next thing he knew everything in his house was lashed together. It had taken him the better part of an hour, but the only knots left now were the ones in his stomach.

The computer monitor was divided into fourths. Preston Wescott was in the upper-left corner. The agency chief in LA was in the upper right. The two bottom slots were filled by California agents.

The LA chief was apparently no more prone to preamble than Wescott. He said, "We're expecting a last drop before the company sells. Probably within the next couple of weeks."

"Any idea yet who's working with Gordon?" David asked. The frozen faces on the screen told him that they all had the same idea. They still thought it was Libby.

"We've made contact with Jamison's CFO," one of the agents said. "Still preliminary, but it looks good."

'Good' meaning what? David wondered, but didn't ask.

"Are you in, Rogers?" the other agent inquired.

It wasn't likely he meant "in love" or "in too deep"—two things David could probably give a positive answer to.

"In with Jamison."

David didn't have to ask what the agent meant by that. He meant that David was in trouble.

As David listened to the latest developments, he was sure that the CIA still wasn't having any more success in their overt attempts to prove

Libby guilty than he was having in his covert attempts to prove her innocent. But he knew also that as the stakes grew, so did their determination. David's jaw set as he made note of the next phase of his assignment.

"Get right on it," Wescott instructed him in closing.

What he needed to get, David told himself as he drove over to Libby's neighbor's house after school the next day, was a new job. One that didn't involve lying to everyone he knew, spying on people he liked, and generally feeling rotten about himself and the world at large.

He might have quit the night before—he really might have—if not for the steely determination with which the men had talked about nailing Libby. As it was, he rolled to a stop in front of Estelle's house and cut the engine. Calliope's head emerged from a flowering bush. Her amber eyes narrowed to slits, but never left David's face. "Hey," he told the cat, "I'm the good guy, remember?"

Trying to remember it himself, he leaned into the back of the HMV for the box he'd brought for Estelle. It contained a telescope. Attached was a sophisticated infrared camera that, once installed and activated, would record the movement to and from Libby's front and back doors 24/7. Added to the additional bugs he had placed in her house and car today (by ditching school while the kids were with her at the library) and the taps the government had on her phone and Internet, Libby couldn't sneeze or let out her cat without somebody knowing about it.

Estelle's house, like Libby's, had been built in the early 1900s. It was two-storied and its most distinctive feature—the one that would be of use—was a narrow widow's walk that ran the length of the second floor and provided a clear view of all Libby's property and most of the rest of the town.

As he climbed the stairs to the porch, David hoped that Estelle really was as crazy as she seemed. She'd *have* to be crazy to believe the story he was about to tell her. The old woman hadn't been as overtly hostile to him of late (of course, she hadn't seen him climb in Libby's window yesterday), but he still hoped that she would answer the door unarmed.

She did. Her empty arms crossed atop her ample bosom. "Captain Skulker."

He affixed his brightest smile. "You can call me David." She didn't. "I, uh, brought you something." He lowered the Trojan horse of a gift. "I, er, hoped to get on your good side." Not that he thought she had one. "It's a telescope."

The face beneath the pink foam rollers changed subtly at last, but David couldn't tell if the expression was born of excitement or suspicion. Or both.

"Why'd you want on my good side?"

"Well, you have the best view in town up on that balcony. I hoped you'd let me set this up and bring the Scouts over to work on the astronomy merit badge."

"Hootie patootie!" She pushed a sausage-sized finger into his chest. "Don't think I don't know what this is *really* about. You want me to put in a good word for you with Libby. It's as clear as the mud on your face." She leaned toward the box. "A telescope, you say?"

He nudged it through the door with his knee. "A good one. I can set it up for you, show you how it works and—"

"I'm on to you, Captain Rogers." Estelle spoke in a whisper though there was nobody else around. "You want me to help you spy, don'tcha?"

The breath David drew grew stale in his lungs, but he couldn't expel it.

"I knew it! I knew it the day you first set foot in this town!" Her voice rose with her excitement. "The very minute I heard about you I told Libby, 'The government didn't send that man to teach school. Uncle Sam sent that man to spy.' That's what I told her!"

Perhaps the only thing David understood at that moment was what it meant to be struck senseless.

"Guess Libby will believe me now!" She considered David's stunned face for a second and then lowered her voice again, conspiratorially. "We can let Lib in on this, Captain, can't we? Or is it top-top secret?"

"Uh—"

It was the expulsion of air held too long, but Estelle interpreted it as a negative response. Her chin doubled and tripled as she nodded solemnly. "Gotta keep it hush-hush, huh?" She pulled the box out from under David's hand and lifted the flap. "Lib'll understand that we're doing our patriotic duty. She's always the first one in town with her flag up on the Fourth of July."

A single word finally formed in David's mind as Estelle peered into the box. The word was *impossible*.

Estelle pulled out the telescope's main cylinder with awe. "I won't press you, Captain," she said, stroking the tube, "but tell me one thing: why did it take NASA so long to send you?" When he didn't respond she added, "I must have wrote them a dozen letters telling them the ten tribes are gonna land any day." She held the telescope up to her eye then, disappointed, looked back in the box for a lens. "I always have thought Uncle Sam oughtta have a little advance notice. We wouldn't want 'em launching nuclear missiles up at the brethren, now would we?"

"No," David said at last. He leaned against the door frame. In another minute he was going to collapse laughing at himself.

"Not that I approve of spying," she continued as she pulled the box into the hall. "But when you're spying on somebody for their own good, that's another ball of ear wax. Right?"

The words had a sobering effect, as did another glimpse of the cat that had crept closer to the open door. "Right. This kind of spying is different," he told Estelle and Calliope. "I swear it is."

chapter 15

Love is laid some place in the world where one
would least expect to find it, and yet it is always found.

— *Good Luck Can Lie in a Pin, 1869*

"Done," David told Estelle as he slipped the screwdriver back into his pocket. The telescope was firmly attached to the rail, which meant that the innocuous-looking little camera attached to its base was perfectly aligned with Libby's house and yard. He wished he could tell Lib about it when he saw her walking home from the final carnival meeting—or at least caution her to keep her blinds lowered after dark—but he couldn't. Nor could he very well explain his new-found relationship with Estelle.

Not that he worried much about explanations since Estelle would likely handle them for him. Now that they were "colleagues" she had not only welcomed him into her home and heart, she'd felt honor-bound to fill him in on her decades of investigation into the ten tribes. David was sharp enough to realize that much of the old woman's "research" had come from watching reruns of *Battlestar Galactica*, but he was too sharp to say so. The whole town knew she was delusional, of course, and humored her. But wouldn't he be the first to join her in the delusion? What would Libby think about that?

* * *

What was Captain Rogers doing on the deck with Estelle? Libby wondered. She paused in front of her house, her hand on the gate, and stared. When he waved, Libby lowered her eyes and fumbled with the latch.

Calliope jumped up on the low wall and watched Libby with interest. "I can't open it because I'm a ninny," Libby told her. "All right?"

As long as Libby's infirmity didn't impair her from operating a can opener, Calliope could let it pass. She jumped down onto the garden path, ambled halfway to the front door and then turned to see if Libby would follow.

Mastering the lock at last, even under David's amused gaze, Libby pushed open the gate and beat Calliope to the door. "What is it about that man?" Libby asked the cat when they were inside.

Because they both knew that any discussion about men was best held in a kitchen, Calliope led the way and Libby followed. The cat jumped up on the countertop and the woman opened the cupboard above it. Unfortunately, she missed the can of whitefish reaching for a jar of fudge sauce.

"I'm not attracted to him, if that's what you think," she told the cat.

It's hard to think on an empty stomach. Calliope mewed.

"Well, I'm *not* attracted to him." Libby opened the fudge sauce and inserted the tip of her index finger thoughtfully.

Calliope raised her front leg. Dinner was at stake. This was no time for soft-pawing. She sank her claws far enough into Libby's arm to be felt—a littler further than usual since fudge was a powerful anesthetic and Libby was thinking about the two-legged tree-climber again.

"Oh, Calliope! I'm sorry. You're hungry, aren't you."

The cat turned in a circle on the counter then sat back down. She mewed a third time as Libby's hand paused above a can of shredded chicken.

"Is it Wednesday already?" Libby asked. When Calliope rubbed against her, Libby removed a different can. "Whitefish it is." She opened the drawer for a spoon and removed two—one for the cat food and one for the fudge sauce. "What's wrong with me?" she asked the cat as she placed the can on the can opener, then paused to stare into space.

Calliope nudged her with her head. Nothing was wrong that a little attention to detail couldn't solve.

Libby pushed the lever and the can spun around. "I'm not falling in love with David Rogers," she repeated, gauging Calliope for a reaction.

The cat licked her lips.

"Oh!" Libby cried, "What am I going to do?"

Calliope eyed the open can. Her suggestion would be to use the spoon.

Libby did. She plunged it into the jar of fudge sauce. She'd taken the first bite when she heard a knock on her back door. She turned and tried to smile at Estelle around the sticky spoon still in her mouth.

The old woman had opened the door and invited herself in. It was then that Libby saw that David was with her. He looked from her mouth to the jar in her hand. "So we're in time for dinner?"

Libby pulled the spoon from between her lips and tossed it into the sink. "I'm, um, feeding the cat."

Calliope plopped down on the counter.

"Aren't you going to ask what we're doing here?" Estelle demanded happily.

"Yes," Libby said, leaning against the sink. "What *are* you doing here?"

"You're my best friend in all the world, Lib."

Libby nodded at Estelle's words, but her attention was focused on David. He had taken two steps toward her and Calliope. She edged sideways toward the table and pulled out a chair, torn between sinking into it and holding it out in front of herself like a lion tamer. She did not want to be in love. Look how it had turned out last time.

Estelle continued, "I told Captain Rogers we were friends. Didn't I, Captain Rogers?"

"Yes," he said, reaching over to remove the can from the can opener. Calliope sprang up hopefully. "Do you have a dish?" The cat's head nodded from the can to the countertop and the tip of her tail flicked as if to point.

"And when Captain Rogers was leaving just now," Estelle bubbled on, "I begged him to please include *you* in our secret."

Libby's hand tightened on the fudge sauce. "Me?"

"A dish?" David asked again.

Unwilling to look at him, Libby shook her head. Calliope mewed insistently and, with a shrug, David spooned the cat food onto the counter top.

Libby didn't notice. "Include me in what, Estelle?"

The woman looked around the tiny room and peeked through the door into the dining room. Reassured they were alone she blurted out, "We're spies, Libby!"

What did she say they were? Libby wondered. *Wise? Flies?*

"Captain Rogers and I are government spies!"

"You *are?*"

Estelle clapped her hands gleefully. "Yes!"

Finally, Libby looked at David. "You are too?"

He smiled, but there was something in his face besides mirth. "Yeah, me too." After a second he advised, "Have some fudge sauce."

She set the jar down on the table. "Government spies?"

"Yes!" Estelle sang out. "Isn't it too exciting, Lib? Do you want to spy with us?"

"What are you spying on?" Libby forced a smile for Estelle, but her voice was frigid as she addressed David. "If you don't mind my asking."

"Uh, you'd better tell her, Estelle," he said.

The old woman beamed. "The ten tribes, Libby! Who else?"

Who else indeed? "You're spying on the ten tribes, Captain Rogers?"

To his credit, David looked pretty darn sheepish. "I, uh, set up the telescope."

"And he's coming back tonight to show me how to use it!" Estelle exclaimed. "You come over too, Lib!"

"No, thanks." Libby made a mental note to keep the blinds drawn henceforth and forever. "I'm not spy material, Estelle," she added, hoping to diminish her friend's obvious disappointment, "but I appreciate you telling me about your new, um, mission."

"I had to tell *you*, Lib!" Estelle said. "I told Captain Rogers that I *had* to tell you—didn't I, Captain?" When he nodded she continued, "I told him that I couldn't keep a secret like that from my best friend in all the world. After all, you told me *your* big secret Lib, and—" Horrified at what she'd said in front of David, Estelle clapped both hands to her mouth. From beneath them came the words, "Oh, Libby!"

Libby glanced toward David's face and then away as she tried to process what she'd seen in the brief glance. He didn't look surprised or even curious. If anything, he looked uncomfortable. Careful not to meet his eye, she pushed the chair back under the table so she could move to Estelle's side and slip a slender arm across her quivering shoulders. "It's all right, Estelle," she soothed. "You didn't say anything wrong."

"I didn't tell!" Estelle said a little too loudly. "I'd never tell!"

"I know you wouldn't," Libby said. She'd confessed to being Elisabeth Jamison before her first trip back to LA so the old woman could reach her if there was an emergency. Estelle *hadn't* told anyone. Not that anyone would believe her, any more than they believed that the ten tribes would return from points beyond the North Star.

"I need my blood pressure medicine," the woman decided. "Too much excitement isn't good for my heart, Lib."

"I know, Estelle." Libby turned to David and her voice cooled perceptibly: "Maybe spying isn't the best business for her."

"Oh!" Estelle protested, "but it *is*! I'll be fine once I take my medicine." She waddled toward the door. "See you at eight-thirty, Captain Rogers. You think about coming too, Libby."

"I'm not coming," Libby told her again. When Estelle's head bowed she added, "But I'll come over in a little bit and bring you some cookies. Okay?"

The pink foam curlers bobbed happily. The moment Estelle was safely across the veranda and down the stairs, Libby spun on David and carefully enunciated every one of her next words: "What do you think you are doing?"

He crumpled the paper towel he'd been using to try to clean up the remaining whitefish. Calliope stretched and purred beneath his free hand. "Feeding your cat?"

So that was why Calliope fell all over him. Really, that cat was so gullible. So fickle. So *easy.* "Don't touch my cat!" she commanded.

David set Calliope on the floor and took a step away for good measure. "Sorry."

Libby was sorry herself—sorry that he wasn't standing near enough the open door to shove him out it, that is. And sorry that she'd been so shortsighted. The jar of fudge sauce was the only chocolate in the house. If she heaved it at him now she'd have to go to the grocery store.

"You're sorry for what?" she said. "For walking into my home like you own it? For making a mess in my kitchen?" Another question drummed in her brain but mercifully did not escape her lips: *Are you sorry for the way you make me feel about you?* She was furious at him—and at herself. "Or are you sorry you're taking advantage of a simple, sick old woman?"

David looked as though she *had* thrown the jar and hit him squarely between the eyes. He opened his mouth, closed it, and opened it again without speaking. "I don't want to take advantage of Estelle," he said finally, and Libby was almost convinced he meant it. "I brought her a telescope, but using it to spy on the ten tribes was her idea."

"Was playing government agent her idea too?"

David held out both hands, palms up. "Believe me, Libby, playing government agent was never *my* idea."

Libby shook her head hoping to dislodge the inclination to trust him. The odd thing was, she couldn't look into his eyes and not believe him. Quite. He wasn't lying to her, nor was he telling her the truth. She didn't know how she knew it, but she did. "You may not have suggested Estelle's latest fantasy," she said, her anger cooling a few degrees despite herself, "but you certainly encouraged it."

"Then I'm glad we have something in common." The words were accompanied by a grin that should be registered somewhere as a deadly weapon.

"*I* don't encourage Estelle."

"Oh? You believe that the ten tribes travel by flying saucer?"

Libby shook her head impatiently. "Of course not."

"Then you've told Estelle that she's delusional? Gotten her professional help?"

"Well, no, but—"

"Okay," David said, "you don't believe her fantasy, but you've never done or said anything to discourage it. How's that different from what I'm doing?"

"For one thing, I never gave her a telescope and secret decoder ring!"

David's face was unreadable when he said: "They've stopped putting decoder rings in spy kits."

This was ridiculous. He might not sound sarcastic, but he mocked her. "You're impossible to talk to." Libby retreated two steps and placed her hand on the side of the open door. "You don't take anything seriously."

At least he recognized a cue when he saw it. She let out a sigh of relief when he walked silently over to the door and out. But before she could swing it closed behind him, he laid a firm hand over hers. "You're wrong, Libby," he said. "I take a lot of things very seriously." His fingers tightened over hers before he withdrew them. "You have no idea."

Fudge sauce, she thought as he walked down the stairs and toward Estelle's. But she wasn't thinking of the jar on the table. She was thinking of the sweet depths of David's incredible brown eyes.

chapter 16

Four-leaved shamrocks grew there; there were seven specimens close to each other. When fortune comes, it often comes in a heap.

—*"The Will-o'-the-Wisp is in the Town," Says the Moor-Woman, 1865*

The sky was blue, the sun was warm, and the carnival bustled with activity. Late in the day Libby paused between tasks to greet Max as he looked around in satisfaction.

"Best carnival we ever had!" he declared. "Looks like you covered all the bases."

Libby began to nod, but then caught sight of Calvin on his way to the next booth. In his hand was a skewer that had been speared through a slice of former beast. The grease ran down his arm and dripped from his elbow onto his blue jeans. Libby blanched.

Max shook his shaggy gray head. "You can't win 'em all, Lib. I'd have been amazed if you'd won that one."

Libby sighed, well aware of the brisk business that LaDonna and LaVerne did over at their rogue "Pig on a Poke" booth. (Though *why* the gamy taste of barbecued javelina would appeal to anyone was simply beyond her.) She looked up at the familiar sound of a gong to see another soggy sixth-grader fall with a squeal and a splash into the dunk tank. Captain Rogers grinned at the surfacing boy as he stuffed yet another ticket into the top of the plastic milk jug. Judging by the several already-full receptacles, his booth was the most popular at the carnival.

Libby frowned. The frown, she told herself, had nothing to do with the fact that LaRae Flake was plastered to his side. When she saw that Max's eyes had followed hers, Libby forced up the corners of her mouth. "Cute couple."

"Do you think so?"

"No."

Max guffawed and wrapped an arm around her shoulder for an affectionate squeeze. "That's my girl." He lowered his mouth to her ear. "How much longer are you thinking you'll make Captain Rogers grovel before you give him a chance?"

Libby pulled back quickly. "I don't know what you mean."

"How many times *has* he asked you for a date now, Lib?"

She pushed the hair back behind her ear. "He isn't serious, Max. He's—"

"How many times?"

"I don't know."

"You thinking you might ever say yes? November, maybe? Or will it take Christmas to put you in the mood to give 'goodwill toward men' another try?" He jiggled her a little to dislodge the frown from her face. "It's time to get over it, Lib and move on. David Rogers is a good man."

LaRae saw Libby look toward them again. She wrapped her arm tightly around David's. If he was bothered by the overt affection—or noticed it—he gave no sign.

Libby turned away. Now that she wasn't staring at David and LaRae, she noticed Shenla up on the improvised stage brushing back the hair from today's flowing black wig as she uncoiled the microphone wire. "I need to help Shenla," she told Max, grateful for the excuse to end their discussion. She hurried across the playground, but by the time she arrived on stage the microphone was in place.

"Testing?" Shenla said. At a piercing mechanical whine, everybody in a three-block radius covered their ears.

"You're too close to the amplifier," Libby said. "Move back a little."

"Say what?" The next screech from the speakers caused coyotes out on the desert to grit their teeth.

Libby grabbed Shenla's arm and pulled her to the center of the stage. "You're standing too close to the amplifier," she repeated. By now, every eye on the playground was on them. The only eyes Libby felt were David's, but she didn't have time to fidget. From this vantage point she could see that a fiery red convertible had just turned the corner down from the school. She gasped at a glimpse of the driver's familiar blond hair.

"Something wrong, Libby?" Shenla asked into the microphone.

Hearing the question bounced back at her from the brick walls of the school kept Libby from going into shock. "No," she said. "Everything's fine." Thankfully, the crowd turned away. She cupped her palm over Shenla's mike and added, "I have to, um, check on the ice for the sno-cones. And count the tickets. And see about—"

Stop lying, Libby commanded herself. *Start thinking.* Her brother-in-law had pulled into the parking lot. Frank coming to Amen could be nothing but bad. Possibly awful. Her first thought was: *How dare he come here?* Then: *What if something's happened to Geneva or Chelsea?* The color drained from her face and she had to clench her fists to keep her hands from shaking.

"I have to go, Shenla," she said as calmly as she could. The look on her friend's face told Libby that her "calm" was as transparent as it felt.

Libby didn't know as she descended the stairs that Shenla had also seen the car, so she didn't see her concerned gesture to Captain Rogers a moment later, silently directing him toward the parking lot and Libby's surprise guest.

* * *

David stiffened instinctively as Libby bolted down the stairs and wove her way through the crowd.

"Ooh!" LaRae exclaimed, squeezing the tense muscles in his upper arm. "You're so strong."

Give me a break. David hadn't been away from Houston long enough to have grown completely unaccustomed to vacuous women on his arm, so when shaking LaRae off had proved impossible today he had mostly been able to ignore her. Mostly. Now he withdrew his arm from the vise without sparing her a look. Then he hoisted himself up on the dunk tank's platform for a better view.

Libby had reached the edge of the parking lot and approached a good-looking man in an incredible sports car. David couldn't tell who it was from this distance. It could be Frank Gordon, or it might be the former fiancé. Whoever it was, as she neared him, Libby's steps grew faster. He watched her stop a little short of the man with her hands clasped together at her throat, but at his first words, the arms dropped to her sides and she glanced back at the crowd before leading him toward the library.

David dropped from the platform and ignored LaRae's rapid-fire questions. He needed an excuse to follow Libby. His gaze landed on the milk jugs full of tickets and he scooped them up. "Gotta turn these in," he told LaRae. "I'll be right back."

"Wait!" she cried. "Wither thou goest, I will—"

David brushed off her fingers. "No. I need you to run the booth for me. Please?"

LaRae turned happily to the children in line. "He *needs* me!"

Fortunately, David had never had a strong gag reflex. He skirted the crowd and sprinted across the parking lot. Since it was on the other side of the school from the carnival, the sidewalk in front of the library was empty. David moved as close as he dared to the open door.

* * *

Libby had weighed the benefit of closing the door for privacy against the distasteful thought of being alone in a locked room with Frank, and had opted for the lesser evil—being possibly overheard by a passerby and exposed for the fraud she was.

She stood impatiently between him and the door as he outlined the lengths to which he had supposedly gone to visit her today. Her nose wrinkled in distaste. "You've been drinking, Frank," she said. "It's lucky you didn't wrap that rental car around a saguaro between here and Phoenix." *Lucky for the cactus, I mean.*

He reacted with faux injury. "You know I haven't had a drink since I married Geneva. An incompetent waitress spilled wine on my suit when she was serving my associate." He brushed at a nonexistent stain on his thigh and flashed his best smile. "Lucky for me it was white wine."

"Then it seems to be your lucky day all the way around." *It isn't mine.*

"You don't know how glad I am to hear you say that, Elisabeth."

Something in his voice, or perhaps in his face, caused Libby to take an instinctive step back. She halted total flight only through force of will. *I am not afraid of Frank Gordon,* she reminded herself. *He bullies Genie, but he won't intimidate me.* "Why are you here, Frank? What do you want?"

It was as if the man flicked an imaginary "charisma" switch. He moved closer and Libby thought she could smell the charm as it oozed from his pores. It was a bouquet of liquor, expensive cologne, and growing desperation.

"We need to . . . talk . . . about you selling the company," he said.

She ignored the hand he extended. "Talk fast. I'm in the middle of a carnival."

"I hoped we could go someplace . . . private."

What was that note in his voice? As his leer moved slowly from her face to her ankles and back Libby knew and felt chill. Perhaps she even shuddered because Frank's mouth curved upward in satisfaction. "Someplace . . . intimate." Both his hands were extended. "Your house? I imagine your little rooms must be very lonely. I imagine quite a lot about them, in fact." He took another slow step forward.

From his spot outside the door, David suddenly didn't care that it was his job to spy on Libby and learn everything he could about her and Frank Gordon. His first thought was to holler at the creep to hold it right there, but at the last second he garnered enough presence of mind to hit the milk jugs together to announce his approach before he barged into the room. "Is this where I, uh, bring the tickets?"

His eyes were on Libby because he knew that her first reaction to his interruption would be the genuine one. There was no way to mistake her expression. She wasn't guilty to have been caught or frightened to have been overheard. She was merely surprised and obviously relieved. David wished he had a hidden camera like any decent spy. One picture of her lovely face at this moment should be worth more than a thousand words in convincing the CIA that she was as innocent as they already knew Frank was guilty.

Gordon's face was as easy to read. This guy had issues.

"Dunk tank business is booming," David told Libby, though he glared at Gordon. "I thought I ought to turn in some of these tickets. They go in here, right?"

They didn't, but Libby extended her hands to take them. "Yes."

As she turned to set them on her desk, David sized up her brother-in-law. Frank's starched, monogrammed shirt was rolled up to his elbows to display a diamond-encrusted Rolex on his wrist. The light from the doorway glinted off his blond hair and bronzed skin. There was no doubt he was a golden boy. David supposed he'd gotten that tan in the Caymans where he went to count his share of the diamonds from the madman in the Middle East. Just looking at him made David ache to put his black belt in tae kwon do to good use. If Gordon didn't stop leering down at Libby in about two seconds, he was going to find himself flat on his back looking up.

Libby was clearly uncomfortable now that her initial relief had worn off. "This is my brother-in-law Frank," she said as she pushed her hair behind one ear. "Frank, this is Captain Rogers. He teaches here at Alma."

A manicured hand shot out faster than a new missionary's. Albeit reluctantly, David took it, noting as he did that it was as cool and dry as snakeskin.

"What brings you to Amen?" Frank asked with forced affability.

David smelled charm himself. Or maybe it was sweat. Small beads of perspiration had formed on Frank's forehead. David almost said, *What makes you think I wasn't born here?* Apparently, Libby and Leonard weren't the only ones who had read the private investigator's report. He said, "I live here. What brings *you* to town?"

Frank's green eyes narrowed as his lips formed an imitation of a smile. He was so polished he positively glowed, but David suspected that the veneer of civility was brittle and very thin. "I was in Phoenix on business and dropped by to surprise my favorite sis." His smile changed when he turned it toward Libby. "Elisabeth and I don't see nearly enough of each other."

I should have flipped him when we were shaking hands, David thought. With that opportunity lost, he fantasized about applying his elbow to the creep's solar plexus and putting an end the niceties right now.

Libby's sudden lack of color seemed to bolster Frank's confidence. Even in front of a stranger he did a poor job of concealing the mixed loathing and lust he felt for his wife's sister. He said to David, "I had an unexpectedly free night and couldn't think of a better place to spend it than with Libby."

The color returned to her face in a rush. Before David could react, violently or otherwise, she said, "You're not welcome here, Frank."

That's for sure. David aimed his elbow toward Frank's gut in case he needed to make her point any clearer.

But Frank moved closer to Libby and spoke in her ear, "I worry about you, Elisabeth." His fingers brushed the hair from her neck. "Way out here . . . all alone."

This time David's reaction was immediate—if impetuous. He pulled Libby from Frank's side to his own, knowing as he did so that he risked her protesting elbow in his own plexus. "What makes you think she's alone?" He was slightly more amazed than Frank when Libby leaned against him. He slipped his arm around her waist and hoped he looked confident rather than stupefied.

"Good-bye, Frank," Libby said. "Give my sister my love."

"Be sure to pick up some of that pig on a poke on your way out of town," David added.

Gordon hesitated for almost a minute before walking toward the door. "I'll look forward to your visit to LA next week, Libby. Good-bye, Captain Rogers."

Once her brother-in-law left the room, Libby moved so quickly away from David that his arm was suspended in air for a full second before it dropped to his side. "I'm sorry," she said. "I didn't think. I . . . "

David didn't know what to say, only what he wanted to do. He wanted to take her in his arms and make all they had implied to Frank Gordon come true. But when he moved toward her she retreated.

"Frank is . . . " she began, "I mean, my sister is . . . I . . . you . . . "

Again with the 'he, she, you, me,' David thought. For a Stanford graduate, this woman could be downright inarticulate. At least he had *some* comfort to offer. He reached for the front pocket of his denim shirt and withdrew a Hershey's chocolate bar. "I was saving this for later," he said. "But now might be a better time to pass it on." When she didn't respond, he extended it. "Take it. I bought it for you."

"For me? Why?"

"Well," he said, unwrapping the top of the bar and handing it to her with a grin, "I couldn't help but notice that I seem to bring out a craving for chocolate in you and—"

"That's ridiculous," she interrupted.

"—you never know when you might win a date with an astronaut. You bought a ticket, right?"

"Thanks, I guess," she said, casually breaking off the H and popping it in her mouth, "but I don't crave chocolate, and if I did, it certainly wouldn't have anything to do with you."

"Uh, huh," David said.

"And if it was part of the raffle prize," she continued as she swallowed the E, "you should have saved it for LaRae. I only bought one ticket. I hear that she bought a hundred or more."

Suddenly David could almost feel LaRae's vise-grip on his arm and smell her fragrance of Eau de Javelina. "Could I, uh, have a piece of your chocolate?"

Libby broke off the R and handed it back to him, suppressing a smile as he took it like a pain reliever.

"I don't feel any different," he said. "How long before it takes effect?"

"It's not morphine," she said. "It's chocolate. And you don't swallow it whole—you savor it." At David's dubious expression, she broke off the S. "I'll show you. Close your eyes and open your mouth."

David smelled the sweet chocolate on Libby's breath mingled with the vanilla-and-autumn-leaves scent of her hair as she leaned toward him to place the square of candy on his tongue.

"Don't bite it," she said quickly, "let it melt so you can taste it."

His lower lip stung where her fingers had brushed it while placing the candy in his mouth. He probed the sensitive spot with the tip of his tongue as the chocolate dissolved on the center. Even with his eyes closed—especially with his eyes closed—he could see Libby. He imagined her moving closer. His arms encircled her slender waist and pulled her close. Her hair fell back over her shoulders as she lifted her lips to his and—

"Do you feel anything?" she asked from several paces away.

Oh, yeah. But the candy—or something—had cemented his tongue to the roof of his mouth and made speech impossible.

"You can swallow now," she suggested as he reluctantly opened his eyes.

I wish.

"Now do you understand chocolate better?"

The FDA ought to require a warning label. He smiled.

"We need to get back," Libby said. She offered him the remaining sliver of candy.

"Keep it," he managed. "It's time for the raffle, and you might win that grand prize."

She popped it in her mouth on the way to the door and David followed her out with a rueful grin. One of these days he was going to do more than daydream about holding Libby James in his arms. And he was going to do more than fantasize about decking that creepy brother-in-law of hers too. But first he'd better hope she won that raffle. Wasn't it Thoreau who said that it's okay to build castles in the air as long as you put foundations under them? An orchestrated first date might not be much of a foundation for eternal marriage, but a guy had to start somewhere.

chapter 17

. . . and on the book glowed one shining word, and only one, the word BELIEVE.

— *The Philosopher's Stone, 1859*

David didn't return to the dunk tank when Libby climbed the stairs to the stage. Hoping to keep a carnival between himself and LaRae, he stood at the edge of the crowd with Max Wheeler to watch Shenla draw the first ticket from the box.

As the poor soul who won the Garden of Eaten gift certificate made his way to the stage, David noticed the grease spot on his bishop's shirt. He made a face. "Don't tell me you sampled that wild pig."

"Don't tell me you got away without sampling it."

David shrugged. "I happened to remember I'm a vegetarian."

"A vege . . . " Max's face lightened with new respect. "Why didn't I think of that? Imagine all the years of suffering I could have spared myself!"

Shenla drew the next ticket and a Laurel was awarded a large pumpkin from Younts' Farm. David didn't think it was much of a prize for the girl unless it happened to come with five white mice and a fairy godmother. Still, the girl positively glowed when Derek Yount, a newly returned missionary, bounded up the stairs to carry it down for her. It was a better prize than he'd thought. David applauded with the others.

The bishop asked, "How many tickets did you buy for the big one?"

David paused in mid-clap. "I, uh—"

"I bought fifty," Max said. "Put Libby's name on every one."

"You did?"

"The wife bought at least that many." Max smiled. "She's the romantic. I'm just helping out a friend." He clasped David's arm. "And knowing as we both do that God helps those that help themselves, I'd be surprised to hear that a bright young . . . vegetarian . . . like yourself wouldn't recognize an opportunity when he saw it."

"I bought a few tickets," David admitted as the next prize was claimed. He shrugged under the bishop's amused gaze. "A few hundred, that is." When Max guffawed he confessed fully. "Okay, so I bought a thousand and I would have bought more but I had to stay up late two nights as it was writing her name on them. I ran out of time."

"That's my boy."

David glanced up at the stage. "I keep wondering what will happen if Libby recognizes the handwriting on the back of the ticket. If she does, she'll probably have the carnival people pack me off with the dunk tank."

"Shenla won't show her the ticket," Max said. "Don't worry."

But Shenla had hoisted a star-covered box and David was hard-pressed at the moment to follow the advice not to worry.

"It's the event we've all been waiting for," Shenla crowed over the loud speaker. "The grand prize drawing!"

If there was a murmur in the crowd, David was too busy looking at Libby to notice it. She was smiling and David took her good cheer for a good sign. If she knew he'd tried to fix the raffle—with a little help from his friends—she'd have called it off days ago. If she even suspected she wouldn't be smiling. He wondered if she'd still smile when she won.

IF she wins, a traitorous little voice pointed out. *It's not a sure thing*.

David generally paid no attention to negative little voices, but he couldn't help but wonder if this one was right: would Libby go through with the evening, even if she won?

She might turn you down in front of the whole town, the voice taunted. *Not that* that *would be anything new.*

David was so engrossed in tuning out imaginary voices he didn't have the presence of mind to tune in actual ones. He missed Shenla's invitation to join them on stage. He didn't miss Max's rough hand on his back urging him forward.

"Good luck," the bishop said. "I'll cross my fingers."

If he'd had any real faith in fairy tales, David would have crossed his own fingers—and toes—as he made his way to the stage. Instead, he crossed his eyes at Tansy seated on the bottom stair and felt a little better when she giggled.

Once he was in place, Shenla shook the large box so vigorously that one of the glitter-covered stars fluttered onto the platform at David's feet. "Our most popular prize ever!" she told the crowd. "Somebody is going to win Captain David Rogers!"

Please let it be Libby.

Shenla shook the box a couple more times without reaching into it and David resisted the urge to shake *her.*

"Draw my name!" LaRae called from the dunk tank.

"Why don't we let you do the honors, Captain Rogers?" Shenla suggested.

It was fitting, David supposed. If he drew one of LaRae's tickets he'd have nobody to blame but himself. He stuck his arm in the hole and rejected the impulse to remove the first ticket he touched. Instead, he sought inspiration with his fingertips. There were more than two thousand tickets in that box. How would he ever . . . ?

Now.

David had to trust that it was the genuine voice, not the rotten little complainer who pretended to be everything it wasn't. He withdrew his hand, a single blue ticket pinched between his thumb and index finger.

"Read the name," Shenla urged.

Read it? He was afraid to look at it. Wordlessly, he passed the ticket to her.

As she read the name on it, her red lips formed into a perfect O.

Oh, no. Feeling his shoulders sag, David straightened them to Annapolis specifications. He was Navy, after all. One disappointment, one minor setback, one—

"Libby James!" Shenla announced triumphantly.

Libby?

"*Me?*" The microphone fell toward Libby's knees.

Shenla steadied it. "Congratulations, Lib!"

"But I only bought one ticket—"

"One ticket is all it takes!"

To David's horror, Shenla passed her the stub. He watched Libby turn it over and straighten her faltering smile with the same deliberation with which he had squared his shoulders a moment before.

"Well," she said to the crowd, "isn't that nice?" She swallowed—apparently with difficulty. "Anyway, thank you all for coming today and . . ."

David didn't hear the rest of what she said. Shenla had pulled him over to the side of the stage and shoved the star-covered box into his arms for safe-keeping. "That was her ticket," she whispered.

"What?"

"That ticket you drew. That's the very ticket Libby bought from me. I saw her sign the back of it myself."

"You're kidding."

"Lucky, isn't it?"

Lucky wasn't the word for it, but David didn't know what was.

"We did it!" Shenla said, then raised one finger discreetly heavenward. "Or He did. At least, it got done." She lowered the finger and tapped it on the box. "Get rid of the rest of those tickets, Captain. Fast. LaRae's on her way up here and none of us can pass an audit."

* * *

Putting a carnival together takes hours. Disassembling it takes minutes. David's dunk tank was emptied and on the carnival company's flatbed truck by the time he returned from his mission to stow the incriminating tickets. (He'd dumped them the only place he could think of on short notice—underneath the desk in his classroom.) As he strode across the playground toward Libby, LaRae intercepted him, several leftover pigs on pokes in her hand.

"I looked everywhere for you!" she pouted. "Why did you run off?"

"I—" Even if he'd had an explanation he cared to share, one look at LaRae made speech difficult. Javelina juices congealed in the creases at the side of her mouth and ran under her chin in long yellow streaks.

She raised a fistful of meat skewers. "Take one. They're even better cold."

David hadn't eaten since breakfast and it was a good thing. His empty stomach churned but held. "No, really."

LaRae used her free fingers to grasp the hand David held up to ward off the pig. Her greasy lips moved back into the pout, but at least she changed the subject. "I put every penny of my tips into that raffle. Almost six whole dollars. Of course, that wasn't enough for Mama." She batted her lashes and tried to look coy. "Can you keep a secret?"

A better question was if he could keep down the cornflakes. The gum she chewed so noisily had done little to remove the strong smell of wild pork from her breath.

She continued as if his silence was a vow, "Mama drove all the way into Phoenix to buy a whole roll of blue tickets! Wasn't that nice? After we put my name on them, Aunt LaVerne took them to school and sneaked them in the raffle box." The gum rolled to the front of LaRae's huge teeth when she smiled. "We *couldn't* buy them from Shenla. Mama says that would look desperate."

David couldn't disagree. It had felt desperate when he'd done it.

"Do you have any idea how long it took to write my name on all those tickets?"

He nodded slowly.

LaRae dropped her meat sticks and raised fatty fingers to his chest. "I didn't win," she pouted, "But you can change that. You can still have me all to yourself." The fingers rose to caress his cheek.

He caught her hand. "LaRae, look, I've tried to tell you this before . . . " The words trailed off at Omar's approach. The coach paused and David knew how it must look. But if he released LaRae's hands she'd be all over him and that would be worse. He couldn't believe that after one date and several weeks of too much inattention on his part, things had come so far. He wouldn't let them go farther. He gripped LaRae's hands tighter. "Yeah, Omar?"

"This, it would not be a good time?"

"Uh, no," David said, stating the obvious. Trying to hold onto LaRae's fingers was like trying to hold five greased pigs. He moved his grip to her wrist before she could squirm away and start running those piggies through his hair. "Give us a minute, okay?"

LaRae sighed and lay her bushy head in the hollow of David's neck. "We'll be longer than a minute."

"No," David said, moving back. "We won't."

Omar nodded uncertainly. "Please excuse the interruption. Miss LaRae, I shall give you as many—" he turned to David, "—or as few minutes as you desire."

As Omar departed, LaRae kissed David's chin. "Mama says that PDA—Public Displays of Affection—are tacky. Do you think they're tacky?

"Yes!"

She glanced over his shoulder at Libby then kissed his ear. "I don't."

David risked dropping both her hands so he could reach for her shoulders and push her out to arm's length. He wished his arms were longer. "Listen to me, LaRae . . . " He looked into her hopeful face and the words trailed miserably away. This was why he never dated a girl more than once or twice. He wasn't very good at being a heel. He might not have been able to be honest now if it weren't for the obnoxious little voice in his head pointing out, *You're gonna have to either dump her or marry her.* It wasn't the Spirit, but David felt certain that the two voices might concur on this one occasion. "LaRae, I'm not going to marry you. I don't . . . love . . . you." He had almost said "like" and was grateful for the intervention of the real Spirit. Her hands moved toward him again and David tightened his grip. He didn't want to hurt her but he was beginning to suspect that she was stronger than he was.

"You'll be crazy about me after we're married."

No matter how long eternity was, it wasn't long enough for that. "I'm in love with Libby." He had never meant to say those words and even the sudden stilling of LaRae's hands didn't make him glad that he had.

"You may *think* you are—"

"No, I'm pretty sure. In fact, I'm certain."

LaRae was so perfectly calm and David was so perfectly amazed at his confession that he released her. That was a mistake. One greasy hand flew up and walloped the side of his face with a crack that might have been heard in the outskirts of Denver.

David stroked his cheek with his fingers and rotated his jaw as LaRae stalked toward home. When he had reassured himself that his teeth were intact and that the ringing in his ear would eventually abate, he looked for Omar. The coach stood beneath a striped canopy a few steps away from Libby. David walked over to join them.

Libby turned at his approach. David tried to grin nonchalantly around the handprint on his cheek. "I, uh, finally told LaRae that I . . . er . . . I'm a vegetarian."

Libby bent quickly to open the plastic ice chest at her feet. She pulled a leftover can of pop from the water and extended it to him.

"Don't you have any root beer?" he asked. "I think I need something stronger than orange soda."

"The ice has all melted, but this is still cold." She moved forward and raised the can to his cheek. "It'll help stop the swelling."

He wondered how long she would stand this close to him if he never took the can.

At last he raised his hand and covered hers. "Thanks, Libby." Her fingers slipped away, but not as quickly as he might have expected. When she turned to untie a knot in the rope holding the canopy he asked, "What's left to do?"

"There's this to take down and the spot where we held the pony rides to clean up." When she looked back at him there was a smile on her lips that, while not unattractive, wasn't promising either. She motioned with her chin. "There's the shovel, Captain."

He picked up the pooper-scooper with his free hand. "I don't have to ask if you saved this little chore especially for me."

* * *

Eventually Libby wished that she had saved the pony chore for herself. Since attention to detail was not only unnecessary in that line of work but distinctly unpleasant, Captain Rogers was left with plenty of time to think and stare. He was staring at her, Libby knew without turning, but she couldn't imagine what he thought. Was he remembering what had happened in the library?

Her mind replayed the time she'd been alone with Frank. Why had he come today? It didn't make sense. Certainly he couldn't be so desperate to hold onto his position at Jamison Enterprises that he'd resort to . . . what *had* he come to do? Maybe, Libby thought, if she could concentrate she could decide.

But she couldn't concentrate. When she tried to think about Frank she thought about David and those thoughts were hopelessly muddled with girlhood fantasy. She could almost imagine sun glinting off his armor as he charged into the room to rescue her from the . . . um . . . evil baron. His chest was as firm as chain mail and when he pulled her close she felt protected and cherished and . . . *stop!*

Libby tugged sharply on the rope, not noticing that Omar steadied his side in alarm. Not only was *Brother* Rogers no knight, she was no damsel in distress. She was from the new school of damsels—the one that turned out maidens who need men as desperately as dragons need bifocals.

How many times had Elisabeth Jamison proved that she could take care of herself? *Ask Wall Street how tough I am,* she challenged the universe. *Ask around at Jamison Enterprises. Ask the LAPD. Ask anybody.*

Anybody but her.

Frustrated at the stubborn knot—but more particularly at herself and her romantic daydreams—Libby braced her legs and tugged harder. When the canopy collapsed and she felt herself pitch backwards, she was too surprised to keep from crying out. She fell into the dirt with the heavy canopy draped over her head. Then she heard Captain Rogers call her name and the sound of his approaching footsteps. Back on earth—figuratively as well as literally—Libby struggled with the rough canvas but couldn't move it.

"Libby!" David said from the outer edge of the tarpaulin. "Libby, are you okay?"

"Yes!" she called. "I'm fine. I can take care of myself, thank you." One edge of the canvas lifted and she saw daylight—and David's face. "I don't need your help."

"But—"

"I don't need you," she repeated to convince herself.

The triangle of sunlight grew slowly smaller as he lowered the canopy. *Good,* Libby thought. *I like it here.* But the darkness lasted only a moment before it was cut by a long rectangle of sunshine.

"I am not helping *you,*" David said as he lifted the canopy. "I am helping Omar finish up so he can leave." The muscles in his arms bunched as he folded back the heavy material. "Omar happens to be one of those lucky guys with a life. He wants to go home." As he lifted the tarp from over Libby's head static electricity caused her fine hair to fly up with it. "Which is why I'm helping *him,*" he told her.

"Not you." The task was almost complete. "I hope I've made that clear."

Libby felt her hair stand on end and used both hands to brush it back down. Then she sat with her fingers clasped at the back of her neck. It was the best way to keep from using them to cover her face.

"I do not know if I am helping you or not," Omar said solemnly from his side of the tarp. "Please forgive me, Miss Libby, if I am not."

He was so serious and so sincere that Libby at last saw the humor of her situation. She shook the hair back over her shoulders and looked up at the fluffy clouds in the perfect sky. The one above her head looked almost like a dragon wearing glasses. She laughed.

After laying aside the canvas, David extended his hands. "Let me help you up." He caught himself. "No, 'help' isn't the word I was looking for. I meant—"

Libby reached up and let him pull her to her feet. "Thank you."

"I know you were fine under that tarp."

His eyes were amused, but Libby didn't mind since they were also as warm and steady as his hands. "Yes, I was." With "was" being the operative word. She wasn't sure she was half as fine now. She needed her hands back. She needed her mind back. No, she thought, and felt spots of color burn into her cheeks, what she truly needed back was her heart. "But thank you anyway."

"I always wanted to rescue a damsel in distress," David said. "Promise you'll call me if you ever *do* need rescuing."

"First fire-breathing dragon I see I'll send your way."

"In the meantime, let me drive you home."

Libby shook her head and withdrew her fingers.

"I'm going to Estelle's anyway," he urged. "Spy stuff. Top secret."

He wasn't the most honest man in the world, Libby thought, but he might be the sweetest. She knew he offered to escort her home because of Frank. Captain Rogers wanted to make sure he'd left Amen and wouldn't give her any trouble.

"I'll be fine, David," she said. Her hair tumbled over her shoulder as she tilted her head to look up at him quizzically. "What?"

"You know my first name?" He grinned like a schoolboy. "Congratulations! For guessing correctly you win my firstborn child. You'll have to marry me first, of course."

Libby's lips parted.

"You haven't read *Rumpelstiltskin?*" he asked. "Then I suppose you *could* choose second prize wherein I drive you home. But first prize—"

"You can take me home," Libby managed.

"Can I keep you? You'll have your own pumpkin shell."

"I never should have loaned you those fairy tales," Libby laughed. "And the book is overdue, besides. You owe the library—"

"A sixpence?"

"I want that book back, Captain Rogers."

"Ah, I must owe you a golden egg then."

"Aren't you ever serious?"

"Only about you."

He looked earnest enough, but Libby knew better than to believe it.

Before she could respond he added, "What if I promise to obey every rule of chivalry toward princesses?"

"You can drive me home." Despite herself she raised a finger to the welt LaRae had left along his cheekbone. It was all she could do not to kiss it to make it better. "But you'd better remember those rules. I have a pretty good swing for a damsel, and you still have one unmarked cheek."

chapter 18

"My name is Cupid," said the merry boy. "Don't you know me? There lies my bow. Look, the weather is getting fine again—the moon is shining."

— *The Saucy Boy, 1835*

The sky had faded to violet when the harvest moon rose over the mountains. David trained the telescope and stood back. "That's the largest of the maria," he told Estelle. "It's called the Ocean of Storms."

The old woman pressed her eye to the lens with a coo of satisfaction. "Is that where the astronauts landed?"

"No, they set down on the Sea of Tranquility. It's to the right and down a little." When he saw the telescope move he smiled. "I don't think you'll be able to see the American flag even with that lens."

She squinted, just in case. "How far away did you say that thing is?"

David squared his shoulders. "It's 225,744 miles at perigee," he recited, "And 251,966 miles at apogee." He moved the telescope back into position with his finger. "See that bright spot in the Ocean of Storms?" When she nodded, he said, "A meteoroid hit there some 800,000 years ago. It's the largest crater on the moon and was named after Copernicus."

Estelle looked up in admiration. "Does Libby know how smart you are?"

The question caught him off guard. He'd been trying to keep his mind on the moon and his eyes from the light in Libby's kitchen window. Not that he wouldn't keep watch on her house all night via his computer modem to make sure Frank Gordon wasn't lurking in the shadows. His suspicion that he knew exactly what the man wanted from Libby had brought him here to Estelle's to personally watch over Lib for a little while, to be sure she was safe.

"Lib'll be here any minute," Estelle said. "We have potluck together every Saturday night." She winked. "I made carrot sticks and ice water. Libby's bringing roasted chicken and potato salad. Stay to dinner. You haven't lived until you've tasted Lib's potato salad." She adjusted the lens. "And if your friend's still in town invite him too."

"Friend?"

"The man at your house this afternoon," Estelle prompted. "Fancy car."

Gordon? "When did you see—?"

"When I came home to take my heart medicine. You didn't expect me to stay at that carnival all day, did you? What if the ten tribes returned while everybody was down at the school?"

She waited for an answer, but David didn't have one. "About that man. How could you possibly see—?"

"Through the telescope. I don't miss anything now, thanks to you."

If he hadn't been worrying about Frank Gordon and what he could have seen in his apartment, David might have worried about this new menace he'd released on Amen. But he was busy going over a mental checklist. His computer was so secure he had trouble getting through all the passwords himself, so Gordon couldn't have opened it. David always had the hand-held version on him, so that was okay too. The Glock pistol, bullet-proof vest, and rest of the so-called tools of the trade were in a steel box in the back of his HMV, secured with a lock that a blowtorch wouldn't faze. No problem there, either.

But there *was* a problem. On a whim, David had printed off one page from Libby's case files—one with a picture taken by a hidden camera. It was great candid shot of her going into her niece's private school. He'd taped it to the mirror in his bathroom. What if Gordon saw it and was smart enough to wonder where it had come from? David knew he had blown it. Wescott was going to have a fit.

He leaned back against Estelle's air-raid siren as his mind continued to process the report he'd have to give the CIA. Their first assumption would be that Gordon had come today to conspire with Libby. David didn't think so. He wondered now if he'd come to Amen to check him out and only harassed Libby out of a perverted sense of fun. Say that was the case, David told himself, and say Frank had been in the john and seen the picture. So what? No matter how deep Gordon tried to dig, David's cover was airtight and his support line error-proof.

Even as he told himself that, he looked up at the moon and knew that he was wrong. That's what everyone had thought about the support line for his space walk. It was a false assumption that almost cost him his life.

David looked down only when Libby emerged from her kitchen with a covered basket. Thoughts of his own life disappeared in half a second. Her life was the important one to him now. He'd do whatever it took to clear her and make a place for himself in her world. He didn't care how long it took or how much it cost.

*   *   *

Libby looked from the pair on the widow's walk to the moon. Had it ever been so large? She didn't need a telescope to see its amber glow in the western sky, or to discern the craters of molten brass upon its surface. What was it about the moon tonight?

The moon is Hamlet on a motorcycle.

Libby had forgotten the poet and the rest of his poem. Her tastes ran more toward the classical—Thomas Moore and Elisabeth Barrett Browning, but it would take a poet to explain the way she felt right now. She'd already waited thirty minutes beyond Estelle's customary mealtime hoping Captain Rogers would leave. But there he was under Hamlet's headlight.

To be or not to be.

Not to be, Libby decided. She'd almost melted this afternoon, but her emotions had cooled by evening. To moon over any man—even this astronaut—after what she'd been through with Karlton would mean she was daffier than poor Ophelia. She'd get herself to a nunnery before she'd become romantically involved with David Rogers. She turned and took a step back toward home.

"Lib-by!" Estelle called from the widow's walk. "We've been waiting. I'm hungry!"

Libby couldn't let Estelle starve. She'd deliver the food to the
door, say she was tired, and go home. Simple enough.

It would have been simpler if Estelle hadn't sent David to the
front door to meet her. "Little Red Riding Hood, I presume?" He
reached for her basket.

Libby clutched it instinctively. What big eyes he had.

They twinkled as he said, "Don't worry, I won't eat you. But your
food smells great. Let me carry the basket."

Libby relinquished it and took a step back. "Tell Estelle I—"

"Come in and tell her yourself." He pulled her into the foyer with
his spare hand and pushed the door closed with his foot. "Come on,
already. I'm starved."

Almost an hour later, Libby watched David stick the last shred of
chicken into his mouth and lick his fingers. "I thought you said you
were a vegetarian."

"Nope," he said around the fingers, "I said I told LaRae I'm a
vegetarian."

Libby couldn't help but smile. This Scoutmaster probably was
loyal, helpful, friendly, courteous, kind, obedient, cheerful, thrifty,
brave, clean, and reverent, but she wasn't about to believe he was
trustworthy. She leaned back in her chair. Maybe it didn't matter that
he wasn't trustworthy. Maybe it was enough that he was handsome
and charming and able to make her laugh. She didn't necessarily have
to trust him to enjoy his company for one short evening.

Estelle interpreted Libby's sigh as a yawn and leaned across the
table to pat her hand. "You poor thing, you must be exhausted. I
don't think I've ever been to such a carnival as you put on today. The
whole town must have been there!"

"Almost." Libby's voice softened at the thought of a person who
was conspicuous only in his absence: Aaron McKracken.

David was apparently also a mind reader. "Tansy told me that Aaron
stayed home today to save his strength for a surprise." When Libby asked
what it was he smiled. "If she'd told me that, it wouldn't be a surprise."

"How're the McKrackens doing these days?" Estelle asked.

"Quite well," Libby said with a quick nod toward David.
"Thanks to Brother Rogers. Somehow or other he convinced Moses
to let some of the Scouts help bring in his harvest this year."

David had swallowed the last spoonful of potato salad. "Remarkable how he's selling so much of that harvest to health food stores, isn't it?" The look on his face said that he didn't think it was remarkable at all. "It wouldn't bring half that price anywhere else."

"Organically grown produce is in demand," Libby said.

"Sure it is." David folded his napkin and lay it on his empty plate. "But I wonder how those people in Phoenix found out about the 'organically grown' produce and came all the way out to his house to ask for it."

Libby met his eyes at last. "Do you suppose it was the same way the antique dealer found out about his carpentry skills and started bringing out furniture for him to repair?" She hadn't thought to call an antique dealer herself, but she had a pretty good idea who *had* thought of it.

"What about the boy?" Estelle interrupted. "How's Aaron?"

Libby and David both looked away. They knew their combined efforts had probably put Moses financially ahead enough to eventually buy Aaron a motorized wheelchair.

"He's not any better, Estelle," David said finally.

Her tongue made a soft clucking sound. "That's too bad. But when the tribes come, maybe they'll have medicine more advanced than ours and—" She lowered her voice at the look on David's face. "Is that classified, Captain?"

David was trying to suppress a smile. Libby made it harder by looking mystified as she asked, "Is it, Captain?"

"Uh, probably," he said.

"I'll keep a look-out," Estelle asserted. "But not tonight. My programs are on TV tonight you know." She consulted the wall clock and pushed her chair back from the table. "Besides, the brethren won't return on a Saturday night. Says so in the holy scriptures."

"It does?" David asked Libby.

She took a quick sip of water to try to avoid the giggles. "Um, probably."

"You two come in and watch TV with me," Estelle suggested from the door.

"Another time," Libby said. "I *am* tired. I need to go home."

"And I'll clean up," David volunteered, "since all I contributed to the potluck was an appetite."

"A man who does dishes," Estelle pointed out to Libby. "You ought to grab hold of him right now."

"Good advice," David said as their hostess waddled away in search of her remote. "Grab away."

Libby pushed dirty dishes into his outstretched hands instead. "The kitchen's that way, Cinderella."

But Libby not only followed him into the kitchen, she stayed and helped him wash dishes. She'd never believed the tales that a full moon caused otherwise sane people to behave irrationally. Until tonight, that is. Tonight she might believe anything.

chapter 19

"Nothing will happen," said the prince, "unless I kiss her, and that I will not do, for I have strength to resist, and a determined will."

— The Garden of Paradise, 1838

David stood with Libby outside Estelle's house. The once-large moon had been spirited from the sky and replaced by a luminescent pearl. In Libby's garden, the moonflowers opened, casting a spicy scent of cloves upon the breeze, but the evening stock were not impressed by the quasi-darkness and held their petals closed to await a true night.

The dishes were done and all that was left to do was to say good night. David couldn't say it. Nor could he kiss Libby—and that was the only thing on his mind.

"Let me carry your basket home for you," he offered. His hand covered hers on the handle and if she wanted to free her fingers she had no choice but to agree.

When they came to the garden gate Libby looked from her frost-white flowers to the glass globe that hung above them, suspended from the tree and glistening in the moonlight. It was the witching ball and Libby felt herself bewitched by it and its giver. Instead of passing between the low stone walls, she sat upon one side of them and released a sigh as soft and warm as the night. She felt so—

Her mind searched for an adjective to describe her emotions and settled at last on "content." She was more at peace in this moment, and with this man, than she'd been in as many moons as she could remember. If only it wasn't about to end.

Fly not yet; 'tis just the hour
When pleasure, like the midnight flower
That scorns the eye of vulgar light,
Begins to bloom for sons of night
And maids who love the moon.

The words were Thomas Moore's and much more beautiful than a metaphorical motorcycle. She looked up at David beneath lowered lashes and almost recited aloud:

Oh stay! Oh stay!
Joy so seldom weaves a chain
Like this to-night, that oh 'tis pain
To break its links so soon.

"Penny for your thoughts," he said. Her face was serene and her eyes nearly closed. He smiled when they opened, soft and gray and more radiant than the moon above. "Okay, a nickel then. You can apply it to the money I owe for the overdue book."

"I . . . I was thinking about a poem by Thomas Moore."

"Tell me."

"Hmm . . . I forget." When she saw that he interpreted her amnesia as his cue to depart she patted a spot on the wall next to her and said quickly, "Tell me about the stars."

"Huh?"

"Have you forgotten that I won the raffle?"

He cleared his throat. "Not exactly."

"Can't you give me a preview at least?"

David set down the basket, eased himself onto the wall next to Libby and looked up into the sky. He searched a moment for a constellation—any constellation—without success. At last he said, "The moon is too bright tonight to—"

"Tell me about the moon then."

"Uh, okay." He drew a breath. "At apogee, the moon is about 250,000 miles away and—"

She nudged him gently. "Tell me something I can't read in a science book."

So much for Estelle's notion that she'd admire his capacity for memorization. If she was into poetry she'd want idyllic descriptions in lyrical prose. Too bad his degree was in aeronautics.

"I'm no Thomas Moore, Libby," David said. "I'm sure poets have seen more of the moon from earth than I ever did in outer space." He shrugged. "I can tell you one thing—the moon is not Hamlet on a motorcycle."

Libby started. Then she laughed. "I'm very relieved to hear that." She tucked a leg under herself to get more comfortable and said, "Come on, Captain. I'm not asking you for an ode to the cosmos or a dissertation on astrophysics. I simply want to know what you saw from the window of those space shuttles."

Though his efforts faltered at first, David was more of a poet than he confessed. Libby was enthralled with his description of the seventeen days of his life lived in space. But more than she appreciated his answers to her many questions she liked to watch how he answered them. When he spoke of landing the shuttle, for instance, his face shone like that of a boy describing his first bicycle flight downhill. But when she asked about his infamous space walk he looked away.

"We don't have to talk about that," she said quickly. "I mean, I saw it on the news." She and everyone else on earth.

"It was a series of freak accidents," he said, trying to make it seem like no big deal—even if it was a big deal.

"What happened?"

He'd tell her only the facts she could cull from an old *Newsweek*. "First off, we blew a maneuver with the mechanical arm and dinged the satellite. I went out with the project engineer to fix it and my O^2 pack sprung a little leak that sent me careening off the side of the shuttle. That's when we discovered that the latch on the tether was faulty too. The combination of those things can send you off on a longer walk into space than you'd planned." When she drew a sharp breath he said quickly, "No big deal. They finally maneuvered around enough to snag me with the shuttle's mechanical arm and pull me in. End of story."

End of story? Not likely. Libby thought that if she reached up right now to touch his carefully composed face it would shatter, so she touched his hand instead. "What did you think when you started to drift off into space?"

"You mean did my life pass before my eyes?"

Libby didn't know what she meant. She only knew that this had been a defining moment in his life and she wanted to understand it.

He said, "My first thought was that I was an idiot for not triple-checking the pack and the line myself. My second thought was a wish that the radio in my helmet had blown too so I wouldn't have to listen to all the frantic little voices telling *me* to stay calm." He looked down at his lap and saw that her hand was on his. How far gone must he have been not to have noticed that before? When he looked back up, her beautiful eyes were still on his face and he felt compelled to add something more. "Anyway, I tuned the voices out and raised the solar shield on my helmet. If you're going to take a one-way trip to nowhere you might as well take in the sights."

She smiled encouragingly, but she couldn't imagine how it must have felt to be so vulnerable and so alone.

"That's when I saw the earth." He drew a slow, deep breath at the memory. "I mean, I really *saw* it. I can't explain it, Libby, but it was miraculous. I looked at it and suddenly knew that it hadn't just 'happened.' You know? Somewhere, there was a *Creator*." He turned his hand over and wrapped his fingers around hers. "And I began to wonder who He was and if He knew me." Her face showed that she knew what he was trying to say. "My mother taught me 'I Am A Child of God' when I was little, but I'd forgotten both the words and the message somewhere along the way."

Having come this far, could he tell her the rest? "It was awesome, Libby. And awful." He relaxed the grip on her hand. "Awesome because I finally knew the truth and awful because I knew *all* of it— that I probably wouldn't get back to earth and I'd spent a quarter of a century blowing the only chance I'd get at mortality."

Now she squeezed his fingers in encouragement.

He concluded, "As grateful as I was to know that God loved me and wanted me back, it was still a shock to realize that there wouldn't be one person among all the billions of people here on earth who would care—really care—that I was gone."

Libby's heart ached at the certainty in his voice. "But your family—"

"I don't have a family, Libby. My parents died in an accident and I never had brothers or sisters. My grandfather raised me."

"Your grandfather," she said. "Surely he—"

"Lib, my grandfather's a four-star admiral of the old guard. He could have cheerfully killed me himself for screwing up on international TV and tarnishing the Rogers' spotless name." At last David smiled. "Anyway, as you can see, I survived both the space walk and Grandfather's welcome home. And I recognized the things in my life that needed to change. I went to church—back to church—and promised my Heavenly Father that I would do something *real* with my second chance, something that would make this world better for me having been here."

"Is that why you volunteered for Teach For America?"

No, that was why he'd gone into the CIA—to make the world safe for democracy and all that—but he knew better than to say it out loud. Still, he couldn't look into Libby's lovely face and lie—any more than was necessary, at least. "I didn't, uh, volunteer to teach. I was drafted. But it was the best thing that ever happened to me." That was the whole truth and it was true on more than one level. "I'm not half the teacher I ought to be, but when I see those kids *get it,* it feels like the most important thing in the world. You know?"

Libby did know. She moved a little closer, deeply touched by all he had said. Moved by him.

"So, I'm glad I'm here," he said with a self-deprecating shrug. "I'm really glad I'm here."

"I'm glad you're here too."

Libby thought at the time it might be eons before she understood what she did next. She placed her palms on each of David's cheeks, pulled him forward and kissed him full on the mouth. When his arm encircled her shoulders, she lowered her hands from his face to his chest, perhaps to push him away, but she didn't push. Instead she melted into a kiss that made her light-headed. It may have been seconds or hours or days before he released her and she slowly opened her eyes. There were stars all around, but it was impossible to tell which were in the sky and which were only in his eyes.

"Was it something I said?" he asked huskily. "I'd like to repeat it."

"I . . . you . . . we . . . "

He raised a finger to her still-tingling lips. "You, me, us. Got it." He patted his shirt pocket. "Sorry. I'm all out of chocolate."

.

Libby knew that this was a juncture that called for that legendary Jamison diplomacy. Unfortunately, she'd lost it with her power of rational thought. She brushed her hair back behind her ear and willed her head to stop spinning. It was one little kiss and it hadn't meant anything.

That, unfortunately, was not true. It had meant *everything*.

"I," she began again as calmly as she could. "I mean, you—"

David stood before she could tell him it was one little kiss and it hadn't meant anything. He knew better. He picked up her basket from the ground and rested it on the wall next to her. "Now you're repeating yourself." He caressed her cheek with his knuckles in farewell. "Good night, Lib."

She had to say something to explain herself. She couldn't let him walk away and think . . . whatever he would think. "You have to understand . . . "

He nodded as though she had finished the sentence. "I do."

Libby sat under the moon and watched him walk away. When his broad shoulders ducked beneath the willow tree and disappeared around the side of the house she rested her elbow on her knee and cupped her chin on her palm. "I hope you do understand, Captain Rogers," she whispered after him, "because I certainly don't."

chapter 20

"I told them that the safest and most convenient course was to give up the honor, and do nothing at all."

— *"The Will-o'-the-Wisp Is in the Town," Says the Moor-Woman, 1865*

Libby raised the blinds in the Young Women's room on Sunday morning then stood with the cord in hand. She saw what was happening out in the parking lot and yet she didn't believe it. Moses McKracken had not only brought his family to church, he had come himself. And David had been waiting for him.

She watched David open the passenger door of the McKrackens' truck and lift Aaron out and into a battered wheelchair. When Moses circled the vehicle to shake his hand it seemed like the most natural thing in the world for the two men to meet at church.

Libby's lips couldn't decide in which direction to curl. Captain Trustworthy out there had fibbed about not knowing Tansy's secret. On the other hand, it *was* Tansy's secret and he clearly was at least partly responsible for getting all the McKrackens to sacrament meeting for the first time this century. Perhaps she should think about calling him Captain Marvel.

No, I shouldn't think about him at all, Libby decided at once, since it was impossible to think about David without thinking of his kiss. She chewed her lower lip to give the nerve endings there a sensation besides the remembrance of his lips' caress.

It was nothing! she reminded herself. Somehow she had to get herself to believe it or she wouldn't be able to face him today.

Libby smoothed back her hair. *We're both mature, responsible adults and it was one quick, innocent kiss. It didn't mean anything.* Libby felt her cheeks burn and was annoyed at their betrayal. *It was that stupid moon,* she thought. *The word 'lunatic' was coined with good cause.*

* * *

David sat outside the bishop's office and carefully folded a meeting program into a paper airplane. It gave him something to do while he waited for Libby. He intended to talk to her about last night's kiss if he had to wait all day and into the night—which was beginning, at this point, to seem likely.

He'd tried to speak to her all morning but she'd come into sacrament meeting at the last possible moment, substituted in Sharing Time for Primary, then escaped into the sacrosanct halls of Young Women. Now she was ensconced in Bishop Wheeler's office, with the "Do not Disturb" light on, no less.

He tossed his airplane down the long hall. It took a steep sideways dive, ricocheted off the wall, hit the water fountain, and skidded to a stop not more than three feet from where he'd thrown it. David knelt to pick it up and then forced himself to sit patiently on the chair for nearly two whole minutes while he wondered what they were talking about in their YW PPI. He hoped it wasn't him.

But he wasn't willing to bet it wasn't. He adjusted the angle of the crease along one of the airplane's wings and glanced at his watch. He'd like to think that Libby was taking last night's kiss way too seriously, but he was probably the one guilty of that. He'd been reading too many of her stupid fairy tales—stories that she apparently didn't read herself. If she *had* read them, she'd know that there are no plot twists between "the first kiss of true love" and "they lived happily ever after."

In other words, she had this story all wrong. Would *Sleeping Beauty* have become a classic if after the kiss Aurora kicked Philip out of the castle and hung a "do not disturb" sign over the moat? Not likely.

He glared at the yellow light next to the bishop's door, tossed his paper plane back into the air and, when the door opened, watched it drop to the carpet and land at Libby's feet. As he bent to scoop it up he felt a pulse from the paging feature on the hand-held computer/phone in the pocket of his suit coat.

Now I get a call. He weighed the chances of it being the President of the United States or the Head of the Joint Chiefs of Staff, decided the odds were negligible, and ignored the page. "Hi," he said to Libby and the bishop. "Did you have a nice meeting?"

Bishop Wheeler chuckled. "We only talked about the Young Women, Brother Rogers, if that's what you're getting at." When the phone on his desk rang he seemed further amused to have a reason to excuse himself and close the door.

"You have the joint activity this month," Libby said as she walked around him.

"Huh?" He wanted to talk about their kiss—well, he wanted to talk about eternal marriage, but he'd better start somewhere this side of a first date—and she was bringing up a joint activity?

"It's planned," he lied. Seeing her eyes on his paper airplane he stuck it in his pocket. While his hand was there he hit the "acknowledge signal" button on the phone to get the stupid thing to stop vibrating. "Now let's talk about why you're avoiding me."

"I'm not avoiding you," Libby said. She was as truthful about that as he had been about the activity. "Why would I avoid you?"

"I don't know. Why?"

Libby clutched her scriptures. "I wouldn't."

"Glad to hear it. I'll walk you home."

"I'm not going home. I'm going—" A whine from the vicinity of David's thigh interrupted her words. "Is that your cell phone?"

"Uh, yeah," he said, reaching into the pocket. "Ignore it. You were saying?"

"I'm going to—" The sound continued, but the tone changed.

The tone, David noted, signaled "urgent." He pulled the minicomputer from his jacket at last and glanced down at the screen. It said, "Urgent."

"Is that a cell phone?" Libby asked, moving a little closer in curiosity.

David flicked the cover over the screen. "Yeah."

"Who do you talk to, the space shuttle?"

"Well, you never know when those ten tribes will show up." To prove he was joking he added, "I told you I'm a spy."

"I'm beginning to believe it." Libby almost smiled, and that was a good thing. Then she held out her hand and asked, "May I see it?" and that was a bad thing.

"It's just a combination phone/palm planner thingy." David stuffed it back in his pocket. "Nothing you can't buy at Radio Shack."

Libby's brow arched suspiciously. "I'll be sure to browse through the next catalogue they send me."

David rubbed his fingers across his forehead. Even if he told her what it was he couldn't admit to Gretel here that Hansel took calls from the gingerbread witch. "Look, Libby—" His words were interrupted by an even more insistent wail.

"That shuttle certainly wants to reach you," she said. "I'll see you tomorrow at school."

As she walked away, David hit the "acknowledge signal" button again to buy another fifteen seconds. Then he yelled after her, "Can I call you?"

When she turned back, her eyes were on the thing in his hand. "It wouldn't surprise me if you could call Jupiter."

Was that a yes? he wondered as she turned the corner, *or a no?* He frowned at the device and ducked into the first empty classroom. Then he closed the door and looked out the window before making himself relatively comfortable atop a classroom table. Finally hitting the "reply" button, he thought, *I hope this is half as important as talking to Libby.* He doubted it could be no matter what the Central Intelligence Agency had to say.

* * *

Because it was a lovely day—not because she was afraid that David would call if she went home too soon; she wasn't avoiding him after all—Libby delayed the Personal Progress interviews with her girls to walk down to the river bank on the edge of town. The only sounds were the calls of birds and frogs and the determined gurgle of the Hassayampa River deepening its bed among the roots of the cottonwoods. This was one of her favorite spots for reflection. Surely not even the Sacred Grove could have been more serene or welcoming to answer-seekers. Libby sank down on a rock and looked up at the trees.

She was careful not to close her eyes. If she did she might relive David's kiss. She might even fall asleep. That could happen when you'd been awake all night staring at the moon and thinking about an astronaut. Still, the leaves of the trees shimmered in the sun until she was forced to lower her lids. Now she saw only stars. If she'd thought that all of last night's feeling had been invoked by the moonlight she was wrong. The real magic lay in David's touch and in the gentle strength of his lips on hers. She'd never been kissed that way before and she never wanted to be kissed any other way again.

A frog leapt from the water and landed with a gentle plop only inches from Libby's shoes. She studied its wide mouth carefully, reminding herself that she had never wanted to be kissed at all. Hadn't she learned anything from Karlton? Sure, some women could kiss frogs and turn them into princes, but when she'd last kissed a man she thought was a prince, he'd turned into a toad.

If it had happened once, it could happen again. She'd forget kissing David Rogers. She'd stick to frogs and take her chances.

* * *

"They're Frick and Frack," David told Preston Wescott again with as much patience as he could muster. "Those two couldn't work for the Keystone Cops, let alone the al-Quaida."

"They were pretty effective spying on you," the chief pointed out without humor. "You didn't know they were there."

Point taken. David *hadn't* seen Homer and Guy nosing around the edge of Libby's yard last night while he was kissing her. Chances are that under the circumstances, he wouldn't have noticed the Shah of Iran or Estelle's ten tribes either. But if he *had* seen Homer and Guy, David thought, he'd have knocked their crazy old heads together. He still might.

"If they weren't there to make a connection with Jamison," Wescott continued, "what were they doing?"

"Trying to settle a bet," David said. He yanked at the knot in his tie. It bugged the heck out of him that not only did Wescott and who-knew-how-many agents know he and Libby had kissed, but by now most of the town must know it too. He'd expected the former since he'd installed the cameras himself. The latter was an unpleasant surprise.

"What are they betting on?" Wescott asked.

On whether Libby would agree to a date with him before the first frost on the pumpkin (Homer's wager) or the first frost in you-know-where (Guy's assertion).

When David told his boss a version of the same—somewhat embellished to make it look as though he'd made more progress than he had—and pointed out that the footage clearly showed that Elisabeth Jamison kissed *him*, Wescott finally chuckled. "Glad to hear you haven't lost it, Rogers." He shifted papers. "Back to your report on Gordon."

David had hoped they wouldn't get back to his report on Gordon.

"He said nothing incriminating to Jamison? You heard every word?"

"Not every word," David admitted. "They might have talked between the parking lot and the library. And I didn't get to the room the same second they did, obviously."

"How much time did they spend together outside your earshot?"

As he had when he'd first reported Gordon's visit, David felt like he was on a witness stand. He knew too, that if this case didn't break soon he would be—at Libby's trial.

"Three minutes," he guessed. "Five, maybe. But—"

"Plenty of time to plot—"

"They weren't plotting," David interrupted. "As I told your assistant last night—"

"And as I've told *you*," Wescott interrupted, "we know Gordon's a pawn. Somebody with power's pushing him around the board."

"Not Elisabeth Jamison."

"So you say."

In the interview that followed David said it again. Then he repeated it once more. But he knew his opinion carried little weight. He'd thought he could sit back and wait for the CIA's lack of hard evidence to prove Libby innocent. Now he knew that would never be enough for them. They wouldn't believe her guiltless until they knew who *was* guilty. But he had access to all the files they did. Maybe, David thought, he could clear Libby by solving this thing himself. It was worth a shot.

chapter 21

*If he could but solve the puzzle he would win the
whole world and a new pair of skates besides.*

—*The Snow Queen, Book the Seventh: The Palace of the Snow
Queen & What Happened There At Last, 1845*

Homer and Guy looked up from the twin rockers on Homer's
front porch when David arrived home at his bungalow.

"There he is!" Homer crowed. "The guy that won me ten bucks!"

Guy spat toward the railing. "One little kiss don't mean nothin'.
Lib'll send him packin' faster than you can count to ten."

"Captain!" Homer called. "Hey there, Captain Rogers! Tell this
blind old coot that you've got that gal eating out of your hand."

David paused at his front door but he didn't reply. He wanted to
tell them something, all right, but since it was the Sabbath he'd wait
until it could be something at least partially civil.

"She's crazy about him," Homer told Guy with paternal pride.

Guy's derisive "huh" reflected David's own assessment of the situation. He grasped the door handle.

Homer called out, "Saw your friend over to your house yesterday.
Some car."

Gordon?

David turned, but before he could say anything, Guy spit onto
the path between the two houses. "Blood-colored sports job? Reckon
I met up with him too then." His eyes narrowed. "Can't say I much
like the company you keep."

"He's not my friend," David said quickly. When both men waited for an explanation, he regretted the hasty response. He couldn't very well tell them the man was Libby's brother-in-law. He said, "I, uh, went to school with him."

"He must've been a slow learner," Guy observed.

David flinched. Gordon was at least ten years older than he was. Didn't Guy miss anything? It got worse.

"Didn't mention you," the junkman continued suspiciously. "Said he was a stranger up from Phoenix, checking out the hunting in these parts." Guy set the rocker into a gentle motion, but his arms were folded across his chest. "He come in to buy a gun. Said it was for dove season."

A gun? What would Gordon want with a gun from a place like Guy's? The answer came almost instantaneously: because he thought he could get it with no questions, no registration, and no way to trace it.

As if reading his mind, Guy said, "Dove season's over."

"So, did you, uh, sell him anything?" David leaned against the door and hoped he sounded at least five times more casual than he felt. What he felt was scared. Libby was going to LA next week. He'd thought all along that the greatest danger she faced was from government prosecution, but he was beginning to think otherwise.

"I wouldn't sell that dandy a slingshot."

Guy wouldn't, but David knew there were plenty of people around who would sell any kind of weapon to a stranger with ready cash. It was a sure bet that if Frank Gordon wanted an unregistered gun, he had one by now.

"I sent him packin'."

"Good for you," David said to close the conversation. He wanted to report this to Wescott and download all the Jamison files he should have paid more attention to in the first place.

Preston was still in his office, but only mildly interested in the new information about Gordon. He refused to believe Libby was in danger because he refused to consider any scenario besides the one where she was the mastermind behind the plot. "I've got a feeling, Rogers," he said. "Every little piece of this thing is gonna fall into place one of these days, you mark my words."

Comparing the case to a puzzle was Wescott's favorite metaphor. It always made David think of the impossible puzzle the Snow Queen had given Kay in Andersen's fairy tale: spelling "eternity" from pieces of ice. He hoped this story would end as well as it did in the tale, but the fictional Snow Queen was just playing games; Gordon and his cohorts were real and they were playing for keeps. If they could sell blueprints for mass destruction to American's chief enemy, he could only imagine what they might do to one innocent woman who stood in their way.

Wescott popped a malted milk ball into his mouth then held up a stack of pictures. "You looked at these?"

David leaned closer to the screen to see the images of Libby's parents lying dead in the galley of their sailboat. He looked away. "Yeah," he said. "I saw them when I first went through the file."

"It's another part of the puzzle."

"I thought the police called it a botched robbery."

"They did," Wescott confirmed. "Because we told them to."

David wondered how he had missed that detail. He supposed he had read it, but not paid attention at the time because it seemed irrelevant to his facet of the case.

Wescott tapped the top picture, of Libby's mother, then slipped it under a picture of her father. David kept his eyes averted as much as he dared. "Believe you me," the chief said, "it was an execution. It happened soon after the first drop to the Iranians. My money's on old man Jamison finding out what was going on."

Now David was incredulous. If they suspected Libby of espionage, did they also suspect her of patricide? "You don't think—"

"In this line of work, Rogers, you have to think *everything*."

You have to think everything, David reminded himself a few minutes later as he sat at his computer going over every single word of every single page of Libby's file and forcing himself to stare at all the pictures of her parents and not to stare at any of the pictures of her. He'd better come up with the solution to this puzzle pretty darn fast or Libby would be in prison. Worse, she might accidentally stumble upon the same information her father had and end up in more jeopardy than even the United States government had in mind for her.

He hit the button to go back to the beginning of the actual police report—not the faux-official one given to the family, company, and the ten o'clock news. Every indication was that the murders were carefully planned, executed, and committed by someone the Jamisons knew. There was no struggle and probably no surprise until the very last minute when the semi-automatic pistol was drawn and aimed. The pistol, no doubt, was now at the bottom of the bay. Nobody aboard any of the other pleasure crafts in the vicinity heard the muffled shots, nor had they seen anything unusual on the clear summer day.

An experienced sailor who always piloted his own craft, Jamison wasn't missed until his boat began to drift into a shipping lane— hours after the time of his death. Even forensics came up blank, which wasn't surprising since if Jamison knew his killer it would stand to reason that all the fingerprints and DNA gathered at the scene could be traced to the family and friends who were frequent guests on the small yacht. Which family member or friend had gone aboard that fateful day? David's finger itched to point at Frank Gordon, but the man had an unimpeachable alibi: he'd been en route to San Francisco at the time. Both Leonard Kelley and a Jamison Enterprises pilot could swear to it.

David drummed his fingers on the keyboard as he frowned at the screen. He was missing something here and he needed to know what it was before Libby left for that board meeting in LA. He took a second to roll up his shirt sleeves before scrolling back to the beginning of the several files. He'd continue to read through this thing as many times as it took for the puzzle pieces to finally fall into place.

* * *

Libby had spent most of the afternoon visiting girls in their homes to check on their Personal Progress. Most of them were progressing better than she was. She still hadn't been able to put David out of her mind.

She dropped her notebook and keys in the basket beside the door, let Calliope out into the yard, and picked up her phone to check for messages. Leonard Kelley had called. He never called on the Sabbath to discuss business, so Libby knew that he must have picked up her psychic vibrations all the way from LA. Nobody in the world was more attuned to her emotions than Uncle Leo.

She curled up on the sofa and punched a number into the auto-dial on her phone. She should have called him sooner. Leonard would reassure her that her fears were about Karlton, not David. She shouldn't need his approbation to give this relationship a chance—certainly her heart hadn't asked her brain's permission to fall in love—but she did need it. She greeted him almost breath-lessly.

"Elisabeth," he said. "I'm glad it's you at last."

"I'm glad you called me, I—"

"I'm sorry it's not social." He must have sensed her disappoint-ment because he said, "I didn't mean to cut you off that way, Princess. Is there something you want to tell me?"

"I . . . no." Libby straightened. "What is it, Leonard?"

"Montgomery's had an accident."

"Jason?" Libby's hand flew to the base of her throat. The CFO of Jamison Enterprises had been with the company for more than a decade. She'd known him most of her life. Jason Montgomery had done more than anyone but Leonard to help her step into her father's large corporate shoes. "Oh, Uncle Leo! What happened?"

"One of our small planes went down a couple of hours ago," Leonard reported sadly. "A problem with the fuel line maybe. The pilot was killed, Lib. Montgomery's in ICU, but comatose, and they tell me he won't make it through the night."

Libby's heart contracted in physical pain. Because it would do no good to cry out the real question in her mind—why it had to happen—she asked an irrelevant question instead: "Where were they going?"

"Pleasure trip. You know Jason and his addiction to golf."

"Their families . . . " Libby began, but couldn't continue.

"Let me handle this for you, Princess," he said. "I know how hard it is."

"I want to be there . . . if there's anything I can do for Jason."

"Of course. I'll let you know." He paused and Libby knew this must be harder for him than it was for her. He and Jason had worked together many years. "Under the circumstances," he continued at last, "will you want to postpone Friday's public meeting with the board and SynQuest?"

Libby nodded, then managed to say "yes" aloud.

"As your financial advisor, I have to warn you, Elisabeth, that the delay might torpedo the deal. They're anxious to close."

"If they can't wait a week or two we'll find another buyer."

"That's what I thought you'd say," Leonard said approvingly. "Your father would be proud of you, you know. People always did come before profit to him."

Again Libby nodded, lost in her thoughts. Life was so tenuous. First her parents and now her friend and co-worker—gone before she had thought to say how much she loved them.

"Libby?" Leonard said. "Are you all right, Princess? I could kick myself for calling to break it to you this way. I should have come out there myself. I can be there in a couple of hours if—"

"No, Uncle Leo," she interrupted. "I'm fine. You'll let me know about Jason though, won't you? If there's *anything* I can do for either family, you'll tell me?"

"You know I will. Try not to fret. I'll call you as soon as I hear anything."

"Uncle Leo," she said, "I love you."

"I know that, Princess." His voice was gruff. "And you know I love you."

Libby turned off the phone and stared at it. Her heart ached and she desperately needed comfort. She knew that she could call Shenla or Max or Estelle, but she didn't want to. She wanted to call David. Yesterday in the library and last night beneath the moon Libby had felt a sense of well-being she hadn't known since before her parents' death. More than anything she wanted to fall into his strong arms and let him shield her from the world. But she'd fallen once before and it had been too fast and too hard and she'd landed unceremoniously on her face.

Dare she risk it again?

* * *

David punched the button on the computer to take the incoming call. It would be the third time in five hours that he'd talk to Preston Wescott. Did the guy live in that office, or what?

"We have a development," the chief said in the longest preamble David had yet heard. "A Jamison Enterprises plane went down."

Across the room, the kitchen phone rang. David ignored it as he asked, "Who was on board? Not her sister or—" Another ring interrupted his sentence.

"It carried Jamison Enterprises' chief accountant," Wescott told him. "He's dying. The pilot's dead. The pilot was the guy who could alibi Gordon the day the Jamisons died. We'd just initiated contact. We're not convinced this thing was a coincidence, Rogers—or an accident."

The phone rang a third time.

"One more thing," Wescott said. "They'd filed a flight plan for the Deer Valley airport northwest of Phoenix. It was supposed to be a golf trip, but so far we haven't come up with a tee time for Montgomery anywhere in the state. They may have been headed over to see Jamison." He turned to listen to someone in the office. "That's her on your phone!" he barked. "Pick it up, man."

David upset his chair but reached the receiver before the fifth ring.

"David? It's, um, it's Libby."

His throat tightened at the pain in her voice. "Hi, Lib."

"I, um, called because, well, I . . . " She drew a deep breath that ended in a sob. "Could you come over? If you're not busy, I mean."

"I'll be there in a minute."

"This could be big, Rogers," Wescott said from the computer. "Be sure you—"

David didn't wait to hear the instructions. He cut the connection and punched in the security code. He'd told Libby he'd be at her house in a minute, and he didn't intend to miss that mark by a second longer than he had to.

chapter 22

It is a strange thing, when I feel most fervently and
most deeply, my hands and tongue seem alike tied, so
that I cannot rightly describe or accurately portray the
thoughts that are rising within me.

— *What the Moon Saw, 1840*

"Is it a national emergency?" Estelle called hopefully from her front porch as David vaulted the low wall rather than take the time to fiddle with the latch on Libby's gate.

"No, Estelle," he said. "I'm just visiting."

"Shall I come over? We could play a hand of Rook."

"Maybe later, okay?" He took the stairs to the veranda in another leap then had to execute some fancy footwork to avoid tromping on Libby's cat. Calliope's tail bristled in warning. "I was invited this time," he told her as he regained his balance. "Honest."

The cat didn't believe it and David wasn't sure he believed it himself. Of every person in the world Libby could have called, she'd called him. Perhaps some part of her knew how deeply he cared. Did he dare tell her that he loved her—that he'd do anything for her—when he didn't dare reveal what he *was* doing: risking his job, his reputation and his life in the hopes of keeping her safe?

With the words "I love you" on the tip of his tongue, he raised his hand to knock. Libby opened the inner door before he could lower his knuckles. Through the screen he could see that she'd been weeping, and every syllable he'd ever known left his mind in a rush.

His hand fell to his side. Forget sweeping her into his arms, he could only stand and stare and ache all over.

"I'm sorry," she said, brushing self-consciously at the corner of one wide, pewter eye. "I shouldn't have bothered you." She made no move to open the screen. "It's just that a friend was in an awful accident today."

A single tear glistening on her cheek and a soft sound that might have been a hiccup or a sob brought David to his senses. He pulled open the screen door himself and followed Calliope into the living room. "I'm sorry about your friend, Libby, but I'm glad you called me. I have to tell you . . . " She looked so vulnerable and afraid of what he might say that the words of love died on his lips. He began again: "Tell me how I can help. I'll do anything."

It was like trying to fix one little drip and breaking the whole automatic sprinkler system. Libby's tears flowed in earnest. "You want to help everybody!" she cried. "Me, the McKrackens, Estelle, everybody! Why do you always have to be so *nice?*"

If David thought he was at a loss before, he was dumbfounded now. All he managed to say was "Uh—" and he was surprised that he could be that loquacious.

"You got my cat down from a tree," she pointed out tearfully.

"Well, it—"

"And you fed her."

"I only—"

"And you fixed the McKrackens' roof and helped Moses in his fields and you gave Estelle a telescope and you built a boat. The kids at school all *adore* you."

Her words were delivered amid sniffles and sobs and David wondered if an apology would help.

"And yesterday when Frank . . . I . . . you . . . well! And when I called you today you came and here you are, and—" Anything that might have followed was unintelligible under another torrent of salt water.

There was a box of tissues on a nearby table. David picked it up.

Libby snatched two from the box he extended. "*See?* You're being gallant again." She blew her nose on one tissue and dabbed at her swollen eyes with the other. "What am I supposed to do when you act like this?"

"I, uh, don't know."

She collapsed onto her chintz-covered sofa. "I don't know either!"

They might be speaking the same language, but David sure as heck didn't know what they were talking about. "Do you have any fudge sauce?" he asked hopefully.

"I don't want fudge sauce! I want—"

"Tootsie Rolls? Chocolate milk? Cocoa Puffs?"

"Don't make me laugh!" she said. "That's what I hate most about you."

He joined her on the couch as the sobbing subsided, but sat cautiously in case yet another spigot broke loose and he had to swim to safety. He wanted to gather her into his arms, but he was afraid to touch her hand. Worse, he didn't know what to say that might possibly help. "I really am sorry, Libby."

Wonder of wonders, an apology *did* help. Within another minute or so even the sniffles ceased. She accepted another tissue then brushed the hair behind her ear with fingers that trembled only a little. "No, I'm sorry. I don't know what I'm saying. You must think I'm a ninny."

What he thought was that he'd never imagined a woman with red-rimmed eyes and tear-stained cheeks could be so beautiful. Libby's swollen lips were so appealing he had to force himself to look away from them. "Believe me, Libby, that's not what I'm thinking."

"David . . . you . . . I . . . we . . . "

He smiled in spite of himself. "Start with 'I.' That's the only part I'm worried about."

"I . . . " Her eyes faltered with her tongue and she looked toward the doorway where Calliope waited with remarkable patience for a feline inconvenienced by so much emotion at suppertime. ". . . I don't want to be alone right now. Are you hungry?"

She was asking either Calliope or him, but David didn't know which. "I am," he admitted when the cat didn't immediately respond. "And I'd offer to buy you dinner if it wasn't Sunday. And if there wasn't only one restaurant in town. And if LaDonna didn't own it." He grinned. "And if I didn't know you'd turn me down like you always do."

"I could warm up some soup," she offered with a tentative smile. "And make sandwiches."

"That would be great. Can I help?"

"Yes. You can feed Calliope." Libby rose from the couch to lead the way to the kitchen. "But use a plate this time."

He followed her through rooms filled with plants and books and glowing antique wood. Her house was tidy but not immaculate, and only feminine enough to make him want to guard it with his life.

The saucer Libby handed him from the china hutch in the kitchen felt fragile. David set it quickly on the countertop before he dropped it. "Pretty," he said, meaning the dish, the home, and especially the woman standing next to him.

"It's Blue Willow."

He admired the dish only long enough to note that it matched the rim around the irises of Libby's silver-flecked eyes. Eyes he couldn't look away from. "Very pretty."

Her lashes lowered as she picked up the plate. Calliope meowed in protest, but Libby ignored her. "It tells a story—a Chinese fairy tale."

"Tell me."

She lay a tapered fingernail on the largest pagoda and the storyteller in her emerged. She told him about the Mandarin's daughter, Koong-shee, and her secret meetings under the willow tree with Chang, the commoner with whom she fell in love.

David listened to the story, and as Libby's hand moved from one image to the next, he imagined it with a gold wedding band—his— on its slender finger. When she told how the couple at last escaped the wicked Mandarin he said, "And they lived happily ever after?"

"Well . . . " Libby laid the plate on the countertop with a sigh to match Calliope's hopeful purr. "The lovers both die, but the gods are sympathetic and turn them into birds to kiss eternally over the willow tree where they first pledged their love."

The eternal kissing didn't sound too bad, David thought, except for the part about them being birds, of course. Kissing was still on his mind when Libby turned away to take an avocado from the windowsill.

Over her shoulder she said, "The cat food is in the cupboard. Today's Sunday, so Calliope will want turkey." Next she opened the fridge. "Is that okay with you?"

David was about to say that he didn't care what the cat ate when he realized that Libby was talking about his sandwich. "It's great."

And it looked great. He could recognize the avocado, tomatoes and sprouts that she piled on top of the sliced turkey breast, but the golden-green leaves that rested between the turkey and the toasted bread were a mystery and he said so.

"It's purslane," Libby told him. "A World War II victory garden manual called it America's worst weed. Then they found out that not only does purslane grow anywhere, it's delicious."

"It's a weed?"

"It's a vegetable. It's crunchy and nutty and has more omega-3 fatty acids than any other plant source." The corners of her mouth turned up just a bit. "A vegetarian like you ought to know these things." She turned to remove the corn chowder from the stove and pour it into a ceramic tureen, then pulled a few leaves from a pot of something growing in the windowsill and sprinkled them over the hot soup.

"You're sure into growing stuff."

"I suppose that some women dream of passion and pearls and Paris, but me, I dream of purslane and peas and parsley."

"I've always wanted to be a farmer," David said, prepared to hitch a team to a plow at dawn if it would assure him a place in Libby's dreams tonight.

"Sure you have," she said, but the smile widened. "You're a very good liar, Captain Rogers." She covered the tureen and set it on a tray with the sandwiches, bowls, and plates. "Shall we eat outside?"

"Lead on," he said as he picked up the tray. "And if you don't believe anything else I tell you, Libby, at least believe this: I'll follow you anywhere."

* * *

By late dusk they'd talked about the weather and the school, the youth in the ward and the toad lilies that grew along the far wall. In fact, they'd talked about everything but cabbages, kings, and the reason Libby had called David over in the first place.

She'd called him because she loved him. Libby was so sure of it now that she'd actually entertained the notion of inviting him to LA with her next week. To take him, she'd have to tell him who she was. She drew a breath at the thought.

David squinted toward the moon garden. Then he moved forward on his chair. "That's the weirdest bird I've ever seen. It looks like it's drunk."

Libby followed his gaze and tried not to laugh. "It's a bat."

"I knew that," he said self-consciously. "But how come it came out of that funny-looking birdhouse?" He looked again and Libby saw the realization dawn that what he was looking at in the trees were her bat boxes. "You raise *bats*?"

"I don't raise them exactly," she said. "I put out homes for them."

"*Why?*"

"Bats control insects—I never use pesticide—and the guano, bat dung," she clarified, "is great for the garden." She watched another small brown bat, a pipistrelle, emerge from the box followed by half a dozen more in rapid succession. "But even if bats weren't essential for the environment, don't you think they're cute?"

"Not really," he said. "Do they bite?"

"Only when they're sick or hurt. If I find one on the ground I cover it with a basket and call Jenn."

"Bats," he repeated. When his eyes turned from the bats to her, Libby felt the warmth all the way to her toes. "You're surprising, you know that?"

Something in his voice nudged her toward a decision. If they were to build a relationship it had to be based on honesty and trust. "David, there's something I want to tell you about myself that *is* rather surprising."

"You're really Batgirl?"

"Well, more Bruce Wayne perhaps." He waited quietly for her to continue and Libby bit her lip. If she told all now there would be no going back. If only she was certain she was ready. Certain he was ready.

"Hello?" Estelle called from the wall. "Hello!" she repeated as she waddled down the path to the veranda. She paused at the foot of the stairs, a pack of Rook cards in her pudgy hand. "Oh, did I miss supper? Why didn't you call me, Lib?"

"I, um, wanted to talk to David alone for a few minutes." At the hurt look on the older woman's face, Libby concluded, "but we haven't had dessert yet. We were waiting for you."

"I don't want to barge in," Estelle said, lifting her chins. "'Specially when you've secrets to tell that don't concern me."

"You know my secrets, Estelle," Libby assured her. "I was only telling David—"

"That you're an *heiress?*" Estelle gushed, "and that you're the head of one of the biggest corporations in the whole *country?*"

Libby bowed her head. She was going to say "about the bats" but Estelle's revelation might better cover it. David was silent and Libby was afraid to look up. She heard rather than saw Estelle clomp up the stairs and fall into one of the wicker chairs.

"I've always wanted to tell *somebody* that secret! And, my! Doesn't it feel grand to have it off our chests at last?"

Libby raised her chin enough to see David smile fondly at Estelle. The old woman's eyes narrowed. "You believe it, don't you?"

"I'd believe it if you told me she was a princess who turned into a swan every third Tuesday," he said.

"David," Libby said quietly, "I am Elisabeth Jamison of Jamison Enterprises." His only reaction was to nod. Either he didn't believe it or he didn't know what it meant. Or maybe he cared for her enough not to care what it meant; or—

Frankly, she had no idea what he was thinking. She lay her palms on the glass table top and spread her fingers. "Say something, please!"

He was amused. "Okay, heiress. Put a prenuptial agreement in front of me and I'll sign it in blood."

"David!"

"Not ready for marriage? Then what say *you* pay for our first date?" Libby's hands dropped to her lap in frustration and David's look turned to one of concern. "What do you want me to say, Lib?"

She didn't know. Then she looked deeper into his unfathomable brown eyes and did know. She wanted him to say that he loved her— not jokingly or lightly, but like he meant it. And she wanted him to say it over and over again forever.

For a dizzying blink of time Libby thought he *would* say it and her breath caught in her throat. She breathed again only when Estelle exclaimed, "Well, now that that's over with, shall we play cards?" She pushed aside the soup tureen with her pudgy fingers. "What did you say we're having for dessert, Libby?"

"Um, ice cream," Libby decided. "With fudge sauce."

Loads of fudge sauce. She'd cleared the dishes from the table—and Calliope from the kitchen counter—when the phone rang. It was Leonard. "Play without me," she called to Estelle and David through the open window. "I'll be out as soon as I can."

"Jason died," Leonard told her. "I'm sorry."

"So am I." Libby was glad that her tears, at least for the time, were spent.

"His brother will have to come in from back East," her Uncle Leo continued, "so the mass won't be until Friday. The pilot's funeral will be on Tuesday, but his wife's insisting on a graveside service. Family only."

The pilot, Libby repeated to herself. She didn't even know the man's name. "Have you—"

"Yes," Leonard said to spare her the words. "Everything that we can do we've done. But I gave his wife's name and address to your secretary since I know you'll want to write to her."

"Yes."

"There's nothing else to do, Princess." He paused and then asked, "Have you talked to Geneva?"

Libby didn't want to admit that she'd scarcely thought about her sister. "She didn't know Jason, did she?"

"No," Leonard said. "I'm glad you understand. I was afraid you'd be unhappy that she's going ahead with her plans for the stockholders' gala on Saturday night even though we've canceled Friday's meeting."

"We've postponed the meeting," Libby said absently as she stooped to scratch Calliope behind the ears. "Formally, at least."

"I don't see how we can complete the sale now. Jason had all the figures and—"

"Please don't tell me he was the only accountant at Jamison Enterprises." Libby wasn't sure why she spoke sharply unless it was that niggling little worry she couldn't shake. She'd already decided to spend Friday morning at Jason's funeral, but Friday afternoon at Jamison Enterprises. She'd turn it inside out if that's what it took to either find out what was wrong or put her concerns aside once and for all.

But it had nothing to do with Leonard. He'd only helped her and she'd snapped at him for it. "Uncle Leo, I'm so sorry—"

"You never have to apologize to me, Elisabeth. You know that. Shall I tell Geneva that you'll stay the weekend, or will you go back right after the services?"

"I'll stay at least until Saturday morning," Libby said. "I'm not sure about Genie's dinner party." She glanced out the window. Dare she ask David to go with her? "I might bring somebody," she told him impulsively. "Someone I want you and Geneva and Chelsea to meet."

The pause was so long that Libby thought they'd been disconnected. At last Leonard said, "Is it the astronaut?"

"Yes! I told him who I am—a few minutes ago—and he doesn't care. Uncle Leo, I think he . . . I . . . we . . . "

Leonard's efforts to restrain from mumbling his displeasure were both amusing and endearing. Libby knew that he was the one person in the world more afraid that she would be hurt than she was herself. "You'll like him," she promised. "Even if he *is* military." That, she thought, would be Leonard's only reservation about David once he knew him. Since his service in Vietnam, Leonard had been vehement in his dislike of the military—so much so that he and her father had agreed years ago that Leo's subordinates would handle all public aspects of his work with the defense contracts.

"Captain Rogers," Leonard said. The way he said it sounded as though it left a bad taste in his mouth. "I never thought . . . I should have warned you, Princess. Please forgive me."

"Warned me?" Libby addressed Leonard, but the yellow eyes she met in dread were Calliope's.

"I didn't tell you everything I learned when I had him checked out." She heard him shift uncomfortably in his ancient leather chair. "I never dreamed you might become . . . involved . . . with the man after . . . everything . . . or I would have told you about his reputation sooner."

Wasn't the weather too mild and the evening too lovely for this to be the end of the world? "Tell me now," Libby said, but her voice said that she didn't want to know.

"Suffice it to say that he is well-known among the ladies of Houston," Leonard confided gently. "And Cape Kennedy, and Annapolis and—"

"I understand."

"That's not to say that he isn't in love with you," Leonard hastened to add. "A man would have to be blind and stupid not to fall in love with you, Libby. I simply want you to approach this thing—if there is a thing—with both eyes open. You'll always be my Little Princess, you know."

The "Princess" set the phone down on the countertop a minute or two later and stared blankly at the open carton of ice cream on the counter top. Calliope looked up and mewed her concern.

"It's nothing," she told the cat. "Nothing I didn't already know." She picked up the scoop. "You saw the way LaRae hung all over Captain Rogers, right? And how he took it for granted?" Calliope was quite the cat-around-town and couldn't deny that she had seen it, so Libby continued, "And kissing him last night ought to have told me that he's had more than a little practice."

Calliope looked away, distracted by a moth or embarrassed for her housemate. Either way, the cat was right. Kissing David was the last thing Libby should be concentrating on right now. She needed to think what, if anything, Leonard's "revelation" meant. After all, Uncle Leo had said himself that a former girlfriend or two—or two hundred—didn't mean that David didn't love her now.

"It's silly to worry about," she told Calliope. "Did Cinderella fret about all the girls crowded into the ballroom hoping to marry *her* prince?"

She did not.

"Did Rapunzel ask her knight in shining armor how many damsels he might have kissed before stumbling across her tower?"

Not likely.

"And who knows what that Beast was up to before Beauty kissed *him*, they might have called him Beast for more reasons than one." Libby scooped out enough ice cream for one dish and then reached for the fudge sauce. "Besides, it's not like *I've* never been involved with another man."

Calliope mewed, and Libby dropped the spoon in dismay. "Oh, Calliope!" she said. "You're right. I'm a terrible judge of men!"

What had come over her? Here she was reciting fairy tales instead of remembering the lessons from her own life. Her eyes moved back toward the window and David in despair.

In a moment he felt her stare and turned. The grin faded from his face and he pushed out his chair and came immediately to the open door. "Libby, what is it?"

She turned away, hoping that she had at least been among the most challenging of his conquests. She heard him cross the room and stiffened when he laid a hand on her shoulder. She said, "I just got a call that . . . my friend died." Her friend and her naïve illusions, both at once.

"I'm sorry."

She shrugged out from under his touch and was grateful when Calliope moved between them. "I want to be alone," she said. "I have a headache and—" What was there to add? That her heart ached worse than her head and that she felt another onslaught of sniffles? "I want to be alone," she repeated. "I need to lie down. Will you please tell Estelle?"

"But—"

"I'll see you at school tomorrow."

Unless there was a way to avoid it.

After a moment of silent consideration, David left the kitchen. When Libby heard the door close behind him, she fled to the bedroom, heedless of the ice cream and fudge sauce on the counter top. She regretted her hastiness later that night when Calliope—who neither forgot the ice cream nor could bear to let it go to waste—woke her with regret of her own.

chapter 23

He was such a distinguished person that if anyone of inferior rank dared to talk to him, he would answer nothing but "Pt" and that, of course, has very little meaning.

— *The Nightingale, 1844*

David sat at his desk and flipped through Libby's book of fairy tales while his class worked with uncharacteristic quiet in their workbooks. The little book in his hand was so *her* that he'd had no intention of returning it to the library since the day he'd checked it out. But if it was the only excuse he could find now to see her, then he'd have to make the sacrifice.

Winning a "date" with Libby on Saturday afternoon had been lucky. Saturday night had been magic. Sunday evening had looked like the beginning of happily ever after. Today, however, was Monday and he was out of the story again—or at least back on page one. The page that read *Once upon a time . . .*

He glanced at a picture of a castle and closed the book. If anything, the metaphorical moat around Libby's heart was twice as deep and probably three times as wide. The drawbridge was up, the "do not disturb" sign flashed neon orange letters, and he wouldn't put it past her to find a fire-breathing dragon or two to keep him in the next county.

David would gladly swim the moat and face the dragons, but Leonard Kelley was more formidable. After all, he couldn't refute the man's observations without telling Libby that he'd listened to a tape of their conversation. Actually, he couldn't refute Kelley anyway because, frankly, everything the man said was true. David *had* dated a whole lot of women before coming to Amen and meeting *the* woman. A woman he never thought existed outside a fairy tale.

He stuck the fables under his science book, but it didn't stop him from reviewing them in his mind. He knew firsthand that an unsuspecting commoner can still, from time to time, be smitten by an unattainable princess.

But what they never tell the swineherds is why the princess has a problem with relationships. She meets up with one or two trolls in her life and then figures that every man who comes along has crawled out from under the same lousy bridge.

Under the circumstances, he couldn't blame Leonard for warning Libby or her for being cautious. But he could blame Karlton Fisk for breaking her heart. And he did. A vivid, recurring daydream in which he fractured the creep's aristocratic nose was the singular bright spot in David's otherwise dismal day.

His foul mood probably contributed to the strange quiet in his classroom. Even Tansy and Calvin were silent. The latter was also turned around in his chair, staring out the open doorway. David cleared his throat theatrically, but the boy didn't respond. "Calvin."

"There's this big, shiny car in front of the school, Captain Rogers, and—"

"And there's a workbook in front of you," David interrupted before any of the other kids could look. "I suggest that you turn around and pay attention to it."

"But—"

"Let me rephrase that. It was *not* a suggestion. Turn around now." Calvin did, albeit reluctantly.

David was congratulating himself for discovering how effective irritability could be as a disciplinary aid when Libby appeared in the doorway.

"Captain Rogers," she said, her face almost as awed as Calvin's, "there's somebody here to see you. Max—Mr. Wheeler—asked me to take your class." As David rose she added, "He's waiting for you in the office."

David's curiosity about the visitor wasn't strong enough to override his pleasure at seeing Libby. As they crossed paths he started to reach for her hand then froze when he glanced out the window and saw the car Calvin had found so interesting.

"Don't worry," Libby said. "It's not bad news. Your grandfather's here in person."

David stared at the long, black Suburban with the US Navy seal on the side and American flags flapping from twin poles on the front. He wondered what part of the news of his grandfather's visit wasn't bad. He drew a deep breath. "Be right back."

"Take the rest of the day," she urged. "The admiral must have come a long way to see you."

Even as David nodded, he knew it would take ten minutes— fifteen tops—for his grandfather to complete his business here and be back on his way to wherever he'd been headed in the first place. The only time the Rogers men saw one another casually was on the occasional holiday, and with Christmas months away, the chances of this being a social visit were slim to none.

David paused outside Max's tiny office to tuck in his shirt, straighten his tie, and run his fingers through his thick hair—hair that was easily a half-inch longer at this point than the military standards he'd been held to all his life. Then, continuing to ignore the petty officer who ignored him, he straightened his shoulders, lifted his chin, and gave a single sharp rap on the door. When it opened, his eyes were aimed straight ahead and focused on nothing in particular. "Permission to enter, sir."

"Granted," Admiral Rogers barked at the same instant Max said, "What?"

"David," Max said when the young man took a single long step into the room, "I was telling your grandfather how fortunate we are to have you here at Al . . . " The word trailed off as he realized that his sixth grade teacher stood at attention. The bemused smile that was his first reaction disappeared as he watched the four-star admiral circle his only grandchild.

"Disgraceful, Captain," Admiral Rogers said. "Simply disgraceful."

I'd have got a haircut and polished the playground off my shoes if I'd known you were coming, David thought. *You're the last person I expected to see here.*

Max said quickly, "Captain Rogers is a sterling example for the children. He—"

"Thank you, Mr. Wheeler," the admiral interrupted. "I appreciate the use of your office for a moment of privacy."

Max looked from the admiral to the burly petty officer that stood at attention outside the door and was of the impression that he could leave or be escorted out.

"Excuse me," he said. "I have . . . things . . . to do. Stay as long as you like."

"We won't be here long." When Max was on the other side of the door, Admiral Rogers instructed the petty officer to close it. "At ease," he allowed when he and David were alone.

Fat chance. David widened his stance and clasped his hands behind his back in the classic military semblance of casualness.

"Hello, David."

"Grandfather."

"You seem relatively fit."

And you are undoubtedly within two ounces of what you weighed when you left Annapolis forty years ago.

"Let's talk about why I'm here."

Yeah, David thought. *After all, I saw you just ten months ago. We covered the pleasantries then.*

The admiral crossed his arms. "What are you doing here?"

I thought we were talking about what you're *doing here.* "I'm teaching school, sir."

"Without my knowledge or permission."

David's role was so deeply ingrained that he answered automatically. "I contacted your office when I got the assignment with Teach for America, sir. You were on tour in the Pacific and—"

"There is no earthly reason for you to be here."

None that you know of. The admiral's security clearance was not quite as high as his grandfather thought it was, but David would never tell him that—or much of anything else. He said, "After my last mission—"

"I know everything about your last mission; I saw your blasted walk and I've read your blasted file!" Admiral Rogers hit his fist into the palm of his other hand. "That file was a hatchet job. There was no reason to ground you. We'll leave now. I'll have you back at NASA tomorrow morning."

David would have liked to think that was impossible, that he'd be in Amen as long as Libby was, but he knew the stubborn old man too well. Faced with the choice of pulling him from the mission or having Admiral Rogers rage in every office from here to Washington, the government just might pull him. But they wouldn't do it today.

David knew it was too soon to worry about what he couldn't control, but time to do what he could himself. He swallowed. He'd never stood up to his grandfather. He'd never known anybody who *had* stood up to his grandfather—or at least anybody who'd stood up to him and escaped the bowels of a submarine engine room long enough to tell about it. Nevertheless, David brought his feet back together and dropped his hands to his sides. He raised his chin and focused on the fishing hat Max had hung on the far wall. He said, "I prefer to stay in Amen, sir."

This time Benton Rogers slammed his fist onto the desk. "I won't have it!"

Talk about irritable, David thought. Maybe it wasn't a very good disciplinary aid; it didn't do a thing for him right now. "This is an official assignment, Admiral," he continued levelly. "I signed on with Teach for America through the end of the year and I will honor my commitment."

His grandfather was no longer irritable. He was livid. "There is no honor in playing nursemaid to a bunch of ragamuffins."

"Respectfully, sir," David said, thinking now not only of Libby but of Calvin and Tansy and the rest of the kids in his class, "I disagree."

The admiral drew himself to his full height. "You will not disagree with me, David." His voice was as cool and smooth as the steel of a ceremonial sword, but the edge was sharper. "You will *never* disagree with me."

David blinked but did not waver. "I'm sorry, Grandfather," he said. "I will."

* * *

"Please open your . . . " Libby didn't finish the instruction to the class because her mind was on what she'd seen beneath his desk. There was a box with at least a thousand tickets for the carnival raffle in it that bore her name, and most of them were in handwriting that matched the scrawl on David's lesson planner. She didn't know whether to be pleased or appalled.

"Open what, Miss James?" Tansy asked.

Libby picked up the first book she saw as she rose from his chair. "Your science books. We'll turn to page . . . " She didn't finish this sentence, either. Now she was engrossed with looking out the window at the scene outside the principal's office. It hadn't been ten minutes and already the admiral was leaving. He didn't wait for the driver to open his door and Libby could hear him slam it all the way across the playground. David was nowhere to be seen.

"What page?" Calvin asked.

"Um . . . " She watched David exit the small administration building as the Suburban left the parking lot. He stood for a time looking after it, then turned toward his classroom. Libby stepped quickly away from the window.

"What page?" the children repeated.

"Never mind," she said. "Captain Rogers is coming." She met him at the door and handed him the book. "We were about to begin science." It wasn't what she wanted to say. She wanted to ask what his grandfather could have said to leave such a look of dread on David's face.

He accepted the book wordlessly.

"Are you . . . ?" she began. She felt the children's interest on them and still she could not move away. David had come so quickly when she'd needed him. How could she abandon him now? "Can I . . . ?" Could she what? Hold him in front of all these children? The whole town was already talking about them. She retreated through the door. "Never mind."

Don't look back, she commanded herself. If she looked back now she might again see the apprehension on his face and never leave his classroom—or his side. She needed time away from David to think—to sort out the past and clearly evaluate the present before she could begin to think of the future.

For the first time since arriving in Amen, Libby wanted nothing more than to get away from it.

* * *

"I can't let her go to LA alone," David told Max on Thursday evening. "It's too dangerous. And I can't go with her when she hasn't told *me* that she's leaving." He sat across from the bishop's desk and hoped that the CIA hadn't bugged the church without telling him. If they had, this would be the last conversation he'd have outside of an interrogation room for a very long time.

"Dangerous?" the bishop asked. "Dangerous, how?"

"Whoever's been selling the microchips is getting nervous," David said. "We think they've committed at least two more murders to cover their tracks."

"Do you have any idea who's responsible?"

"We know Libby's brother-in-law's involved," David said, "but Gordon's not smart enough to pull it off by himself."

"Then who?"

David shrugged. "My boss is convinced it's Libby."

Max didn't consider it worthy of comment. "Who do you think it is?"

"I don't know. Somebody we're not aware of. There are thousands of employees at the Jamison plants and thousands more in their corporate offices. A couple hundred of them have legitimate security clearance and probably a few dozen more could sneak into the classified plant. My best guess is that it's somebody the CIA hasn't looked at yet. It's always the last guy you suspect."

He didn't mention that Jason Montgomery, the man who had died in the plane crash on his way to see Libby, had been one of their chief suspects. At this rate, David thought grimly, they could nab the bad guys by waiting around to see who was left alive.

The bishop placed his elbows on the desk and leaned forward. "Does Libby have so much as an inkling about any of this?"

"I don't know," David said again, aware that it had become his standard answer of late, both to the bishop and his boss at the CIA. "I hope not." He studied his hands under the bishop's probing look. "Libby doesn't exactly confide in me. Since Sunday night she doesn't exactly talk to me." He spread his hands. "The whole truth is that she's inhabiting the same planet as me only because she doesn't know how to get off it."

"It's not you, David," Max said kindly. "You've got to give her a little more time."

If David thought he had time to spare, he'd give it to Libby gladly. His fear was that his days in Amen could be numbered in the single digits. He'd heard yesterday that his grandfather was pressuring the Navy to have his assignment not only to Teach for America revoked, but also the one to NASA. The admiral was now denigrating the record he had previously defended and insisting that David be returned to training—probably to a submarine in the middle of the Indian Ocean. It seemed unlikely that he'd be sent any further than Houston, considering the time and money NASA had invested in his space training. But Houston was still two states away from where he wanted to be: in Amen.

David wished he could count on the CIA to step in and block the transfer, but knew that his performance in this assignment was too lackluster thus far to assure it. There was no doubt in his mind that if he wanted to stay on the job and try to protect Libby, he'd darn well better figure out a way to be in LA with Libby tomorrow. And he'd better come up with something to interest Wescott once he got there.

Max was of the same mind. "Libby's leaving for California in the morning. What are you going to do about it?"

"I came in hoping you could tell me."

"Go with her."

"That, uh, may be a little difficult. Did I forget to mention the part about Libby not speaking to me—or the part about her not knowing I'm a CIA agent?"

Max said, "Okay, so you don't go with her. You follow her there."

"I do?"

"Why not? She told you herself that she's Elisabeth Jamison. The funeral was announced on the national news and the Jamison building is the biggest one downtown. How difficult could she be to find?"

"Won't she think it's strange, me showing up?"

The bishop managed a hint of a smile. "I doubt it. You've been following her all over this town for the last couple of months, why not LA? Besides, you've asked her out a hundred times and bought a thousand raffle tickets just to get one date."

"She doesn't know about the tickets."

"Yeah, she does. She saw them under your desk Monday when she took your class." Max grinned at David's widening eyes. "It's sloppy housekeeping, Captain, but all in all a good thing. It proves you're obsessed."

"Uh, huh. And when she calls in a SWAT team to deal with my obsession?"

"She won't." At David's skeptical expression he repeated, "Trust me, she won't. Besides, do you have a better idea?" When David didn't he said, "I'll take your class. Think you can get a flight?"

That David knew he could do. "I can get a plane from Luke Air Force Base."

"Do it." When David rose, Max said, "Sit back down for a minute, son. I'd like to give you a blessing."

By the time the bishop had removed his hands from David's head, the younger man knew that he could see this thing through. He felt warm and strong and at peace. Funny how he spent so much time worrying and analyzing and trying to figure everything out for himself when the source of all truth and knowledge was ever so much closer than he sometimes realized.

David determined to look there first the next time.

chapter 24

She possessed a gift which all the others lacked. This was the determination to throw herself entirely into whatever she undertook.

— *The Philosopher's Stone, 1859*

Libby's secretary depressed the button on her phone and fixed her most fetching smile on her pretty face. "Ms. Jamison is still occupied I'm afraid."

Across the room, David looked up from the computer in his hand. He'd temporarily stopped reading the transcripts of Libby's phone calls, and was about to win his fifth game of Free Cell. Or was it the fifteenth? Fiftieth? He had lost track about the time the sun set.

"No problem," he said, as he had each time she told him Libby wouldn't acknowledge his existence, let alone admit him to her inner sanctum. At least Max had been right. Libby had ignored him ever since she'd walked into her office, but she hadn't called a SWAT team, or even security.

"It's nine o'clock," the secretary said. "I'm going home." She rose and smoothed her short skirt over her considerable curves. "Want to come with me?"

"No, thanks," David replied politely, as he had to all her previous offers of various and sundry "hospitalities."

"I won't be back until Monday."

David shrugged. "I may be here." And the truly remarkable thing, he thought as he stood to loosen the kinks from his legs, is that there

wasn't anywhere he'd rather be. Standing fifty feet away from Libby—
though separated by steel girders and oak doors—was better than
being anywhere else with anyone else. He wished he could tell her
that.

He pushed a button on his computer to see what she was up to
now and made a second wish. He wished that she would stop calling
every officer and contractor on staff before she accidentally called the
wrong one—the one who was stealing government secrets and killing
innocent people to cover it up. As David looked down at the text of
her most recent conversation, he had no remaining doubts that she
suspected something was amiss at Jamison Enterprises. It was equally
clear by her words however that intuition—or the Spirit—was all she
had to go on.

Just in case a genie lurked somewhere amid the enameled lamps
on the end tables, David made a third wish: he wished that someday
Libby would understand he was there only because he loved her.

** *

Libby hung up the phone and pushed it across the glass-topped
desk. Then she tossed the pen after it. She'd taken three pages of notes
she'd never look at again since she'd heard nothing but petty griev-
ances, transparent flattery and/or sympathetic comments about the
tragedies that had plagued her company and her life. In other words,
she thought with a sigh, she had devoted the last ten hours to
learning she was delusional at best and cursed at worst.

She leaned back in her father's massive chair and was practically
enveloped in the soft leather. *It's too big for me,* she thought with
despair born of sadness and fatigue. *This whole job is too big for me. I
can't run this company and I can't sell it and—*

Before the pity party could get well underway, Libby ended it.
She scooted forward until her feet rested solidly on thick carpet, and
she smoothed any errant locks of hair back into the severe bun at the
nape of her neck. She *could* do this. She *had* done it. It had taken
hours and hours on the computer and phone from Amen, but eigh-
teen months after her father's death Jamison Enterprises prospered.
Yes, the deal with SynQuest was shaky, but they weren't the only

prospect in the world. She would eventually sell the company and—
And what?

Libby looked toward the closed door and her heart beat faster. When she opened the door, would the answer she longed for still be there waiting?

* * *

David stuck the small computer into the pocket of his jacket as he stood and stared out the floor-to-ceiling window. From the top of Jamison Enterprises, the Los Angeles skyline stretched as far as he could see in every direction. To his surprise, he didn't like it. How many nights had it been since he'd stopped missing city lights and started admiring the stars from earth? How many days since he'd begun to find the croaking of frogs more soothing than the noise of traffic? Not long ago he would have been out on the town at this time of night, if not in orbit above it. But now it was his bedtime and he wanted his feet on the ground. Only the thought of Libby being here in this chrome-and-glass tower kept him in it.

"When I was a little girl," she said from the doorway to her office, "I thought that all those lights were stars and that my Daddy's office was up above them all." When David turned she looked past him into a night sky made artificially dark by the illuminated city below. "I was wrong of course."

Elisabeth Jamison's carefully tailored suit and immaculately coifed hair were designed to make her look older and more businesslike, but David had a hard time deferring to her ensemble. To him she looked like Libby; as fragile as Blue Willow.

"You've waited a long time, Captain Rogers," she said with a glance at the gilt clock above the divan. "And now I have to tell you that if you're in LA to buy shuttle parts for NASA, you've come to the wrong company."

"I'm not here for NASA."

"Why are you here?" Her voice was calm. The single indication that she cared desperately about the answer was in the whitening of the knuckles on the strap of her attaché.

David didn't see her hands. He looked at her face and then beyond it to the three men who had arrived at the door to the outer office. He scowled. *Three lousy minutes*, he told the imaginary genie. *Was three minutes alone too much to wish for?*

He stuck his left hand into the jacket of his suit coat. "I said I'd follow you anywhere, Lib," he said as Frank Gordon entered the room followed by Leonard Kelley and a burly security guard. "I meant it."

Libby turned, looked back at David then said to the men, "Excuse us for a minute, please."

Leonard went to Libby's side and wrapped a paternal arm around her shoulder. "Not a good idea, Princess. You've had a terrible day with the funeral and all. You're exhausted. We've come to take you home."

"You thought it would take an armed guard to convince me to leave?"

Leonard chuckled and pulled her close. "I thought it might, Princess. I know you."

She kissed his jowl. "We'll go in a minute, Uncle Leo. David—Captain Rogers—has come a long way and waited hours to talk to me."

"A few more hours won't matter then." The look he cast David left no room for disagreement. He released Libby and extended his hand. "We'll have to forgive Elisabeth's manners tonight. She's overwrought." As they shook hands he said, "I'm Leonard Kelley. This is Elisabeth's brother-in-law, Frank Gordon."

David's hand dropped to his side. "I've met Frank."

The look Leonard gave Gordon caused Kelley to rise immediately in David's estimation. Anybody who so clearly disliked Frank was okay in his book.

"I'm sorry," Libby said. "I suppose I am a little . . . overwrought." She smiled, but it lacked conviction. "Uncle Leo, this is Captain Rogers. I, um, told you about him. He's teaching at Alma School with me this semester. David, this is Uncle Leo. He's my financial advisor and fairy godfather all rolled into one."

Since David's goal in life was to get Libby to look at *him* the way she looked at Kelley, he knew he'd better start apple-polishing here and now. "It's nice to meet you, sir. I'm glad that Libby has somebody here in LA to look after her." He cast Gordon a meaningful glower.

Kelley said amiably, "Then you'll understand me spiriting Elisabeth away from you now."

Before David could respond, her attaché was pressed upon Frank and Leonard had his arm once again around her shoulder. David had seen Dobermans that were less protective, but he didn't blame the old guy. After all, Kelley already thought he was a ladies man. For all he knew, David might be a crazed stalker as well. "I understand," he said, and meant it.

Libby was reluctant to leave. "Are you going back to Arizona tonight?"

David removed the hand from his pocket. "No. I'm not going back to Amen until you do." He extended a chocolate bar. "Open this soon, okay?"

"You don't make me crave chocolate," she said, but the smile that accompanied her words gave David more joy than he'd felt in days.

"Promise you'll unwrap it," he repeated as Leonard pulled her away. When she nodded, Leonard frowned.

Let him send the candy to Jamison's labs for analysis, David thought. *Just so long as Libby gets my message first.*

* * *

His message was written on the inside of the brown candy wrapper and contained a ten-digit telephone number with half again that many words scrawled below it: *Call me any time day or night. I'll always be much closer than Jupiter. Love, David.*

Libby put the cocoa-scented paper on the nightstand beside her bed and flicked off the lamp. A moment later she turned the light back on and reached for the phone. It was the third time she'd repeated the drill—and the last. She was going to call David this time . . . or not. She switched off the light, propped herself up against the pillows and looked out the open window at the waning moon.

How much closer are you than Jupiter? Or was it a witty reference to that weird phone-thing he carried around? And what did *Love, David* mean? You didn't close a business letter that way, but you would write it on the bottom of a note to Great Aunt Myrtle and not mean it romantically.

And that, she thought, *is precisely the problem.* She didn't know if she was the love of David's life or the punch line of a long-running joke. He'd said repeatedly that he was "serious" about her and often asked to marry her, but he'd also said he was a government spy.

*He said he'd follow me anywhere and came all the way to LA to prove it. Surely **that** was romantic.* She pulled the pillows from behind her back and rested her head on them. *Or obsessed.* She turned off the light. *Or something.*

Libby closed her eyes with a sigh. After such a long, emotionally draining day, lowered lids was all it took for her thoughts of David to slip into dreams of him where all her questions were answered.

* * *

"Who's David?" Chelsea asked with an eager bounce on the bed a mere six and a half hours later. "Do I know him?"

Libby's eyes flew open.

"Hi, Aunt Libby!" the girl exclaimed. "Who's David?"

Before Libby could reply, the candy wrapper Chelsea had just read was crumpled into a ball and her niece's arms were around her neck.

"I missed you so much! I wanted to wait up for you last night, but Mother said I had to go to bed early so I'd be able to behave better than a common barbarian today." She bounced back on her bottom to fill Libby in. "Mother's a wreck because of the party tonight. The caterers are incompetent, the florists brought us mere weeds, and the string quartet simply *will not do*—we expected a chamber *orchestra*, for goodness' sake!"

It was such an excellent impression of Genie that Libby couldn't help but giggle. "Is that all?"

"Well," Chelsea confessed, "She's not happy about the weather either. It might rain and you know how easily silk spots."

"We have a covered driveway and valet parking," Libby said. "How bad could a little shower be?"

Chelsea shrugged expansively. "Don't ask me. I only live here. Except not today I don't. Mother says that if I stay out from underfoot today I can dress up tonight. She bought me a new dress." Her grin was wide and excited. "Where shall we go, Aunt Libby?"

Libby had planned to spend only the early morning with her sister and the rest of the day persuading the CEO of SynQuest that a delay of a week or two shouldn't be enough to cause them to pull out of the buyout.

"You're busy," Chelsea saw at once. When Libby began to shake her head she said, "No, that's okay Aunt Libby, I know you are. I'll hide out in my rooms and Mother will never know I'm here. I have to pack after all." The joy returned to her features in a rush. "I can't *wait* to go to Amen with you tomorrow! Is Tansy excited to see me? Does Calliope still go up in our hideout?"

Libby reached forward and ruffled the white-blonde hair. "Tansy is beside herself, Chillygator. And, yes, Calliope is probably chasing the birds out of your tree house even as we speak."

"I'm going outside for a little while," Chelsea decided, "while you get dressed. Maybe I'll find a rat or something to take Calliope as a present. It's not polite to visit without taking a gift to your hostess." She grinned. "That's a joke. But I'll meet you downstairs for breakfast, okay?"

"Okay. Shall we say thirty minutes?" As her niece bounced off the bed, Libby saw an edge of candy wrapper peeking through the child's fingers. "Chelsea!" she called. "May I have that paper back please?"

Chelsea opened her hand and served the wrapper back like a shuttlecock. "Betcha I can find out who *David* is before breakfast!" she sang out as she headed for the grand staircase.

"Betcha can't," her aunt called back.

Since Libby had a tendency to underestimate Chelsea's pluck and David's perseverance, it would turn out that she was wrong.

* **

"Thanks," David told the gatehouse guard—and fellow undercover agent—as he exited the men's facilities. After a night in a car outside the high electrified gate that surrounded Libby's estate, David might not be fresh, but thanks to the sink in the small restroom he wasn't quite as frightening as he might otherwise have been.

He walked along the fence for exercise, but paused when he saw a girl out on the rolling velvet lawn. Her fair hair stood out at all angles and she wore a purple-and-pink paisley skirt with an orange T-shirt that said PRINCESS in bright blue rhinestones.

The girl had seen him too. She raised a croquet mallet in greeting then used it to thwack a red wooden ball in his direction. When it rolled between the bars of the fence to within a few inches of his shoes, David picked it up.

The girl arrived almost as quickly as the ball. "*You're* David."

Obviously, Chelsea's informants were better than the CIA's. "As a matter of fact, I am," he said. "Who are you?"

"Chelsea. Are you in love with my Aunt Libby?"

He almost dropped the ball.

Chelsea cocked her head to the side and rested it on her bony shoulder. "Do you understand the question?"

"Uh, yeah."

"Do you prefer not to answer it on the grounds that it may incriminate you?"

"I . . . " Her coloring was Libby's, her hair—after making contact with a brush for more than a second or two—would be Libby's, and her gray eyes were definitely Libby's. "Yes," he said, "I am in love with your Aunt Libby." His eyebrows rose as the child danced upon the lawn like an elf. If only he could count on her aunt to take the confession that well.

"But she hasn't kissed you!" Chelsea exclaimed after a final spin of celebration. "I know she hasn't because you look like a prince. I think it's your curly hair. It's very princely. And your face isn't green." She rested the head of the mallet atop a big toe and explained: "Aunt Libby says that *every* prince she kisses turns into a frog." She extended her hand for the ball and David passed it carefully between the bars of the fence. "I think that's a joke," she said.

He smiled politely despite the realization that Libby had undoubtedly meant it allegorically rather than humorously.

"You can call me Chilly." Chelsea pulled a lock of hair toward her lips and nibbled on the already-frayed ends. "My name's Chelsea Gaye, but Aunt Libby calls me Chillygator. That's the name on my E-mail too. Do you like to write E-mail? We could write back and forth while I'm in school. Do you know where I go to school?"

"No," David lied.

"Do you know *anything* about me?"

"No."

"That's okay," Chelsea said magnanimously. "Aunt Libby didn't tell me anything about *you* either." Her brow furrowed. "Why do you think that is?"

"She wants to surprise us?"

"Let's surprise her first!" Chelsea flashed a smile that would put a pixie to shame. "Does she know you're here?"

"I don't think so."

"Good!" Chelsea skipped toward the front of the gate with a motion for David to follow. Standing on tiptoe, she pushed a series of buttons on the security pad until the high gate swung open. "We're supposed to meet Aunt Libby in ten minutes." She saw David scan the imposing mansion. "Suits and ties are optional for breakfast," she assured him. "Unless you're Frank. Then you'd wear a tie when you took a shower." As she waved David through the gate she said, "That's a joke." She reached for his hand to hurry him along. "Do you think Aunt Libby will be surprised to see you?"

"I'd say, Chillygator," David replied conservatively, "that she will be stunned."

chapter 25

The golden crown on her head glittered like small stars from heaven and her cloak was made of butterfly wings—and yet she was far more beautiful than all her clothes and jewels put together.

— *The Traveling Companion, 1842*

Libby's trip to LA had been full of surprises. When she returned to the estate about five the following evening, the biggest surprise—and delight—was to find that there was nothing much for her to do but retire to the library for a few precious minutes of quiet. She picked up a book before sitting down, but didn't read it. Instead she stared at the words on the page and thought about David.

The only people more surprised than her at Captain Rogers' arrival at breakfast were Geneva and Frank. Genie immediately set off a fuss—snagging an astronaut for her dinner party was a social coup d'état—and Frank disappeared into his office to fume. Libby was pleased and grateful when David, who Geneva invited not only for the evening but to stay as a houseguest, offered to take the endlessly chattering Chelsea on a quick jaunt (by plane) with him to Edwards Air Force Base to pick up a dress uniform. Although Libby might have liked to go with them, she was equally relieved to be rid of them. It gave her the chance to spend the day charming the CEO of SynQuest, and now the deal looked golden.

She hadn't yet told the Gordons, or even Leonard, of her mission or her success. It wasn't that she possessed David and Chelsea's fondness for surprise. It was more a desire to avoid confrontation as long as possible. She'd make the announcement publicly tonight when she could count on Genie and Frank to be gracious in front of the Jamison stockholders. Then she'd retreat hastily to her rooms and escape for Amen with Chelsea early the next morning. By the time she brought her niece home, Leonard would have worked out the details, Geneva would have taken out her frustrations on the clerks on Rodeo Drive, and Frank would be either resigned to unemployment or out of their lives for good. Libby hoped it would be the latter, so the smile she gave Genie when her sister entered the library was genuine.

Geneva dropped into the chair with an exaggerated air of exhaustion. "Look at me! I'm a wreck!"

Libby inserted a finger between the pages of the book and teased, "Yes, you look like you tumbled off the cover of *Vogue* and landed among *People*. Thank goodness you have a hairstylist and makeup artist waiting in your suite."

Genie frowned at Libby's book. "When do you plan to dress for dinner?"

"In another couple of hours. You know it doesn't take me long."

Geneva acknowledged the truthfulness of the words with a pained expression. "Have you decided what you'll wear?"

Libby shook her head and reopened the book. Thanks to her sister, her closet here in LA was stuffed with gowns; finding something to slip over her head was the least of her worries.

Geneva smiled. "If you don't want to talk about gowns, let's talk about you and Captain Rogers."

That was the greatest of her worries. Libby tossed the book aside, prepared to discuss fashion for the rest of the visit if it meant avoiding this more personal subject. "Shall I wear that new dress you brought me from Paris?"

"Have you had it fitted?"

"No."

"Then it will hang on you like a sack." Geneva looked at her sister more critically then said, "Or not. Have you put on a few pounds, Lib?"

Drat that lousy fudge sauce.

"You look good," Geneva allowed as Libby pulled her skirt up over her knees to examine her legs for evidence of flab. "In fact, you look better than I've ever seen you. What's your secret?" Her finely plucked brow arched as she studied her sister's face. Finally, her lips rose knowingly at the corners. "So that's it. The magnificent Captain Rogers." She leaned forward. "Let's knock his socks off."

"Excuse me?"

"Come on," Geneva said as she stood. "It will be fun."

"If you're suggesting that I try to impress a *colleague* by having my hair and makeup done—"

"I'm not suggesting," her sister said, reaching for her hand, "I'm insisting." She stared down at Libby's ragged cuticles, made a face and tugged harder. "*Come on!* I hate to put this so bluntly, dear, but you haven't a moment to spare."

At the end of two hours, Libby tingled from the top of her gelled head to the tips of her freshly pedicured toes. She stood before the mirror and raised a finger toward her polished lips. Geneva slapped her hand before she could nibble on the new acrylic nail.

Libby dropped her hand to her side with a sigh. "It's not *me*, Geneva."

"Libby, you're *gorgeous*. There won't be a woman in the room tonight who wouldn't kill to look like you."

"Isn't it a bit . . . much?"

"It's *perfect*. You're perfect." She turned to remove a heavy diamond pendant from the box of jewels recently delivered from the safe downstairs. "Now be a dear and latch this for me. The reception line will form without us if we don't hurry."

Libby turned gratefully away from the mirror to help her sister with the necklace. She finished just as Chelsea entered in a rush of velvet and crinoline.

The girl pulled a ringlet out from her head, released it and hollered "Sproing!" when it coiled back into place. "I look ridiculous! Where did you *get* this dress, Mother? Saks Fifth *Outlet*? If you think I'm going to . . . *Aunt Libby!*"

Libby made a helpless gesture meant to convey that Chelsea's mother had dressed her too.

Chelsea's mouth dropped open wide enough for Libby to count her bottom teeth. "Do you know what you look like, Aunt Libby?"

Libby tried to rein in some of her flowing gown. She knew what she felt like. She felt like she was about two weeks early for trick-or-treat.

"You look *exactly* like my Millennial Princess Barbie!"

"Geneva!" Libby lamented.

"That's a compliment," her sister said calmly. "Do you know how much those dolls cost? Bob Mackey designs their little gowns." She took a last peek in the mirror and headed toward the door.

Chelsea grasped Libby's hand. "You look *bee-oo-ti-ful*, Aunt Libby."

Libby looked down into the glowing face and smiled. "So do you, Chillygator."

"Did I tell you that Captain Rogers showed me the *actual* space shuttle?" the girl asked as they followed Geneva into the hall. "The one that was in outer space on *Tuesday!*"

"You did," Libby said, "but I was having a facial at the time and I couldn't see your pretty eyes light up, so tell me again."

This child who had slept through Disneyland Paris and complained through Disneyland Tokyo had been enthralled by an Air Force base in the middle of the desert. Or more likely, Libby thought, she'd been enthralled with the handsome young officer who'd escorted her around like visiting royalty. If Libby hadn't already fallen in love with David Rogers, she might have solely because of the way he had treated her niece today.

"*He's* at the foot of the stairs talking to Leonard," Geneva reported from the top of the long, winding staircase. "It's time for your grand entrance."

She'd never been trick-or-treating, Libby realized with a start. What was she doing dressed up for it now? She grasped the polished rail in alarm.

"Are you all right?" Chelsea asked.

"No," Libby said. "I have a headache." And a stomachache and heartburn and indigestion. Possibly she had malaria. She'd better skip the party and go right to bed.

"Go on!" Geneva urged Libby ahead with her fingertips. "It's Captain Rogers who's going to need a doctor. I promise you, Libby. He'll never know what hit him."

* * *

David didn't know what hit him, though he suspected a meteorite by the way it left him reeling.

"You're supposed to say something charming, Prince," Chelsea whispered from the sidelines.

David opened his mouth but no sound escaped the black hole. Libby's hair was the color of the sun and her dress was surely made of moonbeams. The single diamond that sparkled like a nova from the hollow of her throat could not begin to compete with the stars in her eyes. He couldn't blink. He couldn't breathe. And he didn't think that his heart had beat once in the minute or so it had taken her to descend like a goddess from Mt. Olympus.

"*Say something!*" Chelsea insisted.

"I don't believe the young man can speak," Leonard observed from a pace away. He looked from David to Libby and back before settling his gaze on Frank Gordon. A hint of a smile was all that acknowledged the younger man's brief nod.

"You look nice," David managed at last. Before the words were out he choked on them. He hadn't said "nice" had he? The Sistine Chapel is "nice." The view from outer space is "nice." He didn't know how to describe the vision before him now—beautiful, breathtaking, and stunning didn't do Libby justice—but "nice" was *not* the word he wanted.

"You look nice too," Chelsea said to cover his faux pas. "I like your uniform." She turned to Libby. "Don't you?"

Libby did indeed. David's dress whites accentuated his dark hair, broad shoulders and narrow hips. Wherever the line formed tonight, to be near this prince she was willing to stand in it. "You do look nice, Captain Rogers," she said carefully. "I'm glad you could join us."

"It's very nice all the way around, isn't it?" Frank said with the joviality of a funeral director.

David scarcely spared him a glance. The man had been drinking and his enunciation was not nearly as crisp as his tuxedo. He'd bear close watching, as would all the guests at tonight's event. One of them—or more than one of them—must be Frank's partner in mayhem.

"The guests are arriving, madam."

If David had assumed that butlers were extinct outside of movie theaters, he now knew better. And if he'd believed that Camelot had drifted into the mists of Avalon, well, he knew better than that too.

He scanned the huge, marble hall and wondered where they kept the round table. He'd known all along that Libby was rich and that she owned an estate, but seeing it was something else. This wasn't a big house; it was a small kingdom. He couldn't help but feel conspicuously out of place in it.

"Shall we?" Chelsea asked, wrapping her bony arm securely around his elbow.

David startled from his thoughts to see Geneva walking ahead with Frank, and Libby following on Leonard's arm. "Charmed, Miss Chillygator," he said.

Chelsea giggled. "I'll be your date until Uncle Leonard lets go of Libby. He doesn't like you, you know." She stood on tiptoe to whisper, "I saw him look at you the same way he looked at Charlie."

Karlton he'd heard of, but who was Charlie?

"Charlie," Chelsea volunteered happily, "was the snake Aunt Libby gave me. I had to give him away when I went to boarding school."

David didn't wonder why Libby would give her niece a snake. He did wonder why anyone would send a great little girl like this across the state to a boarding school. As he touched Chelsea's nose with the tip of his thumb he remembered that his grandfather had sent him across the country to military school. Leonard, he figured, would probably like to send him twice that far if he thought it would protect Libby. Her fairy godfather ought to get together with his autocratic grandfather. Together they might be able to land him a permanent post on the Russian space station.

More than an hour later, David still stood dutifully at his post next to Geneva. He'd extended his hand any number of times and said all the things that were expected of him.

Yes, he had piloted the Atlantis *and the* Endeavor. *Yes, he had walked in space.* After the first stockholder or two, he had added *Yes, I'm sure the government recognizes the vital role Jamison Enterprises plays in national security.* There wasn't much diversity, but at least none of these businessmen and socialites asked him how astronauts use the bathroom.

Another perk to constantly repeating himself was that it kept his eyes free to rove over the room and his brain free to process what he saw. The thing that most interested him at the moment was a whispered discussion between Frank Gordon and a man who'd been introduced earlier as Jamison's chief stockholder. They were several paces away, but David overheard the man say that he had spoken with Libby that afternoon. He frowned when Gordon's face reddened at the rest of the report.

When another hand slipped into his, he never looked away from Gordon. "Nice to meet you. I'm sure the government appreciates the vital role Jamison Enterprises plays in national security."

"I'm pleased to hear that," Libby replied. "But before we were interrupted last night, you were telling me that you didn't come to California on business?"

David looked into her face, smelled the subtle tones of her perfume, and felt light-headed.

"The guests have arrived," she said. "Your duties on the reception line are finished. Let's skip the social hour. I'll show you through the gardens and you can tell me why you *are* here."

Houston, we have a problem.

One reason he was here was because it was the best opportunity he'd ever get to observe Libby's associates first hand. With all the pieces in one place, he hoped to at last solve the puzzle. But the other reason he was here was just as important. He was here because he loved her. She was giving him the opportunity to tell her that now, but she was doing it when he had a job to do—and an inferiority complex to overcome. He was supposed to be a special agent protecting his country, not a swineherd courting a princess. But being here with Libby dressed like that, he felt more like a swineherd.

Before David could begin to solve his problem, it got bigger.

Geneva gasped, "Oh, my goodness!"

When the guests who heard the exclamation turned toward the door to see what had drawn her attention, others turned with them until everybody looked at the tall, attractive man silhouetted in the entryway. He smiled as though attention was his birthright and adulation his due.

"A movie star?" David guessed. It wasn't anybody he knew, but he'd never paid as much attention to leading men as he had to their leading ladies.

"No," Libby said, but the word was not an answer as much as it was a moan.

David's grip tightened on her hand. "Who—?"

"I didn't invite him, Libby," Geneva said quickly. "I promise you I didn't. I'd heard he was coming back to town, but I'd never . . . " Her words trailed off as the man saw them and made his way across the crowded room.

"Who is that?" David asked again.

"Karlton," Geneva whispered as though the name alone contained volumes of information.

Which it did. Unfortunately, David wasn't supposed to know even a line from one of those volumes, so he tried to keep his face blank as the cretin approached—tried and failed.

Nor was Libby successful at hiding her emotions. David suspected that if he weren't holding so tightly to her hand, she might have fled. He considered letting her go—or better, taking her away from here himself, but before he could move, Frank Gordon stepped forward and embraced the man like a long-lost brother.

A wave of a magic wand couldn't have had more effect on Libby than that greeting. Her fingers relaxed in David's palm. Her chin rose and her spine straightened. Her bristling reminded David of Calliope and he smiled, hoping that she'd use those new nails of hers to scratch Karlton Fisk's eyes out.

"Elisabeth!" Karlton reached for Libby's hands to pull her toward him. He grasped the one, but David would not relinquish the other. The result was awkward and Libby disentangled her fingers from both men and took a step back.

"Karlton," she said. "How . . . interesting . . . to see you here."

"I just got back in town. I came from the airport when I heard you were home."

If that was true, David thought, he'd traveled standing up. Fisk's tux didn't have a wrinkle in it. What's more, the thing was custom-tailored and the diamond-and-platinum cufflinks genuine. Whatever Fisk had been doing since he left Jamison Enterprises, he'd been doing it very well. David knew he shouldn't jump to conclusions, but he couldn't help but think that the missing piece of the espionage puzzle had conveniently sauntered in the front door.

Karlton sized Libby up and liked what he saw. He let out a low whistle. "May I say it was worth the trip?"

You may not. David opened his mouth, but before he could produce a sound, Karlton continued.

"You've changed, Elisabeth. Or is it only impossible for a mere mortal man to recall how beautiful you truly are?"

That beat "nice" by a moon shot. David wouldn't expect her to buy the line except for the fact that it was delivered with the sincerity of a papal address.

Still, Libby didn't buy it. She took another step back when Karlton advanced. "You haven't changed, Karlton."

"I have," he assured her. "The thought of almost losing you was more than I could bear. The months we've been apart have changed me."

He looked repentant, even to David.

Karlton again extended his hands. "I'm a new man, Elisabeth. Come let me tell you everything I've done to make myself worthy of your love."

It was like a scene from a play. David was aware of the people beside him looking on with rapt attention. They had been around for Act I, he figured, and were now waiting to applaud the tender kiss that would signal the curtain to fall on the end of Act III. He scowled in earnest, but when Libby grasped his elbow with both hands he discovered it was only Act II and she meant to introduce a plot twist.

"Forgive me for being rude, Karlton," she said as she pulled David forward. "I'd like to introduce Captain Rogers. My fiancé." She pressed the point of her elbow into David's side to remove the look of astonishment from his face. He extended his hand automatically.

Karlton didn't see David's hand. He'd turned to look at Frank who glared at Geneva who gaped at Leonard who frowned at Libby.

"Fiancé?" they said as one.

"See what you've done, Karlton?" Libby said with mock dismay. "You've ruined our surprise. We planned to announce our engagement after dinner tonight. Didn't we, David?"

"I've wanted to announce our engagement for weeks," David mumbled.

Libby forced a smile. "And now I suppose we have."

The audience reacted with excited whispers and a round of applause. Except for the small group in the front row.

"Elisabeth," Leonard said before Geneva could recover, "may I speak with you? Privately."

The expression on the patrician's face dared David to challenge his spot in Libby's heart, but he loosened his hold on her only when she nodded.

Geneva grasped David's hand as Libby excused herself and Frank took Karlton aside. "Captain, I had no idea! You must tell me the whole story at dinner!"

"That'd be, uh, great," David said slowly. "I'd like to. But maybe you'd better ask Libby to tell you. She's a much better storyteller than I am."

chapter 26

*"That is the wife for me," he thought, "but she is too
grand and lives in a castle, while I have only a box."*

— *The Brave Tin Soldier, 1838*

Sometime between the entrée and the chocolate mousse—about the
time Geneva gave up trying to pry from him the details of the make-
believe engagement—David looked down the long, linen-covered table
and realized again how far out of his own orbit he'd drifted.

He nudged a fork discreetly toward the edge of the table with his
elbow, caught it as it fell toward his lap, and slipped it into his jacket
pocket. He'd figure out how to return the monogrammed silver later.
David had lost track of which utensil to use to eat which thing in the
six-course meal and had resorted to stealing leftover spoons in an
effort to look less ignorant of social graces than he was.

Libby, seated at the other end of the table between Leonard and
Karlton, had been born knowing that the silver spoon in her mouth was
for caviar. She was unceasingly poised and unerringly gracious. During
the salad course, David had silently applauded her poise in dealing with
Karlton, but now, when she laughed at something the miscreant said, his
eyes narrowed. It had been—what—two hours since their betrothal?
How fickle was that? Sure, Fisk was handsome and charming and rich—
and well aware of which utensil to pick up—but that didn't mean—

A woman at David's left lay a bejeweled hand on his arm. "Where
did you meet Elisabeth?" she asked. "Majorca? Monte Carlo? She
spends most of her time out of the country as I understand."

More like out in the country, David thought, *planting moon gardens, hobnobbing with the peasants, enchanting unsuspecting swineherds . . . stuff like that.*

All at once David knew why he felt so miserable. He'd fallen in love with Libby James, ignoring the fact that she was also Elisabeth Jamison. Or maybe there was a difference between knowing who she was in theory and *seeing* who she was in fact.

The swineherd in a fairy tale had more in common with a princess than he had with the beautiful woman at the end of this table. And the swineherd's chances of winning the princess were better too. Here he'd spent weeks supposing that Libby was playing hard-to-get when actually she'd been being what she was—unattainable.

"Captain Rogers?" the woman at his side persisted. "I asked where you met Elisabeth."

"Uh . . . " *What were the choices again?* David was tempted to choose Majorca then realized that despite teaching geography to sixth-graders, he didn't know where it was. "We met in England." England was good. He spoke the language, could name the capitol, and knew the approximate spot on earth where it was situated.

"Were you presented to the queen?"

"Uh, no."

"Then surely you—"

David was grateful when Geneva rose. Now at least he wouldn't have to lie about doing whatever it was the woman thought he'd "surely" done.

Libby's sister announced the program of music that would follow, then linked her arm through her husband's to lead the way into the conservatory. The rest of the guests followed and, unable to see Libby in the crowd, David brought up the rear flank. He was about to enter the room when Libby reached for his hand from behind.

"Hurry. Before anybody notices that we're leaving."

Puzzled, he followed her back the way they had come, through double doors and into a long, undecorated hall. "Are we lost?" he asked as they turned a corner and he saw nothing but more hallway. "Or was dinner to fatten me up so you could finally feed me to that fire-breathing dragon?"

The cynical note in his voice gave Libby pause. She said, "I keep the dragon up in a turret to guard my vast horde of gold and jewels."

He couldn't bring himself to smile.

"Okay then," she said, "I confess. I'm taking you down into the deep, dark dungeon from which no man has ever emerged. Are you afraid?"

He was, but mostly of how he'd live without her now that he knew he had to.

She took a dozen steps more and pushed open a door. "Captain Rogers," she said, "this is everyone. Everybody, this is David."

"Everybody" didn't live in a dungeon. Or, if they did, it was the nicest, best-smelling dungeon anyone had ever called home. The spacious kitchen in the servant's quarters was filled with people. Chelsea waved exuberantly from a corner of the room where she played Mah Jong and, between bites of chocolate cake, related again all she had seen and done at the Air Force base that afternoon.

Libby introduced the maids, handymen, and chauffeurs, then slipped her arms across the shoulders of a middle-aged Asian couple. "These are two of the dearest people in the world," she said, "Mei and Tat Jook. Mei raised me when I wasn't in boarding school, and Tat, well, both his thumbs and all his fingers are green. Almost everything in my garden at home came from his."

A ginger sauce bubbling on the stove made David's mouth water. "Tat taught you to garden and Mei taught you to cook," he guessed.

"Yes," Libby smiled. "I wish I were half the cook she is." She noted that he sniffed the air. "Are you hungry?"

"Without doubt he is hungry!" Mei exclaimed, turning toward the stove. "Those fish eggs and rabbit leavings that your sister orders for her fancy dinners are not food!" She muttered vague disparagings about the caterers in English and Chinese as she fished plump, pork-stuffed won tons from a pot and slathered them with savory sauce. She carried the plate and two forks over to a table, shooed away the people who were sitting there and motioned to Libby and David. "Sit. Eat."

David went obediently to the bench and Libby slid in beside him. Mei and Tat sat on the bench across from them. Tat removed pictures from the pocket of his worn coveralls. "Our children," he said to David. He pointed to a picture of a handsome young man in a cap and gown. "Our son, the soon-to-be doctor. He is in residency at UCLA." As David, his mouth full of won ton, nodded and tried to make polite sounds of acknowledgement around the delicious food, Tat presented the next picture. "Our daughter."

David swallowed. "She's beautiful."

"She is smart," Mei said. "She is a sophomore at Stanford University. You've heard of it?"

"Yeah," David said with a grin.

"Our little Lib went there." Mei's almond-shaped eyes were bright with pride.

"Yes," David said. "I know." He knew too, who encouraged these children of laborers to follow in her footsteps and paid the tuition so that they could.

"Our Lib is smart too," Mei said.

"And beautiful," Tat added. "And good."

David knew all of that. The won ton caught in his throat and he nodded.

Tat leaned forward. "Chelsea tells us that you will marry."

Mei's face filled with accusation. "This is something Lib did not tell us herself."

"Oh!" Libby said, with a long took toward her niece, "I didn't realize . . . " She glanced at David then away. "We're not engaged, Mei. David is a . . . he's . . . "

David waited to hear what he was—friend, associate, swineherd? He doubted that anything Libby would call him would be something he could live with.

She didn't finish the sentence. Instead, she began another. "Karlton showed up unexpectedly." At Mei's "Wah!" she added hastily, "I didn't know what to say and I didn't want to deal with him. So I lied and said that I was engaged to David. Fortunately for me, Captain Rogers is too much the officer and gentleman to deny it."

David remained silent trying to be the gentleman she had said.

Satisfied, Tat rose from the table. "I'll get you those iris bulbs I promised."

"Must you leave tomorrow?" Mei asked. "And so early?"

Libby turned for a glimpse of the clock. "After I make another announcement in a few minutes—a true one this time—Geneva may ask me to leave tonight."

"It's *your* house—"

"Don't worry, Mei." Libby reached across the table to squeeze the older woman's hand as she rose. "I was exaggerating. But I did sell the company! Mr. Laurent and the top three stockholders agreed this afternoon. That's all I needed. We'll sign the papers and begin the transfer to SynQuest by the end of the month!" She danced around the table, hugged Mei and accepted congratulations from everyone in the room.

Only David couldn't muster a smile. Elisabeth Jamison had no idea that she was about to make the most dangerous announcement of her life, but he knew it. He knew it all too well.

* * *

"Lock your door," David told Libby.

She smiled. When the party ended—rather abruptly after her surprise announcement—he'd walked her to her suite, opened the door for her and then spent several minutes supposedly searching the rooms for a mouse she hadn't seen and he couldn't locate after the first glimpse. Now he paused at the open doorway and gave this odd instruction.

"The grandfather clock is down the hall," Libby teased. "If I lock the mouse in with me, how will he run up it?" She'd hoped to elicit one of David's knee-weakening grins, but it was nowhere in evidence. Even the moonlight that poured in through a high, arched window at the end of the hall lacked appeal since it seemed only to etch the grim lines in his handsome face.

"I'm close. You have the number of my cell phone?"

"Yes." Libby's perplexity grew. He'd behaved strangely all evening, but this locking of doors and reminding of phone numbers was the strangest of all. She looked past him through the window to the moon and the garden below. Their first kiss was all she could think about, but his mind was clearly on something else. She tried to remember when she'd first noticed him acting odd, and Libby realized at once that she had yet to explain her impetuous announcement at the reception. "Karlton and I were engaged," she said quickly, pleased when the words got his attention. "It ended . . . badly. As you heard me tell Mei, I didn't want to deal with him again, especially in front of so many people, but I'm sorry I dragged you into it that way."

"It was nothing."

She leaned back against the doorjamb and the moonlight spilled between them. "That's all you have to say? 'It was nothing?' No witty comeback? No offer to marry me to make me an honest woman?" Her brows drew together. "What's come over you tonight, Captain?"

"Nothing."

Again with "nothing." But "Karlton" had got his attention and "marry" had made him flinch. She was making progress. Libby studied him silently and saw that the "nothing" he looked away from was her designer dress, heirloom jewels and $500 slippers.

"I see," she said slowly. "You've seen Batgirl's alter ego for yourself and you don't like it very much." So much for Geneva's plan to knock his socks off.

He neither confirmed nor denied her guess, but Libby knew she was right. She clasped her hands together at her waist and, in sudden inspiration, pulled off her sister's dazzling dinner ring. Holding it between a thumb and forefinger she moved it slowly back and forth in front of his face and then chucked it toward the staircase.

The brown eyes widened. Astonishment wasn't what she was going for—she wanted him to look at her the way he had last Saturday night in the garden—but it was a start.

He watched mutely as she removed the diamonds from her wrists and around her throat and kicked off her shoes. Then she pulled the gold combs from her hair and dropped them at his feet with the rest. She said softly, "It's really me, David. I took you down to that dungeon for a reason. Didn't it tell you anything about who I am—even here?"

The grim lines had softened into something else. "I . . . " he said, "you . . . "

"So at last we speak the same language." Libby ran her fingers along his jaw line and felt the thrill of touching him travel up her arm to her spine, then down to her bare toes.

"Libby?"

There was still a question mark after her name and Libby couldn't bear it. She had kissed him first, after all. Couldn't she now confess her love first too, if that's what it would take to remove the question from his mind and the doubt from his eyes? She moved closer.

"Didn't you read *The Goloshes of Fortune*? It's the second story in the book you stole from my library." Her fingers closed over the knot in his tie and she tugged playfully. "I want that book back, Captain Rogers." Then she flattened her hand and moved it to his chest as she raised the other hand to join it. "But not until you've read the story."

"I've read it."

His voice was as rich and deep as his shining brown eyes. Libby caught her breath while she could. "Do you remember it? Was there perhaps a line that stuck in your mind?"

"There was one line I remember," David said. His hands encircled her waist and drew her the rest of the way to him. His lips were almost as close as she wished them to be. "'She loved no wealth but fairy tales and me.'"

"That, Captain," Libby said as she settled into his strong arms, "is precisely the line I was thinking of."

Her lips met his in a kiss eloquent both in need and promise. She felt dazzled and dazed and delighted. This was no frog. Without benefit of a magic lamp, talking horse, or fairy godmother, all Libby's dreams had come true. She'd sold her company and found true love at last. All that was left was to turn the page and write "they lived happily ever after" across the parchment in a flowing golden script.

Or so she thought.

chapter 27

She loved no wealth but fairy tales and me!

— *The Goloshes of Fortune, 1838*

"Can I drive?" David asked as he carried his bags and Libby's across a tarmac in the private sector of LAX Airport early the next morning.

Libby looked from him to the business jet and back. "You mean my *airplane?*"

"Well, yeah."

His grin was boyishly hopeful and she melted even though she knew he was intent on distracting her from the scene that had taken place earlier. Geneva had appeared in Chelsea's room this morning with puffy eyes—and a more disturbingly puffy face—and forbade her daughter from going with Libby to Amen. Chelsea screamed and cried and called her mother mean, and there was little either woman could do to calm her.

Libby didn't think Geneva was mean. Perhaps she was weak. Possibly she was petty, and certainly she was stupid to stay with Frank when he had coerced her into using her daughter as a pawn. But she wasn't mean. That Chelsea would have to return to Kendicott for her vacation was regrettable; that Geneva would choose to stay with Frank was frightening. But Libby couldn't control either situation. She could only pray for her family and go back to Amen with David.

Back to Amen with David! Despite her regret, Libby's heart beat a little faster. She was in love. *They* were in love and very little else—no matter how urgent—could remain long in her mind when he held her hand and smiled into her eyes. She paused at the foot of the stairs and smiled back at him. "You're asking me to let you fly my million-dollar airplane?"

"The government lets me fly their billion-dollar space shuttle." The grin alone would have won him the title to the plane. "But if you're worried about my experience, shuttle training aircraft are modified Gulfstreams like this one. I've taken off and landed one of these babies more than a thousand times."

"You can fly the plane," Libby said, preceding him up the stairs.

"If I do a good job will you give me a permanent position?"

"I thought you had a job."

He paused at the door to the jet, relinquished their bags to the flight attendant, and tried not to stare in amazement. The inside of this plane looked like the lobby of a hotel.

"Didn't you say you've spent hours in a Gulfstream?" Libby teased.

"There, uh, wasn't a grand piano in ours."

"Geneva's afraid to fly. Music soothes her."

"Too bad she can't afford a CD player."

"Isn't it?" Libby's smile widened. "I'll consider hiring you, Captain, but first you'll have to find the cockpit and, second, you'll have to tell me why you're applying for a new job."

David pointed toward his left. "Cockpit." Under his breath he added, "They haven't fussed that all up too, have they?"

"I wouldn't know. I've never been in the cockpit."

He took her hand and pulled her along. "You're in for a treat."

"David, no. I prefer the—"

"How do you know you like the backseat if you've never sat in the front?"

When he pushed open the door to the cockpit, the young pilot turned in his chair then jumped to his feet. "Miss Jamison!"

"Hi, Jess," Libby said, reading the man's name from the tag on his uniform.

"I'm sorry about Mr. Montgomery."

Libby lowered her head. "Me too." Then she introduced David. "He wants to fly the plane. He's, um, applying for a job."

The pilot was dubious. "Have you seen his license?"

David had already removed it from his wallet along with his NASA ID. He passed them over.

"You're a shuttle pilot?" Jess asked with reverence. "Will you tell me about it on the way into Phoenix?"

"I'm sure he will," Libby said. "There's nothing he'd rather do than talk. Enjoy yourselves. I'm going back to first class where weary CEOs belong." She smiled as Jess abandoned the captain's seat with alacrity. "Let me know if you think Captain Rogers might work out for us."

Libby had released her seatbelt after takeoff, drunk a glass of orange juice and opened her scriptures when there was a low beep in the headrest of her seat. She reached for the armrest and pressed a button. "Yes?"

"Found her seat on the first try," she heard David tell Jess. "Hello there," he said to her. "This is one sweet little glider you've got, Miss Jamison."

She felt giddy and knew it wasn't the altitude. "I'm glad you like it."

"How about that takeoff? Smooth, huh?"

"Smooth," she repeated. Libby nestled her head into the headrest so it would seem as though he was whispering in her ear this morning as he had last night.

"Want me to do a loop or take a dive or something?"

She sat up straight. "No!"

"You sure?" She could see his teasing grin in her mind's eye. "I want to convince you I'm perfect for this job."

She leaned back, but not trusting him completely, refastened her seatbelt. "What's wrong with the job you have now?"

"Just a minute."

She heard him ask Jess to check the gauge on some piece of equipment that was apparently located elsewhere because next she heard the other man agree somewhat reluctantly and leave the cockpit. "Is everything okay?" she asked nervously.

"Of course," David said. "I'm flying, remember? I could land on a dry lake bed if I had to." He waited for her to laugh then said, "As Chelsea would say, 'That's a joke.' The shuttle often *does* land on a lake bed."

"What did you send Jess to check?"

"Oh, that? Don't worry about it. If he's any kind of pilot at all he knows I was trying to get rid of him."

Libby relaxed her grip on the armrest. "Why were you getting rid of him?"

"So I could tell his boss that I love her. It's been at least thirty minutes since I kissed you and I was afraid you'd forget."

It would take more than a plane crash to make Libby forget his last kiss.

"And to answer your previous question, my commission expires in a few months. I've been thinking that I might be ready to spend the rest of my life on terra firma."

When she didn't immediately respond he asked, "What do you think?"

"Truthfully?" Libby had closed her eyes so she could see his face behind her eyelids. "I'm thinking that the terra in my life isn't quite as firma with you on it."

"Does that mean I'm hired?" His voice was husky. "There aren't a whole lot of jobs I'll qualify for when I leave NASA."

"I hear," she said above the steady rhythm of her heart beating in her ears, "that you're a pretty fair teacher. Have you considered sticking with that? Say, somewhere like Amen?"

"I don't know," he replied slowly. "Amen's a pretty small town. After running away with the school librarian this weekend, my reputation may be shot."

Libby's eyelids flew open. "David!" It had never entered her mind what some people—meaning LaVerne—would think about them leaving and returning simultaneously. Until now.

He chuckled at her cry of dismay. "We're a little south of Vegas. I could change course so we could elope there. No, never mind," he continued before she managed to respond. "We can't get married in Las Vegas. It's Sunday. The temple's closed."

"Temple?"

"You don't think I'm dumb enough to give you a 'death do us part' clause?"

"Be serious, David."

"Libby," he said, "how many times do I have to tell you that I *am* serious?"

"I need to think."

"You're not thinking," he said. "You're obsessing. And you can stop. I was teasing you. Your car is at the airport, but my truck's at the Air Force base northwest of the city. You'll beat me home by three hours, easy." She heard the door open to the cockpit. "Besides, you told everybody that you were going to your sister's. I told LaVerne that I was going to get away to fly airplanes for the weekend. And I *have* flown a couple of them."

For a moment Libby entertained another obsession—the one about how much fiction might be wrapped up in every fact David related.

"The pressure is 6.9," she heard Jess report as he slid back into the copilot's chair. "Well within normal."

"Thanks for checking," David said. "You can't be too careful."

That was probably true in matters of affection as well as aeronautics, Libby thought. But when he said, "Well, Miss Jamison, do you think I'll do?" she couldn't suppress the sudden expansion of her heart.

"Yes, Captain Rogers," she said. "I think I *will* keep you."

chapter 28

She conjured only a little, and for her own amusement.

— *The Snow Queen, Book the Third: The Flower Garden of the Woman Who Could Conjure, 1845*

David sat in a BYC meeting a week later studiously doodling suns and moons and stars on the margins of the agenda to keep from looking at Libby. He wished the meeting would end. Then he could go over to Estelle's house as he had yesterday and the day before and the days before that and sneak from there over to Libby's kitchen—the only spot on earth where she would acknowledge that she loved him.

Talk about a person who didn't believe in public displays of affection. Libby still publicly turned him down for dates even. She'd asked David to keep their relationship strictly private for now and he'd had little choice but to agree, though he felt bad when Homer had lost the ten-dollar bet to Guy who continued to prophesy that the Second Coming would occur before David's first date with Libby.

In the meantime, the sale of Jamison Enterprises grew closer and Preston Wescott grew more demanding. He and David spent long hours tracking dead-end leads and pouring over the mismatched pieces of an impossible puzzle. They held electronic meetings every night to go over everything that happened in both LA and Amen in excruciating detail. Though they disagreed on several points, one view they shared was that Karlton Fisk's return to the picture smacked more of conspiracy than coincidence. Personally and professionally, there was nothing that David would like more than to nail the guy to the same wall as Frank Gordon.

"Brother Rogers?"

Calvin, the president of the deacon's quorum, had slumped down in his chair and the full focus of the youth committee was now on David. Only Libby was smiling, and that was in amusement. If they'd been alone, David would have taken great pleasure in kissing that teasing smile from her face. As it was, he filed the thought away for later in the day.

"We were talking about this week's joint activity," Bishop Wheeler said. "Your deacons are in charge, I believe."

"Oh, yeah," David said. That would be the service project they had never planned. Organizing flying monkeys would be easier than organizing those Scouts. David always figured he was magnifying his calling as a Scoutmaster if he managed to keep them busy and mostly out of mayhem. "Oh, yeah!" he said, grateful when inspiration struck. "We've planned a fix-up project at the old church house." It was a project Shenla had been after him to work on. She headed a committee that wanted to register it as a historic landmark. He hadn't forgotten that he owed her a favor from the carnival.

"We planned that?" Calvin asked.

"Yeah." David reached over to rest a hand on the back of the boy's neck. "Remember?"

Calvin suddenly did.

Everybody in the council agreed to the plan, but nobody was more pleased with it than Libby. In her enthusiasm, she forgot herself and allowed David to walk her home.

"My ancestors helped build this chapel," she told him as they paused in front of the one-room edifice on the way to her house. She looked up at it fondly. "The bottom half is adobe. The pioneers knew they couldn't afford to buy enough wood so the women made the bricks down by the river and laid them along the banks to bake in the sun. Then the men carted them up here and built a house of God."

Libby spoke of it as though it were a temple when what it was, David thought, was an eyesore. "It's, uh, great."

"Yes," Libby agreed. "It is." She began to smile at the way he must see it—and her—but immediately sobered. She pushed her hair behind one ear and asked earnestly, "David, do I seem relatively . . . well balanced . . . to you?"

He cupped his hand tenderly under her chin. "Aside from your taste in architecture, you seem relatively perfect to me."

She reached for his hand and held it as she confessed, "Lately I've had the strangest thoughts."

He was about to make an offhand remark when he saw the depth of concern on her pretty face. "Like what, Lib?"

"I don't know," she said helplessly. "It's been going on for weeks, but it's getting worse." She looked up at the sky. "It's like glimpsing something from the corner of my eye, and turning my head and it's not there. I don't know for sure if it ever was there."

He thought of the surveillance cameras and bugs she must look at every day and not recognize. David's hand tightened around her fingers.

"Mostly I've felt that way about people," she continued. "Sometimes I look at someone and think that I should know something about them that I don't."

No matter how hard he tried, David could not meet her eye. He looked down at his shoes and prayed that she would think that he was considering what she'd said. They were almost through this conspiracy thing—almost to the time that he could tell her the truth. But it wasn't that time yet. If anything, as the sale of the company approached, it was more dangerous for her than it had ever been before. Because he needed to know how much she suspected he swallowed and said, "People? Who for instance?"

"You think I'm crazy, don't you?"

"No." He thought she was sensitive and perceptive and clearly in tune with the Spirit, but he didn't for a second think she was crazy. "What worries you?"

She didn't hesitate. "Something tells me I should know who murdered my parents. And I think I should know *why* they were killed."

"Libby." It was all he said, and all he could say.

"The shooting wasn't random. I'm sure of it."

Her eyes had filled with tears and David couldn't seem to lift a finger to wipe away the first that rolled onto her cheek. If she did know, or if she somehow found out—He couldn't bear to finish the thought.

"But I *don't* know," she concluded in a rush. "And I don't know what to think about that or any of the other odd . . . feelings . . . that I have."

When David found that he could move again he gathered Libby into his arms. "You know what I think it is?" he said as the scent of her hair and softness of her skin filled his senses and threatened to bring tears to his eyes as well. "I think you're in love."

She nestled her head in the hollow of his neck with a contented sigh as he held her close. "Do you suppose I'll ever get over it?"

"No," he said, tightening the embrace. "Never. No matter what happens." He pressed his lips to the top of her head and fought back his own apprehension: Fear that the CIA was not yet convinced of her innocence. Fear for her safety. Fear that when he finally told her the whole story she would not see at once that his love for her was the one truth that never faltered. And fear of the unknown because Libby was right. Her parents' murder hadn't been random. And the murderer hadn't been found.

* * *

Libby leaned her broom against the door of the old chapel and brushed the dirt from her hands. The service project was a success.

"What do you th-think, Sister James?" Aaron asked as he white-washed what of the old adobe brick he could reach from his wheel-chair. Nearby his father and several of the priests nailed the last few boards into place along the doorjambs, windows and eaves, while the rest of the deacons and Beehives weeded the churchyard and the Laurels, Mia Maids, and teachers whitewashed inside and out. Deaf Old Ezra told a story of how he'd once brought a horned toad here with him to Primary. The only person conspicuously absent was the Scoutmaster, and Libby wondered where he'd gone.

"I think it's beautiful, Aaron," she said, trying not to think about how a few months ago the boy would have been the first one up the ladder to work on the roof. "You're doing a fabulous job. Everybody is." She glanced around the yard once again. "Where is Brother Rogers?"

"I think he went around the to the b-back," Aaron reported. "I d-don't know what he's doing."

"What *are* you doing?" Libby asked him a minute later.

David almost dropped his phone. "You startled me."

"Are you talking to Jupiter again?"

He stuck the phone into his pocket without a word of farewell to the person on the other end of the line. "So what do you think?" he asked, ignoring her question as well as her puzzlement. "Are your ancestors happy with what we've done for the old place?"

"Yes," Libby said. "It's wonderful. *You're* wonderful, David. Not only for planning this project and getting Moses to come but—"

He moved closer and Libby felt her pulse accelerate when he interrupted with, "Please tell me that the next reason will be more personal."

Libby knew that one of the kids could show up at any second. She took a prudent step away from him. "As a matter of fact," she said, "as wonderful as I think you are personally, I have some bad news. I can't offer you that pilot job. After this week, I won't own a jet." She had to force herself to keep her distance rather than fall into his arms in excitement. "Leonard called before I came this afternoon—the deal is done with SynQuest! I'll fly to LA Monday morning to sign the papers. From that moment on, I am officially and forever the librarian at Alma School!"

Libby could hear the youth chatter happily in the front yard, the river burble down the embankment and the wind move through the cottonwood trees. He was so quiet she could almost hear his heart beat. "David? I thought you'd be happy."

"Hey," he said too quickly, "you just told me I'm out of a cushy job. That jet had its own piano."

The grin looked forced and Libby had yet another of those inexplicable and disconcerting flashes of she-didn't-know-what.

"It's great about the sale, Lib," he said. "I'm glad." He didn't seem glad, but he seemed sincere when he added, "I want to go with you to LA."

"It's only for the day," she replied. Why couldn't she shake this odd feeling? Wasn't the breeze suddenly cooler and David more distant? But he didn't have an interest in Jamison Enterprises. He couldn't.

Could he?

Libby shook her head to dislodge thoughts of Karlton's deception. Even after all this time they still came sharp and unbidden. She had to forgive herself for that misjudgment, painful as it was, forget it and move on. David loved her. He'd loved her before he knew she was Elisabeth Jamison.

And yet.

"Who were you talking to when I interrupted?" she asked.

"Nobody," he said. She must have looked as dubious as she felt because he pulled the device from his pocket. "It's a remote Internet device. See?" She didn't see because he stuck it back in his pocket faster than he'd pulled it out. "I was checking the weather. With all the complaining Moses is doing about his leg I wanted to make sure we weren't in for rain. I'd hate for all the kids' work to go for nothing."

Libby had two choices: she could believe David and sleep well tonight or she could suspect him of lying to her and lie awake wondering why he would.

It was going to be a long night.

* * *

David didn't know what was urgent at seven o'clock on Saturday night, but he tapped the security code into his computer and waited impatiently for the connection that would allow him to find out. The hand-held version of the computer was on the table beside the laptop and his elbow was next to it.

When the urgent light flashed he had been on his way to Estelle's for the weekly potluck (Libby was taking spaghetti and breadsticks and Estelle was grating Parmesan cheese). David was already late because of an overly long look he'd been taking at the newly compiled dossier on Karlton Fisk. Frankly, all the time he and Wescott spent trying to solve the puzzle made him feel a little paranoid. Despite the imminence of the sale, everything seemed to be in hand and none of the suspects, including Karlton, had made a move. He had to stop expecting the worst. Tonight he had to make himself relax and enjoy the evening with Libby so as not to raise her suspicions any higher than they already were. He thought she loved him, but wasn't half so sure she trusted him.

When Preston Wescott came on-line, David knew by the man's face that he had decided too soon to relax.

"We're making some changes, Rogers."

Didn't the man ever say hello? "Sir?"

"You're off the case."

David had felt this way once before. It was when he'd taken a T-38 twenty thousand feet up and then dropped so sharply toward earth that he was weightless for twenty seconds. When gravity again took effect it was like having a boulder drop from his head to his shoulders and come to rest in his lap.

Wescott continued, "Sorry to throw this bogey at you, Captain. You're a good man and you've done a good job."

"Then—"

"It's not us. It's the military. You were on loan, so to speak, and there are some heads too high to see over."

What he meant, David realized at last, was that one crotchety old Navy admiral who couldn't bear to be disobeyed had rattled enough sabers to make his personal agenda take precedence over national security. "My grandfather—"

"Had a meeting today with the head of the Joint Chiefs of Staff," Wescott finished for him. "We're all on the same side, Rogers, but not all of us know it." David could tell by the tone of voice that the chief didn't like this blow to his mission any better than David did the thought of leaving Libby. But Wescott added firmly, "You're out of there. Tell Max Wheeler there's an emergency and they need you back at NASA."

"But Libby—"

"Don't tell Jamison anything. That's an order. We're probably going to have to bring her in, and I don't want anything to spook her beforehand."

"I can't just—"

Wescott interpreted David's reaction from squarely within his own paradigm. "I know. And just when the case was about to break wide open. I wish there was another option, but at this juncture I don't see it."

"But—"

"End of conversation, Captain. Be in my office at 8 A.M. sharp tomorrow for debriefing."

David pushed back his chair and stood. His head spun worse than after a session in the altitude chamber. Maybe a little fresh air would clear it and let him think. He'd walk over to Max's house to tell him about the "emergency" at NASA and hope the bishop would be inspired in their behalf. So far, the only solution David could come up with to stay with Libby involved high treason. Not that he wouldn't consider it if it came right down to it.

With his concern throbbing in his temples, David pulled open the door and left without turning off the light or noticing that he'd left his satellite phone on the table. Five minutes later, when the shrill whine indicated a message more urgent than the first, David was too far away to hear it.

chapter 29

*Here in the dark night sits the man who measured
the mountains in the moon; He who forced his way out
into the endless space, among the stars and planets.*

— *The Thorny Road of Honor,* 1856

By nine o'clock Libby had seen all the TV she could bear and left
Estelle enjoying the rest of the sci-fi fare alone. She'd been home
almost an hour now and hadn't seen David nor been able to reach
him by phone—traditional or the one he used to call Jupiter.

"He's not coming over," she told Calliope around the thumbnail
in her teeth. "And don't look so disappointed. I wouldn't let him feed
you. You're getting pudgy." At Calliope's mewl of protest Libby said,
"Well, you are."

Speaking of pudgy, she was not going into the kitchen for fudge
sauce. The love of her life had behaved strangely all week, then stood
her up tonight without so much as a phone call, but so what? There
were any number of perfectly reasonable explanations for his
actions—none of which she could name.

"Let's go to bed, Calliope."

Libby had turned off the porch light when she saw headlights at
the end of the street. "It's about time," she told the cat as she drew the
blinds. "But don't act like we were sitting here waiting for him. Act
casual." The cat licked her forepaw. "No," Libby said, "that's what
you do when you break flowerpots." Calliope lowered her paw. "Oh, I
don't know!" The car pulled to a stop in front of the house. "Can't

you pretend to sleep or something?" For her part, Libby dropped down on the couch, scooped an unread novel from the table and opened it to the middle.

"Come in," she called to the insistent rap at the door. When it opened she looked up—casually—and dropped the book. "Geneva!"

"I've left Frank." Her sister's face was white beneath her makeup and her voice wavered.

Libby leapt to her feet. "Oh, Geneva, I'm so glad!" They weren't the right words, but truer ones were never spoken.

Geneva's tear-filled eyes overflowed and Libby was at her side in an instant. "I'm sorry, Genie," she said, grasping her sister's hand. "I shouldn't have said that."

Geneva stared back through the open door at the limo and her voice was scarcely above a croak. "No, Libby. I'm sorry. Please. Please forgive me."

"What? I—"

"Chelsea's in the car," Geneva interrupted with a nervous glance back toward the street. "She's asleep. I think she might be ill. Can you come out and help me carry her inside?"

"Sit down, Genie," Libby said in concern. "You look like you're about to collapse. I'll get the driver to help me with Chelsea."

"No! I'll help you."

On her way down the path Libby thought that it must at last be nearing fall here in the desert foothills. The stepping stones felt cool beneath her bare feet, the air was almost crisp, and since it was a new moon, the stars sparkled in the velvet-dark sky.

Libby reached for the car's door handle and heard her sister stifle a sob. Though her heart ached for her sister's sorrow, Libby was pleased and grateful Geneva had come to her instead of flying off to the Riviera. There was no better place in the world for Genie and Chilly to begin a new life than Amen.

The first thing Libby saw when the overhead light came on was Chelsea slumped against the far door. She was fast asleep, but her breathing was shallow. Libby leaned into the car in concern. It was then she saw Frank Gordon on the facing seat. Along his arm was a dated but efficient semi-automatic weapon. It was pointed at her heart.

"Get in the car, Elisabeth," he said. "We're taking a little business trip."

* * *

Most of David's thoughts over the last couple of hours were could- and should- and would- have-beens. Max hadn't been home, or in his office, or down at the school, the only places David knew to look for him. He finally lowered himself onto a rock in front of the recently restored adobe chapel at a loss to know what to do next.

How would his life have differed, he wondered, if his parents had raised him instead of his grandfather? Would he have become a pilot? Or might he have pursued a different course altogether—one that would have kept him on earth instead of sending him up to the clouds and, eventually, into space to try to rub shoulders with the man in the moon?

As he sat silently, listening to the frogs harmonize with the crickets and looking up at the stars, he wondered how a man's lifetime was measured out. Was it this much choice and this much chance and that much of the influence—for good or ill—of others? Was life truly as out of one's control as it seemed right now? How could it be so harsh and unforgiving and impossible to understand?

David knew that because of his grandfather he couldn't live in Amen with Libby. He knew too, that because of the fate that had brought him here, he couldn't live without her anywhere else. Realizing at last that he had surpassed his own resources David did what humble, intelligent men have done in all ages. He bowed his head to pray.

Give, and it shall be given unto you; good measure, pressed down, and shaken together, and running over.

He couldn't remember when he might have read it and didn't know where in the scriptures it was found, but the verse about Christ's measure gave David more peace than he'd dreamed he could have since Wescott's call. There *was* a plan, he thought with gratitude, a plan that ran through life—the good and bad of it—to steady the course and right the wrongs over which one had no control. It was that plan that had brought him to Amen—and to Libby.

Libby.

The Spirit repeated her name and David's heart beat faster. He would be violating a direct order—and probably committing treason—

but he had to at least call to tell her he was leaving Amen. He reached for his phone and knew in a split second that he had left it behind.

Suddenly, that wasn't all he knew. David's heart hammered in his chest.

Libby.

He jumped to his feet and covered the few blocks to her house in better time than he'd ever posted on the track at Annapolis. He didn't have to vault the wall because the gate was open, as was the front door to the house. He sprinted down the path and took the stairs as one. The lights were on in the living room but it was empty.

"Libby?"

Calliope came out from the rear of the house so David walked to the end of the hall and called again, louder. When there was still no response he searched the small home and backyard with a growing sense of dread. *She could have stayed over at Estelle's,* he reminded himself desperately, *or gone to help somebody who called her on the phone, or...*

He knew in his heart she had done none of those things.

In the kitchen, he picked up Libby's phone and punched in the numbers to Wescott's secure line as Calliope looked on accusingly.

The chief answered on the first ring. "Where have you been, man? We've been trying to reach you for two hours—ever since Gordon got on the plane in LA. He's on to you, Rogers. We thought you were dead."

Frank Gordon has Libby. David couldn't speak. If it had felt as though a boulder had fallen on him during their earlier conversation, this felt like a mountain.

"Glad you're still with us," Wescott allowed. "It looks like you were right about Jamison all along. We got a bug in the rental they took from the airport. Jamison's probably as clean as you say, so with her and the little girl along it's a hostage situation."

David knew he didn't have a moment to panic if he hoped to act. "Where are they now? Where are they going?"

"They're on their way to Deer Valley," Wescott said. "From there Gordon's planning on South America. That, of course, is a no go. We've already pulled the pilot."

"You'll need another."

"A guy's on the way from Phoenix SWAT."

"No," David said. "Me."

"In the first place, Gordon's on to you. He'd planned to kill you in Amen."

And he might have, David thought, *if I'd been with Libby*. Or maybe, if he'd been with her, she'd be safe now in his arms. "He'll have to take me if I'm the only pilot in a hundred miles," David said to interrupt thoughts that were costing him precious seconds. "Make that happen."

"In the second place," Wescott continued as if David hadn't spoken, "they've got a twenty minute head start on you by now. I don't want to keep Gordon waiting around the airport. He's got a short fuse and I've got innocent people."

"They have to take the highway," David said, "I don't." His truck wasn't called a High Mobility Vehicle for nothing. By cutting across the desert he could shave off at least half the linear distance. "I can get there first, Preston." The silence told him that Wescott was considering it. He pressed, "I'm the best you can get and you know it. I'm getting there before Gordon, and I'm flying that plane. You worry about the support."

David dropped the receiver before hearing the reply and was across Libby's yard and on his way to his truck before the chief hung up the phone. He'd made it from earth to space in eight and a half minutes. If there was a world record for travel time between Amen and Deer Valley, he'd shatter it too.

* * *

Libby held the sleeping Chelsea close and looked down at the top of the girl's head to avoid her brother-in-law's steady leer while she tried to figure out what was happening. At this point, all she knew for sure was that Frank had a big gun, her sister was terrified to the point of hysteria, and her niece must have been drugged. Chelsea's pulse was a little too slow and her breathing a little too fast. "She needs a doctor," Libby told Frank.

He yawned. "First one we come across in Bolivia."

"Bolivia?" Libby had been silent to this point, wanting answers to her questions but unwilling to give Frank the satisfaction of hearing fear in her voice when she asked.

"Don't worry if you left your passport behind . . . with your shoes." Frank ran the toe of his wingtips languorously across the top of Libby's bare foot. "It's an uncharted flight to a field Customs has never heard of."

Libby pulled her feet under the seat, and forced down her growing dread. "Are you crazy, Frank?" Stupid question, she berated herself. The answer was self-evident.

But Frank was willing, even eager, to reply. "You thought I'd sit inside your comfy little estate and wait to be arrested?" His hand stroked the gun in his lap. "Or did you think I'd be 'honorable' like you and cooperate?"

"Arrested? I don't know what you're talking about."

"I *told* you she doesn't know!" Geneva cried.

Frank slowly clapped his hands together three times. "A stunning performance, Elisabeth." His eyes narrowed. "I'm anxious to see what you can do for an encore."

Libby turned toward the window but there was nothing to see; even the stars were obscured by the deeply tinted glass.

"Where's your 'fiancé' tonight?" Frank asked while Libby's thoughts raced to keep up—to make sense out of any of this. "I'd hoped to kill him before we left."

Libby's eyes swung back in shock and alarm. "David?" she gasped. "You . . ."

"No," he said, clearly interested in her reaction. "I said I *hoped* to kill him. Where *is* that spy who kissed you?"

Was he deliberating talking in riddles, or had he truly lost his mind? "Spy?"

It was almost a minute before a slow smile spread across Frank's face. Then he laughed—so long and so hard that Libby thought the gun might slide from his lap and she would have a chance to make a grab for it. She waited her chance, but it didn't come.

"It's too good, Genie!" Frank said between sputters. "She *doesn't* know. I don't think I can stand it!"

Even if he had dropped the gun, Libby couldn't have reached for it now. She sat mute and perfectly still knowing that whatever it was that had flitted outside her consciousness for these last few weeks was about to be revealed. She prayed silently for the strength to bear whatever she must.

At last Frank stopped laughing long enough to say, "The man you think is so much in love with you, Elisabeth, works for the CIA. I thought you two were in a sting, but I see now I was wrong. *You* must have been their prime suspect. Captain Tall, Dark and Charming was trying to nail *you*."

Libby felt neither dubious nor distraught. She felt nothing at all. It was easy, then, to keep her voice level when she asked, "Nail me for what?"

"It seems, sis," Frank smirked, "that you've been sneaking little tiny microchips from your precious top-secret defense plant to Iran." He patted a leather attaché case that was on the seat beside him. "You're about to make your last delivery to your friends in the al-Quaida—thanks to that sale to SynQuest you insisted on. A deal you made against my best brotherly advice, I might add."

Libby was too intent on her thoughts to see Frank's gloating eyes travel over her. Her father had been sharp enough to uncover the plot early on, she knew at once, and that is what had gotten him and her mother killed. Likely her CFO, Jason Montgomery, suspected too, and the plane crash was no accident. Who else knew what went on at Jamison Enterprises better than she did herself?

The government.

David.

Libby pulled her thoughts away from him as from a flame, but the name seared her heart and mind, and left a pain she could scarcely have imagined she could endure.

Frank shook his head in mock sympathy. "Poor little Libby. When *will* you stop falling for men who only want to use you?"

chapter 30

The boy was frightened and tried to say a prayer, but he could remember nothing but the multiplication table.

— *The Snow Queen, Book the Second: A Little Boy & A Little Girl,*
1845

At last David saw headlights in the distance. He rose from the lower steps of the boarding ramp and stood at its foot. A voice in his ear said, "This is it."

The small airport had been cleared of everyone but government agents and an essential staff of maintenance workers and flight controllers. The Gulfstream stood empty, minimally fueled and cleared for take off. Sharpshooters, invisible in black gear and black masks, lined the top of the terminal, but David knew they would never get a clear shot. With Libby and Chelsea to shield him, Frank Gordon would get on that plane. What happened after that would be up to David.

No, he thought. *It will be up to God.*

The car rolled to a stop on the runway not fifty feet from where he stood. A rear window hissed down and the chrome barrel of a semiautomatic weapon pointed at his head.

"I'm the only pilot you've got, Gordon," David said. He extended his arms slowly from his sides and raised his hands toward his shoulders to indicate that he was unarmed. "And I'm the only one you're gonna get. Take it or leave it."

For a long moment David expected to die. Then the gun was withdrawn and the door swung open.

"I wouldn't have it any other way," Frank said. As he pulled Libby from the car, his fingers dug deeply into her slender upper arm and the barrel of the gun pressed against her neck to force her chin toward the night sky. "In fact, we were just talking about you, *Agent* Rogers. Weren't we, Elisabeth?"

David's stomach clenched with his fists. He had sworn to himself over the last several weeks that he would protect Libby—that he would keep her so far from the dangers of Jamison Enterprises that she would never suspect anything was amiss until it was over, she was safe, and he could explain. Even if he hadn't expected his plan to be flawless, never in a millennium did he expect the course of events to take such a sickening, horrifying twist. "Lib—"

"Shut up," Frank commanded. Geneva had struggled from the car with Chelsea as the driver sat, probably paralyzed with fear, in the front seat. "Take the kid."

David scooped Chelsea into his arms the moment Geneva dropped her. Judging by the way she swayed on her feet, he suspected Libby's sister would have a difficult time making it into the plane herself. Libby, however, stood tall and unnaturally calm. The single hint of the terror she must feel was in the size and luminosity of her eyes.

"Move," Gordon said.

David preceded him up the steep stairs into the plane. A whimpering Geneva followed as best she could. When Frank shoved Libby toward a double seat in the lounge, David bent to set Chelsea down beside her. As he rose, he looked searchingly into Libby's face. The depths of shock and mistrust he saw there were more physical than a slap and he recoiled even before she turned away.

Frank cast a disdainful glance at his cowering wife and motioned David toward the cockpit with the tip of his weapon. "We have a rendezvous to make, Captain."

With a long backward look at Libby, David made his way toward the pilot's chair. Among his fervent prayers was one that, given the circumstances, he could remember how to fly an airplane.

* * *

Libby listened to the thrum of the jet's powerful engines carry them farther above the earth and tried to attach a name to the emotion that wrung her heart. If she could define the agony, perhaps she could overcome it and once again wish to live—even if that wish would be only to keep Chelsea and her sister alive.

When Karlton had betrayed her, the defining word was "mortified." She'd realized almost at once, even at the time, how little pain there was in losing the person; the hurt was all to her pride. This time—though she'd been doubly stupid in trusting David—the wound was to her heart, and pride was nothing. It was the man she feared she could not live without.

Libby squeezed shut her eyelids and forced the tears so deep that they might never fall. The word she sought to describe her feelings, she realized at once, was "desolate."

At Libby's side Chelsea stirred. Libby released the girl's seatbelt and turned her enough to see into her face. It was disoriented, damp with perspiration, and much too pale.

"Aunt Libby?" Chelsea looked around and saw her mother. "Where . . . ?"

"We're in the jet, sweetheart," Libby said, knowing that the rest would be too hard to tell. "We're taking a trip. Try to relax."

Libby couldn't obey her own instruction because the plane took a sudden stomach-twisting lurch. At the same time she reached to re-secure Chelsea's seatbelt, Libby heard the intercom click on in her headrest.

"I don't know what it was," she heard David tell Frank above the other man's curses. "Go check the gauge on the wall outside the cockpit. Tell me where the needle's pointing." When the man refused he said, "Fine. You fly the airplane and I'll go."

She heard Frank rise from his chair with another oath. When the cockpit door opened David spoke very low and very fast.

"I can't take us out of the country," he said. "Our only hope is landing this side of the Mexican border. I'm dumping the fuel over the desert now, and then we'll glide in."

Libby looked toward the window. With no moon it was almost pitch black. A safe landing would be almost impossible, even for David.

"I can do this, Lib," he said into her ear. "It's going to be okay." His voice was so tender she thought she might sob after all. "Take

Chelsea and Geneva and get to the tail section—as far back as you can go. Strap in and put your head down between your knees."

He planned to take the plane in nose-down she realized at once. That might protect the tail section, but would surely demolish the cockpit. Her fingers fumbled for the response button on the armrest. "David—"

"Libby, you have to believe that—"

Whatever words might have come next were interrupted by Frank opening the door to the cockpit. "The needle's right around the seven," he said. Libby heard the apprehension in his voice. "Is that bad?"

"Yeah," David lied. "That's bad."

As Libby pulled at the latch on Chelsea's safety belt she heard Frank curse and David respond, "Go ahead and shoot me, Gordon. But I'll tell you one thing, this plane's going down and she isn't going to land herself." After a brief pause he added, "I'd give us three or four minutes, tops."

The latter was for her benefit, Libby knew. She pulled Chelsea to her feet and supported her with one arm as she reached for her sister's wrist with the other hand. "Genie, come on!"

Geneva looked up blankly. The events of the evening coupled with her terror to fly had left the woman dazed and barely functioning.

"Genie," Libby repeated, appalled at the note of terror in her own voice, "you *have* to come with me. You have to!" She tugged desperately on her sister's arm and prayed for her and Chelsea and David all at once. "You have to help me!"

At last Geneva rose and supported Chelsea's other side. Together the sisters half carried and half-dragged the girl to the rear of the plane and deposited her in one of four crew seats behind the galley. Whether it was disassociation or discernment that kept Geneva quiet and cooperative Libby never knew. But as she slid into her own seat, her mind was scarcely on her sister, her niece, or herself. Her thoughts were all on the plane's captain. She knew she couldn't bear it if he died, but thought she couldn't bear it if they lived and—

The plane took a steep dive and somebody screamed. Libby didn't know if it was Chelsea or Geneva or herself. As the plane leveled out, she heard one engine sputter and cut off and then the other. She pushed Geneva and Chelsea down and then rested her own head upon her knees as she prayed. The prayer was silent, wordless, and the most fervent she had offered in her life.

* * *

David was grateful for each of the more than 1200 landings he'd made in a Gulfstream because it made his motions instinctual and left his mind free to pray. If he could hold the belly of the jet just right, and if they hit soft desert sand and nothing bigger than a prickly pear, they'd all survive. If he brought it in too steep or hit a boulder the plane would crumple and/or break apart.

David knew that he controlled everything he could. The fuel tank was empty, negating the chance of an explosion on impact. He'd come out of the descent into a slow, manageable glide, and though the darkness forced all reliance onto the instruments, he'd used them before and trusted them more sometimes than he did his own eyes. What he knew he couldn't control—and couldn't see, even—was the landscape. Only God knew what lay below and only He could dictate whether or not David's best efforts would be enough.

Since bracing for an impact was the worst thing a pilot could do, David forced the muscles in his arms and legs to relax as the lights flashed and the needle indicated they were now fewer than a thousand feet above the desert floor. Then he gritted his teeth, pushed forward on the wheel, and tried to land Libby's million-dollar jet somewhere in the middle of the Sonoran Desert sometime in the middle of a pitch-black October night.

* * *

The first jolt threatened to rip Libby from her seat. The second drove the seatbelt deeper into the lower part of her body until she felt that she must surely have been cut in two. The cabin lights flicked abruptly off as the forward momentum continued and she heard every unsecured item that had just slammed into the ceiling fall back to the cabin floor and slide toward the rear of the plane. A metal cart from the galley smashed painfully against her leg and then, as suddenly as the chaos had begun, it stopped and all was quiet.

* * *

David had made worse landings, but not for a long time and never outside of a Houston flight simulator. There, the only indication that he'd wrecked the shuttle and killed everybody on board was a flashing light on a digital screen and a voice over the intercom saying, "Let's take it again, Captain."

At first, all David saw was the flashing lights. Then, against the advice of his throbbing skull, he opened his eyes and slowly remembered where he was. His first truly lucid thought was that if he was alive here in the cockpit it couldn't be too bad in the rest of the plane. He'd done it. The jet was intact, at least, because the dim emergency lights had come on along the floor.

David raised a hand to wipe the blood out of his eyes and at the same time tried to swivel his seat toward the cockpit door. At first he thought the seat was jammed and then he realized that movement was impossible because his legs were caught in the badly twisted metal. As he struggled without success to free them, he couldn't help but note that there was little pain anywhere besides his head and chest, which meant that the injury to his lower body wasn't bad, or else was worse than he wanted to imagine.

At a movement behind and to his right, David turned as much as he was able. He saw Frank Gordon stumble to his feet, cast a murderous look in his direction and then fall back to his knees. He was looking, David knew, for the gun. He also knew what would happen when Gordon found it.

* * *

When the emergency lights came on Libby saw at once that, like her, Chelsea and Geneva were shaken up and bruised, but uninjured. She reached for her seatbelt. "Stay there. Help will be here in a few minutes. Until then don't move, no matter what."

"Where are you going?" Geneva asked anxiously. "What are you going to do?"

Libby didn't know. She knew only that David had safely landed the plane. But things could be much worse in front. He could be dead. Or, if he were alive and if Frank was also, then—

She stood abruptly and pushed the cart out of the aisle. "Stay here." Running through the cluttered cabin barefoot in such dim light was out of the question, but Libby made her way as quickly as she could through the debris, looking as she went for anything she could use as a weapon.

In the main cabin the grand piano had been torn from its anchor and had demolished the seats she and Chelsea had occupied earlier. Libby shuddered. If David hadn't sent them to the back of the plane, they would never have survived the crash.

David.

Though she looked desperately among the wreckage, there was nothing Libby thought she had the physical strength to use against Frank. *If he lived. If either of them lived.*

Libby pushed the thought away, but it returned as it became apparent that the damage here in front was greater than in the tail section. She'd come to the short hall that led to the cockpit when she heard Frank's voice. At the same time she heard the sound of helicopters in the distance. Frank would probably never get away, but she didn't doubt for a second that he would indulge in the satisfaction of killing David before the first helicopter landed.

Libby bent and grabbed what she saw—a broad-barreled curling iron that lay amidst the ruins of Geneva's cosmetics case—then she pushed her way past one door that had been flung backwards by the force of the crash; and squeezed through the opening of another.

Though Libby didn't have time to look for the gun herself, she saw at once that Frank didn't have it. Instead, he held an iron bar that he raised slowly toward his shoulders as he approached the man in the pilot's chair. Libby looked quickly away from David's blood-covered face, knowing that she could not think of his injuries and do what she must.

She raised the curling iron and thrust it with all her might between Frank's shoulder blades. "Put the bar down, Frank," she said, praying that her voice would sound steadier than her hands felt. If Gordon suspected for a half-second that she didn't have the gun, David would be dead before those helicopters set down.

Frank didn't obey, but he didn't move, either.

"Drop it," she repeated.

"Saint Elisabeth," he said scornfully. "To the rescue."

Libby felt her palms grow damp. David didn't rise to help her—couldn't rise, she realized in a sickening flash—and she wasn't strong enough to loop the curler's cord around Frank's throat or do much of anything else to stop him once he realized she had no weapon.

"Do you expect me to believe that you could shoot me, Elisabeth? *You?*"

Frank began to turn, and though the sound of the helicopters landing was deafening now, Libby knew it was too late for her and David.

"You could never shoot me, Libby."

"*I* could shoot you, Frank," Geneva said from the doorway. Her voice was surprisingly steady and carried clearly over the sound of the rotating blades. "I think I'd take great pleasure in shooting you."

Libby watched Frank complete the turn and blanch. Geneva had raised the gun to her shoulder and her manicured finger curled around the trigger.

"Move Libby," Geneva said. When Libby couldn't immediately respond, she moved further into the cockpit herself so that her aim at Frank's chest was unobstructed.

He dropped the bar. "Genie—"

"Shut up, Frank."

Libby watched in amazement as her sister moved slowly toward David's side.

"Are you okay?" Geneva asked him. When he said he was, she passed him the gun. "Then it's better, Captain Rogers, that you're holding this instead of me when your friends break down that door."

It would be a matter of minutes now, Libby realized, though none of the muscles in her body obeyed her brain's command to react. At least two helicopters had landed and men were prying open the door on the outside of the jet. The desert was flooded with light and still Libby couldn't move or look at David when he said her name. She couldn't even think.

"Libby," Genie said, "go to Chelsea. Take her away from here before she sees Frank and me arrested. I—"

The rest of the words were lost in a sob, and Libby regained her senses. "Not you, Genie," she said, reaching for her sister's hand. "You didn't do anything wrong." The look of devastation on Geneva's face froze Libby to the core.

"I knew," Geneva said. "Frank told me. But he said the man who was in charge would kill us—and you and Chelsea and Uncle Leo—if we didn't cooperate. I think they killed our parents, Libby. I was afraid to say anything, or do anything. I—"

"I'll call Leonard," Libby said. "We'll get you the best lawyer in the world, Genie. You saved . . . " the word stuck in her throat, " . . . Agent . . . Rogers's life just now. And you'll tell them everything."

Geneva nodded quickly with tears running down her cheeks. "Go to Chelsea. I don't want her to be afraid. I don't want her to see . . . " She couldn't finish the sentence. "Take care of her for me," she sobbed. "Promise me you'll take care of my baby!"

"You know I will," Libby said, torn between responding to her sister's anguish and the panic Chelsea would feel when the heavily-armed CIA boarded the plane.

When Geneva pushed her toward the cockpit door, Libby fled. She stumbled back through the rubble and was immeasurably grateful to find Chelsea in her seat, awake, but dazed and much under the effects of the drug. She put her arms around her niece as she heard the jet's door give way at last. The crash was followed by the sound of big men scrambling up the emergency ramp.

"Chillygator," Libby said, "sweetheart, everything's going to be all right." She clasped her niece more tightly, buried her face in Chelsea's tangled hair, and prayed that—somehow—God would make it so.

chapter 31

They cut out large pieces of air with their big tailor's scissors. They sewed away with needles that had no thread in them. At last they said, "Look! The clothes are ready!"

— *The Emperor's New Clothes, 1837*

David stood in front of the candy machine in the lobby of the infirmary at Fort Huachuca Army Base. Located some fifty miles outside of Tucson, Huachuca was the closest military installation to where he'd taken down the jet, and thus where they'd been flown for medical attention. His scalp was stitched up and his chest taped to help alleviate the pain of a hairline fracture in his second rib. But he could stand, and Libby and Chelsea were unhurt. All things considered, David thought his last landing was his best one.

Because of the drug, Chelsea was in a nearby room where doctors—and Libby—had kept her under close observation all night. The girl's mother and Frank Gordon were back in LA by now. If Geneva knew anything significant, or if Frank talked under interrogation, the mastermind of the espionage might soon be arrested and this nightmare would finally end. Except for the worst part, of course. The part where Libby never forgave him as long as he lived.

David peered into the candy machine, dug in his pocket for change when he spied chocolate, and withdrew his hand without any quarters. Not only were these not his clothes—his own bloodstained shirt and ruined pants had been replaced by Army-issue—but it was a futile gesture in the first place. Libby had left the crash site with

Chelsea while paramedics were still cutting him out of the wreckage. She had refused to speak with him here at the base and he knew it would take more than a seventy-five cent Hershey bar to change her mind.

Right now his boss, Preston Wescott, was in the room with her outlining the CIA's newest plan, and trying to get her to change her mind. Come to find out, under the right circumstances, one *could* go over some of the highest heads in the Pentagon. It only took a higher head to do it. With A) homeland security topping everyone's agenda since the tragedy at the World Trade Center, B) David the only agent with ties to Libby and Amen, and C) this case within days if not hours of being wrapped up, he had been re-reassigned to the mission.

Assuming, that is, that Wescott accomplished the impossible task of getting Libby to agree to her part in it. David wished him luck.

* * *

"I'm not sure you understand, Miss Jamison," Wescott said.

Libby ran her fingers over Chelsea's cool forehead, grateful that the child now slept peacefully, then withdrew the hand when she saw that it trembled. She glanced over at the CIA chief, and then past him at the agent—*David's partner?*—who had accompanied Wescott into the room. The woman stood silently after introducing herself as Agent Roberta Compton. Libby couldn't help but see how attractive she was.

"At least," Wescott continued, "I'm not convinced that you fully understand."

Libby felt ill with understanding. She knew now that her brother-in-law was a thief, a kidnapper, and a traitor to his country, and that her sister had known for some time about the espionage but had been too terrified to act. She knew that whoever controlled Frank had killed her parents, and now, according to the CIA, might wish to kill her as well—and Chelsea and Uncle Leo. And, what hurt the worst and frightened her the most in all this horrifying "understanding" was the revelation that David was not the man with whom she'd fallen in love. He'd acted a part to gain her confidence and trust. Now the CIA wanted her to act a part as well, but she would not. Captain Rogers was the professional liar, not she.

"I do understand," Libby said at last. "And as much as I appreciate your concern for our safety, your plan is unacceptable." Wescott had broached a strategy for her protection twice now and twice she'd refused it. Why wouldn't the man take no for an answer? She looked down at her lap. "I will not return to Amen with Agent Rogers."

"Then I can't allow you to return to Amen."

Libby's head snapped up.

"You and your niece will be placed in immediate protective custody," Wescott continued, "until such time as Gordon reveals his connections or our investigation turns up the other people involved." He rose from his chair. "I'll arrange for your transfer to Los Angeles as soon as possible. Your estate is out of the question because of its size, but the accommodations will be adequate if not luxurious." His hand was on the doorknob before Libby could swallow. "I appreciate the cooperation you've given me thus far, Miss Jamison, and assure you that I will stay in touch with additional questions about your knowledge and involvement. Good day."

"Wait," Libby said as the door opened. "Wait, please . . . ." Was he saying that they suspected her? And protective custody? What did that mean—a glorified jail cell? She looked at Chilly and knew she owed her niece a sense of normalcy, no matter what the price. She drew a deep breath. "Perhaps, sir, I've been hasty."

"Perhaps," Wescott said with the open door in hand, "you have. Would you like to hear what I have to propose once again?"

"Yes," she said humbly. "Thank you."

Wescott stuck his head out the door and called for David. Libby gripped the sides of her chair and looked studiously at the chief as he once again took his seat. She would not look at David as he came into the room. It was more than she could bear to see that his forehead was bandaged in the spot she had once tended for cat scratches, and that his handsome face was cut, swollen, and surely painful.

But it had nothing to do with her, she reminded herself. Agent Rogers had done his duty by landing that plane—just as he'd done his duty when he came to Arizona and made her fall in love with him. If she looked, she'd see the triumph reflected in his eyes. But she wouldn't look. She'd agree to whatever she must to take Chelsea home to Amen, and help right the unspeakable wrongs at Jamison Enterprises, but she would never look into David Rogers's brown eyes again.

Wescott outlined his plan. David would fly back to Deer Valley immediately and from there return to Amen with the story that he had been injured four-wheeling in the desert the night before. Libby would follow in the late afternoon with Chelsea and Roberta Compton. The agent would pose as her sister. Libby would tell people she had persuaded Genie to stay with her during the breakup of her marriage. They'd been in LA, according to the CIA script, retrieving a few things she and Chelsea would need during their stay—things that the CIA had already obtained from the downed jet.

Libby looked at Agent Compton and realized with a pang that she did resemble Geneva. Roberta would accompany Libby everywhere she went and do everything she did. David, in the meantime, would be close by to watch over Chelsea in his class at school, go over Jamison personnel with her, and oversee the operation as a whole.

"Do you have any questions?" Wescott asked at last.

Libby shook her head and then said, "No," but it was the first of her lies. She had dozens of questions. The one that mattered, however, was how she could manage to be close to David. She felt his eyes on her—warm and sympathetic—and stiffened. Surely he didn't think she was stupid enough to fall for that ploy again. The game was over and he had won: Love/Nothing. He got love, she got nothing— she would not engage in a second round.

"Captain Rogers tells me that your niece is bright and that she's successfully kept your secret the several times she's visited Arizona," the chief continued. "He believes that she'll be able to handle her part in this, even in light of the . . . unfortunate . . . circumstances with her mother. Do you concur?"

"Yes," Libby said quickly. Like the other Jamison women, Chelsea would do what she must. For the first time, Libby considered it a blessing that Chelsea had been away at school and therefore never very close to her mother. "I'll explain it to her and she'll be fine."

"Then at last we have an understanding." Wescott again rose from his chair and walked toward the door. "There's a plane waiting for you, Captain," he said when David made no move to follow. The chief tried not to smile. "You'll forgive us, I hope, if we provide the pilot this time." To Libby he said over his shoulder, "We'll leave you to get acquainted with Geneva." When Libby started at the name he added, "The sooner you become comfortable with one another the better. Rogers?"

David hesitated a moment more before turning to precede Wescott out the door. Only then did Libby relax to any degree.

The relaxation was short-lived.

"Whoa!" Agent Compton said as the door swung closed. "Hot stuff." She fanned a hand in front of her face and smiled broadly at Libby. "I'd heard about David Rogers—everybody has—but I never saw the legend for myself before today. What's he look like when his face isn't bashed in?"

Libby opened her mouth to respond, but no words came out of it.

"Uh, oh," Roberta said sympathetically. "Sorry." She appropriated the chair recently vacated by her boss and pulled it forward. "Would it help any to hear that you're not the first to survive Hurricane Rogers?"

Survive him? Libby thought. What made this woman think she'd survived?

* * *

To: drogers@nasa.gov
From: chillygator@jamison.com (Chelsea Gaye)
Subject: a FAN letter

Dear Captain Rogers:

Thank you 4 giving me your e-mail address so I could write 2 you. I want 2 say that you are a genuine All-American HERO. (Do you get lots of letters that tell you that? You deserve them if you do.) The way you landed that airplane without breaking us all into bits was STUPENDOUS. I don't think anybody but a real astronaut (and a HERO) could do THAT. I wish I could tell the whole WORLD but Aunt Libby says that I can't tell anybody. Not even Tansy and she's my best friend. (Did you know that?)

I can't WAIT until tomorrow when I can be in your class. Uncle Leonard wanted me 2 go back to boarding school. (Don't tell Aunt Libby I was listening in.) But Libby says that I am safer here. (With you.) Uncle Leo wants Libby 2 go back 2 L.A. and hire a whole army of bodyguards, but Libby says that we will stay right here for right now. I think it's cuz she is in love with somebody whose name I am not allowed 2 say but his initials are DR and he is a HERO.

Deep down, Aunt Libby thinks you are a hero 2—or maybe even a knight in shining armor—so don't feel bad because she treats you like a warty frog. We women are like that. (That's a joke.) I am not like that at all. I have loved **Aaron** 4-EV-R and I don't care who knows it. He doesn't know he loves ME yet, but I can wait. I am a Very Patient Person (VPP).

I hope that you are a VPP 2!

I will see you 2morrow, but I had to tell you that I think you are a HERO 2night because 2morrow I can't say ANYTHING. Unless I raise my hand. (That's a joke.) But the rest of what I wrote—I was NOT KIDDING.

LUV U 4-EV-R, Chilly

David hit the "reply" button, thought better of it, and turned off the computer. The problem was that he was not a "Very Patient Person" and having to give his word of honor to be strictly professional until the case ended was more painful than his lacerated head, bruised legs, and broken rib combined. On the other hand, Wescott hadn't gotten where he was by missing anything, and David felt fortunate to have been given nothing more than a lecture and an oath before being allowed to resume his assignment. Right now, however, he ached all over, and didn't feel like he'd been thrown from a vehicle as in the official story, or trapped in the wreckage of an airplane as in the truth, but had instead survived an apocalypse. That was another version of truth. No way could he imagine the end of the world being any worse than what he'd seen in Libby's face last night on that airplane.

Unless it involved knowing that he deserved her distrust. He'd spent so long telling himself that he was doing the wrong thing for the right reason that when he'd finally stopped telling himself it long enough to consider how he'd feel if their situations were reversed, he finally understood that the end hadn't justified the means after all. Especially since the end had turned out to be *the* end. Of his world.

David slammed down the lid of the laptop and looked around his spartan apartment. He'd be sure to pick up his scriptures from the end table, but other than that he probably couldn't take anything with him. It was suspicious enough that he had another computer and a duffel bag of essential clothes out in his Hummer. At least that would be suspicious anywhere but in Amen. Here there was nary a soul who would suspect arson when his bungalow went up in flames sometime before midnight.

The furnishings were meager, the walls were warped and unpainted, the carpeting threadbare, and still David felt like a louse. The government would reimburse Homer for his destroyed property eventually, but his landlord was a simple, good man who didn't deserve deception and destruction in exchange for his overtures of friendship. If there were any other way, David would take it. But despite his prayers, he and Wescott had been unable to devise another plan that moved him into Estelle's house except to destroy this one and throw himself on the old woman's compassion. As much as he regretted Homer's loss, David would do whatever it took to put himself in the best possible position to protect Libby and Chelsea, and that was from next door.

It was almost ten o'clock, so the volunteer fire department would be sawing logs by now. Exhausted himself, he decided to get it over with. He'd just reached for the bag of supplies when there was a knock at the front door. Nobody would be out at this time of night in Amen except maybe a cat burglar, and David doubted the town boasted one of those. He'd left the service pistol and Kevlar vest in the HMV which, now that he thought about it, wasn't particularly bright. On the other hand, weren't assassins—and cat burglars for that matter—more in the habit of inviting themselves in than knocking? David zipped closed the bag and tossed it aside on his way to the front door. "Max?"

"Hey," the bishop said. "I heard about your accident and came by to see how you are." He took in David's battered face and troubled expression and shook his head. "Right offhand I'd say you're not very well." When David stood mutely with his hand on the knob the bishop added, "Mind if I come in?"

"Uh, no." David took a step back. "Please." He offered the bishop the one ratty, stuffed chair in the living room and retrieved a folding chair from the kitchen.

"Are you all right?" Max asked in concern. "You've seen a doctor?"

"Yeah," David said. "I'm fine. Great."

"What happened, exactly?"

David hadn't been able to lie to the bishop so far. "I had an accident," he said. "I was . . . stupid." That was the truth if ever he'd uttered it.

The bishop ran a hand through his shaggy hair. "I'm not going to ask you what's going on. Just like I didn't ask Libby about it when I was over there just now to meet her sister."

Only the sharp pain in his rib cage kept David from slumping forward in relief. The bishop's office hadn't been bugged, but Libby's house was a veritable recording studio. "Thank you, Bishop."

"This thing's gonna work out," Max said, although he didn't look like he believed it as much as David wanted him to. "I'm more concerned about what's happened between you and Libby." His blue eyes darted around the room and he almost whispered, "She knows about you now?"

"She knows," David said, his voice flat. "She's never going to forgive me."

"She'll come around," Max said quickly. "I'd bet—"

"Don't. You'll lose your money faster than Homer did." It was the closest he'd felt to tears since childhood and it made his words sharper than he'd intended.

"David—"

"It's all my fault. It's no more than I deserve."

The bishop sat silently for more than a minute, seeming to feel David's pain as deeply as the younger man. Finally he said, "Your body will heal, son, and so will Libby's hurt. Right now you need to rest. Don't plan on coming into school tomorrow."

"I have to be there," David said too quickly. "I've got to—"

"Uh, huh," the bishop said. "That's what I thought. And it brings me to my reason for being here."

Why was it, David wondered in consternation, that he always had to spill his guts before this man got to the point?

"I met with Sister Dyson this evening," Max said.

"Estelle? You've been busy."

"This was a welfare concern. Estelle's on a fixed income and as her health deteriorates, I can't help but feel it's unwise for her to be in that big house all alone."

The small hairs along the back of David's neck rose. He knew what was coming, although how it had come about was simply beyond him. Maybe God *did* hear his every prayer regardless of evidence to the contrary.

"I suggested to her that she take in a boarder," the bishop continued. "I suggested she take you." The hint of a smile played at the corner of his lips. "I hear that the two of you have a great deal in common, spying on the ten tribes and all."

David ignored Estelle's "breach of national security." "She agreed?"

"Wholeheartedly. She has a room waiting for you now. She doesn't think you ought to be alone tonight in case you have a concussion from that accident. I think she's right. Besides, won't you sleep better over there than you ever will here?"

David thought there was a double meaning to the bishop's question, but wasn't willing to swear to it, or answer it.

While the bishop waited David paused only long enough to pick up two items: his scriptures and the computer picture of Libby. As he placed the picture between the pages of the Doctrine and Covenants, a familiar verse caught his eye.

. . . If it had not been so, thou wouldst not have come to the place where thou art at this time . . . Be patient; be sober; be temperate; have patience, faith, hope and charity . . .

Could it be true? If he was a Very Patient Person like Chelsea had counseled—and a faithful and hopeful one as the bishop had said—*would* he get another chance with Libby? Maybe time—and Gordon talking—would release him from his vow of stoic professionalism and maybe the Spirit would bless him with the right words to convince her that all he'd done had been for her.

David knew it would take a miracle to get Libby back. But hadn't he had more than his share of those lately? What was one more?

chapter 32

To trust in thyself and God is best,
In His holy will forever to rest.

— *The Philosopher's Stone, 1859*

Libby didn't know what Chelsea and Tansy discussed so earnestly up in the tree house, but it caused her to gaze up repeatedly from her Saturday gardening. Surely Chelsea would never tell their secrets, but the conversation seemed so earnest and intense that Libby couldn't help but call out to them. "Why don't you girls come down and we'll go inside and make popcorn balls for Halloween?"

They'd been back in Amen for a week now. Libby had postponed the sale to SynQuest and spent painstaking, painful hours with David every day after school going over each person on Jamison Enterprises' considerable staff. Captain Rogers was a consummate professional. He never made a personal comment or alluded to their former relationship. That wasn't what made the sessions painful.

Or maybe it was. It had begun to dawn on Libby that while David had obviously never loved her she might never stop loving him. Still, she'd had no other choice but to endure his closeness. Geneva had told the government all she knew, but it hadn't been much, and Frank refused to speak to anyone but his attorney. Six days after the terrifying kidnapping, the CIA was no wiser and she and Chelsea were no safer.

Libby couldn't stop worrying about the girls in the tree. "Chilly!"

Roberta looked up from her chair on the porch. Although it was Saturday afternoon and still rather warm in southern Arizona, she wore one of Geneva's cashmere sweaters over her T-shirt and designer jeans. She wore it, Libby knew, to hide a small service revolver that was strapped to her side. David also wore a suit coat that he never removed in public. And while Libby never went close enough to him to ascertain for certain what was underneath it, she knew, and the knowledge kept her awake nights.

Or so she told herself. It was easier to believe that she woke up anxious and unhappy because she feared for her life than it was to believe that she couldn't sleep because she feared for her soul. Had she, like the Little Mermaid, given up her heart in the hope for eternal love? Since mermaids have no tears, they suffer all the more. Dry eyed, Libby lay awake each night and looked out the window at the ripening moon and wondered how she could continue to long so desperately for a man who'd only used her to do his job.

"Anything wrong?" Roberta asked, noting Libby's troubled expression. She moved immediately to the edge of her chair to follow Libby's line of vision into the tree.

From where he worked at the corner of Estelle's yard, David's hand moved instinctively to the waistband of his jeans. Libby knew at once where his gun was when he wasn't wearing his suit. "Everything's fine," she said loud enough for him to hear. She turned back toward the tree and called out, "Popcorn balls! What do you say?"

The two figures in the tree hesitated longer than was normal for preteen girls offered a chance to make a gooey, delicious mess. "Come on," Libby urged. "Halloween is Monday night. We'll dye the popcorn balls orange and make them look like jack-o-lanterns. Then we'll dress up like the three witches from Macbeth to hand them out. Won't that be fun?" She ignored Roberta's sarcastic remark about the simplicity—or simpletons—found in small towns and smiled as the girls at last came down.

"What were you doing up there?" Libby asked Tansy a few minutes later as she pulled the heavy iron kettle out from a lower cupboard and sent Chelsea to the pantry for popcorn and Karo syrup.

"We were talking about Aaron."

No wonder the serious faces. Tansy was devoted to her brother, and Chelsea adored him.

"Everything's the same," Tansy volunteered morosely. "Every day he says he's going to walk and every day he tries to get up. Every time he tries he falls down flat and lies there until one of us comes along to help him back to bed or his wheelchair." Her face was flushed and her eyes were filled with tears of confusion and frustration. "Sister James, it isn't *fair*! Aaron is the best person I know. He's always done everything right. Now the rest of us are doing things right too—my Dad reads the scriptures with us every day—and *nothing's happening*!"

The last words were delivered in a wail and Libby set the pan aside and took Tansy into her arms. "It isn't anything you're doing or not doing, sweetheart," she said, fighting back tears of her own. Tansy was right about Aaron being faithful and worthy and determined. If Libby could donate her own strong legs to him, she'd do it willingly. But she couldn't, and that was a principle Tansy needed to understand.

She stroked the girl's wild, orange hair. "God isn't Santa Claus. You can't just 'be good' and expect him to bring you just the blessing you want." How well she knew that for herself. "You have to do your best to be obedient and then trust Heavenly Father to give you the blessing He knows is best for you."

"But you *do* have to ask Him for what you want," Chelsea said from the doorway to the pantry. "That's what you always told *me*, Aunt Libby." She came the rest of the way into the kitchen. "And you should ask for a priesthood blessing. You said that too."

"Yes, I did," Libby agreed, wondering where this was going. Before she could say more, Chelsea flew to the kitchen door and screamed at the top of her lungs for Captain Rogers.

Roberta was in the kitchen in a flash, her hand under her blazer as she visually searched every inch of the room. David vaulted the railing of the veranda not a full minute later and burst through the doorway. "Libby!"

"I called you," Chelsea said calmly.

He scanned the room. By this time, Roberta had withdrawn her hand from beneath the blazer. She smiled into his anxious face. "False alarm."

"No it's not," Chelsea insisted. "We need you. Thanks for coming so fast."

Assured that there was no immediate danger from terrorists, hit men, or Martians, David leaned back against the doorjamb and tried to slow his breathing for the sake of his battered rib cage. "I'll come every time you call me, Chillygator. What's up?"

He's so gallant, Libby thought, *and so patient and so* . . . She turned away.

"Tansy and I want you to bless Aaron and make him walk."

Libby spun back and saw David's knuckles whiten when he drew his hands unconsciously into fists.

"Did you hear me?" Chelsea asked after a moment.

Tansy's hands were clutched too—almost prayerfully—and her green eyes were huge. "Please, Captain Rogers! Aaron hasn't had a blessing. Dad said in the hospital that nobody was going to bless his son but him and . . . well . . . he won't be able to for ever so long— Mama says at least a year. But Chilly and I thought that if *you* asked Dad, well, he'd say that it would be okay for *you* to make Aaron walk."

Roberta, Libby saw, was simply astounded at the request, but no more so than David. His face paled beneath the lingering bruises on his forehead and cheek.

"Tansy," he said at last, "Chelsea . . ."

Libby saw he wanted to say the right thing. Whatever else he had lied about, David Rogers's concern for Aaron was genuine. "Girls—" she began.

"No," David interrupted quietly, "they're right." He turned toward Tansy. "I'll ask your father if Bishop Wheeler and I can give Aaron a blessing tomorrow. If that's what Aaron wants." David swallowed. "But girls, I'm not promising you anything. Priesthood blessings are God's will, not ours. Understand?"

As they nodded, Roberta apparently forgot that she was supposed to be Chelsea's mother and a member of the church. "You're a, a *priest?*" she asked David in astonishment. "No wonder you never—" She caught herself at the warning expression on his face and colored. "I mean—"

"I'm an elder, not a priest, Geneva," he said meaningfully, with a glance at Tansy to gauge her reaction. Thankfully, she paid no attention to the adults as she and Chelsea hugged. He moved closer to Roberta and lowered his voice so as not to be heard over the girls' squeals. "Why don't you read up on the Church instead of movie stars? You might learn something you could use personally as well as professionally."

"Yes, sir," Roberta whispered meekly.

Despite herself, Libby smiled.

"Okay," David said aloud. "I guess I better get back to clearing that landing spot for the 'brethren.' Estelle expects them on Halloween for some strange reason." He rolled his eyes and they lit on Calliope. "Don't forget to feed the cat," he said. "It's Saturday. She'll want chopped liver."

Libby couldn't say why the words tore at her heart. She nodded and reached for a Blue Willow saucer.

"I hope," he said quietly as he turned to leave, "that Chinese guy knew how good he had it as a bird."

Libby caught her breath. The reference to the doomed lover in the story of the Blue Willow was the only personal remark he'd made since they'd returned to Amen.

As he departed, Roberta gazed after Captain Rogers's broad shoulders. "My goodness," she said at last. "If you don't want him, Libby, I certainly do."

I should say, "You can have him," Libby thought as she put the pan on the stove and resisted the urge to stare after David herself. *That's what I should say.*

But she couldn't say it.

* * *

"Roberta has a thing for you, you know," Chelsea reported to David on their way back to Amen from driving Tansy home.

David didn't respond. His mind was on Aaron and tomorrow's promised blessing. He wished they'd let him anoint and ask Bishop Wheeler to pronounce the blessing, but Aaron's preference was clear. The boy hadn't forgotten David's rash promise that he would walk again. David hadn't forgotten it either, but regretted it more than ever. He regretted too, what could happen when these kids' perfect faith collided with the Lord's perfect will.

"Roberta wears those tight jeans and low-cut blouses because of you," Chelsea continued. "And she says that when the case is over . . . " She frowned at David. This was important and he wasn't listening. " . . . you're going to run off to Jupiter and rule together over Estelle's ten tribes."

At last David's face swung slowly in her direction. "Huh?"

"I'm warning you about Roberta. She has a thing for you."

"Call her 'Mother.'" His eyes returned to the empty road. "And she does not."

"She does so! We women know these things."

Only the ringing of his phone saved David from the possibly fatal blunder of telling Chilly that she was as close to womanhood as he was to canonization. He pulled over to the side of the road and stopped the truck before answering the phone.

"We lost Fisk," Wescott said. In spite of the lack of confirmation from Gordon, Karlton Fisk had remained their top suspect.

Mindful of Chelsea, David asked cautiously, "What are you saying?"

"That he disappeared. He left his hotel early this morning and got in a cab. We lost the cab and he hasn't turned up in any of the places we've had staked out."

David glanced at his watch. "It's been, what, ten hours?"

"Twelve."

"He could be most of the places on earth by now."

"Including Arizona."

Including here. David made it back to Amen in record time. The three women were on the back porch setting out the weekly potluck supper. Estelle had brought potato chips and mustard and Libby had baked beans and rolls and was about to barbecue hamburgers.

"Quiet?" he asked Agent Compton under his breath. When she nodded he glanced at Libby's unhappy face and added, "Then you know where I am."

Estelle looked up from her knitting as he turned to leave. "Hold it, Captain. This isn't a hen party. The least you can do is help Libby with those hamburgers." When he didn't obey, her brows knit more furiously than her fingers and she glared all around. "You little chickies better invite him then. He won't listen to this old biddy."

Roberta and Chelsea were quick to beg David to stay. Libby said the right words but with the wrong inflection.

David might have stayed if he trusted himself more. But he'd slipped up this afternoon and mentioned the Chinese fairy tale. If he did nothing else, he had to see this thing through for Libby's sake, and that meant being nothing but professional. He'd keep his distance to ensure the safe operation of his mouth. To keep busy he'd concentrate on clearing a safe landing site for the ten tribes. It was as good an excuse as any to spend all his time in the backyard, watching Libby's house.

He was at the garden wall when his phone rang again.

"Fisk is our man," Wescott said. "We turned up microchips, cash, and a couple of diamonds in the search of his hotel room."

David sat on the wall, remembered the night he'd sat there with Libby, and stood. "If he was bailing, why would he leave cash and diamonds behind?"

"Probably figures to come back."

"Back from where?" Though he didn't say so, David began to wonder if it might have to be from the dead.

"That's the question," Wescott agreed. "But him being the kingpin fits the puzzle. He's intelligent enough. He's been abroad—including stays in Saudi Arabia and Iraq. He has all the right connections. And he has a motive besides greed—revenge on Elisabeth Jamison."

David frowned. "Isn't his disappearance now a little *too* transparent?"

"One thing you'll learn in this line of work, Rogers, is that puzzles aren't always complicated. You just have to have all the right pieces."

David couldn't help but think there was a piece they were missing—besides Karlton, of course.

"If Fisk's not already in Arizona," Wescott continued, "he's on his way there. This thing ought to go down in the next twenty-four to forty-eight hours. We've put a 'crew' to work on the highway outside of town and commandeered a couple of National Guard helicopters for 'maneuvers' in the area. You've done a good job for us, Rogers, so I'm making this your call. The code word is 'phantom.' We mobilize on your signal."

Something about this didn't feel right to David, but he had little choice but to agree. After cutting the connection he walked back over to the grill. "I changed my mind about staying," he said, taking the spatula from Libby's hand. He tried not to sigh as she fled to the porch and Roberta hurried down from it. Chelsea made faces behind her back and David wondered again how long he could go on honoring his word and being a Very Patient Person when his first inclination was to grab Libby and take her somewhere far, far away—whether she wanted to go with him or not.

* * *

David was apprehensive and Libby wished she knew why. Every barking dog and each sound of the wind caused him to look up from his hand of Frog Juice, Chilly's favorite card game. Estelle had gone home to watch her shows and Roberta had claimed to hate games, but sat down at the table when David did. She seldom took her eyes off him. More than once Libby resisted the urge to spill cold cider in Roberta's lap or "accidentally" kick her under the table.

For Libby to admit to feeling ambivalent would have been an understatement. One moment she would wish that David had gone with Estelle to spare her these pangs of jealousy, but the next moment she couldn't be more grateful that he had stayed. The shadows on the wall seemed ominous tonight and Libby couldn't deny that having David at her side made her feel safe.

"I'm going to cast an Enchantment Spell!" Chelsea announced triumphantly as she laid a card from her hand face-up on the polished dining room table and then placed two more cards beside it. "I have the Maiden and the Prince." She turned to the person at her left. "Roberta—"

"'Mother,'" David corrected her immediately.

"But—"

Libby had never known that a mortal being could silence Chelsea with a single look. Her surprise must have showed on her face because he said dryly, "I practice that glare on Calvin every day."

Ten days ago Libby would have laughed, but David was always so serious now that any remark of his that neared the outskirts of humor made her want to cry.

"*Mother*," Chelsea began again, "do you have a Stardust & Moonpowder card?"

"No." The agent pulled another card from her hand. "But I do have a Witch and she's going to sweep your Prince off his feet." Her voice was as triumphant as Chelsea's had been and she winked at David as she reached for the girl's card.

"Witch Wash!" Chelsea shrieked. She waved a neutralizing card in front of Roberta before grabbing her own cards and clutching them to her chest. After a moment of stunned silence around the table, Chelsea began to sob. "You can't *have* our prince!" she wailed. "Y-you *can't!*"

"Chelsea!" Libby was shocked and somewhat appalled by her niece's outburst, and not knowing what to do, turned to David. But he had apparently thought it through by the time she caught his eye.

He held out his arms to the girl and said gently, "Chillygator, it's okay."

Chelsea was around the table and in his embrace almost before Libby saw her move. Although most of the words she sobbed into his shoulder were unintelligible, Libby got the gist of enough of them to realize that Chelsea wasn't coping with the strain of losing her mother and being guarded by the CIA as well as Libby had thought she was. She'd seemed so happy with Tansy, and generally unaffected over the last several days, that Libby had put away the tugging of the Spirit and relied instead on what appeared to be true. She wondered now if she could trust anything she merely saw with her eyes or heard with her ears.

Chilly eventually calmed under David's quiet reassurances and used the back of both hands to wipe away her tears. That's when she saw the mangled cards in her fist. She lay them on the table and stared down miserably. "Now I've ruined the spell."

David smoothed out the creases as best he could. "No you didn't, Chelsea. A little wrinkle or two never hurt a good enchantment." At her tentative, soggy smile he held up the remaining two cards in his own hand. "You should have asked *me* for the Stardust & Moonpowder card."

"You have it?"

"Well duh." His grin was contagious. "Who but an astronaut would have the Stardust & Moonpowder card?" He put it beside Chelsea's Maiden and Prince. Libby felt the warmth begin in her cheeks and spread throughout the rest of her body. She might have said something—or reached for his hand—but before she could he added, "All I have left now is this Frog Juice card. Tell me what spell can you do with Frog Juice again."

"Disappear," Libby whispered, praying that he would not. But the word caught in her throat. Perhaps that was why he misunderstood it so completely.

"I guess I better do that." David lay his card on the table and pushed back his chair. "Thanks for dinner and the game." To Roberta he said, "I'll be listening. If you so much as *wonder*—" He looked from Chelsea to Libby and his eyes grew darker than Libby had ever seen them. "Could I talk with you outside for a minute, Geneva?"

As Agent Compton rose eagerly, Libby watched David pull something that looked like a piece of putty from his shirt pocket and stick it securely in his ear. He *would* be listening. Since all her dreams were of him, Libby hoped that she would talk in her sleep. It might be the only way she'd get the difficult words of love from her heart to his ear.

As he and Roberta walked through the kitchen toward the backyard, Libby wished she had an earpiece of her own. She wanted desperately to hear what they'd say.

* * *

"She's certifiably Looney Tunes!" Roberta declared, casting a disparaging look next door.

"You mean Estelle?" David asked. He'd given Agent Compton her instructions and needed nothing more than a polite way to end the conversation. It occurred to him that Chelsea might be right. Roberta did seem to be artificially prolonging this time alone. Still, Estelle was his friend and David felt obliged to defend her honor. "You don't know Estelle."

"Thank goodness!" Roberta exclaimed. "I don't want to know her *or* the Weird Sisters."

"They would be?"

"LaThis, LaThat and LaOther." Roberta leaned forward. "Did I tell you they brought over a *possum casserole* and tried to talk me out of 'divorcing my husband'?" Her face contorted to show her disgust. "Has anybody ever told you that a woman can't get into the celestial kingdom—wherever that is—without a man?"

"Was Libby listening?" David asked hopefully.

"Jamison's as weird as the rest of them!" Roberta waved an arm toward the trees. "Do you know what lives in all those boxes? Bats!" She shook her hands out to indicate an advanced case of the willies. Then she moved closer to David. "And if Batgirl, the Weird Sisters and the Space Case weren't enough, there's this wheezy old geezer—"

"Guy," David guessed.

"—who hauls junk in the front door so Libby can give him food before she sneaks his garbage out the back." She threw up her hands in bafflement. "And that whacked-out school of theirs!"

"Alma? What's wrong with Alma School?"

She cast him a look that said that if he weren't adorable she'd include him on her list of the hopeless. "Well, let's see . . . you call the principal 'bishop,' the librarian is an heiress, one teacher is a movie star, the PE coach is an Egyptian sheik, and you—you're a Navy-fighter-pilot-turned-astronaut-turned-secret-agent!"

David grinned. "So our faculty seems a little unusual to you?"

"Are you *kidding?*"

David leaned back against the willow tree and discovered that he wasn't kidding at all. Everything she found bizarre now seemed normal—perfectly normal—to him. "But you left out Homer and the McKrackens and Deaf Old Ezra. Not to mention the javelina." David's grin broadened when she didn't smile. "Welcome to Amen. Remind me sometime to tell you about the strange parts."

Roberta responded warmly to his smile if not his invitation. She slipped her arms around his waist. "Just tell me how soon we can get out of here."

David scarcely noticed Roberta's embrace. What he noticed was how close "soon" and "get out of here" were in her sentence. His stomach dropped. He'd be gone from Amen before he knew it. What he'd once wanted more than anything, he now wanted less. He took a step away. "We'll leave when we've done our jobs."

* *

"She's practically attacking him!" Chelsea reported from the dining room window. She rapped sharply on the pane with her knuckles.

"Chelsea," Libby said, but it was perfunctory. She hoped her niece wouldn't obey her instruction to come away from the window.

"Aren't *you* going to do something?" Chelsea demanded. "Don't you *care?*"

"No," Libby said. "And no." She felt warm despite the cool evening. "Yes. But what can I do? Captain Rogers never loved me." She had no idea she'd murmured the words aloud until Chelsea spun from her seat at the window.

"He does love you, Aunt Libby!" she exclaimed. "I asked him if he loved you and he *told* me he does!"

"It was part of his job to say that, Chilly. He was acting."

Chelsea shook her head. "I've seen him act and he's not very good at it."

"But—"

"Tansy says Captain Rogers looks at you the same way I look at Aaron."

Libby smiled. "Tansy says that?" *Oh good, Elisabeth*, she berated herself. *Now you're grasping at romantic threads spun by twelve-year-olds.*

"He loves you, Aunt Libby," Chelsea insisted. She jumped down from her seat and ran to Libby's side. "Kiss him!" she said. "You'll see. David won't turn into a frog."

Libby was lost in her thoughts. She had already kissed him and ended up with Stardust in her eyes. She gazed out the window at the waxing moon. In two nights it would be full for the second time in a single month. A blue moon. How was that for providential? She wondered how to go about gathering up its Moonpowder. If she raised a palm full of it to her lips and blew it over David, might it be enough to complete the Enchantment and make the astronaut Prince hers forever?

"Kiss him," Chelsea urged. "How else will you know for sure?"

Might it be as simple as that? Libby wondered with the beginning of a smile. Would one more incredible kiss beneath Monday's blue moon be the strongest enchantment of all?

chapter 33

The Book of Truth lay open before him, but its pages were to him as blank paper.

— *The Philosopher's Stone, 1859*

On Halloween morning Alma's school yard was full of ghosts, scarecrows, prom-dress princesses, and every other character that could be contrived from a linen closet or trunk in the attic. Shenla wore a dress that had once been to the Academy Awards, without her in it of course. Omar decked himself out in a sombrero and serape—a bizarre Egyptian bandito—and Max donned his waders, fishing hat and multi-pouched vest. He'd come as what he most wanted to be—retired. As she'd promised Chilly and Tansy, Libby was a witch. David alone was conspicuous in non-participation. He sported sunglasses as his only concession to a costume.

Possibly the glasses were a costume, Libby thought as she peered out at him through the library window. More likely they were to disguise his bloodshot eyes. If that man had slept since last Friday night, Libby didn't know when he had done it. From what she'd seen from other windows at home, he'd spent most of both Saturday and Sunday nights outside her house keeping watch.

Watch for what? she wondered. *Or for who?* Impulsively she walked over to the door and pulled it open. "I'll be with David," she told Roberta when the agent rose. The woman's face lighted and Libby had to suppress a frown as she quickly added, "I want to speak with Captain Rogers alone."

It was true—and impossible. But at least she could stand near him for a few minutes with only an entire playground of children around them. Certainly nobody could hear their words above the excited din. He was so far gone she had to nudge him to get his attention. "David?"

His head rolled toward her tiredly but snapped to attention when he saw she was alone. "Where's Geneva?"

"I told her I'd be with you." Before he could begin the lecture she added, "Don't you have a calendar, Captain? Today's Halloween. You're supposed to wear a costume."

He pushed the sunglasses up the bridge of his nose then moved the finger to tap the ear with the plastic receiver in it. "I did wear a costume. I'm a secret agent."

She didn't smile because he didn't. But she lowered her voice when she said, "On Halloween the idea is to dress up as something you're not."

He let out a long breath between his teeth. "My point exactly."

He was not only desperately tired, she saw at once, he was desperately discouraged. She followed his line of vision toward the two little witches huddled together in the corner of the playground and thought she knew the source of his discouragement. She wanted to throw her arms around him and tell him how good and kind and faithful he was, but all she could do was edge a little closer. "Nobody expected Aaron to jump right up and walk after your blessing yesterday."

"Some people did."

Yes, Libby thought, some people did. He must have been one of them. "You've done everything you can, David," she said fervently. "From the first day you got here." His face moved toward her again and Libby wished she could see his eyes through the sunglasses. Did he understand what she was trying to say? Did he know that she'd never have to forgive him his deception because now she understood it?

"I'm sorry, Libby," he said, and the depth of emotion in his voice made her think he did understand, at least in part. "I couldn't do it. No matter how hard I tried, I couldn't solve the puzzle."

Her mind flew back to the story in the book of fairy tales. Kay had solved the Snow Queen's puzzle by spelling "eternity" from shards of ice. He should have won the world and a new pair of skates besides. David looked as if he'd just lost the world, the skates, and his very soul.

"You and Chilly will have to go into protective custody tomorrow," he continued. "It's too dangerous to stay here now that . . . " He turned away. "I'm sorry, Libby."

"We'll go," she said quickly and grasped his arm to turn him back toward her. She'd gladly take Chelsea anywhere he wanted to take them if it would remove the desperate, haunted look from his face. "But why?"

"We thought Fisk was the threat."

"Karlton?"

"Yes. He disappeared from LA on Saturday. We expected him to turn up here."

"Which is why you've spent the last two nights in my yard with the bats?" At his shrug she asked hesitantly, "Did he turn up some-place else?"

"Yeah," David said. "He turned up in LA. Dead." His voice was very low when he added, "Ballistics says it was the same gun used to kill your parents. It was never pitched in the bay like we thought." Libby hugged herself as she watched his shoulders sag back against the wall. "Nothing lately has been what I thought and now we're fresh out of suspects."

"What about Uncle Leo?" When his eyebrows rose above the rim of his glasses, she said quickly, "I mean, shouldn't he be protected too? Geneva says they've threatened his life as well as mine."

"It would be a good idea for him to go with you," David agreed at last. "I'll get somebody on it."

At last Libby relaxed. With Chelsea and Leonard safe and David at her side, she could live happily ever after even in a modified jail cell. "Where will we go?"

"I don't know." David's face was pointed toward the girls as he tried to make his voice expressionless. "They'll take you back to California probably. That's where the base of operations is."

Libby hadn't heard a word beyond "they." "You're not coming with us?"

"No."

Why would he? Libby thought in despair. Chelsea was wrong. He'd never loved her and all the moonpowder in the galaxy couldn't change it. She tried to raise her voice above a whisper and was unsuc-cessful. "What will you do?"

"Swab the bowels of a submarine if my grandfather has his way," David said ruefully. "Otherwise I'll probably go back to space. Who knows, maybe they'll ask for volunteers for a mission to Jupiter."

Maybe if she begged him not to leave her. Maybe if she spent every penny of her fortune on a love potion. Maybe—

"Captain Rogers!" Max lumbered around the corner of the school, moving arthritic joints faster than Libby would have believed him able. He grasped David's elbow as he stood scanning the school yard. He saw at last who he sought and cupped his hands to his mouth. "Tansy! Come here please. You too, Chelsea!"

Libby thought she might burst before the two girls finally skidded to a stop in front of the principal. "The whole town's gonna know before long," he said, bending down eye-level with the girls, "but I promised to tell you first. Your mother called me, Tansy. She was helping Aaron dress for school just now and he moved his big toe."

The significance was immediately apparent to Tansy and Chelsea. They fell joyfully against David as one. He looked over their heads at Max. "Are you saying . . . ?"

"Yes!" Libby cried, her joy as great as the girls'. "That's what he's saying, David!"

David leaned back against the wall as the girls ran to spread the news. A spot of moisture glistened against the rim of his sunglasses as his chin dropped toward his chest. Libby looked on in concern, then realized that he was praying and that gratitude to God was a singularly appropriate response.

A few moments later, Max looked from Libby to David and back. "Glad to see you two talking. I knew things would work out. When's the first date?"

David looked toward the horizon because it was probably how far his mind was from her and Libby looked down at the slippers on her feet because she thought it might be how far her heart had dropped. Max blew a whistle and all the scarecrows and ghosts and princesses scampered toward the classroom doors. The witch gazed for another minute at the secret agent, found she could not speak, and fled toward the library.

A few minutes later, once the threat of tears was past, Libby considered canceling her morning classes. She wished to use the time to tell Guy about Aaron and to take him all the jams and jellies in her pantry. Then she'd spend the rest of the day telling Max and Shenla and Estelle how much she'd miss them.

Libby looked across her desk at Agent Compton and knew that her wish was out of the question. With a sigh, she chose a book to read aloud to the third grade and tried to compose herself for her last day in the library in Amen. Tomorrow she would leave this beloved town and never come back. By the time the protective custody ended David would be gone. Libby would stay away as well. Neither her books nor her garden nor even her friends could fill the void she would feel here in his absence.

* * *

Before the first pint-sized goblin toddled out at dusk with his pillowcase in hand, the whole town had heard about Aaron McKracken. Guy drove out to the farm with Homer, Deaf Old Ezra, an old bag of books, and new outlook on life. Others had already arrived. Everyone who went was personally welcomed by Moses.

Libby hadn't gone—it was too painful to even think about leaving them—but she talked to him and Hannah on the phone. She'd also laughed through an exuberant report from Tansy, who'd rushed home after school to see her brother, then returned to town to celebrate Halloween with her best friend. Besides the big toe, Aaron could now feel pins and needles in the soles of his feet. On Wednesday his parents would take him back to Phoenix to see the neurologist who'd said any sign of movement was a sign of a possible recovery. "Possible" is all Hannah had prayed for in her humble life and now it would prove enough. "Possible" meant that her son might now kneel with them at the temple when Moses's priesthood was restored and they were sealed as a family for eternity.

Eternity.

She had been thinking about the puzzle in *The Snow Queen* ever since David had sent Calvin to the library that afternoon to return the book. Though she had lived her life with words, she found that there were none to describe what she felt when she held that little book in her hands and turned the pages that David had turned, and reread the fairy tales that he had quoted—often erroneously and always to suit his own ends. The thought of him keeping this book so long made her smile, and weep. When she left tomorrow she would take Chelsea and Calliope and it. Nothing else mattered.

"The dry ice is going out!" Chilly reported, startling Libby from her thoughts. Sure enough, the cauldron on the front wall no longer boiled and bubbled. Chelsea's green mud-masked face peered down at it in consternation.

Libby hadn't yet told her niece about the protective custody. She'd told her only that Uncle Leo would come tonight for a visit. She didn't want to overshadow Aaron's good news with bad, and she wanted Chilly to enjoy to the fullest the last night she would spend with her best friend.

"I poured the punch over it again," Tansy said. "It didn't work this time."

Libby walked over to examine the pot of dry ice and green limeade. "The ice has a crust on it." She took the wooden spoon and cracked the outer layer of frost. The green liquid bubbled and a fine mist rose once again toward the full moon. "I think you've seen your last trick-or-treater, though," she said. "It's getting late. We need to go in."

"Can't we stay out a few more minutes?" Tansy begged. Her eyes moved toward the house next door and Libby knew that the girls had hoped David would come over. Estelle was out on the widow's walk with her telescope trained toward the stars, but Captain Rogers was apparently downstairs in his room where he'd been ever since school let out. Libby didn't know what he was doing there, but she hoped for his sake he was sleeping.

* * *

Once or twice today David thought he knew the answer to the puzzle. It had been *right there* in his subconscious, but when he reached for it consciously it was gone. And he was out of time.

He ran the palm of his hand across his face and into his hair. He didn't feel the stitches, so intent was he on the computer screen in front of him. Wescott was wrong. They had all the pieces to this thing; they just weren't putting them together right.

"He's here," Agent Compton reported in his ear.

Thank goodness. David glanced out his window to confirm Leonard Kelley's safe arrival. It would have been more than Libby could bear if something had happened to him. Still, Leonard had refused an armed escort and David doubted there were many times the distinguished gentleman didn't get his way. That was one reason he was so glad Leonard had agreed to enter protective custody with Libby. Undoubtedly he would do a better job of caring for her than David had been able to.

He considered using Kelley's arrival as a pretext to walk over to Libby's house, then put the thought away. He'd kept his vow to this point with one minor slip, but wasn't sure he could continue to under the circumstances. Besides, there was the pain to consider. A man who couldn't stop beating his head against the same wall deserved brain damage.

David called up the next screen and stared into its blue-green glow. If he could figure this thing out in the eight and a half hours he had left, Libby could stay in Amen. If he could do this one thing for her, at least he could live with himself—even if by himself—tomorrow and all the days after that.

* * *

Leonard accomplished what Libby could not. He not only persuaded Tansy and Chelsea to go inside, but to transform themselves from witches back into girls in pajamas. Libby knew that she too would have done with alacrity anything he asked for the promised reward: a cup of his famous "killer hot cocoa" and *The Monkey's Paw* told in the dark as only Uncle Leo could tell it. She curled up on the sofa to wait and rested her chin on her arm.

"Are you all right, Princess?" Leonard asked.

"It's nothing that can't be cured by a cup of your cocoa," she lied. "Shall I help you make it?"

"And learn my secret recipe?" He clutched his heart in mock horror. "Never!"

"That recipe is all I asked him to leave me in his will," Libby told Roberta as Leonard made his way toward the kitchen. "He makes cocoa with whole milk and cream and then melts in a chocolate truffle."

"How much cholesterol is there in a cup?" Roberta asked warily.

"You won't care once you taste it," Libby said. "You'll just die happy."

The cocoa must have been as divine as she had promised. Libby watched a look of bliss cross Roberta's face at the first sip. The girls drained their cups quickly and asked for more. Only Libby's cocoa grew cold on the table. Leonard had used the Blue Willow tea set and Libby found she could scarcely touch it. Instead, she listened to him tell *The Monkey's Paw*, a horror story about the danger of getting what one wishes for, and hugged herself disconsolately. In her shock at learning he worked for the CIA, Libby had rashly wished David out of her life and now it had happened. She looked down at the "killer cocoa" and knew that two more loves of her life would go with him. She'd never enjoy Blue Willow or chocolate again.

* * *

How'd that story go? David wondered as he pushed out his chair, stood and stretched, hoping to revive his body enough to jump-start his brain. He tried to recall the details of Andersen's story about a blind girl who went around gathering up every grain of truth from the earth. There was something in there about her suffering the "beatings of a heart engaged in good action" too. He walked over to the window and looked out at the moon. In the end, the truth she collected and the heartache she endured combined to give her perfect vision.

In his ear, David heard a microphone pick up Libby's voice. He flinched. Without question, his heart had taken a beating while engaged in what he'd thought to be good action. Why, then, hadn't he been given clear sight? There must be a grain of truth he had missed.

Resolutely, David returned to his chair, his computer, and his task. If the grain was there to be found, he would find it.

chapter 34

Oh, were I rich in lovers' poetry, To tell my fairy tale, love's richest lore!

— *The Goloshes of Fortune, 1838*

Libby sat up in bed and gazed out the window at the blue moon—an event that happened so rarely that it passed into folklore. This moon was yellow-white and high enough in the sky to look very much like Hamlet on a motorcycle.

She swung her legs over the side of the bed and sank her bare toes into the braided rug. She couldn't sleep, and she wouldn't lie here and mourn a moment longer. She'd get a cup of warm milk and the most boring book she could lay her hands on. At the foot of the bed Calliope looked from Libby toward her warm, recently vacated pillow and chose to keep company with the latter.

"Don't get comfortable," Libby told the cat as she slipped into her robe, "I'll be back." But it wasn't true. She'd need more than warm milk and the essays of Cicero to help her sleep on this, the last night she would ever be close to David.

Roberta didn't suffer from insomnia. Probably, Libby thought, the strain of the last few days had finally taken its toll. She slept soundly on the daybed in the next room.

Libby walked through the quiet house to check on the girls. Not even Leonard's spine-tingling story had been able to keep them awake long. They were out by the end, and Libby had covered them with soft afghans and let them sleep where they lay. Now she tucked the blankets more securely around their bare arms then picked up a couple of dirty teacups to take with her into the kitchen.

With the moon so bright, she didn't bother to turn a light on. As Libby went to put the cups in the sink, she saw from the corner of her eye a form move in the shadows. She dropped the china and stifled a scream when one cup shattered on the white porcelain sink.

"Uncle Leo!" she cried as she turned with both hands clasped to her chest. "You frightened me to death!" She looked toward the kitchen door, expecting Roberta to arrive with her gun drawn. The house remained quiet.

"You should have drunk your cocoa, Princess," Leonard scolded her fondly. "You'd have been able to sleep. We have a busy day tomorrow."

"I see I'm not the only insomniac," she replied. Her computer was on and her attaché case open on the table. "Or is there so much to do to keep Jamison Enterprises solvent that you have to stay up all night to do it?"

His only response was to cross the room and put his arm around her shoulder. He smelled of cocoa, a long-familiar after shave, and that one smelly pipe he simply would not give up in the evenings. Libby leaned into him and felt like a child again. If only he could kiss her forehead and take her hurt away. "Uncle Leo . . ."

"Let's get some air," he suggested. "I'll tell you a bedtime story like I used to."

* * *

"Are you sleeping, Captain?" Estelle asked from the door to his room.

David sat up straight. "No!" he said. "Yes." He shook his head to clear the cobwebs from his brain. "I don't know if I was or not."

He raised a finger to his ear, but heard only steady breathing. The last thing he clearly remembered picking up from the microphone was the end of Leonard's ghost story. They must have gone to bed after that. And no wonder. According to the clock on his computer screen it was well after midnight.

"Do you have an earache?" Estelle asked in concern.

David dropped the finger back to his lap. "No. I . . . uh . . . well, okay."

"I'll get you some clove oil." But she couldn't seem to move her bulky frame from the doorway where she'd paused in fatigue and discouragement of her own. "Think I ought to stay up and watch a little longer? I felt in my bones that the brethren would come tonight. You did such a good job of getting the yard ready, and I took Libby's cookies from the freezer."

And she had twenty packets of cherry Kool Aid and ten pounds of sugar waiting in a plastic punch bowl in the kitchen, David knew. It was Estelle's idea of the perfect reception, and her disappointment at the absence of the extraterrestrial guests of honor tugged at his heart. "Let me watch for awhile, Estelle," he said. "I'll sound the air-raid siren if there's any sign."

"You were up all last night on Ten Tribe patrol," she pointed out. "And most of the night before."

"Well," David said sheepishly, "when you feel something in your bones . . . " He trailed off without finishing the thought. He wondered instead what it was his bones—or the Spirit—were telling him now. Every nerve in his body was suddenly on alert, but apparently without cause. He looked automatically down at the computer screen, but the dossier open on it now was only of Leonard Kelley. David reached down to click it off. *Only Leonard.*

Only Leonard.

David froze. He'd thought "only Leonard" because Leonard Kelley was the only one at Jamison Enterprises he'd never looked at. Thought about. Suspected.

Everything that had been "almost there" all day suddenly was there— and in a rush that made David reel. Leonard had been on the Jamisons' yacht. He'd been on the plane with Gordon and the now-dead pilot. He'd worked with Montgomery. He'd introduced Karlton Fisk to Libby. He'd worked with everyone and known everything and been everywhere.

And now he was next door.

Struggling to quash the first numbing wave of panic, David rose from the chair, crossed the room in about a second and pushed past the baffled Estelle. As he raced down the hall he pulled the phone from his pocket. "Phantom!" he called into it sharply. "Phantom!" Then he discarded the phone to reach instead for the pistol in the holster beneath his jacket.

* * *

Libby watched Leonard use the toe of his shoe to set the porch swing into a gentle, lulling motion and wondered why he hadn't at least put on slippers. "You haven't dressed for bed. Don't you plan to sleep at all?"

"Probably not, Princess," the older man said. "I didn't drink the cocoa, either."

Indian summer had passed, even here in the low desert, and Libby felt chill. She pulled her robe a little tighter.

"Shall I tell you that story?"

"Yes." Determined to set aside her unhappiness, Libby settled herself against Leo's side. "But not something scary. And not anything sad."

Leonard leaned comfortably back in the swing and smiled up at the moon. "Something happy for my little Libby then." The tale he related was the fable of a man who wanted more from life than a meager, rocky farm, so he abandoned his family, sold his ancestral home and searched the world over for fortune. At the end of life, bent and broken and bitterly disillusioned, the man learned that diamonds had been discovered in the fields behind the house he'd left so long ago.

Not surprisingly, Leonard told the story like a master, but Libby hardly listened to the gruff, beloved voice. She already knew the moral. Looking across the lot toward Estelle's house, she knew that all the treasure she wanted in the world slept just beyond that wall.

As she looked, she thought she saw a movement in the shadows and leaned forward. But Leonard leaned forward too, to remove something from his pocket, and obstructed her view. When he pressed a small, velvet pouch into her hand, Libby looked instinctively down at it instead.

"That bag is full of diamonds, Elisabeth," he said softly. "A king's ransom for my Princess."

"Diamonds?"

"The man in the story was a fool." Leonard's voice was suddenly cool and disdainful. "Who could overlook a fortune in diamonds in his own backyard?"

A new moral? What did it—and the odd tone of voice—mean? And why would Leo give her diamonds?

All at once, Libby's brain began to spin too fast for her to touch upon a single thought, let alone grasp one long enough to think it through. Leonard had come to Amen because she'd asked him to, but he'd used her computer without permission. He'd done something with the papers she'd prepared for the CIA, but he'd made her the cocoa that she loved. He gave her diamonds; the microchips were paid for with diamonds. Leonard was her father's best friend; her father was dead.

"Take them, Elisabeth," Leonard said. "I insist."

Libby clutched the bag as Leonard reached again into his pocket. She studied his face and prayed she was wrong.

It's only Uncle Leo, she assured herself. The craggy lines in his face, Roman nose and sculpted lips were the same features she'd known and loved all her life. The carefully clipped hair was grayer, but thick and familiar. His chin was the same. His—

In the next instant Libby recognized the difference. Leonard Kelley's watercolor-blue eyes had turned to dry ice.

"I didn't want to kill you, Princess," he said softly. "I never wanted it to come to that. If you'd only listened to me and stayed away from Captain Rogers."

The gun in his hand had a silencer and was military issue, left over from what Leonard called the "bad old days" in Vietnam. The days he rarely talked about. The days that had made him distrust the United States government.

But to despise his own country and its citizens?

"You have to believe I never wanted you to die," he said.

The pouch of diamonds slipped from Libby's suddenly lax fingers, slid down the soft satin of her robe and caught in a wide pocket. She felt the weight settle against her thigh. Now she would die like her parents had—killed by the man they'd trusted most—but her death would also be made to appear to condemn her for his espionage. It was funny how little death or disgrace mattered, Libby thought as Leonard grasped her arm to pull her from the swing. What mattered was that David would blame himself and, worse, never know how much she loved him.

"Kelley."

Libby's head swung toward the miraculous voice. The moonlight that shone through the apple tree bathed David in dappled light and reflected off the gun in his hand. Torn between relief and horror she stood mute, scarcely able to catch her breath.

David's pistol was pointed carefully at the ground. "Put your weapon down, Leonard," he said. "It's over. There's no way you'll get out of it this time."

Did she hear helicopters, Libby wondered, or was it the pounding of blood in her ears? She moved toward David, but Leonard tightened the grip on her arm and pressed the gun into her side. "I'll take her with me," he said.

David took a step forward. "You'll have to go through me."

"No!" Libby cried when at last she found her voice. This couldn't be happening. It was a terrible, sick nightmare. The throbbing in her ears increased as blocks away, twin spotlights split the sky and drenched the ground in light. *Is this how it feels to faint?* There was a rosy haze of luminescence at the corners of her eyes. It grew brighter and would soon converge overhead with the frosty pillars of light and soft amber glow of the moon.

Leonard dragged Libby down from the veranda and raised the revolver to her head. "Throw away your gun, Rogers."

David tossed his pistol into the monkshood but took another step forward. "I love her, Leonard," he said as though it made sense—as though it was the only thing that *could* make sense right now.

Libby felt Leo's gun leave her cheek and swing toward David. Frantically, she brought up her elbow. A soft "thwup" was followed by the sharp sound of shattered glass as the witching ball exploded over David's head.

"Uncle Leo!" Libby cried. She wrenched free from his grasp but flung herself back across his chest. "Please! *Please* don't hurt him. I'll go with you. I'll do *anything* for him."

"He's not good enough for you, Elisabeth. He's a government spy."

The gun rose beneath her arm and this time Leonard didn't miss. Libby spun in time to see the bullet hit David in the midriff and propel him backward into the moon garden. She collapsed on the ground when he did.

Leonard reached for her elbow, but she was immovable. Death, life—nothing in all the world would ever matter again. She didn't glance up when, from the widow's walk, Estelle began to shriek.

"It's them!" the old woman hollered. "They've come! The brethren have arrived!" In the next instant she was at the air-raid siren, cranking the handle for all she was worth. Out on the desert, coyotes lifted their noses to the moon and howled in protest. At the dumpster behind the town hall, javelina scattered and ran for their lives. Across town, Deaf Old Ezra sat up in bed and searched for his glasses.

Perhaps the sound was loud enough to wake the dead. David rolled forward, grasped Leonard by the ankle and pulled him off his feet. In another thirty seconds he had the man disarmed and back up, secured by a half-nelson.

The noise was so intense, the lights were so bright, and the events so far beyond belief that Libby had lost all hope for cognitive reasoning and motor skills. Within minutes half the nation's defense corps were in her backyard, trampling her purslane and gazing—at Estelle's hysterical insistence—at the fading red lights of a passing jetliner. Libby, for her part, simply could not think, speak, or get up off the ground.

"Not that I think you need help," David said as he extended his hands with the grin she'd thought she'd never see again, "But—"

"David." She found she could say one word after all. It was the only word she cared if she ever said again.

He bent to lift her to her feet and steadied her with a strong arm when she swayed against him. "I'm sorry about Leonard. They're taking him away now. I think it's going to be a long, long time before you see him again."

She'd have to face all that pain eventually, Libby knew, but not right now. Right now her eyes were on David's chest. "But I saw—"

He released one of her hands so he could unfasten a button on his shirt.

Libby stared at the gray material that lay beneath, uncomprehending.

"So it's not shining armor," he said. "But these days a bullet-proof vest is handier."

Her hand rose to his chest and her fingers sought the spot where the bullet had hit. When she found it—just above his heart—she gasped at the size and depth of the crater. "Are you hurt?" she whispered.

He captured her fingers and pulled them to her lips. "Well, it probably cost me another rib, but I figure a woman like you is worth more than one."

Before Libby could breathe, Preston Wescott himself arrived on the scene. "Captain," he said, "there's an old woman over there who claims that you deputized her as a government spy. She's assaulting my men because they frightened off your space aliens." Despite his ridiculous words, the agency chief's face was stone sober. "If you do not disarm her *immediately*, I'm giving the order to have her gassed. You can explain it all to me later." His lips formed a thin line. "Perhaps you should have legal counsel present when that explanation takes place."

"Understood," David said. He dropped Libby's hands and looked around for Estelle.

She wasn't hard to locate. She'd taken her stand atop Libby's root cellar where she had not only the strategic advantage, but a whole barrel full of ammunition. Estelle brandished knitting needles in one hand and lobbed Libby's apples with the other. The dozen well-armed men who surrounded her were clearly outmatched.

"I'll be back," David told Libby. He saw Wescott glower as Estelle's Granny Smith drew blood with a direct hit to an agent's nose. "Maybe."

The CIA questioned Libby in her kitchen while paramedics examined Roberta and the girls, and most of the citizenry of Amen gathered in her front yard. As the hubbub in front increased, Libby looked toward the stove, saw that there was still a bit of drugged cocoa in a pan on the back burner and considered passing it around.

Or perhaps she should give it all to Estelle. Recently—and regrettably—released by the authorities, the woman was now on the front porch relating to the bishop and others how the brethren had come, been frightened by the government's helicopters, and departed— probably for another millennia. She was so certain and so sincere, Libby wouldn't be surprised if she managed to whip the townspeople into a righteously indignant mob that would follow her to Washington to storm the capitol.

Let them storm it, Libby thought, and let the CIA go through her computer and briefcase and cupboards to their hearts' content. Libby wanted only to know what had happened to David. She'd last seen him accosted by paramedics shortly after he calmed Estelle. Then he'd disappeared with Preston Wescott. Their meeting must have ended, because Wescott had come into the kitchen several minutes ago to confer with the men who were so interested in her computer, but David was nowhere to be seen. Surely Wescott hadn't been serious about arresting him.

At last she saw him through the window. He was on his knees in the dirt out by the moon garden. She glanced around and then, while Wescott was deep in conversation, excused herself to use the restroom, ran down the hall to the bathroom, and slipped out the window.

David looked up at her approach, but didn't rise or move toward her. He said, "After the miracle with Aaron this morning and everything tonight, I thought I'd be able to do it, Lib."

His faced lowered back toward the ground and Libby knelt hastily at his side. He'd gathered up the largest shards of the witching ball. Under the moonlight bits of broken glass sparkled in even lines upon the dark soil. David had dirtied his hands and cut his fingers and spelled ETERNIT.

"So much," he said quietly, "for the whole world and a new pair of skates besides."

She never knew what she might have said if they'd remained uninterrupted a few seconds longer. At that moment Max and Shenla, Guy and Homer, the three Flake women, Deaf Old Ezra, and a couple of young CIA agents trooped around the side of the house following Estelle on the first pilgrimage to the sacred site of the Ten Tribe's Almost-Landing. Most of the rest of the town soon appeared to gaze over their shoulders.

David looked from Libby toward their friends and neighbors and moved quickly away from her by force of habit. The frown that had been on her lips disappeared. She moved close to him and spoke loud enough to be heard by everyone in the recently assembled town meeting. "I asked Estelle to call you all out here so I could ask Captain Rogers for a date this weekend."

"I told you!" Homer crowed as he stuck a bony elbow into Guy's side. "You owe me ten bucks!"

There was a rumble from the crowd, but all the remarks were directed at Homer to be quiet so that everybody, except Deaf Old Ezra, could hear Captain Rogers's reply.

One corner of David's mouth had turned up, and Libby felt her knees melt beneath her. "I might be free," he said. "What do you have in mind?"

His voice was rich and low and infinitely tender. A spot of warmth began in her bosom and spread throughout her body. David loved her! She could see it in the flecks of stardust in those magnificent brown eyes.

Libby's eyes filled with tears as a sudden inspiration filled her heart. She had moonpowder to complete the enchantment! She reached into her pocket and removed the pouch she'd forgotten she had. Untying the string, Libby poured the diamonds into her palm and from there into the dirt at David's knees to form a Y.

His gaze was still on ETERNITY when she fell forward to wrap her arms around his neck. She'd hold on tight this time and she'd never, ever let go.

"Since it's our first date," she said, "We ought to go someplace memorable." Her soul was in her eyes. "How about a sealing room in the Arizona Temple?"

David's arm encircled her waist and his lips covered hers in answer. Everybody but the Flakes applauded.

At last he drew away enough to manage, "You wouldn't tease a special agent of the United States government, would you?"

"No," Libby said, her lips tingling from his last kiss—and aching for his next one, "I'm the serious one, remember?"

"We can kiss forever without turning into blue birds?"

"Forever."

His grin was broader now and almost maddening. "Does anything come between this part of the story and 'happily ever after'?"

"No."

"No wicked witches, poisoned apples, cursed spinning wheels or—"

If David Rogers *had* a flaw, it was that he read too many fairy tales. "Nothing," Libby said as she raised her hands to his cheeks to pull his lips back to hers, "but this." She kissed him so soundly, so thoroughly and so sincerely that any chance that he would disappear—or turn into a frog—was dispelled forever.

This princess had discovered a spell older than the moon and more potent than stardust. Her magic was the sacred enchantment of eternal love.

ABOUT THE AUTHOR

Kerry Lynn Blair lives in West Jordan, Utah, with her husband, Gary, and three of their four children, the fourth being away at college in Arizona. While growing up in Arizona, Kerry spent every Saturday in the old brick-and-stained-glass Carnegie Library in Prescott. It is there that she first fell in love—with Hans Christian Andersen. Books are still the love of her life as she continues to read them, collect them, and sometimes write them. She is the author of three best-selling Covenant novels, *The Heart Has Its Reasons, The Heart Has Forever* and *The Heart Only Knows.*

Kerry enjoys corresponding with other readers, who can write to her in care of Covenant Communications, P.O. Box 415, American Fork, Utah 84003-0416. Readers of *Closing In* can receive an epilogue (in the form of an E-mail from "Chillygator") by writing to Kerry through Covenant.

Without a Flaw

Isabelle Dalton's stomach knotted with fear. Glancing at the clock, she calculated how much time she had left before her husband, James, got home from work. Turning down the vegetables to let them simmer, she gave the gravy one last stir. She still needed to change her clothes, put drinks on the table, and light the candles. She'd have to hurry. The last thing she wanted to do was keep him waiting.

Racing up to her room, she quickly took off her jeans and sweater, hung them up, then pulled on the clingy black jersey dress that her husband liked so much. She hurried to the bathroom, where she brushed her mane of long blonde hair, then twisted it onto her head and fastened it with several glittering rhinestone clips.

She touched up the bruise on her right cheek with some base makeup and glossed on a light coat of lipstick. Checking her watch, she realized she only had ten minutes to get back downstairs and have everything ready in time.

Shoving her feet into her shoes, she scurried downstairs and filled James's crystal goblet with wine and hers with ice and water, set them on the table, then lit the candles. She wasn't much of a drinker, preferring to keep her mind and reflexes sharp, especially when James was home.

The timer on the oven buzzed, letting her know that the dinner rolls were finished and that James would be pulling into the driveway anytime now. Her stomach lurched as she poked the vegetables with a fork, hoping they weren't overdone. He hated it when the carrots were too soft.

A flash of headlights passed the kitchen window, telling her James was home. As she always did before he came through the door, she prayed he would be in a good mood and that she wouldn't do anything to set him off. She'd made his favorite: pork roast with mushroom gravy, new potatoes along with steamed broccoli and carrots, and her delicious dinner rolls.

Taking their dinner plates, she began dishing up their food. James liked to have his meal on the table, waiting and ready, when he got home. After five years of marriage, Isabelle finally had the routine down, but having things just the way James liked them, all the time, was no easy task. And when she disappointed him or didn't measure up, the price was too painful to have to endure very often.

Her nerves tensed and she froze when she heard the doorknob turn and click. Pasting a smile on her face, she waited for James to enter the room before she greeted him, because that was how he liked it.

"Good evening," she said when he finally appeared. She anxiously searched his expression to determine what kind of mood he was in.

"Good evening, Isabelle," he replied.

She walked to him immediately and gave him a kiss, then stepped away. "I hope you're hungry," she said cheerfully, trying to keep the mood light. "I made your favorite."

He glanced over at the stove, then back at her. "I thought we'd decided to have lasagna tonight," he reminded her.

"I know, but, . . ." she swallowed, hoping with all her heart that he didn't get angry, ". . . I was hoping—"

"Isabelle," his voice was impatient. "I give you a menu at the beginning of every week. I expect you to follow it."

"I'm sorry, James," she apologized quickly. "I won't let it happen again."

He nodded sharply, setting his briefcase and the mail—which he insisted on collecting himself every night—on the counter.

"Did anything come for me today?" He looked at her with a piercing gaze that made her stomach curdle.

"No." Her tone was even.

His gaze penetrated deeper. Beads of perspiration broke out on her forehead, and her palms grew clammy.

Without a word, James spun on his heel and left the room to

wash his hands.

Isabelle pulled in several deep breaths to calm her jumbled nerves. James received packages from Federal Express at least once, if not twice, a week. She didn't know what was in the packages; she never asked. She didn't care. But sometimes when something he expected didn't arrive, he made her feel as though it was her fault it hadn't.

With the plates of steaming food on the table, Isabelle stood by her chair, waiting for him to join her, which he did moments later.

He helped her into her chair, then sat in his own chair.

Placing the linen napkins on their laps, they picked up their forks. Isabelle waited for him to take the first bite before she began. This was their routine, night after night. This was how James liked things. He was happier when things went as he wanted them to, and Isabelle was much happier when he was happy. It wasn't worth trying to change the way he liked things.

He nodded after taking a bite of the tender, juicy pork roast. "Very good," he said.

Isabelle relaxed a little and smiled. "I'm glad you like it." She took a small bite of her own slice of meat. Under James's encouragement and tutelage, she had become an exceptional cook. There were few things he allowed her to do, but cooking was one of them. He liked having a wife who could prepare gourmet dinners, especially when he entertained people from his law office.

"So, how was your day?" She asked the same question she'd asked every night for the past five years.

"Fine," he said, taking a sip of wine. He told her about a couple of his clients, and how brilliant he'd been in court that day. She smiled approvingly and said the appropriate words at the appropriate times.

She didn't have much of an appetite; she usually didn't at dinnertime, but she managed to take a few bites of the food on her plate. When James was finished, he placed his napkin beside his plate and told her he'd be in the den watching the evening news while she cleaned up the dishes.

Putting the last pot in the dishwasher, she shut the door and turned the knob for the cycle to begin. Giving the sink a quick scouring, she rinsed the sponge and wiped everything with a paper towel so the chrome faucet sparkled and the porcelain sink glistened.

She was just about to hang the dishtowel to dry when she jumped. James was standing in the doorway, watching her.

Holding her hand up to her chest, her heart beating wildly beneath her fingers, she said with a laugh, "You startled me."

His eyes narrowed in an intent gaze.

"Did you need something?" she asked nervously. She hated it when he stared at her like this. This was a look that frightened her. She scanned her mind quickly for something she might not have done to his liking or how in any way she might have angered him.

"I was looking for my evening paper . . ." he said, eyeing her.

Her heart stopped beating. She'd forgotten to get the paper. He liked having it beside his leather recliner in the den. She'd been so busy getting dinner she'd forgotten to get it off the porch. She was just about to apologize when the phone rang.

She jumped to get it, but James answered it. Grateful it was for him, she rushed to the front door. Grabbing the paper off the porch she took it inside and to the den, hoping James would forget it wasn't there earlier.

Picking up a novel, she tried to read as she waited for James to return. But it was impossible to comprehend anything she was reading. She was too nervous worrying about what he would say to her about not having the paper next to his chair.

Finally, she heard footsteps coming her direction.

"That was Mother," he said. "She wants us to come over for dinner on Sunday." He sat in his chair and picked up the paper.

The only thing worse than trying to please James was trying to please his mother. Mrs. Dalton was as nitpicky and critical as a person could get. "How nice of her to invite us," Isabelle lied, watching closely for a muscle to twitch in his cheek, or his hand to clench, to indicate he was going to flip out about the paper. "Did she mention if she'd like me to bring anything?"

He always read the business section first. "No," he replied, getting lost in his reading. "We just need to be there promptly at six."

"I'd better go·write that down so I don't forget," Isabelle said. Relieved that her forgetting the newspaper hadn't turned into a big deal, she went to her planner and wrote down their dinner appointment. It was bad enough to suffer James's wrath, but adding his mother's to it was the truest form of hell on earth.

The evening was quiet, and as usual Isabelle was grateful to climb into bed that night. Most nights James stayed up late doing work he'd brought home from the office. She was grateful she could slip into the privacy and safety of her dreams. There she was happy and carefree again, as she had been before she'd married James.

Lying in her bed, Isabelle waited for her dreams to overtake her as she considered that her marriage was nothing like she'd imagined it would be. James had a side to him that she hadn't seen before they were married. A dark side. And sometimes, a violent side. He'd been attentive, protective, and involved in her life when they were dating. For a girl whose parents were both now gone and whose older brother had left home when she was a young girl and hadn't been seen or heard from since, she liked having someone to protect her, take care of her.

In the beginning James had swept her off her feet with all his attention and devotion. She'd been flattered by his near obsession to be with her or know where she was at all times. She hadn't understood what his demands really represented. She didn't realize the extent to which his "obsession" would grow.

James's love was anything but gentle and nurturing. It was controlling and dominating and robbed her of her freedom: freedom to associate with others, to pursue her dreams, to be herself. He told her how to dress and wear her hair, whom to associate with, what to do each day, where to go, what to buy, and even whom to talk to on the phone. She knew she'd grown paranoid about his obsession, but she honestly wondered if the occasional reverberation she heard on the phone meant the phone lines were bugged.

With each year they were married, his control seemed to grow stronger, more obsessive. At times she caught him staring at her, as he'd done earlier that night, with a look in his eye that rattled her nerves. And she wondered what exactly that look in his dark, pensive eyes meant.